# THE KINDRED OF DARKNESS

# THE KINDRED OF DARKNESS

*A James Asher vampire novel*

## Barbara Hambly

This first world edition published 2013
in Great Britain and 2014 in the USA by
SEVERN HOUSE PUBLISHERS LTD of
19 Cedar Road, Sutton, Surrey, England, SM2 5DA.

Trade paperback edition first published
in Great Britain and the USA 2014 by
SEVERN HOUSE PUBLISHERS LTD

Hambly, Barbara author.
  The Kindred of Darkness – (The
  James Asher vampire novels; 5)
  1. Asher, James (Fictitious character)–Fiction.
  2. Vampires–Fiction. 3. Kidnapping–Fiction. 4. Horror tales
  I. Title II. Series
  813.6-dc23

ISBN-13: 978-0-7278-8342-1 (cased)
ISBN-13 978-1-84751-497-4 (trade paper)

*All Severn House titles are printed on acid-free paper.*

Severn House Publishers support the Forest Stewardship Council™ [FSC™],
the leading international forest certification organisation. All our titles that
are printed on FSC certified paper carry the FSC logo.

Typeset by Palimpsest Book Production Ltd.,
Falkirk, Stirlingshire, Scotland.
Printed and bound in Great Britain by
TJ International, Padstow, Cornwall.

*For Lucinda*

*Seldom do the Undead entrust the living with the knowledge of who and what they truly are, lest their revulsion at working for the dead, or their honor as men, or their care for their own souls, at length overcome them and turn them against their evil masters; and seldom do the dead employ a living servant for more than five years, before killing him and all members of his family, to protect their secret.*

*The Book of the Kindred of Darkness*

# ONE

'Vampires exist.' Dr Osric Millward swept his auditors with a dark gaze almost hungry in its brooding desperation that they should believe. 'I have seen them. In this city – in these streets – in this modern and progressive year of 1913. Is that so difficult to believe?' He pushed back the silver-shot raven forelock that fell on his high brow, stretched long fingers stained with ink and silver nitrate. 'Every civilization back to the beginning of time has spoken of them: men and women who prolong their existence after death by drinking the blood of the living. For centuries they've walked the streets of London, in the dark hours when law and reason sleep.'

'Yes, but if that's the case,' argued Lady Savenake, slipping her Pekinese a fragment of cracker liberally smeared with paté de Strasbourg, 'why don't we hear about more bled-dry corpses turning up in alleyways?'

Lydia Asher could have answered the question, but didn't. Completely aside from the fact that the vampires of the London nest knew who she was and where she could be found, Dr Millward – whose powerful baritone could stop every other conversation in a drawing room dead in its tracks – had prefaced his remarks on vampires with fifteen minutes on the subject of how the 'emanations' of the female reproductive system made it impossible for women's brains to grasp either the principles of logic or the 'masculine intuition' necessary for such disciplines as medicine or the law. She merely dropped another lump of sugar into her tea, and glanced across the drawing room at her cousin Emily, shyly accepting a plate of biscuits from Terence Winterson.

Since Lydia's Aunt Isobel had commanded Lydia to chaperone Emily to Lady Brightwell's tea in order to bring about precisely that encounter – Winterson's father was a baronet worth ten thousand a year – Lydia reflected that it was probably too early to flee.

'The vampire is a natural phenomenon,' Dr Millward insisted. 'Centuries of records prove this, to those with minds open to understand—'

'Couldn't the same be said of ghost stories?' protested Lady Ottmoor, turning her attention from the spring toilettes on display along Park Lane below the drawing-room windows. 'You're not going to tell us that Anne Boleyn really perambulates the Tower of London with her head tucked under her arm, are you?'

'But I've seen a ghost!' Young Lady Kentacre nearly bounced on her striped satin chair. 'Madame Rowena summoned the spirit of Marie Antoinette only last week! I saw her with my own eyes!'

Millward drew back as if her young Ladyship had spilled a slop bucket on his feet. 'Rubbish!' he boomed. 'This isn't some silly women's nonsense, of crystal balls and mysterious white figures playing the accordion! These are creatures that do murder in the dark—'

'And create others of their own kind from their victims,' added Edward Seabury, Dr Millward's (unpaid) secretary and young Lord Colwich's particular friend. His dark eyes were troubled and sad.

'There are more things in Heaven and Earth,' agreed Lord Colwich, 'than are dreamt of in your philosophy, and all that.' He nodded wisely – as if ruminating upon the originality of the remark – and went back to contemplating the platter of cucumber sandwiches, seed cakes and caviar being held before him by the footman. Aunt Isobel had hoped to bring Cousin Emily to the attention of this tall, powerfully built young aesthete (his father was the Earl of Crossford), before Lord Colwich's proposal, the previous week, to the daughter of an American millionaire. Aunt Lavinnia had observed that his lordship was in any case far more interested in Ned Seabury than in any of the maidens embarking, like Emily, on their 'season' that spring. ('As if Lord Crossford would have considered Emily anyway for his son,' Lavinnia had sniffed. 'Richard –' Lavinnia's brother, Isobel's husband, Emily's father and Lydia's sole maternal uncle – 'hasn't a penny over six thousand a year . . .')

On the second of May, Lydia had received a letter from her aunt, informing her of these developments and of Isobel's subsequent attack of sciatica, and demanding Lydia's attendance in London to chaperone Emily in a revised assault upon the marriage market. *With your husband out of the country you must be in quest of occupation . . .*

None of Lydia's aunts ever referred to James Asher by name,

maintaining the fiction, after twelve years, that if they ignored so lowly a person as a lecturer in folklore and linguistics at New College, Oxford, he would eventually go away.

'I *do* apologize,' said Lady Brightwell, when Lydia and Cousin Emily took their leave. Her Ladyship glanced back into the drawing room, where Dr Millward was declaiming about the courage and dedication one needed in order to hunt the Undead, to the exclusion of every other attempt at conversation in the room. 'Noel brought him . . .'

Lydia followed her nod, but to her myopic vision Noel Wredemere, Lord Colwich, was only a tall, stout blur in a gaudy green-and-yellow waistcoat, now deep in conversation with the graceful shape that could only be Ned Seabury. With Emily's departure, Dr Millward had seized upon the only other male in the room – the hapless Mr Winterson – and was regaling him with accounts of how to manufacture silver bullets in one's rented chambers.

'Honestly, one tries to oblige, but between that *tedious* professor of his and poor Ned Seabury tagging along . . . How *can* he still wear his Eton tie, just as if he wasn't a clerk in some law firm or other!'

Thus Lydia's thoughts on the train back to Oxford that night – Dr Millward's assertions notwithstanding – were far more taken up with how she was going to finish her article on the possible medical uses for the newly discovered element 'radium' for the *British Journal of Medicine* in between taking Emily to fittings for her Court presentation gown, than she was with whatever undead entities might be stalking the streets of London in the dark hours when law and reason sleep.

She'd turned down her aunt's command to accompany Uncle Richard – Viscount Halfdene – and his family to the opera, and since it was Lydia who was paying for Emily's presentation gown there wasn't much Aunt Isobel could say. But there seemed to be no way of getting out of the masquerade ball at Wycliffe House on Saturday night – the eligible Mr Winterson would be there, after all. Aunt Lavinnia – with a daughter of her own to bring out this season – could not be relied upon. (Aunt Harriet, comfortably ensconced with a barrister husband in Maida Vale, was 'out of the question'.) Lydia only hoped that Aunt Isobel's sciatica would resolve itself quickly, though as Aunt Lavinnia had pointed out after dinner, it never had before. ('Mark my words, dearest, she'll have it the rest of the season: so if Emily "takes" she can claim credit for having planned her campaign, and if she ends up come August without being engaged it will be your fault.')

Lydia closed her eyes and leaned back against the tufted plush of her first-class compartment – blessedly empty – as the lights of Didcot flashed by in the magical twilight of a spring evening. Tea with her aunts generally gave her a splitting headache. Lydia had fled their world at the age of seventeen to enroll at Oxford – to her wealthy father's disinheriting fury – and a few years previously would have simply torn up Aunt Isobel's note and abandoned Emily to her fate.

But in January of 1912 – seventeen months ago now – Lydia had herself become a mother. And while she hoped she wouldn't become one of those doting parents who found their child's first steps more interesting than an analysis of pituitary secretions, she did find herself understanding her aunt in a way that she never had before.

Even more startlingly – she noted with academic interest – she found herself looking forward to a game of pick-up sticks with her daughter upon her return home, almost as much as she looked forward to the intellectual challenge of her article. Which was very unlike herself.

*Was* Dr Millward – who had recently called Jamie 'a blind and sterile quibbler' in an article in the *Journal of British Folklore* – correct insofar as that the glandular changes triggered by pregnancy had an effect on the chemistry of a woman's brain?

*He certainly has an extremely inaccurate perception of vampires.* Since her first glimpse of a vampire in a London alleyway in 1907 – the year James had been blackmailed into working for the London nest – she had associated with the Undead on four separate occasions and had the suspicion that for all his scholarship, Dr Millward had never actually spoken to a vampire in his life.

James Asher, though a folklorist and linguist, had no more believed in vampires six years ago than he'd believed the moon to be made of green cheese, and Millward had been absolutely scathing about his monograph on the origins of Balkan traditions concerning the walking dead. As the lights of Oxford glimmered through the trees, Lydia planned her evening letter to James. In his hotel in Venice, she knew he'd smile at both Millward's rodomontade and at his shocked fury at being put on the same level as a fashionable spiritualist charlatan . . .

And she was thus meditating on the subject of the Undead when she stepped from her compartment to the platform, and saw at once that something was terribly wrong.

Ellen – who had been a maid at Lydia's childhood home of Willoughby Close – *never* came to meet trains. On those occasions on which Lydia went down to London by herself (a perfectly respectable activity, she had more than once reminded the aunts and another extremely old-fashioned acquaintance), James would meet her homecoming train with a cab: the Ashers did not keep a carriage. When James was away from Oxford, Mick Bell – who worked in the Ashers' garden – would meet her.

But when Lydia peered short-sightedly around the platform for someone of Mick's stature and coloring – she had not the slightest intention of putting on her spectacles where anyone could see her – she made out not only Mick, but Ellen, Bette the parlor maid, Mrs Brock (Miranda's nurse) and, almost unbelievably, not only someone who looked like little Mrs Grimes the cook but also Tilly the scullery girl, all running toward her through the drifts of dispersing passengers.

*Mrs Grimes?* Lydia's heart seemed to stand still in her chest. Years of navigating the world without the disfigurement of 'gig-lamps', as the other girls at school had called them, hanging on her face had taught her to identify people almost unerringly by the way they moved. There could be no mistake – it *was* Mrs Grimes. *Why would SHE come . . . ?*

*They'd never have left just Nan the nursery maid home with Miranda . . .*

Her hands and feet went cold.

*No.*

She ran toward them, breathless with fear and shock as they nearly collided.

'What happened?'

'I swear it, ma'am, I don't know! I was in the garden, couldn't nobody have got to the house . . .'

*Oh, God . . .*

Dizziness. Shock. Terror.

'Miss Lydia, I took them up a tray at seven . . .'

'We were in the kitchen together, ma'am, and how anyone could have got into the house . . .'

'*What happened?*' She fought the urge to take the cook by the shoulders and slap her.

*This can't really be taking place . . .*

Tears streaking her face, the big maid held out a sheet of folded paper. 'This was on her pillow, ma'am.'

It had been sealed with red wax, the image on the seal – Lydia held it close enough to see its details clearly by the gas-jet on the station wall – a woman planting a tree. The seal had been cracked. The servants had read it already.

Jamie's work with old manuscripts – among other things – had taught Lydia what sixteenth-century handwriting looked like.

> *Madame,*
> *Y'r daughter & ye girl are well & safe & will no be harmed. Yet you must needs speake with me and soone.*
> *Grippen*

# TWO

Cold panic turned to rage so hot it was almost blinding. Grippen.

The Master Vampire of London. Dead since 1555. Since 1666 the ruler – and the begetter – of the vampires of London.

Lydia crushed the note and the hard wax dug into her hand like the edge of a coin. In a calm corner of her heart she knew quite well that it had been no choice of James' to make the acquaintance of the London nest and its sinister master. Nevertheless, for a moment she hated not only Grippen – the man, the thing, the animate corpse that had penned the words – but James as well.

Six years ago, the London vampires had sought James out, and before that bargain was concluded he and she had both come so close under the shadow of the wings of Death, they could feel the fan of the feathers.

*Grippen . . .*

She shook as if the May night had turned to bitter winter. 'Get my bags, please, Mick.'

James would laugh at her for taking, for an afternoon in London, a valise containing rice-powder, rouge, mascaro, distilled water of green pineapples, rosewater and glycerin, a silk shawl, a wool shawl, a change of shoes, three issues of *Lancet* and Curie's 'On a New Radioactive Substance . . .', plus bottles of lemonade and mineral water, and two very large hatboxes – but this, she would point out to him, was only because he was sufficiently handsome that he did not require extensive embellishment to appear presentable. People didn't care what men looked like anyway.

She stood balling the paper tighter and tighter in her hand and shaking as if with fever.

*He took Miranda. He took my daughter.*

She had never understood why women in plays and novels screamed. Now she knew.

*We will stay away from you and yours*, the vampires had said to James, when he had accomplished the task they had needed a living man to do. *It is simply prudence on our part. You could hunt us down eventually, were you willing to give your soul to it, to become obsessed . . . To hunt us would be to hunt smoke . . .*

But she had always known they were there.

*He took my daughter . . .*

Rage and panic made it hard to breathe.

'Who is he, Miss Lydia?' Ellen whispered. 'How could this Grippen have just walked into the house like that? Bette was up to the nursery just an hour before—'

'He's no one.' Lydia took a deep breath. 'Put his name out of your mind. Never think of it again. Mick . . .'

The gardener appeared, laboring under hatboxes and bags.

'Please take Ellen and the others back to the house. I'm going to walk.'

'You can't, ma'am!' Even at age twenty-one, Mick was scandalized. 'It's a good three-quarter mile, and it's near to eleven—'

'Not wearing those shoes, Miss Lydia!' Ellen protested. 'They're not—'

*I really am going to scream.*

'Just go! Please.' She softened her voice with an effort. 'I'll be quite all right, it's right through the center of town and the worst I'll encounter is undergraduates.'

*And a man who has systematically murdered thirty thousand people and drunk their blood in order to stay alive himself.*

*If I'm lucky.*

'That isn't the point, Miss Lydia. What your mother would have said, or your aunts, if I were to let you go walking about the town by yourself—'

Her voice shaking – knowing what would happen to Ellen, or to any of the servants, if they accompanied her – Lydia said, 'Just please do as I ask. I need the fresh air . . .'

It took ten minutes of arguing before they obeyed. Any of her aunts, Lydia reflected, with a chilled detachment as she watched the little knot of servants finally walk away, would have fired them on the spot. *Dear God, please don't let them follow and watch me . . .*

Breathless with the pounding of her heart, when Lydia reached the end of the platform she slipped her silver spectacle case from her handbag, put on the thick, round-lensed glasses that she never let anyone (except James) see her wear. Better a blinky-blind skinnybones (as the other girls at Madame Chappedelaine's Select Academy for Young Ladies had called her) than a goggle-eyed golliwog (her other appellation there). One could get over being a skinnybones if one had the money to hire a really good dressmaker.

She scanned the night beyond the station's gaslights. This was the end of the line for the 9:50 from Paddington, and it was the last train of the evening. As the cars huffed their slow way on to a siding, all cabs vanished as if by magic from the graveled space between the town's two railway stations. The sweet shops and newsagents along Hythe Bridge Street were shuttered for the night. The darkness around her lay unbroken, like clear cobalt glass. Even the roving undergraduates seemed to be either asleep or keeping to their own jumble of little streets and courts further east. Lydia's heels clicked softly on the stone verge as she crossed the bridge, the smell of the river an ache of nostalgia, the willows of the Worcester grounds a dark mass under the starlight.

*Ellen was right; these aren't shoes for walking any great distance in . . .*

James – and others – had told her: this was how one found a vampire. She had no doubt that having left the note in Miranda's crib, Grippen would be waiting for her to do exactly this. To 'promenade herself', as the vampires said.

For six years now she'd worn, under the fashionable high collars of her exquisite dresses, half a dozen silver chains around her neck, a concentration of the metal sufficient to badly burn a vampire's mouth, to buy herself an instant to run, to scream, to twist free. James wore them, too, over fading bite scars that tracked his throat and forearms. Terror filled her, but it went nearly unnoticed under a pure, burning anger so powerful that it seemed to lift the hairs on her head.

*He took Nan . . .*

Miranda's little nursery maid – the changer of nappies, the emptier of bathwater, the server of Mrs Brock's evening tea – was Cousin Emily's age. Seventeen, sweet-faced, slow-speaking and good-natured no matter what was demanded of her. Performing the dirty, heavy chores of the nursery work and taking orders from the crusty Mrs Brock was, Lydia recalled, the girl's first paid employment.

*He wouldn't have taken Nan if he didn't need to keep Miranda well and cared for.*

*If he harms a hair of that poor girl's head . . .*

Tears closed her throat. Tears of terror, less for herself than for her daughter. Tears of remorse, for the traveling companion, four years ago, who had been killed by a vampire.

*If he hurts her . . .*

*If he hurts Miranda . . .*

*Damn Jamie; damn him for being in Venice . . .*

Mist filmed the river, blurred the outlines of the willows.

*I'll bet it isn't even a philology conference.* Bulgaria, Serbia, Montenegro and a lot of other little countries in the Balkans had all been fighting each other since last spring, and James had received a steady stream of notes from the Foreign Office – for whom he had worked before quitting in disgust at the end of the African war – which he had just as steadily been putting on the fire. Then, quite suddenly, he had asked her, was it all right if he went to Venice? A meeting of experts in folklore and linguistics . . .

A man stood at the end of the bridge, silhouetted against the star-soaked mists.

A vampire . . .

*The* vampire of London. He'd been murdering people since before Queen Elizabeth was on the throne.

He stood massive and unmoving, but his eyes caught the distant lights of the station like an animal's.

*It's him.*

Rage flooded her and she lengthened her stride, straight up to him.

His clothing smelled like old blood.

Lydia didn't care. She slapped at his face: 'You give her back! You bastard devil, you give me my daughter back!'

She knew vampires could tamper with the mind, put a cloud on human perceptions, but had been too angry to remember. When he grabbed her, caught her against his body in an iron embrace, it was as if she didn't, for an instant, remember how to struggle or cry out. It was just that suddenly he was crushing her fingers in an agonizing grip; his arm was around her waist as he bent her backwards over the parapet of the bridge. His pock-marked face was inches from hers and when he spoke his mouth reeked with blood.

'You want to bless your stars, Missy, that I've too urgent a use for you, for me to go off and let you think for a week or maybe two about layin' hard names to one who's got your brat in his hand.'

His grip tightened on her fingers until she cried out, and he grinned. Distant gas lights showed her his fangs. Then he threw her from him on to the stone of the bridge, as a child will throw a doll in a fit of temper. The impact knocked the breath from her and she fought not to weep, as she'd fought when, long ago, her Nanna had taken a strap to her. *I will NOT let him see he's hurt me . . .*

The impact had knocked her spectacles off as well. She saw starlight gleam in the round lenses near the parapet, and groped over to pick them up. For a miracle, they hadn't broken. In her smallest voice she said, 'You are right, sir. I should not have spoken.'

This was what she'd always said to Nanna, or her stepmother, and neither had ever seemed to notice that the phrase was simply the literal truth and contained no apology.

The vampire made no move to help her to her feet. Painfully, she used the parapet to steady herself as she rose.

He was tall, as tall as Jamie. His half-seen face was a horror, thick-fleshed and sensual, fangs protruding a little beyond his heavy lower lip and a nose flat, crooked, and sprouting with black hair. He'd been a physician in sixteenth-century London, James had told her. *So he probably started killing people long before he joined the Undead.* Like other vampires she had encountered, he had a quality of stillness to him, more than simply the fact that he didn't breathe. As if he'd been there forever, waiting for you to get near.

And she knew he could get the minds of the living to not quite notice him, unless they were looking for him. Lay sleepy inattention on the thoughts. Trick the mind into not seeing him as he was.

Into seeing him as handsome, or trustworthy, or someone you would be happy to walk up a dark alley with.

That was something vampires did.

She drew a shaky breath. 'And what use is it, sir, that you have for me?'

*May you rot, may you burn screaming for eternity in Hell . . .*

He folded his heavy arms. 'They tell me you can track the Undead in their lairs.' His deep, hoarse voice sounded almost like an American's. James had mentioned this also, when he spoke of dealing with Grippen six years ago. In the sixteenth century, apparently everyone in the south of England used those flat vowels and nasal Rs.

Again Lydia took a deep breath. Either *Yes* or *No* would be a perilous answer. One did NOT go about telling vampires that one knew how to locate their home addresses.

*He wants something. He'll keep her alive because he wants something.*

*Oh, God, don't let me mess this up . . .*

'Only sometimes,' she lied at last. 'Who is it, that you want me to find?'

'Damien Zahorec. Montenegrin, or Serbian: some kind of dago. He's in London now.'

'Does he have a lair in London? Or have you merely seen him there?'

'If I knew it I wouldn't be knockin' on your door, Missy. I've not even seen him – not even I, who knows the names of every beggar that rots on the wharves. He's hid; hid deep. I want to know where.'

He stepped closer. He was built like a bull and seemed larger in his old-fashioned evening dress: frock coat, low-crowned shaggy hat, high collar wound round with a dark cravat. His hands were bare and even as she could see his fangs and the unholy reflective glimmer of his eyes, she could see how his nails had thickened and grown into inch-long claws. She knew there was something wrong with herself because as she stood before this man, this creature, who had killed thousands of people and kidnapped her daughter and who could kill her as easily as plucking a daisy, she found herself wondering about the cellular composition of those claws, and about whether the vampire's eye, dissected (*one would have to do so under artificial light*), would resemble that of a cat.

Those hands had picked up Miranda.

Had held her child . . .

She was trembling again.

'He's been killin' two and three a night sometimes,' the vampire went on. 'The police are startin' to talk. And folk are talkin', down Whitechapel and among the docks. Next they'll be startin' to look about 'em. I can't have that.' One corner of that fleshy lip raised to show a long glint of fang. 'I'll show him who's Master of London.'

'How long since he came to London?'

'Candlemas. I smelt him along the wharves below the City, and that's when the killings began. That's when first I heard whisper of his name.'

'From whom?' asked Lydia, interested. 'If no one's seen him—'

'From those as have no business to know it!' He caught her arm in a grip that made her sob and shook her like a drunkard shaking a child. 'I knew this city when 'twas the size of the Paddington railway sheds and I know every crack and sewer and cellar of her. Yet nary a hair of his arsehole have I seen. I want to know where he's hid, and who it is who's hidin' him.'

'But if you can't find him . . .'

The heavy finger, the long, cold claw, pointed at her nose. 'I want a list of every bolt hole he's got. Every lair, every cupboard where he hides his clothes and every cellar where he changes 'em, and that's *all* I want of you. You're not to put a foot in any of 'em, nor tell man nor woman, livin' nor Undead, where they lie. Just tell me. You put a note in the Personals for me, in *The Times*, under the name of Graves – or you'll never see that brat of yours alive again.'

'Please!' Lydia caught at his wrist. 'I swear I'll do whatever you ask me but give her back. I'll . . .'

She broke off. He was gone. She was aware, with a sensation like waking up, that he'd been gone for some time. She was cold to the marrow of her bones and nearly ill with weariness.

She passed through Oxford like a ghost through a city of the dead, unseeing through silence. The shut-up shop fronts and cobbled pavement of George Street, the dark gables and stumpy tower of Balliol cast not even a shadow on her mind.

*Miranda.*

The child she'd never thought she'd bear. The child she'd never even imagined she'd want, until after eight years of marriage to James she'd found herself pregnant – startled at first and simply curious to observe first-hand the physiological symptomatology on the female nervous system (*Is there anything analogous in males?*). And then suddenly it had come to her: *that is ANOTHER PERSON. I am carrying ANOTHER PERSON inside me.*

Nothing in medical science had prepared her mind for this and when she had lost that child in her first trimester she had been devastated. As if a door had closed, a gate locked against her, sealing off a road filled with wonder. The second miscarriage, in September of 1910, had been worse, like a God she had never quite believed in telling her that she was too defective to bear a child. *Four-eyes, skinnybones, goggle-eyed golliwog . . . No proper lady asks questions like that, no girl from any decent family even thinks about such things . . .*

Fifteen months after that, Miranda was born.

Her magical red-haired child.

Lamps burned in the tall old house on Holywell Street. Lydia had to steel herself to walk that last fifty feet to the front door – far more than she'd had to do in order to slap the Master Vampire of London in the face. The servants adored Miranda and Lydia felt that if any of them even spoke her daughter's name to her, she was in danger of breaking down completely. But the rigorous training she'd received from Nanna and her aunts held good. When they swarmed around her (*Don't be silly, Lydia, five people isn't a swarm . . .*) in the hall, she was able to clasp Ellen's hands, to comfort Mrs Grimes: 'Please, I need to be alone right now . . . Yes, I talked to Mr Grippen . . . I'll tell you about it later . . . No, we're not going to the police . . . Yes, he assured me that Miranda and Nan are both safe—'

*Lying, murdering devil—*

'—Please, I need to be alone right now. Mrs Grimes, could I ask you to have some tea sent up? Yes, everything is going to be all right.'

Mrs Brock, usually so grim-faced and reserved, was weeping, and the sight of her tears nearly broke Lydia's heart.

She lit one of the bedroom candles from the gas-jet in the hall, and carried it up to the study above. Through open windows the air was a soft miracle of springtime. Tea at Lady Brightwell's, dinner with Aunt Isobel, drawing-room chatter about Emily's Court gown . . . She wondered who that had happened to and why she remembered it.

A little girl playing the violin for pennies on the platform at Paddington, who had smiled at her when she'd dropped a shilling in her cup. *Did SHE have a mother?*

*Did Lionel Grippen know HER name?*

Lydia kindled the gas-jet, lit the oil-lamps above her own exquisite eighteenth-century secretaire and sat for a moment, only breathing.

The ormolu clock on the mantle gave the time as quarter to one. The Post Office was closed. Nothing could happen – *nothing* – until morning, and all the night yet to get through.

*Grippen was IN THIS HOUSE.* Her mind repeated the thoughts, stupidly, as if like fingers numb with cold they could grasp only a few things. *He must have made the servants fall asleep.* Some vampires could do that, the older ones, more experienced or more deeply imbued with charge upon charge of psychic energy that they had absorbed from death upon death.

Vampires. Walking corpses, drinkers of lives as well as of blood. Manipulators of illusion, readers of dreams.

*If I hadn't married James . . .*

But she knew she was being silly. *If I hadn't married James . . .* she couldn't even imagine what her life would be. In any case she knew she would never have been happy, vampires or no vampires.

*Grippen was in this house.* She still had braided chains of garlic, wolfsbane, and the desiccated blossoms of the Christmas rose, in a green painted tin box under her bed. *I'd better get them out, festoon the windows like some demented heroine in a penny dreadful . . .*

Lock the bedroom door whose knob and hinges James had had replaced – at startling expense – with solid silver.

All those rituals and precautions with which Dr Millward had bored everyone who came within twenty feet of him, letting them know that he never went to sleep without a wreath of garlic around his throat (his clothing reeked of it) and that he practiced three times a week, shooting moving targets with silver bullets by moonlight.

*What made us trust their word? What made us think this WOULDN'T happen in time?*

*OF COURSE we trusted their word . . .*

She remembered another vampire saying to her: *It's how we hunt . . .*

She wanted to put her head down on the desk and cry.

Instead she searched through five drawers crammed with dress-makers' bills, silk samples, sketches of other peoples' kidneys, three half-written articles on the effects of vitamins on the endocrine system ('I hope you publish under a pseudonym!' Aunt Harriet had protested over dinner), a *Votes For Women* handbill that her friend Josetta Beyerly had given her and invitations to a score of parties to which she was supposed to chaperone Emily. She finally unearthed a couple of Post Office telegraph forms.

On one she wrote the address of the hotel where James was staying in Venice. *And if he's gone on to some secret location in the Balkans I will KILL HIM.*

*Jamie, come home at once. Grippen has done something terrible.*

Even the bare facts would be torture to him, in the three days it would take him to reach Oxford. Grippen's name alone – and the fact that she would wire him to return at once – would tell him that the matter was urgent.

She looked at the other yellow form for a long time before writing anything on it. After she did, she found the teacup (and two of Mrs Grimes' biscuits) on the desk beside her, but couldn't remember Ellen either entering or leaving. So entangled her mind had been, with thoughts of the Undead.

Walking corpses that drank the blood of the living. That devoured the psychic energies released by death.

Beings who could use those energies to make people not see the fangs and the claws and the catlike, shining eyes. Who could make people trust them, or believe their promises, or lust after them with insane intensity . . .

Who could read the dreams of the living, and whisper illusions into those dreams.

Who stalked the streets of London in the dark hours when the forces of law and reason slept.

Grippen had been a vampire since 1555. At an abstemious rate of one victim a week that was eighteen thousand dead, the mortality rate of a flood or an earthquake. Nothing that produced such carnage could be trusted.

*Should* be trusted.

Her reason told her this.

But after a long time, she wrote on the second sheet of paper: *Please come. I need you.*

She folded it up, wrote on the outside:

> Don Simon Ysidro
> 2, Piazza della Trinità dei Monti
> Rome

# THREE

*He was in this house.*

In her dream she saw him – a massive, pockmarked shadow – pass through the kitchen. Mrs Grimes and Tilly slumped unconscious at the scrubbed table, the tray for the servants' evening tea between them. Bread and butter, yesterday's cinnamon cake toasted to revive its appeal.

Gaslight gleamed in the dark of his eyes as he passed up the stair.

The heavy hand with nails like dirty claws on the handle of the nursery door.

*No . . .*

Mrs Brock asleep on the old striped Chesterfield that had belonged to Uncle Ambrose, a tiny dress half-embroidered in her lap. Nan – plump and fair, with a sad tenderness that spoke of a child loved deeply and lost, somewhere in the past that seventeen-year-old nursery maids weren't supposed to have . . . Nan in the chair beside the white-painted crib.

Miranda like a little red-haired marsh fairy against the clean white of the pillows, lashes like long black feathers on pink-stained ivory cheeks.

Grippen stood beside the crib . . .

*NO . . .*

The child woke as he reached down with those long-nailed hands . . .

*NO!!!*

Gasping, Lydia jerked from sleep in time to hear the clock in the upstairs hall chime three.

The oil lamp had gone out. The gas-jets burned low.

*He was in this house . . .*

*And how did he get out of it?* Lydia got to her feet, put on her eyeglasses. *Did he carry poor Nan over one shoulder like a sack of grain and Miranda tucked under his arm? Did he make two trips?*

She frowned.

*He couldn't have carried Nan through the streets of Oxford in his arms.*

*He had an accomplice.*

From panic and fear, her mind became oddly cool. It was a problem to solve, like any medical puzzle.

*The sun didn't set until almost nine. The sky held light for nearly an hour after that.*

Her train had come in just before eleven and she'd heard the station clock strike half-past as she saw Grippen standing before her on the bridge.

*Living accomplices.*

The desk lamps had burned out. She fetched a candle from Jamie's desk, lit it at the gas jet, carried it upstairs to the nursery. The glow of the blue-glass night light showed her the empty cot, the big black-and-white toy bear and the elegant doll called Mrs Marigold, her haughty china features wreathed in corn-golden hair braided into some fantastic coiffure of Miranda's own devising.

*They would have to be living. He'd have to get Miranda out of Oxford, and be back to intercept me, AT MOST ninety minutes later.*

*The Dead travel fast*, Leonore's demon-lover said to her in the ballad, but even they couldn't be in two places at once.

*Living accomplices, to deal with Nan and Miranda after daybreak.*

She stepped back into the hallway's darkness, shielding the candle with her hand.

Trains would be leaving Oxford, either for London or for railway hubs like Nottingham, up until ten. *A horse and gig? Would a sixteenth-century vampire know how to drive a motor car? They could have gone to ground anywhere . . .* But as James had once pointed out during one of Cousin Ritchie's excited accounts of a cracking good book he'd read, it actually takes a good deal of time and expense to hold someone captive, particularly if one wants them to remain in relatively good condition for any length of time. 'It isn't something one can easily do in one's attic.' (Cousin Ritchie's book had theorized that it was possible for German agents in London to do precisely that.) 'The servants would talk.'

*And if Grippen didn't want Miranda to remain in relatively good condition, he wouldn't have kidnapped Nan as well.*

*Vampires may be able to fade into shadow and illusion*, reflected Lydia, *but their human allies are flesh and blood.*

Feeling calmed, she descended the stairs to her room, where she kindled a night light of her own, removed her spectacles, and lay awake, on top of the bedcovers, staring at the tiny pool of amber on the ceiling until the coming of first light.

Mr Polybius Teazle had offices in London's Old Street, near the railway line. Lydia found his address in James' address book. The building was a flat-fronted brick horror, and Teazle's office, two flights up, shared a hallway with a dentist, an accountant, and a manufacturer of false teeth. Teazle himself was about James' age, and had James' slightly downtrodden air of a man whom nobody would notice in a crowd.

But like James, she guessed, he saw more than he let on, and she was very glad she hadn't given him her right name, and had arranged to contact him through an accommodation address.

'Mr Grant tells me that you have operatives to search public records.' John Grant was the name under which James had done work for the Department in England – when he was working for the Department – and Mr Teazle nodded.

'That we do, Mrs Curie.' His voice was like his person, soft and unassuming.

'I'm looking for shipping records,' she said, thankful that the six pounds she'd just paid absolved her from having to come up with a story about why she wanted this information. 'An arrival in this country, probably from the Balkans, with a crate or an outsize travel trunk – anything above four and a half feet in length, weighing over a hundred and fifty pounds. This would be the end of January.'

He jotted something on his notepad. Even at a distance of four feet, Lydia hadn't the slightest idea what.

'I need names and all addresses that you can find. And I'm afraid the matter is urgent. If more than one operative can be put on the task, I would greatly appreciate it.'

'Very good, ma'am.' He might have been taking an order for tea and biscuits at a café. 'You realize you may be dealing with several hundred addresses?'

'Yes, I understand that. If any of these trunks came in through a receiving office, information about their ultimate destination would be appreciated. Do I need to pay you anything extra on account?' She reached for the battered leather handbag that she'd borrowed – along with a deplorable hat and an out-of-fashion chintz frock – from Mrs Grimes, and felt his glance size up . . . what? Her willingness to part with money over and above the retainer, in comparison with her out-at-elbows dress? Her too-new shoes?

Or was he used to people coming into his office, asking for information about shipping records or people's movements and giving accommodation addresses and false names?

'Quite all right, ma'am. I'll send an account at the end of the week.' He rose, and escorted her to the door. 'Do coffins count?'

She hoped her startle wasn't visible.

'A man can transport a deal of effects in a coffin, ma'am, and no customs official will think to open it. Particularly if the owner's thought to put a dead chicken in it, before leaving home. Begging your pardon, ma'am.'

'Definitely coffins.' The thought that any Balkan vampire would do something that obvious hadn't occurred to her, but of course, who would be looking for one?

Except vampire hunters.

'Very good, ma'am.' Mr Teazle opened the door.

As she descended to the smoky heat of the London morning, she hoped wretchedly that she wasn't going to get the poor man killed.

A short cab-ride took her to Broad Street, where another 'Private Enquiry Agent' from James' address book had his offices. Henry McClennan was Scots, fat, brisk and bustling, and assured her in his high, surprisingly light voice that for £6 7s he could have two of his operatives at Somerset House by noon, ascertaining whether any of the properties listed had been willed to anyone since 1907.

If Grippen knew she could track vampires through their property, he'd have changed the ostensible ownership of his own since then.

She turned the matter over in her mind as she walked the hot pavements toward the Women's Temperance Hotel on Blomfield Street.

Vampires didn't rent. How could one risk it, if the smallest ray of the sun's light would ignite unquenchable fire in that pale and fragile flesh?

They needed – demanded – absolute control over their surroundings. No wonder the thought of angry and suspicious dock-workers made Lionel Grippen nervous.

So who *was* hiding this Mr Zahorec?

That morning, as soon as it grew light, she had checked the ground in the open strip of earth behind her house for wheel tracks. The Slipe, as it was called – too wide to be a lane but not quite wide enough to be considered a yard – gave access to the stables, kitchens, and domestic offices of New College, and saw considerable traffic during the day, but Lydia thought she'd discerned the prints of a four-wheeled brougham that had waited there during the night. It didn't tell her much, and Grippen would almost certainly learn of it if she went rushing around Oxford asking if anyone had rented such a vehicle the previous day. But her conviction grew that he had used the living for accomplices, not the Undead. In the six years since Horace Blaydon had wreaked slaughter upon the London nest, the Master of London must have made new fledglings . . .

*I suppose I'd better learn who those are*, she thought as she took her key from the hotel desk, where she had rented a room under another name. Names and initials were the tracks she followed, in tracing vampire property. *He may hold property in their names rather than his own.* With a certain amount of difficulty, owing to the absence of a chambermaid, she changed out of Mrs Grimes' borrowed frock into a stylish celery-green Patou ensemble, rearranged her hair, applied rice powder, the tiniest whisper of rouge, the faintest traces of mascaro and kohl (not enough to elicit comment from Aunt Isobel) and tried to imagine how she was going to get through the next twenty-four hours.

It would be that long before she could reasonably expect to receive any information from her operatives. Two or three times that long before James would be home, if he'd been in Venice when her telegraph reached his hotel. To return to Oxford now would only result in being driven frantic by the anxieties and unsolicited suggestions of her servants. But a claim to be ill would at best spread the saga of her indisposition throughout the family (with speculation that the illness was faked to avoid social responsibilities), and at worst bring Aunt Isobel hot-foot to Oxford – sciatica or no sciatica – to bully her into wellness. Isobel's conviction that Lydia was 'soft' on her servants might easily lead to inquiries that could end with the police being called in.

*It would also be useful*, Lydia reflected as she adjusted her hat, *to know if Grippen's fledglings even know that he's enlisted me to find this Zahorec, and if they approve, or disapprove, of the participation of the living in their affairs.*

*And if* – she locked the door behind her, started down the dingy stairway – *Grippen has sufficient command over them to keep them from killing me before I locate Miranda and get her to safety.*

# FOUR

L uckily, Aunt Isobel was far too self-involved to notice her niece's pallor or the smudges of sleeplessness under her eyes. When Lydia came through the door of Halfdene House at noon, the stout, dark-haired little woman whom her uncle had married – enthroned now in a wickerwork bath chair of marvelous design and attended by a footman, her maid, and a harassed-looking Irish nurse – swept down upon her with a list of accessories Emily's wardrobe would need for her presentation and regaled her, over a luncheon that she didn't seem to notice Lydia did not touch, with a catalogue of the eligible gentlemen expected to be present at Lady Binney's masquerade on Saturday night and the net worth of their parents.

'I'm told Freddy Farnsworth – Lord Varvel's heir – has two thousand a year settled on him but the family's worth a good ten thousand . . . Lawrence Rockland's a trifle old but the Rocklands have at least a quarter million in the Funds. Your Aunt Lavinnia tells me not to be deceived by the Clifford boy; he's obliged to hang out for an heiress . . . What a pity young Colwich got snapped up by that American girl! She has the most frightful accent – if you ask me, nothing can take the place of a good Swiss finishing school . . .'

Lydia recalled her own days in a good Swiss finishing school and shuddered. Cousin Emily said nothing, well aware that this commotion had far more to do with her mother's determination to prove her offspring 'acceptable' than with any desires of Emily's own. Tall and slender, like most of the Halfdenes, Emily took after her mother's sallow coloring: Lydia wondered if she could order her gown in ivory hues rather than the 'snow-princess' satins her mother rhapsodized over.

*After all*, she reflected, *I AM paying for it* . . . Another 'duty to the family', attendant upon her mother's having 'betrayed her lineage' by marrying extremely well.

'. . . entire interior of the house in different colors of marble!' exclaimed Aunt Harriet, setting down her fish fork. 'I never heard of anything so vulgar in my life!' Barrister's wife or not, she remained every inch a Viscount's daughter and knew to a carat's-weight what was vulgar and what wasn't. 'Though how the Crossfords got Colwich to propose to the girl I can't imagine. Noel has always been a little *fond* of that friend of his . . .'

'With a settlement of three million dollars,' retorted Aunt Isobel, whose marriage to Richard, Lord Halfdene, had much more to do with her dowry than her family's non-existent background, 'I don't suppose there was much shilly-shallying. Charles, this water is *cold*! You know what Dr Fielding said about chilled water being bad for the liver! *Honestly* . . . And I don't suppose there was any trouble getting Lady Mary Wycliffe to present the girl at Court . . . Lady Mary Binney, I *should* say!'

'Poor Lady May,' sighed Aunt Harriet. 'Married to that *dreadful* man, but they say her father was all to pieces, with Wycliffe House about to be sold out from under them . . .'

*Grippen can't be keeping them in London*, thought Lydia. *I'm not sure you COULD keep a kidnapped baby hidden – unless he drugged her* . . .

*Dear God, don't let him have drugged her.*

Eight months of internship at a London charity hospital had given Lydia deadly experience in how small children could most easily be kept silent.

*Don't let him have harmed Nan* . . .

She tried to push from her mind the sight of her companion Margaret Potton's body lying, drained of blood, on that high carved bed in Constantinople. Did Miranda's *jailer* even know that he – or she – was in the pay of a vampire? And that vampires had an expeditious habit of cleaning up after themselves in order to keep the secret of their existence?

'Not that it will make any difference to this what's-her-name American – Miss Armistead – millionaire's daughter or not, with that frightful father of hers tagging along to "make sure the job gets done properly".'

'Job indeed!' Isobel sniffed. 'I'm told she's gone to Worth for her gown, so we'd probably better do the same for Emily, Lydia . . .'

*If Grippen was with his human accomplice for the first hour or so, they could have taken the train and no one would notice . . .*

'Crossford's heir or not, Colwich isn't anyone I'd care to see wed to one of *my* daughters,' opined Aunt Harriet smugly. 'Running off to Paris to paint things . . . turning himself into a veritable disciple of that *ghoul* Millward . . . Urania Ottmoor tells me he was at Andromache Brightwell's tea yesterday and prosed *dreadfully*! Spending every penny of his allowance on nasty old books . . .'

'The portion he doesn't spend on kif,' added Aunt Isobel, anxious to dissociate herself from her former plans to wed Emily to the Viscount. 'And I'm sure neither of *your* daughters need fear being proposed to by the Earl of Crossford's son.'

Harriet lifted patrician brows. 'Oh, not with a fortune like Titus Armistead's on offer.' She prodded the cold roast beef set before her, then ignored it as she would have an audible belch in Church. All of Lord Halfdene's daughters – Lydia's mother included, Lydia recalled – gave the impression of living solely on moonbeams and wild strawberries, and regarded their brother's stout wife and her pottery-manufacturing family as unmentionably gross. 'One regrets seeing the spectacle matchmaking society mamas make, scrambling after a title, no matter what sort of man it's pasted to.'

Isobel turned bright pink.

*Grippen is wealthy.* Jamie had told her that master vampires would create fledglings in part to gain control of their estates . . . of the hidey-holes and safety that money would bring. And even the most modest of investments, he had once remarked, would accrue

a startling amount of interest if left to mature for three hundred and
fifty years . . .

That kind of wealth could buy a guard for a woman and child,
and no questions asked. Even as it would buy herself – with luck
– the addresses of total strangers who'd brought large trunks into
England last December.

*Oh, Miranda, I'm sorry.*

She thought of her child . . . *Where? In an attic? In a cellar?*
Nan would never abandon her tiny charge, but Lydia could easily
imagine Nan trying to figure out a way to escape with the child,
and the possibility turned her cold inside.

*Down a drainpipe, across a roof, carrying Miranda in her arms . . .*
*STOP IT THIS MINUTE! They're all right. They'll be all right . . .*

'. . . won't you, Lydia dearest?'

Aunt Isobel was regarding her expectantly.

'I'll certainly try.' Lydia wondered what she'd just let herself
in for.

'Excellent!' Isobel beamed. 'I'll let your Aunt Lavinnia know.
Now you'd best be going, if you're to be at Worth's by two.'

Somehow, Lydia made it through the day. When she returned to the
hotel in Blomfield Street to change clothes ('What your mother
would say,' deplored Aunt Harriet in parting, 'if she knew any
daughter of hers was riding in a common hack . . .') she crossed to
the nearby Commercial Hotel in Finsbury Circus that was one of
her three accommodation addresses, thanking James for everything
he'd taught her about what the Department politely called 'tradecraft'.
Two telegrams from Ellen awaited her, sent at noon, and at three.

No communication from James. Nothing from Rome.

She telegraphed back that she would be staying in London for
the night, and would Ellen please send to this address a parcel with
clean linen, her plum-colored walking-suit (*Is it too late in the
season for plum?*), her black-and-apricot Paquin suit (*Let's be on
the safe side*), the apricot velvet hat with the heron feathers, the
black straw hat with the white flowers (*Does that really go with the
plum?*), the black suede Gibson shoes, the Cuban-heeled pumps,
the black-and-ivory pumps, another bottle of rosewater and glycerin,
four pairs of white silk stockings and her white kid gloves. (*Oh,
dear, that looks like rather a lot . . .*)

At the Christian Railway Hotel on the opposite side of the Circus, she picked up Mr Teazle's first installment of shipping notes, and Mr McClennan's information about which vampire nests had changed hands since 1907. Slender packets enough, but she guessed she wouldn't be sleeping tonight.

Dinner at Aunt Lavinnia's – known as Lady Peasehall to London society at large – and then the Opera, in ostentatious celebration of the engagement of Lord Colwich to his American heiress (Lady Crossford had been to school with Aunt Lavinnia and they were still bosom-bows). That meant having to borrow a dress from Emily, which entailed a long argument with Aunt Isobel ('You can't borrow that one, it's for the Crossfords' ball next week . . . Oh, not the rose silk either; Lady Varvel is sure to be at the Opera – not that she knows Enrico Caruso from Robinson Crusoe – and she'll be sure to recognize it at her Venetian breakfast Monday night . . .')

Lydia wondered if she could invent a headache to get out of the inevitable supper afterwards at the Savoy. If nothing else, she reflected as she washed off powder, rouge, mascaro, kohl and then settled before the fly-specked hotel mirror to reapply them afresh, the information the detective agencies had sent her would give her names.

Vampires changed identities, if they lived long enough. They willed their property to themselves, when the authorities might have grown suspicious about Mr Brown being a hundred and fifty years old. Or they willed their property to the Master who made them, who held over them a sway which could barely be comprehended by the living.

*My darling, I'll find you . . .*

Rattling to Aunt Lavinnia's in a cab, Lydia recalled her own first (and only) 'season' in 1899, before her father had melodramatically cast her out of his house upon the discovery that she had applied – and been accepted – to Somerville College, Oxford, to train in medicine. Dressed in the height of Mr Worth's elegance and rigid with anxiety, she had been borne through the still-bright daylight of the streets of London toward Berkeley Square.

Only on the present occasion at least she had the quiet and privacy of the cab – odiferous as it was – instead of the chaperonage of her stepmother and her Aunt Faith, neither of whom ever shut up for so much as a moment.

*You have dealt with vampires before this, and you survived.*
*Jamie, where are you?*

Dakers – Aunt Lavinnia's butler – bowed as he took her (borrowed) coat and said, with the liberty of one who had known her from earliest childhood, 'You never came in that vehicle, Mrs Asher? Her Ladyship will be most shocked.'

'Only if someone tattles,' Lydia replied, and slipped him a half-crown.

Without change of expression he led the way up the curving oval of stairs, and opened the drawing-room doors at the top. 'Mrs Asher,' he announced.

'Well, here you are at last, dear.' With brittle graciousness, her tiny, perfect stepmother turned from speaking to a man in evening dress whose looming outline – a Stonehenge menhir wrapped in black and white – Lydia did not recognize. Hands outstretched in welcome, exquisite in midnight-blue crêpe de chine which set off her delicate blonde prettiness, Valentina Willoughby rustled over to her late husband's only child. As usual in her presence, Lydia felt six feet tall and all elbows and knees as she leaned down to kiss the powdered cheek. The broad diamond 'dog-collar' necklace that plastered her stepmother's white throat had belonged to Lydia's mother: her father's second wife had undoubtedly worn it to annoy the stepdaughter whom she had – erroneously – thought still disinherited upon her late husband's death . . . and also to enrage that stepdaughter's aunts.

But, as Isobel had pointed out over luncheon, *Valentina knows everybody*, and had to be kept sweet for the sake of Emily's chances of meeting the right gentlemen.

'Mrs Asher –' Valentina's voice handled the name exactly as her fingers would have dealt with a dead mouse – 'allow me to introduce Mr Armistead, of Denver, Colorado. Mr Armistead, my *dearest* daughter. And I'm *sure* I have no need to tell you, Lydia, darling, of his lovely daughter's engagement to Lord Colwich. Their love story is the talk of the town!'

'Long as Cece's happy,' grunted the big man, in a voice like gravel being stirred at the bottom of a well. 'Beats me why every gal in the country's on fire to marry some Englishman or other just 'cause he's got Sir this or Lord that on his name.' Up close, Lydia had an impression of grizzled hair, a broken nose, and a mouth like an iron door.

'Like them paintings you buy over here. Why, they'll ask six thousand dollars for a picture of some woman with a bird that you could have painted up for two hundred in New York, and the New York one's brighter, and livens up a room.'

At that point Cecelia Armistead rustled over – she of the three-million-dollar marriage portion – exclaiming in ecstasies at the beauties of Lord Peasehall's London house. 'That beautiful fireplace in the long drawing room . . . Can you have one made like it, Pa*pa*, for our new house? Pa*pa* –' she carefully emphasized the second syllable, as if her governess had taught her that this pronunciation was more elegant, exactly as Lydia's had – 'has bought the most wonderful house for Noel and me! So ancient! It's practically a ruin!' She clasped her hands before her breast in delight at the prospect.

'I love ruins – don't you?' She smiled at Lydia, Spanish-dark eyes in the creamy oval of her face. 'And there are just *none* in America! When we visited the old priory near Leeds, I begged Daddy – Pa*pa*,' she corrected herself, 'to take me back there after dark, so I could see the place by moonlight—'

'I didn't bring you three thousand miles to have you catch cold,' growled Pa*pa*. 'There wasn't a moon that night anyway. But –' he jabbed at her with a finger like a policeman's truncheon – 'you say the word, honey, and I'll send a man to photograph every square inch of that ruin and I'll build you one just as good at Newport. We've got a summer place at Newport,' he confided to Lydia, as Cece went into further raptures over Emily's ice-blue satin dress. 'Cost me a million-eight, but it's every bit as fine as the Astor place or the Berwinds'.'

Lydia was given ample opportunity to hear more about the summer place in Newport – and about the London house which Armistead had purchased for his daughter and her affianced husband – throughout dinner, as she had been seated between the American millionaire and his business partner, the equally wealthy and recently knighted Sir Alfred Binney.

'Meself . . . *My*self,' Sir Alfred amended, 'I'd kiss the door-knocker of a place that only costs twice what you'd pay new to fix it up, like you're payin' for Dallaby 'ouse . . . House. You shoulda

seen Wycliffe House 'fore I bought it! Had to be half pulled apart
'fore it could be livable – oil lamps, one bog and not a bathroom
in the place – tcha! 'Ere, you, let me have a bit more of that wine,
'fore you takes it away. Bottoms up to the 'appy couple!'

Across the table, Lydia saw her mother's old friend Lady Mary
– formerly Wycliffe, now Binney – wince.

'And I've 'eard that place in Scotland old Crossford gave Colwich
for the weddin's worse still. Grouse moor or no, the roof's fallin'
in, the tower's crumblin' to bits . . .'

Lydia closed her eyes briefly against a pounding headache and
an almost uncontrollable desire to brain Sir Alfred with the epergne.

Across the table, Viscount Colwich, whose *boutonnière* of lily
of the valley accorded ill with his massive six-foot frame, listened
in glum silence to Cece Armistead's gushing account of two English
ladies who had seen the ghost of Marie Antoinette in the gardens
of Versailles. 'Not simply the ghost, but they were actually *transported* back into the past! When they returned to the place a year
later, the paths they recalled were not the same, and both of them
identified the woman they had seen – sketching in front of the Petit
Trianon – from a drawing of the Queen . . .'

Colwich glanced pleadingly down the table at Ned Seabury, who
had clearly been invited to 'make up the numbers' disarrayed by
the unexpected inclusion of Julia Thwaite's hired companion Mrs
Bellwether. Lydia could almost feel the meeting of their eyes.

Carriages for the Opera had been ordered for eight, and Sir Alfred
Binney made sure everyone knew he'd been to the opera in both
Milan and Paris.

At the first opportunity, Lydia retreated to the little cloakroom
adjacent to the ladies' toilet, intending to lie down there – she knew
the room was furnished with a daybed – and be 'discovered' in a
debilitated condition by the next person into the room, hopefully
not Valentina. But she found Cece Armistead there already, stuffing
tissue-paper into the toe of one of her too-long slippers.

'You must excuse Daddy.' The girl looked up as Lydia entered.
'He's such a diamond in the rough. But he has such *feeling* for
paintings, and for manuscripts . . .'

Lydia had formed the impression that the American's 'feeling'
for paintings, incunabula, and medieval manuscripts was largely that
of his accountant, but she said, 'Indeed.' Though she had a hint of

her father's sturdiness, Miss Armistead was a pretty girl, with her
Peruvian mother's dark coloring and a voice – despite a tendency
to drop back into her American accent – both pleasant and sweet.
She was glaringly overdressed for her years – nineteen, her father
had said – and her debutante status: in addition to a gown of claret-
colored silk cut deep in the bosom, she wore sparkling girandole
earrings, diamond bracelets on both wrists over her gloves, a
diamond tiara (Lydia had already seen her stepmother and Aunt
Lavinnia eyeing this with scorn), three strands of very large pearls
that hung almost to her waist, and a 'dog-collar' necklace of
diamonds and pearls that put Valentina Willoughby's to shame.

A single strand of pearls – Lydia could almost hear Aunt Lavinnia
say it to Lady Savenake – was the only thing appropriate for a girl
in her first season . . .

'I'm so grateful to Sir Alfred and Lady Mary for sponsoring me
this way,' added Cece, a little shyly. 'He and Lady Mary met us in
Paris before coming on here. Lady Mary – dang it!' she added, as
her necklaces caught on the profusion of her curls. 'Ow!' The attempt
to pull her hair clear sent the dog-collar slithering to the floor.

'Oh, I hate the catch on that thing! One of these days I'm going
to lose it and then Daddy will be furious . . .'

*Well he might be*, Lydia reflected as she gathered up the glittering
weight in her hands. The thing was easily nine hundred guineas.
'I'll get it.' She moved to put it around the girl's throat.

And as she did so, even without her spectacles, she saw on the
right side of Cece's throat, just above the jugular vein, the small,
fresh scab of two puncture wounds, as if the flesh had been bitten
by an animal.

For a blank second Lydia wondered if this were her imagination.

But Emily, coming in at that moment saying, 'Cece, have you
got a cigarette? After listening to Ned Seabury for two solid hours
I deserve—' then stopped in her tracks and said, 'Cece, what *did*
you do to your neck?'

And Cecelia put her hand over the wound and said, 'Just a stupid
accident with a pin.'

And she smiled a smile of dreamy ecstasy.

# FIVE

*I*s it Grippen?

Light rain, blowing in late, clattered on the window. Across the street, the chime on All Hallows church struck one.

*Or one of his fledglings?*

*What can I do?*

Lydia stared unseeing at the neat pages of handwritten notes before her. *Jan. 12,* Empress Josephine *from Bordeaux, Matthias Barrière and Family, of Bordeaux – 2 trunks 2×2×5½ 275 lb. Same craft, Ottakar Dusik of Prague, trunk 2×17 – ×4 200 lb. Jan. 13* Doksa *out of Athens, Christov Antokolski of Kiev, coffin of his father. Jan. 13,* Sirena *from Venice, Natalia Vatarescu of Sofia, and maid, 3 steamer trunks: 2×2×4 250 lb, 28'×17'×50 220 lb, 28'×22'×3.5' 250 lbs . . .*

*What could I say, and to whom?*

She knew the look in Miss Armistead's eyes. The girl was being lured by a vampire.

Courted in her dreams – as Lydia's companion Margaret Potton had been courted four years ago – with visions of a soulful Byronic wanderer through the ages, who lay the heart he did not think he still possessed at the feet of a living girl who could save him . . .

She wondered if the vampire seducer had grinned to himself all the while at the depth of her eager surrender, tickled at his own power to fool.

She shivered, and drew the room's spare blanket closer around her bare shoulders.

*Ludovico Bertolo of Sofia, and valet, Jan 15, from Cherbourg, on the* Reine Margot, *trunk 28'×18'×6', 300 lbs. Fuad Al-Wahid of Cairo, Jan 17, on the* Great George *out of Bordeaux, with the coffin of his brother . . .*

By and large, vampires fed on people no one would miss. Crossing-sweepers, mudlarks, paupers in workhouses or old men sleeping on alley pavements in the East End.

But neither man nor vampire lives on bread alone. The drunkards, the whores, the irredeemably abandoned were no fun to hunt.

And with all of eternity before them, vampires – she had been told by Jamie, who knew them better – were often and easily bored.

Her skull felt as if it would split.

Cece would deny it.

If Grippen – or one of Grippen's fledglings – was Cece's demon lover, Miranda and Nan would probably die if Lydia asked questions, poked into shadows.

*They'll probably kill me, too.*

*And Cece.*

Would vampires dare kill the daughter of an American millionaire?

*Grippen wouldn't.* That was a thousand times worse than two or three paupers a night.

*But none of his fledglings is more than six years a vampire. Who knows who they are, or how much control he has over them.*

By the end of the evening Aunt Lavinnia had been unobtrusively maneuvering to break up Lydia's conversations with the American girl, lest – Lydia knew without a word being exchanged – her growing friendship with Cece encourage Armistead and his bumptious partner Binney to believe themselves 'accepted' into the Halfdene-Peasehall social circle.

*God, forgive me for not pulling Cece aside this evening, demanding to know what's going on. For not warning her, telling her . . .*

Telling her what?

*5–7 Shoe Lane, willed by William Boyle of Newham Street to Francis Houghton of Priest Row, Nov. '07. 10 Bell Yard, willed June '08 by Cosimo Graves of Rood Lane to Bartholomew Barrow of Rose Street. By the same testament, 2 Rose Street willed to Daphne Scrooby of Parish Street, and 13–17 Horsleydown Street to Nicholas Barger of Rood Lane. 29 Rosemary Lane by deed of gift Dec '09 by Viscount Vauxhill to Nicholas Barger of Rood Lane . . .*

*(Dear Heavens, not Geoffrey Vauxhill! Father wanted me to marry him!)*

*Vampires hunt slowly, when they hunt for sport. They'll court a victim for weeks or months . . . Cece looked FAR too healthy for this to have been going on long . . .*

*I can't let her meet him again!* But even as she thought it, she knew she'd have to. Distantly the clang of the Liverpool Street train yards broke the dark of the sleeping city, and the coal-oil stink of

the lamp smoke vied with the pungency of the dried garlic she'd
hung in garlands around the window.

*I should have hung them in Miranda's nursery.*

Osric Millward – she had heard from Valentina, accompanied by
a tinkling, silvery laugh – had such protections on the windows of
the small chambers he rented in Kensington, on the settlement that
his wife's family still paid to him. 'Honestly, I'm astonished the
poor woman stayed with him as long as she did! She's a cousin of
Honoria Savenake's . . . still lives in Deauville . . . I hope your
husband doesn't keep horseshoes nailed to the doors or strews salt
across the thresholds . . .?'

Dimly, she heard the clock strike again.


She opened her eyes. Sat up. The rain had ceased, and the lamp
had gone out. Something moved outside the window.

Some flying thing that blundered into the glass.

Lydia put on her spectacles, got to her feet.

She crossed to the window, her long red hair hanging down her
back in the ruins of her chignon, the fawn-and-pink silk of her
niece's gown whispering perfumed secrets. Whatever was out there,
it was small and pale, bobbing erratically in the darkness. Sulfur
eyes sparked in the light.

*Is this a dream?*

Feeling strangely unlike herself, Lydia unhooked the swags of
garlic and wolfsbane from the curtain rods. *Did Cece dream something like this? About how she had to go to the window, open it for
whatever that is – that white flying thing out there?*

*Did it whisper like this in her mind?*

She stood for a moment, hands filled with dried blossom, looking
out into the darkness. Then she carried the garlands to the farthest
corner of the room, covered them with the bed pillows, came back
to the window and opened the casements.

Stretched out her hand into the blackness of the night.

It landed on her wrist, a white mantis half again the length of
her palm. Tilted its triangular head to regard her with yellow eyes.
Four little feet pricked the skin as it walked up her wrist, the other
two, tucked centaur-like up under its breast, for all the world as if
it was indeed about to recite a Paternoster for the insects it would
kill.

She brought it inside, set it on the corner of the table where the reflections of the street-lamps did not reach. Wondered again if this was really happening.

The mantis changed, and a man stood beside the table. He was young and very thin, his long hair like dusty moonlight over his shoulders and his champagne-colored eyes reflecting the dim luminosity like a cat's.

Scars marked his cheekbone and throat, as if the wax-white flesh had been sliced with razors.

He said, 'Mistress,' and because this was a dream Lydia stepped forward into his arms.

His flesh was cold through his clothing and his grip like whalebone and steel cable. It was like embracing a skeleton in a two-hundred-guinea suit.

'Hush.' He brought up a gentle thumb to wipe the tears on her face. She realized she was weeping, and could not stop. 'Hush, t'will be well. T'will all be well, Mistress.' The clawed nail touched her skin like a dagger-point. For a time she could only cling to him, terrified that waking would drag them apart, until her tears were all cried.

'He took my child,' she whispered at last. 'Grippen took my child.' Just being able to say it was like a steel band breaking from around her chest.

She didn't have to keep silent any longer, or be strong, or explain.

Don Simon Christian Morado de la Cadeña-Ysidro understood.

He said one word, in Spanish, that Lydia guessed would have taken paint off a gate.

Then, 'What does he want of you?' He handed her into the desk chair where she had been sitting, replaced the blanket around her shoulders. Then he perched one narrow flank on the corner of the table, folded those long hands upon his knee. He had a gold signet ring, worn nearly smooth by time.

'There's an interloper here, another vampire.' She removed her spectacles, wiped her eyes. Replaced them. Simon had seen her in worse state than as a goggle-eyed golliwog, and anyway this was only a dream. 'You got my telegram?'

'Upon arising. Service in Rome is villainous.'

'When will you be in England?'

'Tomorrow night. *Die Todten reiten schnell*, as Burger observes.

One of the few advantages I have ever found in being dead. He wishes *you* to find this interloper?' Another man's brows would have knit – there was only a flicker of shadow in those yellow pupils pleated with faded gray.

'He says he can't. He's a Serb, or a Montenegrin, Grippen says, calling himself Zahorec . . . Simon, before anything else, please, can you learn if Miranda is still alive? She's with her nursery maid; Grippen kidnapped both.'

'Then I should say the odds are good that both thrive.'

'But it doesn't mean she's safe. It doesn't mean she isn't terrified, or hungry, or cold, or alone in the dark. It doesn't mean they haven't murdered poor Nan—'

'Nan?'

'Nan Wellit. The nursery maid.' Lydia wiped her eyes again, propped her spectacles back into place. 'She's only seventeen. Heaven knows what will happen to her – to them both – if she tries to escape. Or if whoever is keeping watch over them panics. . . .'

'Were I employed by Lionel Grippen to guard one whom he wished to keep well,' remarked Don Simon, 'I should take great care how I panicked.'

In appearance, the young man before her was as he had been when death had claimed him, in his mid-twenties, in 1555. Lydia had not seen him in waking life since a November night last year in Peking, and the scars on his face – taken in a struggle with the Master of Constantinople, to protect her – seemed fresh as ever after four years. *How long DOES it take vampire flesh to heal?* He could keep the living from seeing them, though Lydia suspected that they would be visible in a mirror.

She wished she could do as much with her eyeglasses.

He had killed, probably, at least as many people as Grippen had. Drunk the energies of their deaths in order to maintain his own powers to tamper with the perceptions of the living.

Murderer and monster, a walking corpse.

She took his thin hand. 'Please.'

'It shall be as you desire, Mistress.' Inflections of sixteenth-century Castille clung to his whispering voice. 'At this distance, knowing neither your child nor the girl, no, my mind cannot touch theirs. In any case I would hazard that Lionel guesses you will call on me – though to my knowledge he knows not where I am hid – and he will have bestowed the pair of them underground. The thickness of earth baffles our senses. Thus it is, I suspect, that he can find no trace of this interloper himself. London is an old city, and built upon river clay. Underground rivers flow beneath her streets, and the movement of living water confuses perception. Ancient crypts lie deep below the palaces of your progress, and Roman vaults below them. An interloper, whose mind Lionel knows not, could easily hide from him for a time.'

'Since early February, Grippen says. But Grippen's dealt with interlopers before.'

'But interlopers before promenaded themselves upon their arrival, walked the night streets that he might see them, and asked his leave to hunt. I take it this man has not.'

Lydia shook her head. 'Grippen says he's been killing, every night and sometimes twice and thrice—'

'Has he, indeed?' This time the vampire's eyebrows really did go up.

'Grippen said the police – and worse, the people of the neighbor-hood – were getting angry and suspicious—'

'Well they might. There are those among the Undead who would – an they could – kill twice and thrice in a night, and most would hunt every night an t'were possible. But 'tis not. Indeed, without stooping to the vulgarity of a pun, I would say 'tis the chief bone of contention between most Masters and their fledglings that the Master must keep those he has created from over-hunting their grounds, and revealing to the living the existence of the nest. 'Tis curious that this interloper, knowing himself in a strange city with a powerful master, would kill in this fashion. What does he do, that he would *need* to kill so?'

He looked about him at the dingy flowered wallpaper, the narrow bed. 'And where is James during all of this? I take it you are in London—'

'Yes, at the Women's Temperance Hotel on Blomfield Street. James is at a philology conference in Venice, lecturing on Balkan dialects. I wired him this morning.' Already it seemed weeks ago. 'At the same time I wired you, but I've heard nothing. I think he must have gone on from Venice to . . . somewhere else . . .'

Her voice faltered. Another woman might have suspected an errant husband of marital divagation. Lydia's own fears ran deeper than that. James had often said that no one ever really left the Department: working for them was more than something you did. It was something you were.

Since October – according to both Jamie and to her friend Josetta Beyerly – warfare had again raged in the Balkans, as the small nations that had broken from the Turkish Empire in the previous war in May turned on that weakened giant (and one another, James said) with demands for more territory. With Russia egging on the three attackers there was a very real danger (James said) that Russia would be drawn in to fight the Turks – who would call on their allies the Germans, causing Russia to call on *their* allies the French, who for forty years had been waiting for an excuse to attack Germany and retrieve territory lost in a previous conflict . . .

Even as Germany champed like a racehorse in the gate, seeking the first justification to launch itself at France in the hopes of a quick victory and the chance to seize France's possessions in Indo-China, in Africa, on the far-flung islands of the Pacific.

*Europe is a powder keg*, Jamie had said before he'd left for Venice, *waiting for a spark* . . .

Maybe that was why James had finally gone. *Venice is next door to the fighting.*

'Have you sought this invisible interloper?'

'I have detectives going through the shipping records from the end of January. I think he must have fled Montenegro when the fighting started. Once I can find a name, or names, I'll start checking the land registry office, though of course he may not have registered a sale—'

'I never do.'

'What I really need is bank records. I'm guessing Zahorec will have used Barclays Bank, since they have offices in Bucharest and Sofia. I don't know if Jamie can get that information out of his old colleagues at the Department.'

'It may be that I can assist in this matter. One would not wish James' former colleagues – worthy men as I am sure they are – brought in any way to notice this interloper. One never knows what they will do with such information, nor where such trails may lead.'

Lydia regarded him with widened eyes. 'Can you do that?'

'Think you that such matters lie beyond me?' And, when she did not reply, but looked aside with a sudden flood of hope coloring her cheeks, he asked, 'Aught else, Lady?'

She hesitated for so long, her heart pounding (*which he can perfectly well hear, drat him*), that he repeated softly, 'Aught else?'

She almost whispered, 'The Bank of England.'

Stillness after the words, like water frozen to silence. In the street a drunk raised his voice in song, faded again.

'Barclays were more likely, for Zahorec to use.'

'Not Zahorec,' she said. 'Grippen.' She looked back at him. 'That's where he kept his money back in 1907. I won't do anything silly,' she added, a little defiantly. 'But I need to know where they are. Miranda and Nan. I need to know they're all right. I think they're being kept by living accomplices, not his fledglings—'

'Heaven forefend. Lionel is a fool when it comes to the making of fledglings. I'd not trust any of his get, nor can he.'

'All the more reason I have to find them,' she said. 'And I need to know who the fledglings are, so I won't waste my time on false scents. And there's a girl here,' she added, a little uncertainly. 'An American. A millionaire's daughter. She's being seduced by a vampire. Hunted.' Her eyes met his again. 'The way you said once that vampires hunt the living for sport.'

She spoke accusingly, defying him to say he had not played that mocking game. Meeting for champagne suppers, walking by night along the Embankment. Using the psychic glamour of the vampire to make the victim think they were with a living man or woman, make them not notice the clawed nails, the long teeth . . .

Killing elsewhere early in the night so as not to be hungry too urgently, so as not to harvest the victim until the evil sweetness of love and betrayal and tragedy has sufficiently ripened. But loving the smell of the blood, the smell of trust soon to be betrayed.

*Have you done that?*

His eyes were an expressionless labyrinth of sulfur and salt. *I am as I am. What do you think I have done?*

It was her gaze that fell.

'But I can't let Grippen know that I learn anything about his fledglings, you see. Not even that I'm asking. And it might be Grippen that's after her.'

'A man of no logic.' The soft voice was dismissive. 'And a Protestant to boot.' He walked to the window. Though over the real

London – the London of soot and grief and Court presentations and little girls who had to play the violin for pennies on station platforms – the fingernail moon had set hours ago, there was moonlight in her dream. 'If he wants this Bohemian destroyed—'

'He didn't say he wanted him destroyed,' said Lydia. 'What he asked for, specifically, was for me to find Zahorec's lairs and hiding places. In fact he commanded that I not set foot in any of them . . .'

'Did he so?' Don Simon tilted his head. 'Curious. Most curious.'

'What should I do?'

'Tread carefully, Mistress.' He turned back to her, held out long fingers cold as death. 'Remember always that Lionel's fledglings hate him – an emotion not uncommon between Master vampires and those whom they draw into the world of the night, once they discover what it is truly to be a slave. In their hatred they distrust all his works, and will watch you if nothing else, particularly if this girl is indeed their quarry. I will be with you soon.'

She shivered, and drew the blanket about her shoulders again. *It was YOU who drew James into the world of the night. Had you not done that, Miranda would be sleeping safely in her own bed tonight, and I safely in mine.*

When she did not take his hand he crossed to her, and laid his palm to her cheek.

'I beg pardon, Mistress.'

She did not look at him. 'I don't know that I can give it.'

'You need not. Send to your home for things which belong to your child and the maid. I doubt I shall be able to find them e'en so, but I shall make the attempt. I know well that this is in part my doing, and if for no other reason than that I will do all that I can, to make good what I owe.'

Speaking carefully, to keep her voice from shaking, Lydia said, 'I'm not sure there is any way that you can do that.'

'Nor I,' replied the vampire. 'Thus all I can give you is my willingness to perish in the attempt.'

She woke still sitting at the rickety table in pre-dawn gray, chilled to the bone in her cousin's silk evening frock, to the groaning of the trains and the rusty chime of All Hallows, and the grumpy clunk as the hotel's bootboy dropped a pair of shoes outside her door.

# SIX

For two days, Lydia found herself prey to the frequent sensation of being in a dream – or, rather, of being in several dreams, traversing between them by cab rides along High Holborn.

Six years ago, when her husband had first been blackmailed by Don Simon Ysidro into seeking out a vampire-hunter considerably more efficient than Osric Millward, she had gone into hiding in London and out of curiosity had made the attempt to read that classic of vampire fiction, Bram Stoker's *Dracula*. Don Simon had little good to say of the work, which Lydia had found unreadable, but then few things compared to a good solid medical case history in her opinion. One scene, however, remained in her mind. While a prisoner in Castle Dracula, the fictional hero Jonathan Harker witnesses the arrival of a woman before the castle walls, a woman whose child the vampire count stole: she pounds upon the castle gate, crying '*Monster, give me my child . . .*'

A scene of melodramatic horror ('*If Dracula and all three of his wives were living on the excess population of a small mountain village,*' Simon had remarked, '*I doubt he would have left it to the wolves to make a meal of her.*'), but one which returned to her now in her dreams.

*Monster, give me my child . . .*

Had she known where Lionel Grippen slept in his coffin, she thought those first two nights that she would have gone there, pounded on the panels, cried to him: *Monster, give me my child.*

And would have been killed, she reflected despairingly, by the two-legged wolves he was capable of summoning, as surely as that poor Transylvanian peasant-woman had been.

Polybius Teazle knew whereof he spoke, when he'd warned her of the sheer volume of travelers who had entered London at the end of January burdened with a trunk large enough to conceal the body of a man. Patiently, Lydia divided those who'd come singly (*What man would endanger his family by bringing them on such an enterprise?*) from those traveling *en famille* (*And what vampire would trust three or four – some of them children – with his secret?*), and apportioned them by port of origin: Athens, Trieste, Bordeaux, Cherbourg, Amsterdam. Here again it was the names she sought. Few people (James said) had the wits to discard a perfectly good set of identity papers once they'd been used: the temptation was always to use them again. The kidnapping had brought home to her how easy it was for a vampire to utilize human helpers – like the hapless madman Renfield in *Dracula*, like her own poor companion Margaret Potton in Constantinople . . .

*Like Jamie.*

*Like myself.*

She wondered who Ysidro had coerced to help him travel from Rome. And what had become of him or her upon arrival.

*Someone is watching over Miranda and Nan during daylight hours.*

And she would wrench her mind back to the lists. She purchased a tin kettle and a cup at an Italian grocery shop in Wormwood Street, and brewed herself endless pots of tea on the room's minuscule grate, through the gray of dawn. At ten she'd go down the hall to wash, and changed into the chintz dress she'd borrowed from Mrs Grimes, to visit her drop boxes in Finsbury Circus. *If Grippen can't tell where Zahorec is, even, how can I be sure he isn't aware that someone is hunting him?*

*No wonder poor Jamie was driven half mad, living like this.*

There was something at once penitential and militant about the room at the Temperance Hotel, like a cell or a barracks. The tiny deal table, the single broken chair: teapot, cup, and paper bag of tea lined up at the back of the table. The locked suitcase that held the dry, softly crunching wreathes of garlic and wolfsbane . . . the mountain of frocks and stockings and gloves and notes and hats that heaped the narrow bed, and beside which she slept . . . and dreamed.

These were the half of her life. The real half, she thought of them.

At one on Saturday she donned one of the elegant frocks that Ellen had sent her, arranged her hair, applied rouge, mascaro, Recamier beauty cream, rice powder, kohl, rosewater and glycerin to her hands, and the perfume of vanilla and sandalwood that long ago her father had had formulated for her by Houbigant of Paris, and took a cab to Halfdene House. The thought of a masquerade ball – of listening to Lady Savenake on the iniquities of servants and Aunt Lavinnia on the iniquities of Valentina Willoughby while a bad band played 'Yes, We Have No Bananas' – acted upon Lydia as the threat of being chained for a night in a haunted catacomb would have upon the heroine in the average romantic novel: at least in a haunted catacomb one could read a book. But one of the things Lydia had overheard at Aunt Lavinnia's dinner party had been that Titus Armistead and his daughter were staying with the Binneys at Wycliffe House.

With luck, in the course of the evening she would be able to learn the identity of Cece's vampire lover.

'I don't see what you see in the wretched girl,' Aunt Isobel sniffed, when the tea things had been cleared away and Aunt Isobel's dresser laid out half a dozen fancy-dress costumes in the dreamlike gorgeousness of the Yellow Drawing Room. 'In spite of that "superior" governess, she has a terribly common accent . . . Charles, fetch some water for me, it's time for my pills . . . And you see the way she wears her clothes! She made that Poiret she had on yesterday look like a bathrobe. And her *hair*—'

'She's an American.' Valentina's small gesture – merely the turning-over of her lace-gloved hand – held more venom than a pit of cobras. '*I just LOVE that AY-ria . . .*' Her mastery of Cece's flat vowels was devastating. '*That part where it goes Da da dee da DAAAAA-da . . .*' She clasped her hands over her heart, mocking the girl's habitual gesture.

'At least she doesn't pretend to swoon over the parts that she doesn't care for,' Lydia protested, 'just because everyone else says how wonderful Mr Caruso is.'

Valentina – who had invited herself to luncheon – smiled indulgently. 'Well, you never did care much for music, did you, dear? And those *jewels* in the middle of the afternoon . . . No wonder that frightful father of hers has private detectives all over Wycliffe House these days. You aren't going to *wear* that tonight, are you, dear?'

Lydia drew back from the green velvet doublet of Maid Marian's attire.

'That collar will only emphasize your shoulders.' Her stepmother shook her head, and turned her enormous blue eyes back to Isobel. 'Urania Ottmoor tells me the Armistead girl's costume cost two hundred guineas, not counting the jewels, and her father paid for Noel's as well. *Such* a sweet boy he was as a child.' She shook her head sadly, and added, with sugared malice, 'Of course, you wouldn't have known the family . . . I know he's a thousand times more prepossessing now than he was when he left for the Continent, but who knows how long that will last? Did you *see* him last night at supper, Lydia, dearest? I understand opium is a *frightfully* difficult habit to break.'

*But nothing*, reflected Lydia, *compared to an attraction to a vampire.*

And she shivered at the quickness with which the thought rose up: *Simon is different . . .*

Beyond doubt, if challenged, Cece would say the same of the creature that visited *her* dreams.

'Two hundred guineas!' Emily kept her voice low as she and Lydia stepped down from the carriage ('My dear, go to Wycliffe House in a *motor car*?') in the forecourt of the baroque mansion on Queen Street. 'That's more than my Court presentation dress is costing, isn't it? I mean . . .' She blushed at having mentioned money, as they trod up the crimson carpet to the lighted door, followed by Uncle Richard's second footman bearing Emily's Medusa-headed shield and silver-tipped spear. 'I mean, that sounds like quite a lot!'

Brilliant electric light streamed from the doors, lighting up the mizzly gloom of the spring night.

'It sounds like her father wants her to have the best.'

The girl sighed very slightly. 'Like Mama,' she said, as if hesitant to express such unfilial heresy. 'Not just to have the best, but for everybody to *see* that it's the best.'

'Like having her marry an earl's son,' agreed Lydia. A footman in full eighteenth-century fig relieved them of their wraps. 'Is it true what Valentina said, about the opium?'

'It's what Julie says.' With her hair concealed by a papier-mâché helmet, and her slim form robed in a blue-and-yellow peplos and himation, Emily looked surprisingly dignified. 'I know he was a terrible mess when he left for Europe: sort of fat and pasty-looking, with his eyes all puffy. At least since he's been back from Paris he has some energy, and talks about something other than his headaches, even if it is only about all those frightful old civilizations nobody's ever heard about in places like Antarctica, and how vampires are going to take over England. Isn't it awful what Sir Alfred's done to this place?'

She looked around at the foyer in the blinding blaze of electric illumination. Through the open door of the porter's room Lydia glimpsed two burly men in American-looking suits lounging in kitchen chairs smoking cigars: the 'detectives' Valentina had spoken of. Did Titus Armistead really think anarchists were going to storm a fancy-dress ball?

'I remember how it used to be before Lady May–' she used the family nickname for her aunts' old friend – 'married Mr Binney – Sir Alfred,' Emily corrected herself. 'Yes, it was falling to pieces, but it was . . . I don't know. *Real*, somehow.'

Even without her spectacles – which would have accorded ill with the graceful folds of her ivory satin Restoration gown – Lydia had to agree. The oval entry hall at the bottom of the vast double hanging stairway looked like nothing so much as a hotel lobby, the worn marble of its floor masked in gold-and-burgundy Axminster and the walls 'brightened up' with hues that smacked of Liberty's newest catalog. Lady Mary Wycliffe had gone to school with all five of the Viscount Halfdene's daughters, of whom Lydia's mother had been the second-born and most beautiful. Like a dream within a dream Lydia remembered being brought to the crumbling old townhouse, to dodge through dust-sheeted chambers while her mother and aunts had tea with their friend in one of the few rooms still habitable.

Like Emily, she found the sea change wrought by Lady May's Mancusan mining-baron unsettling, and sad.

Cece Armistead was upstairs in the ballroom, ebullient in two hundred guineas worth of Ancien Regime court dress and flirting with Lord Colwich in a fashion that would have got Lydia sent to bed without supper, even from a ball for eight hundred people in her honor. In sharp contrast to his demeanor at supper Friday evening, the viscount seemed in high spirits, flirting back with every appearance of relish. Recalling the fat and profoundly unhappy young man she had seen at one or another of her aunts' entertainments over the past twelve years, Lydia reflected that Emily seemed to be right. When she came close to greet them, Lydia observed – as far as she could without her spectacles – that the powdered wig and lace ruffles in no way rendered the tall, powerfully built young man effeminate, and his manners had improved.

'People don't understand Dr Millward,' he said, when Lydia

commented on his return from Paris. 'Particularly my parents, poor souls.' He glanced across the crowded ballroom toward the Earl and Countess, very correctly got up in modern evening dress. 'They keep asking if it was Millward's idea that I move into Dallaby House – the place Mr Armistead has bought for Cece and me –' he smiled tenderly at his giggling bride-to-be – 'during the restoration; as if they can't imagine why a man would want to live in a place of his own.'

'I'm going to try to talk Daddy into buying *this* place for us.' Cece gestured around her at the mirrors that filled the walls where the Rococo boiseries had been, the high ceiling whose frescoed angels and goddesses had, like the hall downstairs, been 'brightened up' with fresh paint. 'Sir Alfred has talked about tearing it down and putting up a block of flats. Daddy thinks that'd be swell – *good* – but I think it'd be a shame, don't you? It's why Sir Alfred hasn't fixed up the gardens. Have you been in the maze down there?'

'I used to play there.' Lydia smiled a little at the recollection of her solemn five-year-old self, playing Explorer.

'*Honestly?*' The American girl clasped her hands before her bosom in a way that recalled Valentina's exaggerated imitation of the gesture. 'Do you know the little temple in the middle? It's so romantic, like a magical door between this world and others . . . It's all in ruins, but I wish they'd leave it that way . . .'

'Nonsense, nonsense!' Sir Alfred Binney, attired as a Chinese mandarin, thrust himself into the group. 'If I do keep the place I'll have it fixed up – get a smart new statue for it . . . trim those hedges and pave the paths and put in handrails . . . But with property values as they are hereabouts . . .'

'Oh, but it's *magical*, Sir Alfred!' Cece insisted, and turned, to take Lydia's hand. 'You know, Mrs Asher—'

'Please,' said Lydia. 'Call me Lydia.' From beside the buffet table Aunt Lavinnia – in the persona of the Snow Queen – glared daggers.

Cece beamed. 'You know, Lydia, I think the room they've given me there, across the way –' She pointed with her fan to the tall windows, and the wing visible on the other side of the narrow garden – 'is haunted? Not in a *bad* way,' she added quickly. 'By lovers who were kept apart, I think. Sometimes I dream about them. The little boudoir off my bedroom has a portrait in it, of a dark-haired girl with a lily. Nobody knows who she is, but she looks at me with the saddest eyes . . .'

'Piece of trash.' Titus Armistead loomed behind his partner. He at least, Lydia observed, had the good sense to stick with plain evening dress. 'Supposed to be a Quesnel, but my accountant tells me it's nothing of the kind. And anyway, Noel tells me nobody buys Quesnels. Sharp boy, Noel,' he added, with a stiff bow to Lydia. 'Up on all that art stuff . . .'

Lydia wondered if this stiff, grim American had ever seen his prospective son-in-law in his less energetic days, when he'd spent weeks at a time without getting either dressed or shaved, while he pottered with his paints or compared typefaces in decaying manuscripts of the *Malleus Maleficarum*.

Emily came over then with Julia Thwaite, and Lydia effected introductions, moments before her own attention was claimed by Valentina (resplendent, Lydia observed with indignation, in the pretty Maid Marian tunic and tights that she herself had wanted to wear). Dancing had started, and a buffet of chilled caviar, asparagus, cucumber sandwiches, quail eggs, oysters and lobster patties had been laid out on ice at the far end of the room. Lydia glanced again through the windows, across the darkness of the garden, to the opposite wing, and remembered – exactly – which small chamber of that long file of bedrooms had contained the shadowy portrait of the girl with the lily and the sad eyes.

And how easily one could enter that wing from the garden, unnoticed by anyone in the house.

*She'll have his name somewhere.*

*And an address to get in touch with him.*

*I would . . .*

The ballroom was on the *piano nobile* of Wycliffe House's southern wing: the 'noble floor' where all the best public rooms were situated, above the ground floor's business offices and dining room. A fertile source of confusion to Sir Alfred's American guests, reflected Lydia, as she slipped through one of the ballroom's several doors and made her way to the backstairs: Americans would refer to the 'noble floor' as the 'second floor', when Sir Alfred and every other person in England and Europe would call it the first. She gathered her heavy skirts around her, hastened swiftly down. The footmen she passed on their way up politely ignored her, assuming her to be in quest of the ladies' toilet.

She had no doubt that the first thing Sir Alfred had done upon

taking possession of this grand house of his wife's impoverished
father had been to install a dozen bathrooms. There had been none
in the days when Lydia had roved the dusty rooms as a child. Even
the family had used a House of Office at the end of the garden –
separate facilities, of course, for the family and the few servants
that had remained to them, after the Seventh Earl of Pencalder had
gambled away nearly everything the family had owned in 1848.

Once outside, the first thing Lydia did was fish her silver spectacle case from her pocket. Up at the front of the long U that
comprised the house, the terrace that overlooked the gardens had
been transformed into a sort of outdoor bistro, with yet another
band playing 'Yes, We Have No Bananas', and a dozen small tables
set up under strings of electric lights around yet another buffet.
The glare from that, coupled with the brightness streaming down
from the ballroom windows, made the narrow strip of overgrown
pergola between house-wall and maze nearly as bright as day. As
Cece had observed, the garden didn't appear to have been touched
in fifty years: the pergola thickly overgrown with roses, the gravel
underfoot buried beneath a carpet of shed leaves. It took Lydia
several minutes to locate the southern gateway in the twelve-foot
wall of hedge and, once inside it – the wayward masses of foliage
absorbing nearly all of the light – she had to press and fumble her
way until the crunch of the pebble paths, rather than any appreci-
able gap in the leaves, indicated the corners.

The key to the maze was simple, though – even as a five-year-old
she'd deduced it quite quickly – and the maze itself barely a dozen
yards wide. She slipped through the northern gate only feet from the
door that led into a sort of garden room in the north wing. The wing
had been added by the Fourth Earl of Pencalder – Lady May had
told her later – for the accommodation of his mother and sisters,
who objected to his way of life: the sad-eyed girl with the lily had
been one of his several mistresses. From the ballroom windows Lydia
had seen that the wing was entirely dark. Presumably all the servants
– even the detectives – had been pressed into readying the midnight
supper for the guests.

Lydia had brought in her pocket a tin of matches, and the picklocks that James – ever the cautious ex-spy – had warned her never
to leave the house without, but the door into the garden room was
unlocked. She found the backstairs with little trouble, and the light

was better upstairs, leaking faintly from the avalanche of wattage being pumped into the garden. Gently she opened door after door, identifying smells.

Tobacco and leather would be Mr Armistead's bedroom, the fusty comfort of book dust and ink the library. Toward the front end of the wing where it joined the main house were the public rooms: a cavernous drawing room enfiladed with a smaller parlor and an office. Guest chambers soft with the scents of potpourri and black-leaded grates. Presumably the detectives had a lair of their own downstairs. She couldn't imagine any butler in London – not even Sir Alfred's – putting up with them.

Dusting powder, stale cigarettes, and the distinctive scent of Jicky perfume by Guerlain marked Cece's bedroom. The boudoir lay beyond, the Fourth Earl's pretty mistress a pale blur in the shadows. Lydia let down the heavy drapes before she struck a match.

A desk stood beside one window, and by the other a dressing table the size of a kitchen stove. Like the rest of the house the room was wired for electricity, but Cece's desk boasted an immense girandole, its candles showing use. Lydia touched the flame of her match to one, settled with a whisper of heavy skirts in the little chair, and opened the drawers, praying she wouldn't find there the maelstrom that crammed her own secretaire at home.

However, one drawer held some virginal stationery – Cece's letterhead included the address for Wycliffe House as well as addresses in Newport, Rhode Island, and Denver, Colorado – and a pen which obviously had never been used, and the others, nothing. The mess was in the dressing table – old powder puffs, combs, hair rats and switches, face creams, perfumes, *papiers poudrées*.

A man's handkerchief.

And at the back, carefully buried under a stack of old issues of *Harper's Bazaar*, a Morocco-leather notebook. Cece had plainly intended to copy all the addresses that she really wanted to keep and just as plainly had abandoned this endeavor long before she and her father had left Italy for Paris in November. Cards, fragments of notepaper, old dance cards with jotted bits of information on them interleaved the little volume's pristine pages. Lydia thumbed through them quickly, wondering if she should simply steal the whole book . . .

Would Cece blame the maid?

Then her fingers turned over a torn scrap of what looked like the slip sheet from an old book. *Ludovicus Bertolo, Hotel Cecil, the Strand, London.*

Ludovicus Bertolo, she knew, had come to London on the fifteenth of January from Cherbourg, with a valet and three pieces of luggage, one of which was a trunk six feet long and weighing nearly three hundred pounds.

She wondered what had become of the valet.

*He'll have left the Cecil by this time . . .*

She replaced the paper in the book, the book in the drawer. Went to the window, blew out the candle, the scent of wax like a note of music in the sudden dark. Looped back the drapes as best she could. Started toward where the door would be—

And heard the faintest whisper as the handle turned.

There was no line of light beneath it. Whoever was outside stood in darkness.

*Saw* in darkness.

Lydia remembered there was an armoire somewhere to her left but there was no time. She stepped back to the window, rolled herself in the curtain and crouched to the floor, her corset stabbing her mercilessly in the hip-bones as she curled herself flat.

He came into the room and very faintly she smelled the blood in his clothing.

*Oh, God . . .*

*He'll smell my perfume.*

*And the blood in my veins.*

Softly he closed the door. 'And who have we here?' Like Ysidro's, his voice was barely a murmur. But deeper: black velvet, with a slight inflection of Mitteleuropa. Drowsiness crushed her mind, like suffocating in rose petals. Sensual. Hungry for this man's kisses; for the touch of his lips . . . 'I know you're hiding, beautiful one . . .'

'You can't know I'm beautiful,' said Lydia matter-of-factly, and stood up. 'You haven't seen me.'

The reflected light from the window showed her a dark god. A pale face above the blackness of a satin cloak that wrapped him from throat to feet, a darkness of tousled curls. 'All ladies are beautiful,' he said softly, 'met by moonlight.'

*If he touches the silver on my neck or wrists he'll know I know about what he is.*

'Nonsense,' said Lydia briskly. 'And anyway that's electricity, not moonlight. You sound just like Bertie, and I'm perfectly fed up with him—'

'Bertie?' He got between her and the door and made it look accidental.

Her heart was pounding so she could barely think. 'Bertie Mousemire.' She manufactured a sigh. 'Trust Bertie to arrange an assignation and then not be able to find his way up from the terrace. The man is hopeless. And by this time Richard will be looking for me, and—'

He was suddenly beside her – it was nearly impossible to see vampires move – and his hand closed around her arm above the elbow. Through the thick satin of her sleeve his touch was like warm electricity, a shocking sense of his presence. Of need.

'And do you so hunger for love that you must needs seek it with the Berties of this world?'

His eyes were in shadow, but she knew they were blue. Languor flowed over her mind, honey now instead of sparks. A yearning to taste his kisses . . .

*With THOSE teeth?*

'Don't be silly,' gasped Lydia, in her best imitation of her long-departed Nanna, and prayed her voice didn't shake. *He'll probably think it's with passion . . .*

And it was. Irrational, overwhelming hunger for what James never gave her (*but he DOES*), for what no man had ever given her . . .

She pulled free and he didn't hold her. This was seduction, she recognized; the game vampires played.

The game he was playing with Cece.

*Or maybe it isn't.*

*WOULD he kill here at a party?*

*There are nearly a thousand guests, he could hide my body and no one would know I was gone . . .*

'I have never understood,' said Lydia, 'this passion people have for going around kissing total strangers . . .'

He put his hands on either side of her against the wall, pinning her without touching her. But she could feel the heat of his body, which meant, she knew, that he'd fed.

Someone in London had already died. Two and three kills a night sometimes, Grippen had said . . .

'Since you do not understand, will you not open your mind?' He put his hand to her cheek. His face – barely seen in the darkness – seemed weary and a little sad, the face of a man who has survived horrors. 'Why do you so much fear even the taste of a dream? Are you afraid you might follow it?'

Footfalls whispered in the carpet of the hall. Had the vampire been a cat he'd have put one ear back. Lydia took the moment to step away from him, and open the bedroom door. Cece's voice was no more than the scent of the candle wax in the darkness. 'Damien?'

Lydia felt the velvet cloak brush past her, smelled again the halitus of fresh blood. Gaslight from Queen Street filtered into the hallway from its windows, showed her the vampire like a shadow beside the pale shape of Cece Armistead in her lace-clotted gown of gold and bronze. Jewels still twinkled in her powdered hair, but she'd removed the collar of lace that had covered her neck. Zahorec bent his head to kiss her, gentle as a flower petal, on the lips, on the breast, on the delicate skin of her throat. Cece whispered, 'I have . . .' But the vampire touched his lips to hers.

'It can wait. All things can wait.'

Shaken, breathless, Lydia stood in the door of the bedroom as the two shadows merged; heard Cece's soft gasp.

It was two steps to the door of the backstairs and Lydia held down her heavy skirts with both hands, terrified that she'd feel his arms circling her from behind in the pitch black of the staircase. She was shaking uncontrollably by the time she reached the door at the bottom, stumbled out into the shadows of the pergola . . .

*Can he follow me through the maze? Follow me back to the hotel?*

She went straight up the graveled path and across the terrace to the front hall, where she tipped one footman to get her a cab and another to take a note up to Aunt Lavinnia, claiming a splitting headache and the urgent need to return to her hotel at once, and would Aunt Lavinnia see to it that Emily got home? *Aunt Lavinnia will never speak to me again . . .*

Once at the Temperance Hotel, Lydia double-locked the door, dragged the little desk in front of it, wound her garlands of garlic-flowers, aconite, and Christmas rose around the door handle and the window sashes.

And dreamed, for what remained of the night, of Damien Zahorec's eyes.

# SEVEN

*L*udovicus Bertolo. Lydia studied the entry over tea at her little table in the gray of Sunday morning.

Not Grippen, not his fledglings.

He'd arrived from Cherbourg on the *Reine Margot*. He'd come through France.

Checking other entries for those who'd come from France, she found the record of Titus Armistead and Party, with crates enough to transport an army of vampires, also from Cherbourg, on 17 January. Presumably the *Imperatrice* was a higher-class vessel than the *Reine Margot*.

On the *Imperatrice* also had been Noel Wredemere, Lord Colwich, with two steamer-trunks and three crates over two hundred pounds and four feet in length – 'and valet'. Someone last night (Valentina?) had told her that Colwich's beloved Ned Seabury had gone to Paris in the fall because of Colwich's 'way of life'. Had he traveled back on the *Imperatrice* as well, gazing in hungry jealousy as his friend flirted with the American million-aire's daughter?

Or had he returned earlier, and learned of the engagement when he went to the dock to welcome his friend home, and saw him come down the gangplank with that bright-hued bird of paradise clinging to his arm?

As she removed the protective garlands from the windows and sought soap, towel, slippers, sponge bag and pennies for the bath-room geyser among the untidy chaos of the bed, Lydia recalled the look of weary pleading Colwich had thrown his friend along the dinner table Friday night, and the way the two young men had stood together in the drawing-room window Thursday, at Lady Brightwell's with Dr Millward. Were the tender looks and cheerful caresses with Cece last night window dressing only, to keep his wealthy father-in-law sweet?

She remembered Cece's golden shape as the vampire's cloak enfolded her in darkness. The girl's soft gasp.

Of course Cece would accept the proposal of a Viscount. One day she'd be Countess of Crossford.

The Crossfords had property all over England and Scotland.

*He's going to make her a vampire.* Lydia shivered as she thrust coins into the bathroom geyser box and turned on the spigot for her modest fivepence-worth of nominally hot bathwater. *It isn't just seduction. He's biding his time, waiting till she marries.* The Crossford lands were mortgaged and in a poor state of upkeep, but this wouldn't matter to a vampire.

*He doesn't want a victim.*

*He wants a fledgling.*

*Who will leave him property in her will.*

Lydia reached St George's church in Hanover Square just as the congregation issued from their pews to take communion, but after all one went to St George's to be seen by the *beau monde*, not because the sermons were any good. She waited at the back, from a sense of guilt and because, without her spectacles, she couldn't identify the Halfdene pew until the footman in blue and yellow livery wheeled the bath chair into the aisle. Then she hurried down and ducked into the enclosure. 'I'm so sorry . . .'

Uncle Richard smiled as he took her hand. '*I will give unto this last, even as unto thee,*' he whispered, quoting Christ's parable about dilatory latecomers who scurried at that last minute through the gates of the Kingdom of Heaven.

Following divine services, like three-quarters of the population of the West End – or that portion of the population that weren't polishing boots, preparing dinner, pressing Madame's skirt or taking Madame's children for their Sunday stroll – the family of Viscount Halfdene went driving in the Park, Uncle Richard's saddle horse having been brought along tied to the back of the landaulet which had carried them to church. Lydia made all the correct responses when they encountered friends or family among the slow tide of vehicles and horses that flowed along the southern avenue. By the gates she glimpsed, across the road, the massed green-purple-and-white banners of the suffragists gathered outside the Horse Guards, and she thought she saw one of them – undoubtedly her friend Josetta – wave to her, but couldn't be sure at that distance.

But within moments her thoughts returned to Cece Armistead. To that voice like sable velvet: *Do you so hunger for love . . .?*

No matter how many times Lydia told herself, *Actually, no, I don't*, its echo returned. *Why do you so much fear even the taste of a dream? Are you afraid you might follow it?*

No wonder poor Cece wore that goopy smile. Lydia shivered again.

*God knows what Zahorec has told her about what he is. About what being a vampire means . . .*

Beneath the trees of Rotten Row she caught a glimpse of Cece, riding in company with Lady May. No sign of Colwich's bright waistcoat: two-thirty in the afternoon was evidently too early an hour for his lordship to be astir. A stolid detective followed them on what was clearly a rented hack, his brown suit like a baked potato in a plate of petits-fours. Even had Lydia been wearing spectacles the little group was too far off for her to tell if the American girl looked pale or ill, but she seemed to have no trouble controlling her frisky steed.

*He's seen me, in her bedroom. Hiding from 'Bertie', he thinks. And no one he needs to worry about. Unless I speak to Cece and tell her, 'I know you're being courted by a vampire.'*

*Then she'll tell him.*

*As I told Don Simon, when old Professor Karlebach warned me about HIM.*

She wanted to leap out of the carriage and run . . . *where? Back to the Temperance Hotel?* To put up her garlic-blossom garlands again like a madwoman; to sit staring at the peeling greenish trellises of the wallpaper until it grew too dark to see? She didn't know which grated most across her nerves, having to lie when Aunts Harriet and Lavinnia – out driving themselves in Lavinnia's blood-crimson park phaeton – asked her how Miranda was, or encountering Valentina (driven by an admirer and full of backhanded compliments on Emily's dress) and having her not ask about the child at all.

*Three nights she's been . . . somewhere. Crying for me? Hungry? Drugged?*

*STOP IT THIS MINUTE . . . She's all right. She'll be all right.*

'I'm sorry, Aunt.' She pulled her mind back to the present. 'I felt dreadfully about leaving Emily, but I had the most fearful headache last night . . .'

'It could have been the champagne,' purred Valentina, whose admirer happened to pull his natty Tilbury up next to the Halfdene landaulet at that moment. 'It takes some people that way, if they're not used to it. Though heaven knows had *I* been left by *my* husband I'd have done just the same . . .'

'You're sure you won't stay in town and go to the concert this evening?' asked Isobel, when dinner was over. 'Emily could certainly lend you a dress – though not the white tarlatan,' she added, with a worried frown. 'She's wearing that to the Ottmoors' and they're sure to be there tonight . . . Not the ice-blue either . . .'

Lydia refrained from saying that firstly, nothing would induce her to wear ice-blue, and secondly, she had a perfect right to both frocks, having paid for them. 'Thank you, Aunt, but I should be getting back home.'

'Have it your own way, dear.' Isobel poured her out a second cup of tea. 'Though I must say, whatever Valentina said – and did you get a look at those emeralds she was wearing? In the middle of the afternoon, too! – I expect it was all the running up and down from Oxford that brought on your headache last night. Heaven knows the *worst* migraine I ever had in my *life* was when I traveled up to Scotland last August to go shooting at the Wintersons'– I was in bed for *days*! Dr Purfleet had to prescribe veronal for me. When you come back up tomorrow – You *are* coming for the opening of the flower show? We're quite counting on you – you are most welcome to bring your things and stay here. I'm sure Miranda will be just fine without her mama for a few days . . . I remember during the Season, for years, Emily would go *weeks* without seeing me and it never seemed to do her any harm, did it, darling? You could— Yes, what is it, Ross?'

The butler bowed, and extended a polished salver bearing a card. 'Excuse me, Madame, but there's a gentleman here to see Mrs Asher.'

'At this hour?'

'He apologizes for the intrusion, Madame, but explains he has but newly come to London and knew he might find her here. He is a friend of Professor Asher.'

Lydia had already picked up the card. The lettering on it was just large enough for her to read – with a certain amount of difficulty – without holding it up to her nose.

*Esteban Sierra*
*Piazza del Trinita del Monte*
*Rome*

Feeling a little breathless, she said, 'Oh . . . yes, of course.'

Isobel's lips tightened – her own father might have owned a pottery works, but not even she had approved of Lydia's match with a mere lecturer at New College, even if she had been disinherited at the time. But she only said, 'Then of course, Ross, show him in.'

He came into the drawing room and bowed, with perfect correctness for the twentieth century. Aside from the length of his pale, spidery hair he had the appearance of any thin young gentleman, though if she looked at him closely, she could sometimes see the scars on his face. She found it persistently impossible to notice his fangs, or the fact that he did not breathe. He went first to Aunt Isobel, and begged her pardon for intruding upon her at such an hour – 'Professor Asher suggested that your generous hospitality is such that Mrs Asher might well be found beneath your roof . . .' Then to Uncle Richard: 'I'm certain you have no recollection of it, sir, but we met briefly at the Royal Academy Show in 1906. Was the decision to exhibit the Hogarths yours, sir?'

Uncle Richard – whose passion was his membership in the Royal Academy of Arts – beamed.

Only then did Ysidro cross to Lydia, and bend over – without kissing – her hand.

'Mrs Asher.'

She hadn't seen him in the flesh in seven months, and had received only a single brief note from him, upon her and Jamie's return from China, telling her that – contrary to what the old vampire-hunter Karlebach believed – he was well. When he said, 'I trust you've heard from your husband since he and I last met,' she knew it was for Aunt Isobel's benefit. 'Nevertheless, he bade me seek you out and give you his kindest regards when I came through London, and so you behold me, Madame.'

She replied, 'I have heard nothing of him for over a week,' and saw a tiny line, like a pen-scratch, flicker into being between his pale eyebrows. 'But I understand the posts in Italy are frightful.'

'They are indeed, Madame.' He turned then and included his

hostess and host in the conversation, charming them with a wholly fictitious account of where and how he knew Professor Asher ('My father insisted that I do a year at Oxford – Christ Church – and as my chief study was languages a meeting was inevitable') and drawing them out adroitly: Uncle Richard on art, Aunt Isobel on the slings and arrows encountered in presenting a daughter to Society. When precisely fifteen minutes had elapsed, he said, 'But I must not further trespass on your evening, kind Madame. Having discharged my errand to my friend, I must be in Bayswater at nine—'

'Might I prevail on your friendship,' said Lydia promptly, as Ysidro rose, 'to beg a place in your carriage as far as Paddington? No, really, Uncle, there's no need to turn out poor Perkins—'

Perkins was the Halfdene coachman.

'—at this hour.'

There followed a few minutes of polite argument, in which Ysidro made it tactfully clear that his coachman waited for them in George Street, and that he would take it as a privilege and an honor to see Mrs Asher on to her train.

'You don't really have a carriage waiting for you, do you?' whispered Lydia, as Ysidro handed her down the shallow step to the pavement of Berkeley Square, and led her toward the dim shape of a brougham a few houses along.

The warm glow of the gaslight behind them vanished as Uncle Richard closed the door.

'*Dios*, no. There is a cab-stand at the corner of Davies Street, if so be you have no objection to such a vehicle.'

'Not in the least. Aunt would be horrified – and horrified at you, for even suggesting that a lady ride in one. Considering you came with no letter of introduction, even, I'm astonished she didn't give us both a lecture about what married women can and cannot be seen to do with even close and trusted friends of their husbands.'

'I was chosen to come to this country,' returned the vampire, as they climbed into the cab under the gas lamp at the head of Davies Street, 'because I was a diplomat – and the principles of diplomacy have not changed so very much in three hundred years. Have you something of your daughter's, and of this nursery maid who was taken with her? 'Tis early yet in the night for the girl to be asleep, but children sleep at any hour, and the more so, if, as you say, she were to be drugged.'

'Thank you,' she said, as the cab began to move, 'for coming.'
In the darkness he was nothing but the gleam of his eyes.

'Did you not know that I would?'

Heat suffused her face. In her mind she heard again Damien
Zahorec's voice: *Are you afraid you might follow?*

*But follow to where?*

*No good can come*, Simon had told her more than once, *of friendship between the living and the dead* . . .

So why the confusion, she wondered, at the thought that she had
known, down into the marrow of her bones, that if she called him,
he would come?

Why the intense consciousness of him sitting beside her, of his
gray sleeve against the velvet of her cloak?

She took a deep breath. 'I've seen Damien Zahorec. He came
last night to Wycliffe House – that's where the American girl is
staying, Cecelia Armistead. It's he who is seducing her.' As the cab
wove its expert way through the porridge of busses, motor cars,
carriages and cabs on Oxford Street, Lydia recounted the events of
the evening, and her own deductions as to the interloper's motives
and intent.

'He's phenomenally attractive,' she said. 'I mean that literally:
he attracts like a magnet, or at least he did me, in the few minutes
we were together. And obviously he has poor Cece completely under
his thumb. She doesn't impress me as the kind of girl who'd . . .
who'd ordinarily vamp a man into marrying her so that she could
turn over his property to a lover, but it may be that she doesn't
think of it in that light. I assume Zahorec plans to kill poor Colwich
as soon as they're married.'

''Tis more likely he'll be his wife's early victim. That's the usual
pattern.' Ysidro folded his hands as they passed into High Holborn,
watched the hawkers of oranges and dolls on the sidewalks, and a
blind man mending umbrellas in front of the Post Office. 'I was often
in Wycliffe House in the Old Earl's time,' he said at length. 'The
garden went clear to Cadogan Place – not that there was anything
but a lane there, then – and I was sorry, when his grandson built the
north wing and shut it in. I didn't know you knew the family.'

'The seventh Earl's daughter was a friend of our family. My aunts
wrote to me – that was the year I was in school in Paris – about
how horrified they were when she married Alfred Binney, who

wasn't a baronet then, just very wealthy. But that's exactly what my mother did, when she married Father. They said about him everything they said about Father behind my back – and about my mother, too. In spite of the fact that it was Father's money that paid for school for my cousins Ritchie and Charles, and kept Halfdene House from being sold.'

'And kept you from growing up as your aunts did, and Lady Binney.'

Under the calm yellow gaze, Lydia felt disconcerted. *Can I accept his help finding Miranda*, the thought came to her, *without condoning that his ability to give it comes from murder? Just as my aunts accepted Father's money even as they were calling him a vulgar disgrace to his family for going into trade?*

'Come,' said Ysidro, and took her hand. 'Tell me what you have learned so far of this Zahorec, and of what you need yet to learn.'

# EIGHT

Ysidro shrank from touching the blanket Ellen had sent – it was one of those into whose binding Lydia had sewn thin silver chains – but ran his fingers over the tucked white lawn of Miranda's frock.

*No mother in her senses should be able to watch this*, thought Lydia, as he stroked the lettuce-green silk sash. *Knowing what he is, I should be screaming at him to keep away from anything that has touched my child.*

*What's wrong with me?*

*Why do I trust him?*

And she tried not to hear her heart reply: *Vampires hunt by making the living trust.*

He touched the fabric to his lips. Champagne-colored eyes half-shut, he faced the window of her shabby room at the Temperance Hotel seeming almost in a trance.

'Nothing.' He laid the little garment back on the cluttered bed. 'The dreams of children whisper over London like the night sea. I said, did I not, that Lionel will guess that you will call me, and that

I will come.' Beyond him the sooty rooftops were a jungle of chimney pots and ridge poles, touched here and there with the grimy echo of a skylight's glow.

'Myself, I believe he will hide the child outside of London altogether, to keep the matter from his fledglings.'

'Do all masters distrust their fledglings?' Lydia leaned her shoulder against the window frame, gathered the little dress in her arms.

'Not all. Some fledglings learn in time the wisdom of their master's prohibitions. Indeed, some masters take care to choose their fledglings for reasons other than for property, or from desire.'

'Desire?' Lydia's eyebrows twitched together. 'I thought the Undead were sexless. That the generative organs ceased to function.'

'You yourself know, Mistress, how much desire resides in the mind, and vampires in this respect are no more wise than the rest of mankind. Many masters choose those whom they wish to possess, as well as those whom they simply wish to use.' He brushed Nan's gloves to his cheekbone, then tilted his head, eyes half-shut, listening.

'Nothing.' He set the gloves aside. 'Thus it happens that many choose fledglings of lesser intelligence, seeking those who will not challenge their dominion. Then when the master *does* perish, it is often without teaching the fledglings all that they might know about the vampire state. This being so, they cannot pass the knowledge along in their turn.'

'Like the reading of dreams?'

'That and other matters. Walk with me, Mistress.' He took up her jacket from the bed, and held it for her to put on. 'Walk and tell me what you will need, to find this interloper's lairs.'

Obediently she donned the garment, removed her spectacles, locked the door behind them and followed him downstairs, where the lobby clerk sat gazing at his copy of *The Illustrated London News* without seeing it – or them – as they passed.

'I take it your master didn't believe in keeping his fledglings ignorant?'

For a moment, as they went beneath the gaslight in the lobby, she saw his face turn human as he smiled. 'My master – Rhys the White – like myself was curious about the vampire state. He said that he thought the reading of dreams was originally a hunting skill, in the days before there were many cities, to draw prey from far off, or to find sleepers by their dreams. 'Tis a skill that grows slowly,

and not many teach it now. And indeed why should they? We
ourselves are safer in cities, where neighbor knows not his neighbor,
and money can buy protection from those who do not inquire for
whom they work. The poor die unheeded, so what need of stealth
and skill?'

Beside the door of All Hallows church Lydia saw two men lying,
bundles of rags ranged along the wall, asleep on the sidewalk with
greasy caps over their faces, as oblivious to the clatter of the luggage-
vans and cabs rattling within feet of them as the hurrying cabmen
and drivers were to them. Tramps from the provinces, hoping things
would be better in the city. London was full of them.

For a long while Lydia didn't speak.

Then Don Simon asked again, 'Tell me what you need,' in a
voice so gentle she wondered if he read her anger and her confusion. 'Banking records, you said?'

She took a deep breath, let it out. 'A vampire fleeing unrest in
the Balkans would need a means to transfer his money here, if he
wishes to acquire property.'

'And the method described in romantic novels, of paying for everything in ancient gold coin, would cause more talk than the occasional
corpse drained of blood with puncture-wounds in the throat.' He
steered her gently past a crowd of coster Don Juans clustered outside
a sweet-shop, buying ices for their *donahs*. The glare of electric lights
turned the girls' gaudy dresses to jewels. 'At least in London, it
would.'

'We're probably looking for a single gentleman rather than a
company,' Lydia went on. 'Though I expect *you* operate through a
corporation of some sort . . . The name might be Zahorec or Bertolo,
and he'll have started withdrawing cash here around the seventeenth
of January. He came here from Cherbourg, so there may have been
withdrawals in Paris also.'

'Duly noted, Mistress.'

'Can you . . .' She hesitated. 'Can you do that?'

His slow smile in the electric glare was once again completely
human. 'Think you it lies beyond my measure, Lady?'

'How—?'

'How indeed. Do you not trust me?'

'I do.' She was aware that she should be ashamed of herself for
meaning it. 'And I'll need access to records in the Bank of England.'

He tilted an eyebrow.

'I promise I won't do anything silly,' she repeated doggedly.

'Had I a silver coin for every time a woman has said, *I will not do anything silly*—'

'You would burn the skin off your hands,' retorted Lydia. They had crossed the jostling confusion of drays, cabs, passengers dashing to catch the last omnibus in Finsbury Circus, to the doors of the Christian Travelers' Hotel. He handed her up the single shallow step. In a smaller voice, she said, 'I have to know.'

Without answering, he opened the door for her, the Christian Travelers' Hotel not running to a doorman. At the desk, she gave the clerk a shilling and asked if there were any letters for Elizabeth Röntgen.

There were two. One, from Henry McClennan, contained another list of properties: her eye picked out the name of Daphne Scrooby of Parish Street again, of Francis Houghton and Bartholomew Barrow. It was noted that while birth certificates existed for Mrs Scrooby (née Robinson) and her husband, a well-known pub-owner in the Limehouse, no such things existed for Houghton, Barrow, or Nicholas Barger of Rood Lane, to whom Barrow had also willed City property.

It was hard to keep her fingers from trembling as she opened the second envelope, a telegram from Ellen sent that morning.

WIRE FROM MR JAMES SENT VENICE LAST NIGHT STOP SAYS HE IS ON HIS WAY STOP

*He is on his way.*

She woke in blackness, gasping. *NO . . .*

The dream swallowed back into itself.

*The Temperance Hotel . . .*

Reassuringly, the darkness around her smelled of wallpaper mold and the desiccated ghosts of garlic and wolfsbane. Across the street, the clock on All Hallows struck three. *Was that what waked me?* Dimly the groan of the goods trains came from Liverpool Street Station, without cease through the small hours.

It had been cold in her dream.

*Miranda?*

*No.* She'd dreamed of her daughter, a brief, far-off image of the toddler curled asleep in Nan Wellit's arms. She'd taken great comfort from the fact that – although in the dream too it was pitch dark – she could see that Miranda's clothes were clean and her hair combed. Nan was looking after her.

*Good for you, Nan . . .*

It wasn't that which had frightened her.

*Something about Simon?*

After she'd stuffed the telegram from Ellen, and that thin sheaf of information from Henry McClennan, into her handbag, she'd walked with Simon to a café on the other side of the oval park, had sat talking for a time, knowing if she went straight back to her room she would lie awake. She'd asked him about being a vampire, and about reading dreams; about the Old Earl who'd built Wycliffe House and laid out its gardens. About the harper called Rhys the White, who after his death had slept in the crypt of St Giles Cripplegate and had lured his victims with music that they could not tear from their dreams. *There were men in London, living men, who believed him to be a wizard or an angel or a saint, because of the dreams he could visit upon them . . .*

And as he spoke Ysidro had watched passers-by beneath the glare of the café's electric lights, servants making their way home from evening service, soldiers who stopped to buy ginger beer. Observed them the way Jamie observed them, picking individual faces, separate voices: *That man's from Sussex. One of that girl's parents is Liverpool Irish. See how he holds his left wrist? He's a coachman . . .*

Reading their bodies and voices, their mannerisms and their lives.

*James and I understand one another*, he had said. *Many vampires make humankind our study: sit in cafés and theaters and on the benches of the Embankment, watching and listening. To us the Personals of every newspaper are like serialized novels, or like observing the tracks of beasts in the woods. Such awareness is life to us: hunting, or watching for who looks at us twice and thrice.*

When they'd walked back to the Temperance Hotel, she had observed that the beat constable had rousted the two sleepers beside the church wall, and moved them on.

*It was Rhys the White who killed you?* she had asked, and Simon had answered, *Yes*, matter-of-factly, without so much as a pause.

Yet in a dream once she'd felt the paroxysm of light, that was the drinking of the soul of the living by the Undead, and knew there was more to it than *Yes . . .*

*Was that what I dreamed?*

Somewhere in her mind lingered the echo of moonlight through the iron lattices of a barred window, of a man's voice whispering desperately: '*De profundis clamavi ad te, Domine . . .*'

*Out of the depths I cry to you, Lord . . .*

A man clinging to the edge of life as to a precipice.

*The smell of pine trees . . .*

The creak of a hinge as the door behind the prisoner opened and he flung himself to his feet, threw himself at the bars and clung to them with all his strength in the knowledge that his strength would not be enough. *My God, my God, why hast thou forsaken me . . .?*

Trembling, Lydia sat up. She fumbled her eyeglasses from beneath her pillow – rooms at the Temperance Hotel did not include such luxuries as night stands – and rose with care, recalling that she'd left her notes and pencils strewn on the floor around the bed. As she had in her dream two nights ago, she crossed to the window, the baize curtain rough under her fingers, the wreaths of garlic and wolfsbane like dry tissue paper against her cheek.

Through fog and darkness the tangle of rooftops and chimney stacks was barely to be seen. Mists caught the electric glow from the train yards, and by it, like a shadow, she thought she saw three figures, standing on the roof across the alleyway.

Two men and a woman. (*How on EARTH did she get up there wearing a corset and a dress?*) A dozen feet separated them from the window. She had seen vampires leap twice that distance. So great was the darkness, no gleam of light caught in their eyes, but she knew what they were.

*Do they hear me breathe?*

*Detect the pounding of my heart?*

As silently as she could she moved back into the room, opened the suitcase beneath the bed and took from it the jointed rod she'd had made when she'd come back from China last winter, that screwed together into a sort of spear with a sharpened silver point. Whether it would work or not she didn't know, but all weapons used against vampires were more or less only to buy you time to flee, provided there was anywhere to flee to.

There was also a little box of coffee beans, to counteract the vampire's ability to make a victim drift momentarily into a dream-like state of inattention. She'd once heard Dr Millward describing (at tedious length) a silver ring he'd had made, with a little spike on it to dig into his palm for the same purpose, though Lydia person-ally wouldn't have wanted to risk drawing one's blood anywhere near a vampire . . .

She screwed the spear together and sat on the bed, facing the window that was only just less inkily dark than the blackness of the room.

*Grippen's fledglings?*

*Zahorec's, made in some fashion that Grippen couldn't detect?*

*Whoever they are, they know I'm here.*

For six years she had lived with the knowledge that Grippen and his fledglings knew of her. Knew and kept their distance, out of fear of Simon.

*Fear?* She wondered now. *Or was that part of a bargain? That he would leave London, and they would leave me alone?*

*And now he's returned . . .*

After a long time she realized that she could see the pale rectangle of curtained window a little more clearly, and heard the All Hallows clock strike four-thirty.

At five-thirty she unscrewed the sections of her spear and stowed them in her suitcase, took off her spectacles, and lay down once more. But it was long before she slept, and when she did, she saw them in her dreams. Two men and a woman, standing on the roof ridge of the building across the alleyway, watching her window with gleaming eyes.

# NINE

'Have you ever played Fox and Geese, Mistress?' Simon asked her the following evening, as they walked along the Embankment.

'When I was in school, yes. The son of one of the headmistresses would insist on being the Fox, and my friend Josetta – she was the English mistress there – taught me that once one learns the strategy, the Geese can always win.'

'Your friend is wise. The Fox can kill any Goose, but the Geese are many. By working together, and coordinating their attack, they can surround and trap Señor Fox. Multiply that a thousand fold –' his glance took in the sailors and flower vendors and fashionable ladies strolling around them, the rumble of traffic from the Strand above – 'and you have the situation of the vampire.'

It was early enough – not quite ten – that twilight was barely out of the sky. The yellow twinkle from the military yards across the river answered the street lights in the park, and spangled the dark water between. From a barrow beside the curb a man cried hoarsely of nougats and caramels.

Despite Simon's assurance that no one Lydia knew would notice her as long as she was with him, she kept glancing at their fellow strollers, expecting any moment for Aunt Isobel to swoop out of the shadows of the trees in her bath chair, demanding to know what she was doing here and who was that she was with?

*Did Jamie feel like this when he walked about somewhere like Vienna or Berlin, back in his days as a spy?*

'Were the Bohemian to get fledglings,' Simon said at length, answering an earlier question, 'I doubt he could conceal them. Indeed, 'tis more like they would lead Lionel to him. 'Twere more difficult for Lionel to know if this Zahorec has made living allies, and I think that is what he fears even more. The living have freedom of action denied the Undead, and a master cannot constrain his fledglings if they make such alliances behind is back.'

'Would he kill them if he found out about them?'

'Beyond doubt, Mistress. I would.'

Lydia remembered Constantinople, and glanced sidelong at her companion's face, wondering what he recalled.

'Would Lionel's fledglings kill me behind his back? Rebbe Karlebach –' she spoke the name of Jamie's mentor hesitantly, but the vampire showed no reaction at the mention of the man who'd emptied a shotgun full of silver pellets into him the previous year – 'warned us that the Undead usually kill their living helpers.'

'This is because Rebbe Karlebach is an imbecile,' returned Ysidro calmly, 'like many self-nominated Van Helsings. They know only what they tell one another. I doubt he has had more than a dozen conversations with actual vampires in his life, and refused to believe what he heard from them. You are in no danger from Lionel's get, nor yet from Lionel himself.'

'Have you spoken to him since your return?'

'Not yet. But I do not think he has forgotten my words to him, on the subject of yourself, at our last encounter.'

That morning Lydia had dispatched a note to Aunt Isobel, crying off from the flower show and Lady Brightwell's garden reception on the grounds of urgent business in Oxford, and promising to return in time to chaperone Emily to Lady Savenake's ball that evening. It had crossed her mind that morning that if Nan Wellit had somehow managed to escape, and attempted to communicate with her at the Oxford house, she wasn't entirely certain that Ellen or Mrs Grimes would be aware of a subtle message.

But the sight of the empty nursery, the sound of Mrs Brock's muffled sobs, had been more than she could stand. Ellen and the other servants asked her a dozen times that day what could be done, or suggested everything from calling in the police to canvassing London themselves for word of 'this Grippen cove', and went about their duties in a state of such morbid anxiety that Lydia was driven nearly frantic.

*It's been FIVE DAYS!!!*

*Would they be more, or less, anxious if they knew who had kidnapped her, and who I am dealing with?*

She had escaped the house with a sense of deep relief, with two trunks containing gowns, shoes, hats, gloves, and jewelry suitable for operas, teas, flower shows ('You're never going without me to help you dress, Miss Lydia!') and a state dinner for forty to consecrate the bridal party for the upcoming Colwich-Armistead nuptials. Yet upon her arrival at the Temperance Hotel, the thought of seeing Cece Armistead hanging on Colwich's arm all evening at Lady Savenake's was more than she could bear. She had just finished and blotted a note to her aunt, begging yet again to be excused, and was about to carry it down to the lobby when the porter brought her up Don Simon's card, with his familiar spiky, sixteenth-century handwriting: *Would you do me the honor to walk out with me a little this evening?*

She had nearly wept with relief.

''Tis well that James will be here ere long,' he said. 'When you find record of Zahorec's properties, 'twere better we had a man who can easily go into any neighborhood to see these places, than a woman going about alone. Spare me,' he added, raising two fingers, 'the tale of how a woman in these modern days might venture into any street in London without reducing herself to the level of a common trull: I will not stand by and see you harmed. Rather let me ask of you –' he guided her toward the steps that ascended toward the Savoy Hotel – 'if you have among the garments you brought with you to London a green day frock? I thought you might. 'Tis a color that suits you, if I may be permitted to say so. If you will wear it tomorrow afternoon at six, and sit in the Café at the Hotel Metropole, a man from Barclays will come to you. Wear this also.'

From the pocket of his elegantly cut jacket he took a slim box, which contained – when Lydia opened it beneath the electrical lamps outside the Savoy's great doors – a long sautoir necklace wrought of pearls, peridot, and a scattering of emeralds, and sporting as its central pendant an exquisite mermaid of enamel and bronze. She stared at it, shocked – it was Tiffany work, obviously expensive and not the sort of gift a married woman could possibly accept from a man not her husband, even if he *had* been dead for three hundred and fifty years.

'At the sight of this necklace this man – Timothy Rolleston is his name – will, it is to be hoped, lay his soul and his access to the bank's foreign depositors at your feet. 'Twill impress him greatly if you call him by his name ere he hands you his card.'

'*Simon* . . .'

'Show no surprise at anything he says. His dreams are a stew of occult and aesthetics, and worse things I dare say. At the sight of you wearing this jewel he will believe whatever you tell him. I suggest that what you tell him shall consist merely of, *I am forbidden to speak*.'

'Forbidden by whom?'

'He knows that no more than you do yourself. But it sounds well.'

A carriage drew rein before the Savoy's doors and Lydia – even without her spectacles – recognized the team of flaxen-maned chestnuts as Sir Alfred Binney's. She gasped and drew back, but Don Simon put a hand on her arm, and moved one finger to signal silence. Sir Alfred, Lady May, Titus Armistead and Cece passed within a foot of them on the hotel steps, in full glow of the electric lamps, without the smallest sign of recognition.

When Don Simon made to lead Lydia after them into the hotel café, however, Lydia shook her head: 'I couldn't! They're going to Lady Savenake's ball, and if they *did* see me they'll tell Aunt Lavinnia – who has to chaperone Emily tonight as well as her own daughter . . .'

'Are they, indeed?' The vampire looked after them thoughtfully. 'Then perhaps 'twere the moment – if you would be so good as to accompany me, Mistress – to visit Wycliffe House, and see there whatever might be seen.'

They stopped on their way to Queen Street at Guerlain's Bond Street emporium, where Don Simon purchased a small bottle of Jicky perfume. 'An offensive air,' he remarked as he handed it to her, 'but favored by the young Mistress Armistead, I believe. 'Twere best the Bohemian did not scent it in places where a guest of the house would have no access.'

At that hour the lights were on in the front of the house, and on its upper floors. After they dismissed their cab Don Simon stood for a time on the flagway opposite the doors, head bowed, arms folded. A carriage rattled past, and in the opposite direction a woman in a nanny's dark cloak walked arm-in-arm with a soldier. Ysidro did not stir.

*Grippen did this.*

Lydia put on her spectacles and looked sidelong at that thin face like carved alabaster: aquiline nose, pointed chin. Lashes straight and colorless as the spider-silk of his long hair, and his scars – she could see them clearly now – like strokes razored into unbleached wax.

*Grippen stood in the Slipe between New College and our garden gate Thursday night, just like that. Reaching out to the minds of every man and woman in the house, whispering whatever it is they whisper that causes the mind to drift, then the eyes to close.*

He raised his head, met her eyes. Took her hand.

The front door was unlocked. The liveried footman she'd paid Saturday night to fetch her a cab slumped sideways in a chair in the porter's booth off the front hall, profoundly asleep. Don Simon paused to regard the young man, whose lolling head exposed several inches of throat above the snowy linen of his stock: Lydia could see the tiny beat of the vein under the flesh. Her stomach turned even as the vampire moved away.

*He could kill anyone in the house.*

*My God, what am I doing with this man?*

He crossed the blue-and-pink flowers of that garish carpet, looked up at the electric chandelier, the refulgent runner on the stair, the bright splashes of gilt on the sky-blue boiserie panels, and though his expression did not change she saw the shadow that moved in his eyes.

*He sees it as it was.*

*And himself, as he was?*

Then his eyes shifted from genuine grief at the passage of years, to disdain at Alf Binney's taste. '*Dios.* I believe that sound I hear is the Old Earl rolling over in his grave. I have not crossed that threshold in forty years – an instructive lesson in letting the dead bury their own dead. Show me where it was, that you encountered this Zahorec.'

In loyalty to Lady May, Lydia replied, 'It was terrible to see it in the eighties. Everything that hadn't been sold was covered in dust sheets, and cardboard over windows that had been broken . . . I take it vampires don't actually need to be invited into a house in order to enter it?'

'I was invited in 1682,' replied Don Simon, as he followed her through a beautiful little vestibule into the dining room, the long table glinting softly in the diffused light from the windows. 'But no. 'Tis another of those tales the living make up about the dead.'

'Like that one about needing to sleep in consecrated ground – or your own native earth? I don't think that bank vault you rented in Peking was particularly holy—'

'I assure you, Mistress, the world abounds in men who think so.' A rare human smile touched his face.

'But you do need human assistance in crossing running water?'

''Tis a different matter. Our ability to bend the minds of the living fractures with the movement of energy through living water, but that energy shifts with the moon and the tides. At midnight, or the tide's turning, our minds can focus briefly—'

'Is that why you need the help of the living, in order to travel?'

'How not, when the first stain of light will ignite our flesh like a fat-soaked reed?' He held up his hand, ungloved now, regarded the long fingers as if expecting to see them indeed consumed in the postponed flames of Hell. 'A thousand strangers cross our paths, and a thousand things can go wrong, to keep us from shelter. 'Tis no surprise that the living believe that we cannot venture far from our graves. Few of us do.'

'You do.' Lydia halted, her hand on the latch of the garden door. 'I didn't think, when I wired you . . . *Did* you get someone to come with you to England? A valet, a courier . . . Grippen wouldn't harm *him*, would he? Or . . .' A second, worse, fear smote her. '*You* wouldn't . . .'

'Mistress.' He laid his hand on hers, cold as death and clawed like the Devil's. 'I assure you I murdered no one in order to reach your side.' He opened the garden door. 'Ah! Here at least is what I recall of this place . . .' He stepped into the dappled moon glow of the pergola, and reached to brush the hedge with his fingertips. 'Or will it be but a matter of time ere this man Binney mows down the yew maze and lays down a tennis court in its stead?'

'Beast!' She shoved him lightly – as she would have Jamie, or one of her chums in school – and like a dancer he turned out of her way, smiling again. 'You sound just like Cece. I suppose you'd rather the place fell to ruin—'

'Forgive one who has seen too much fall to ruin, Lady.' He took her hand, and crossing the pergola, led her to the little southern door of the maze. 'And too much suffer a sea change into something rich and passing strange indeed . . . and among the things which have so suffered since last I walked this ground in daylight was a church called St Adsullata's Coldspring. 'Twas rebuilt as an inn – called Cold Spring also, or Cold Well – and the ground later sold to the Old Earl. For long the half-ruined shell of it served the house as stabling, with the hay stored in the crypt below.'

They passed through the open ground at the heart of the little maze, thirty feet long and barely ten broad even when the dark walls of yew had been trimmed. Saplings and thrusting branches overgrew it, and in its center the little temple – a mere ring of pillars topped by a dome – had been robbed of its statue even in the days when Lydia had traced her way there as a child.

In its shadow Don Simon paused, and stood as if listening. Then, satisfied, he renewed his grip on Lydia's hand, and plunged into the northern side of the maze.

'Do you think the crypt is still there?'

'I know it to be so, Mistress. The Fourth Earl built the wing for his mother and sisters on the foundation of the stable, and used the crypt as a wine-cellar. They kept butter below it, in the sub-crypt which in its time had been part of a temple: inscriptions there preserve the names both of Jupiter and of the Magna Mater.'

They crossed the northern pergola, lamp glow from the garden room dappling the grass before the French doors.

'Lionel knows this as he knows all things within the city, though he comes seldom to its western end. His domain lies for the most part downriver of the Tower, among the streets he knew of old. Not hallowed soil, but his own.'

A footman – wig off and cravat loosed – sprawled with his head on the little table in the center of the garden room, a burly detective snoring in the chair opposite and a decanter of V.S.O.P. Napoleon brandy and a game of rummy between them. Don Simon spared them a reproving glance; Lydia felt again the sensation of being in a fairy tale, passing like a ghost among enchanted sleepers.

They climbed the back stair and found Cece Armistead's maid – a light-complexioned black woman of perhaps Lydia's own age – sprawled on her back on her mistress' bed, her knickers about one ankle and her skirt hiked past her waist, and a footman in dark-green livery ('Lord Mulcaster's, I believe,' remarked Ysidro) in a similar state of *deshabille* deeply asleep at her side.

Lydia remarked, 'Good Heavens,' and assisted Ysidro to make a more thorough search of the secretaire, dressing table and closets than had been possible Saturday night by candlelight. She unearthed from the back of the closet a quantity of books – Keats, Radcliffe, Machen and LeFanau – and bottles of laudanum and absinthe. A slim gold case tucked under the mattress of the bed proved to contain brown Turkish cigarettes whose tobacco gave off the bitter smell of opium.

'Here.' Don Simon held out to her a slip of paper with the words *Şcoala Neacşu, Ion de Majano, Claro Guinizelli*, and addresses at hotels in Florence and Paris. Lydia copied them down. From there they moved, silent as a pair of shadows, down the hallway to the door of Titus Armistead's library.

'I have picklocks,' said Lydia when Ysidro tried the handle, and fished James' little kit from her handbag. 'Have you ever picked a lock?'

'The nights are long.' He held out his hand for them. 'If one does not particularly care for the company of other vampires, 'tis always a useful thing to acquire accomplishments.'

He had it open in half the time even Jamie would require. *Well, he DOES have hypersensitive touch and hearing . . .*

'What happened to seeping through keyholes in the form of a mist?'

'You have read a great deal too many novels, Madame.'

'They were seeking something in here,' said Lydia as Don Simon pushed open the door. 'Cece said, "I have—" and Zahorec said, "It can wait." But they came in here, so I think what she must have "had" was the key.'

She looked around her at the glass-fronted shelves, the marquetry work cabinets below them. Ysidro switched on the lights, the electric glare showing up more variegated carpeting and expensively uphol-stered chairs. The books themselves were bound sets, stamped in gold, bought with the house: Lydia recalled them from her child-hood. Lady May had told her how in the old days, when a rich man bought a book he'd just buy the pages, and have it bound to match the other books in his library. The few dozen acquired since that time – Dickens, Thackeray, Gibbon, Austen, a thick Latin grammar, five French and three Spanish dictionaries – stood out among them, like civilians in the ranks of the Guards.

Don Simon opened the drawers of the black-and-gold Louis XV table, but his search was cursory. He took the picklocks to the smaller door tucked among the bookshelves on the library's inner wall and, opening it, revealed a stairway going down.

New carpeting, fresh paint, and electric lights amply attested to its recent use to the new lord of the household. In structure it was obviously old, winding in four deep turns. Lydia guessed that under that blue-and-yellow broadloom the fifty-four original stone steps had been filled in with concrete to even out signs of wear.

At the bottom she switched on the lights and said again, 'Good Heavens!'

The long room was clearly, as Don Simon had said, the vault of the old chapel of St Adsullata. Squat Romanesque pillars and stone ceiling groins had been plastered over and whitewashed, but the proportions whispered of great age even to Lydia's uninstructed eye. The wine racks had been shoved higgledy-piggledy to the back of the crypt, and the room was crammed with crates. Boxed-up paintings: huge, flat, and square. A few were uncrated: portraits, landscapes, academy works that pointed up morals or sentimental scenes of faithful dogs guarding sleeping children. Josetta often accused her of having a hollow in her head where others had what the phrenologists called a 'bump of aesthetics': Lydia was always fascinated by the faces of portraits, wondering who these people had been and whether they'd been happy (*Did their wigs itch?*), but couldn't have told a Vermeer from a Monet.

There were books there, too, stacked up on the crates: bindings of ancient leather, dark with age, or crates whose shape proclaimed them as more books, layers of brown paper visible through the tight-nailed wood. Evidently Armistead went in for collecting holy relics as well – a huge gold monstrance which displayed behind crystal a few scraps of cloth and hair, and three large chests of solid silver that made Don Simon back quickly away. Smaller reliquaries of silver, crystal and gold lay among the books, and Lydia picked one up. It contained what looked like a child's tooth.

Hastily, she set it down again.

'No ill investment,' remarked the vampire, 'if this chamber were their goal. The quantity of treasure here is such that a golden crucifix, or that copy of Aretino's *Di Novi*, would not be missed until your American returned to his home country, and then none could say when and where it had vanished. The price of any one of them would easily cover freehold on any property in London. Ah . . .'

With deceptive ease he moved the wine racks aside from the wall.

'I thought this would still be here.'

# TEN

The door was wooden, ruinously old under its coating of white paint. It was barely five feet tall and set two steps down into the floor. Lydia could see its weight in the way even the vampire had to strain to open it a crack.

The smell that rose through it was indescribable: muck, sewage, wet stone. The bright lights of the wine crypt showed her steps, narrow and deeply worn.

Nobody had fixed these up with concrete filler or a Chicago Kidderminster.

'What's down there?' she whispered.

'The ancient baths. Did he lair in this house t'would be here, yet I behold no mark upon the floor, where the door would scrape on opening.'

'Keyhole infiltration?'

'At a guess the keyhole rusted solid sometime in the reign of Queen Anne.' He fished in his pockets for the candles he had collected in the pantry. 'Will you come? St Adsullata Coldspring lay close to the old Tyburn River, and anciently a sewer connected the Roman baths with the stream. 'Tis long since I passed this way.'

The flame from the match he struck seemed to shine through his fingers as he touched it to the candle's wick.

'Such places exist in Prague, and in Roman cities on the Adriatic like Zara. A vampire out of Romania would surely know to look for them.' As they ducked low through the ruinous doorway, Don Simon ran his free hand along the jamb, an inch or so from the stonework. Lydia had to press her own free hand against the clammy wall, to keep from slipping where feet had worn a groove down the center of the steps.

'Why would the Romans have put a bath so deep underground?'

''Twas scarce the depth of a common cellar when first they delved it. London's buildings slowly sink with time. Catacombs lie deep beneath the Camden Market, and the ancient Temple of Mithras under Holborn. Behold.' He raised his candle. Lydia had a dark impression of a very long room, of brickwork arches from which the plaster had long since fallen. In a rectangular pit three or four feet deep, filth-crusted red and white tile could still be dimly discerned. The stone head of a lion at one end of the pit marked where water had once flowed in; a stone culvert showed where it had flowed out.

Rats fled the light. Lydia hastily hiked her skirt up to her calves, and tucked it into her belt.

'I can scarcely see Zahorec crawling out of the sewers through that culvert,' she remarked. 'Unless he has a change of clothes hidden somewhere here . . .'

'I have them hidden all over London.' Simon walked slowly around the perimeter of the room, studying the buckled floor. 'But 'twere altogether a tidier matter to have his sweetheart admit him to the house through the garden door.'

He dropped lightly from the edge of the pit – *It must have been the bath itself,* reasoned Lydia, observing the pit and chimney in the corner that led into the hypocaust beneath – and stood beside the low stone arch of the drain. Though the flicker of two solitary candles showed her barely the outline of the arch, and the vampire's pale profile against the darkness, she knew he could see in that darkness as in daylight, whether there were any scrape-marks of elbows and knees coming up out of the realms beneath.

'It would certainly be a help to be able to get about as mist,' she commented, as Don Simon took two running strides and sprang up the four-foot wall of the pit as easily as she or James might hop up a curbstone. 'Here's the way down into the hypocaust, but it doesn't look like it's been marked. I mean, one couldn't get a coffin down something that narrow, but this far under the earth he could surely just curl up in a corner.'

'He could.' He stretched himself full length beside the circular hole, and peered down it. Lydia's candle showed her notches in the brick sides, which formed a sort of ladder. 'Depending upon how he felt about being eaten by rats in his sleep.'

'Oh,' said Lydia. 'Oh, *that's* why you're so careful about having a coffin or something to sleep in.'

'Once we sleep –' Simon rose and dusted his waistcoat fastidiously – 'we do not wake. The coffin provides another layer of protection. During the Great Fire I slept unprotected for three nights, in hypocausts and crypts such as this . . . But by the third night every rat in London had either fled the city or had other matters to think on. As we age, we toughen, and an older vampire can remain awake for sometimes as much as half an hour when the sun's light is in the sky, if he is protected against its rays. Likewise there are potions we can drink which will prolong wakefulness well into the day, but many of these are dangerous in themselves, and all of them leave one debilitated for days.

'He has been here,' he went on. 'I feel his presence in the stones. But 'tis not how he comes and goes to the house above. Certain it is that he hunts along the underground rivers, coming up only to make his kill and then going below again. Thus it is that he has avoided Grippen's eye. There are entrances to the underworld throughout London. Old churches, and the chapels of monasteries, often had vaults through which one could enter the drains, forgotten now by all save those who hunt the night.'

'Jamie told me about them,' said Lydia. 'He made a study of them, when he was with the Department.'

He led her back to the old ascending stair, switching off the electric lights in the treasure-crypt as they passed through it.

'So if Zahorec is buying properties in London, he'll choose those—'

'Silence.' Don Simon stopped on the long stairway back to the library, held up one finger. 'Stay here.' They were within sight of the door at the top; he reached it in what seemed, to Lydia, like two steps, and switched off the lights. In the blackness she felt his cold fingers around hers a moment later. 'They've returned.'

'Oh, bother! I do hope,' she added, 'Miss Armistead's maid has – um – finished . . .'

'They woke a little time after you and I went below ground. One presumes they went their separate ways. Come,' he went on. 'All have gone downstairs for tea, the servants to wait on them.' The cold hand led her up through the darkness (*And thank goodness those stairs were leveled and carpeted . . .*) then across the plush of the library rugs. Lamps burned in several of the bedrooms and Lydia experienced a momentary rush of panic as they stepped into the hall.

'Do not concern yourself,' urged Don Simon as they walked toward the door of the backstairs. 'We shall not be—'

He was already stepping back as Lydia reached for the handle of the backstairs door. It opened virtually under her hand, and Lydia found herself face-to-face with Cece Armistead's erring maid. The young woman halted, startled, eyebrows plunging together as she faced Lydia – who, at the vampire's gentle tug, moved out of her way without speaking.

'You better have those baths drawn,' snapped the maid, and strode away down the corridor, not waiting for a reply.

Simon guided Lydia ahead of him into the backstairs.

'What . . .?'

'She thought you another of the maids.' He was smiling slightly, a far-off twinkle of brightness in his yellow eyes that she had never seen there before.

*He's enjoying this.*

He was almost laughing as they slipped out into the garden.

'Think you not, that if we can trick the eyes of the living so that they do not see us as we are, we can also – with a little practice – trick them into believing that we are someone else they know? Someone who has every right to be in the upstairs hall? Ere she reaches the parlor with her mistress's shawl, she'll forget that she even saw us.'

'Wretch!' Lydia poked him again. 'No wonder Jamie's worried about one of you hiring on with the Kaiser! And no wonder there are all those legends about vampires making respectable married ladies think they're their husbands—'

'So *they* said,' retorted Simon. '*I* never had call for such a trick.'

'You are dreadful!'

The chimes of midnight were striking from St Michael's as they emerged through the old garden gate into the mews. Lydia found herself trembling, from exhilaration and fright and the bone-deep relief of not fighting her battle by herself. Her heart still ached in terror for Miranda, her fear a shadow that colored the very air she breathed, and yet, for a time, she had been able to turn her mind from helpless dread.

And the rest had brought unspeakable relief.

As much relief, she wondered as Simon hailed a cab, as a young man would have, who was able to forget for a little time that he was a vampire?

To forget that there was no road back to the country of the living which she saw now, suddenly, he had so profoundly loved.


Wearing her green Patou frock, and Simon's mermaid necklace, Lydia arrived at the Café Metropole the following afternoon at a quarter to six and ordered coffee.

And thought, as she waited for Mr Timothy Rolleston of Barclays Bank, about illusion, and deception, and Simon de la Cadeña-Ysidro.

She had dreamed again of the man praying in Latin in the barred moonlight of his cell, and this time had recognized Damien Zahorec's dark curls and aristocratic features. She had smelled in the cold darkness wet snow on pines, the stink of latrines and woodsmoke. Had seen, when he turned his head at the creak of the cell's door, the puncture-wounds on his throat, some freshly scabbed and others weeks old. A woman stood in the doorway and Lydia thought, *She's keeping him here. Playing cat-and-mouse.* The moonlight didn't reach across the cell. Lydia saw only the silver light tipping the ends of furs about her neck, and the animal gleam of her eyes.

*Did that really happen?* she wondered, waking in the darkness. *Or is that only to make me see him as an unwilling victim, not responsible for what he is?*

*Is that the dream he sent to Cece?*

Since her family duty that day had included chaperoning Emily to breakfast at Dallaby House – Titus Armistead's 'wedding present' – she'd had plenty of opportunity to see precisely how deeply Cece was entangled in the intoxicating labyrinth of romantic dreams.

'It's the oldest house in the street.' The girl led her dozen guests up the two worn sandstone steps to its door. 'Noel says it's been here since Elizabeth's time, but the chapel in the back of the house is ancient, part of the old priory of St Mary . . . the church of St Mary Westbourne over on Lyall Street was part of it, too, didn't you say, Ned?' She threw a sparkling glance at Colwich's friend, who followed, doglike, in his lordship's wake. 'Only they've torn it all down and made it smart. Ugh!'

She shuddered elaborately. 'The builders tell me there used to be a secret crypt down below where they held Masses, and a passageway to the old priory, to escape from Cromwell's men! Noel's been looking for it, haven't you, darling?'

Pale as she was – and the vivid pink silk of her shirtwaist, worked high around her throat, seemed further to drain the color from her face – her dark eyes glowed with dreamy light. 'Oh, how I wish that instead of making it all bright and new, Papa would take it back to the way it was when first it was built!'

'You'd sing a different song first time you wanted to take a bath,' growled the mining baron. 'Or use some other plumbing I could mention . . .'

Emily blushed, and Seraphina Bellwether – the other chaperone of the party – looked as if she would take the millionaire to task for speaking of such matters in mixed company, had she dared.

'Oh, plumbing is much of a muchness.' Lord Colwich dismissed the whole subject of convenience with a wave. 'Such a bore, when one compares it with the incomparable vibrations of endless time!'

His smile went straight past Ned Seabury as if his friend weren't present, and caressed his bride to be.

They passed through the bare drawing room, suffused with light from curtainless windows. The walls had been stripped to the plaster and the equipment of the paperhangers littered the uncarpeted oak floor.

'Glad you like it, your lordship,' Armistead grunted. 'But I'm telling you now, I wouldn't have bought it if I'd known how much work there'd be – and at the prices you English charge for a simple job of paint and plaster! In Peru I could have brought in a dozen Indians from any of the villages . . .'

'Now, Daddy!' Cece took her father's arm. 'You know you said, *doesn't matter what it costs.*'

He growled, but when he looked down into her face it was like hearing one of the menhirs of Stonehenge suddenly whisper *I love you* to a child.

'The moment I crossed the threshold,' Cece gushed, turning back to her guests, 'and felt the vibrations of ancient days, ancient memories, whispering to me like a half-heard song across the chasm of the centuries, I knew I could live nowhere else!'

Snow and darkness and Latin prayers . . . A desperate man imprisoned at the mercy of a powerful and terrible woman . . . *It's like those books up in her room*, thought Lydia, as she followed the party down the hall. *Like Camilla, and Christabel, and the Belle Dame Sans Merci.*

Ahead of her, Colwich spread his arms in an expansive gesture as he chatted to the dour millionaire of psychic alignments and the ectoplasmic communications he'd received – under Dr Millward's guidance, of course – at seances held at 'our castle' in Scotland. *And he's as bad as she is*, Lydia reflected.

'I'm going to have our bedroom done up in tapestries and medieval furniture, just as it was in olden times . . .'

*She's practically begging to be hoodwinked, with Gothic shadows and 'vibrations' from the past.*

Sitting at her white-draped table at the Metropole, coffee cooling before her in its gilt-rimmed cup, Lydia turned the mermaid of her necklace in her fingers. *And of course there's no reason a clerk at Barclays Bank wouldn't believe in faerie voices and elder gods and the spirits of the earth as well, or whatever other mishmash of omens Simon's poured into this Mr Rolleston's dreams. 'Occult and aesthetic . . .' A mysterious woman in green, wearing a necklace he's seen already in his dreams . . .*

*He'll be fired without a character if anyone ever finds out he's been giving details of a depositor's account to a stranger.*

Lydia shivered. *And Miranda may die, if I tell him the truth and send him away.*

She closed her eyes, not knowing whether it was Don Simon she hated, or herself.

'I can't like it.' Seraphina Bellwether had sidled up to Lydia as the younger members of the party exclaimed over the breakfast, set out on an exquisite Regency table in the midst of the tarpaulin-draped dining room. 'Colwich may be an Earl one day, but had I a daughter, I should certainly not wish to see her marry a young man of his *reputation.*' She tilted a significant glance at Ned Seabury, who had been trying all morning – unsuccessfully – to get his lordship alone.

Since Colwich had departed abruptly – 'to have a chat with the family solicitor, you know . . .' – the dark young eromenos had relapsed into glowering at Cece from across the bright array of silver and Rockingham china.

'Quite apart from . . . well . . . what one *hears,* I understand his lordship spent the whole of his time in Paris, when he was *supposed* to be studying art – and what business has a young man of his station studying art, anyway? Ogling undraped *grisettes,* more like, which he could certainly have done at home . . . Well, I understand that he kept *dreadful* company, smoking himself into an opium stupor and going about the town with Devil-worshippers. I fear he may lead Miss Armistead into evil habits.'

Lydia remembered the bottle of laudanum at the back of Cece Armistead's closet, and the bottle of absinthe.

And yet, she reflected, Lord Colwich displayed none of the symptoms of opium use with which she had become acquainted in her months at the charity clinic. Most of the morning he had chattered with his prospective father-in-law about the typography in various printings of the *Hypnerotomachia Poliphili,* and blown kisses at Cece.

Left as host, Armistead grunted replies to his daughter's chatter, mostly concerning the prices paid by Vanderbilts and Belmonts for

Gutenberg Bibles and First Folios of Shakespeare, and on his other side Emily went into raptures about the house's 'Gothic shadows'. 'I know it must be haunted,' sighed Julia Thwaite. 'I'm very sensitive to vibrations and I can feel it in the house's ancient bones.'

*Does Cece realize that Zahorec intends to initiate her into the Undead? To put it at its baldest, to kill her?*

*Would she MIND?*

*What has he told her about the vampire state? Does she think it isn't really necessary to kill your victims? Just take a little blood, the way he does from her? And live forever . . . with him.*

*Does she think they'll make love in reality as they do in her dreams?*

*And when she learns the truth, it will be too late.*

*No wonder fledglings hate their masters.*

The acrid whiff of wool long uncleaned and linen unwashed stung her nostrils in the same moment the light from the café's long windows dimmed, and looking up, Lydia saw a man beside her table. Tallish, stooped, neither fair nor dark, his silk hat in his hands to reveal the greasy gleam of dirty hair, thinning away from his forehead. Though she couldn't see his face clearly she saw that his eyes were light within smudges left by poor sleep. He'd made an effort to drown the smell of his suit and flesh with bay rum and the result was nauseating.

She set down her coffee spoon. 'Please have a seat, Mr Rolleston.'

Instead he fell to his knees and took – and kissed – her hand. At the next table, her Aunt Harriet's friends Lady Gillingham and Mrs Tyler-Strachley stopped their gossip and stared.

Timothy Rolleston whispered, 'My lady,' and, thank goodness, took the other chair. Even without her spectacles Lydia could tell he was devouring her with his gaze, staring at the cloisonné mermaid on its green jeweled chain.

*Simon, I am going to drive a stake through your heart for this . . .*

'Command me.'

*How about starting with a BATH?*

'What were you told?' At least a week's association with Cecelia Armistead had given her an idea of the tone to take. *Gothic vibrations. La Belle Dame Sans Merci.*

'That you had need of me.'

She touched her forefinger to her lips. 'You understand that it is not necessary that you understand why we ask these things of you?' She privately thought the *we* a nice touch.

'I understand.' He bowed his head. 'But thank you. Thank you from the bottom of my soul.' A tear glistened in his eye and she felt another pang of rage at Simon, for manipulating this man. His voice was not that of a youth just setting sail on his career, but of a man in middle age, beaten and tired. She could see no ring on his bare and ink-stained fingers.

'It is we who thank you, Mr Rolleston.' She tried to make herself sound like someone in one of Cece Armistead's novels. 'What we ask is simple. We seek a man, who entered this country late in January, from Montenegro or Serbia. He will have transferred money from a bank in that part of the world, Sofia or Bucharest.'

Rolleston nodded, his queer pale eyes not meeting hers but looking away to the side. 'Many did, when the fighting started, my lady.'

'This man goes by the name of Zahorec sometimes, or Ludovico Bertolo, or possibly one of these others . . .' She held out to him a notepaper on to which she had copied the other names Simon had found in Cece Armistead's desk.

'You are to speak those names to no one, but to seek him in the bank's records. Tell me what property he has acquired, and the names of all to whom he has transferred money from his accounts. If he has accounts under other names I wish to know those. If he has traveled from London, I wish to know that. You will find everything about him, and everything about his money.'

'Yes, my lady.' She had the feeling he'd have slipped from his chair and knelt before her again, given the slightest encouragement to do so.

'And you will find out all these same things about Bartholomew Barrow, if he has any dealings with your bank; about William Duggan, about Francis Houghton . . .' She gave him every name under which Lionel Grippen had ever held property that she knew about. 'If they have money, the names of the people they disbursed it to.' From her handbag she took her list so far of Grippen's names and properties, pushed it across the snowy linen to him. 'If your bank has handled transactions involving any of these properties, I want to know the names of everyone involved and where the money went. Do you understand?'

'I understand, lady,' he whispered. 'I shall do as you ask.'

If he'd had any doubts about violating the most sacred rules of his bank, he'd resolved them. Perhaps as he stood on the threshold and saw her, the red-haired woman in green wearing the necklace he'd been shown in his dream by some glowing elf king or elder god or angel . . . With his head humbly bowed, she could see the gray that streaked his hair. For her convenience Don Simon had, with the utmost casualness, put this poor deluded man in danger of ruin.

'I shall be here Friday at this time.' Her voice shook as she spoke the words. *You're a goddess*, she reminded herself. *Or the queen of the elves. Or the reincarnated spirit of this man's sweetheart or wife. Such creatures don't have pity for those who run under the juggernaut's wheels for their sakes.* 'Will you have this information by then?'

'I should. I'll bring you what I have, lady.' He looked down at his own grubby fingers, then quickly took her hand and kissed it again. Without meeting her eyes, he whispered, 'And then I will be free?'

*FREE OF WHAT???*

Fury, pity, helplessness threatened for a moment to block all speech.

*Miranda*, she thought. *Oh, Miranda . . .*

She made herself say grandly, 'Yes. You will be free.'

Tears flowed down his face and he quickly wiped them with a crumpled and yellowed handkerchief. Then he blundered to his feet and hurried from the café with a swift stooped shuffle. Lydia watched his gray form thread between the bright swatches of the ladies who'd stopped here for a cup of tea to recruit themselves for the evening's ball or dinner or visit to the opera. Ladies who'd gone to Select Female Academies with her mother, who'd said *t'sk-t'sk* when Lady Mary Wycliffe – or Catherine Halfdene – had married 'beneath them' to rescue the family fortunes. Ladies who gave lavishly to charities and paid their poor maids barely ten pounds a year, ladies whose worlds began with the gossip of their friends and ended at the dressmaker's.

Ladies among whom, all her life, Lydia had felt like a changeling, a visitor from some alien place or time.

At the next table she was aware of Lady Gillingham giving Mrs Tyler-Strachley a trenchant glance as she rose. Lydia laid the price of the coffee on the table beside her cup, got swiftly to her feet, and left the café. She was trembling.

*Don't any of you DARE speak to me . . .*

She understood to the core of her soul why James had quit the Department.


There was a *musicale* at Lady Stafford's that night, but the possibility that Lady Gillingham might be there – let alone a) her stepmother and b) Cece Armistead – overwhelmed Lydia as she climbed aboard the crowded omnibus to Liverpool Street Station. *I can't do it.*

*Aunt Isobel will kill me. I've abandoned Emily now two nights in a row.*

*And if Simon shows up at Lady Stafford's thinking I'm going to thank him for seducing that poor clerk into jeopardizing his position, I think I'll burst into tears.*

She stopped at her two letter-drops in Finsbury Circus, returned to her hotel room long enough to write a note to Aunt Isobel and change into a traveling costume of tobacco-colored faille, then took a cab to Paddington Station. Her heart wept for the peace of Oxford, for her own house – still and empty as it now felt, the nursery vacant, the servants whispering of this scheme or that to take matters into their own hands. The clock on All Hallows struck seven; there was a seven-thirty express to Oxford. She bought her ticket, crossed the teeming chaos of the station.

Clerks in their shabby black coats and the silk hats they treasured and nursed as their badges of respectability trudged toward the trains that would take them to red-brick suburbs: Basingstoke, Maidenhead, Westbourne Green. Students – fresh-faced, rowdy, slightly intoxicated, headed back 'up' to Oxford – as if London lay in a slough of sin at the bottom of an intellectual hill – sons of dukes and financiers and baronets, 'down' to be briefed by parents as to their duties in the Season. Costermongers shouting pies for sale, children crying as they hung on to their mothers . . .

And – she didn't know what made her look around – a man in brown at the far end of the platform, standing suddenly still.

*James.*

Sixty feet separated them as the train began to move, and she wasn't wearing her spectacles, but she knew him. Groped in her handbag for them even as he strode toward her, and yes, it was him, nobody else in the world moved like that.

She cried, '*Jamie!*' as the seven-thirty to Oxford began to pick up speed, and stepped down off it, into his arms.

# ELEVEN

He listened without comment, thumbed through the sheaf of yellow foolscap from Teazle and McClennan that she'd had in her satchel along with three issues of *The Lancet* and a monograph on blood groups. 'Don Simon has arranged for a clerk at Barclays Bank to go through the bank's records for me,' she said, and he glanced up at the slight tremor in her matter-of-fact voice. 'So I should have a list of Zahorec's properties by Friday. I suspect that he's going to lair up at Dallaby House – do you know it? Titus Armistead purchased it for his daughter and Lord Colwich to honeymoon in. Simon and I broke into Wycliffe House last night and found nothing . . . Well, nothing about vampires, anyway, but a great deal about what servants do when everybody's out at the theater.'

'Does Miss Armistead know that either of us knows about vampires?' James Asher was a little surprised at how calm he sounded. Seventeen years of secret service to Queen and Country had, he understood, taken its toll on him, but somehow he hadn't expected this. His rush of rage had almost suffocated him, when Lydia had told him what the Master of London had done. Yet with his heart screaming his daughter's name, he found he could answer as if he were talking of someone else's child.

'I don't think so.' Lydia picked up her cup of railroad coffee, cold now, as Asher's was – not that it had been particularly warm when the spotty youth at the café had brought it to them, along with a plate of moderately stale biscuits. Asher had devoured his share of them – the last time he'd eaten was, if he recalled rightly, at the Gare du Nord that morning – but noticed that Lydia left hers untouched. By the look of her he guessed she'd been eating almost nothing since the night of the kidnapping.

'I suspect it's time –' Asher pushed a plate of biscuits across to her – 'Isobel's shrieks of outrage notwithstanding – for *you* to develop sciatica and retire to Oxford. It isn't a very long trail that could connect you with the London nest. I'll put myself in touch with Grippen—'

'I don't think I can do that.' She obediently picked up a biscuit, broke off a corner of it, and left both fragment and biscuit on the plate.

Not that he blamed her, given the quality of biscuits served by the Great Western Railway Café.

'I met Zahorec at a ball at Wycliffe House – spoke to him. I think he's been trying to lure me in my dreams.'

The anger returned, a rush of crimson heat that extended not only to the interloping vampire and the London nest, but to Simon Ysidro as well. He heard the steely hardness in his own voice as he said, 'And has Zahorec asked anything of you yet?'

'Not yet.' She broke her biscuit into tinier and tinier fragments without appearing to notice it at all. 'But now that he knows me he might wonder if I suddenly went back to Oxford. And to tell you the truth, I'd rather be where I can do exactly as Grippen asked me: find all Zahorec's lairs. It may be the quickest way to . . . to bring an end to all this. Just give him what he's asking for.'

Asher closed his lips on the words, *Do you really think he's going to give her back?*

'I gave Mr Rolleston – the Barclays man – a list of all the names by which Grippen has done business over the years, and the addresses of his properties. Simon says he'll find me someone in the B of E.' Again the tremor in her voice, the movement of her eyes. Ysidro, Asher knew, could be ruthless. 'That's where Grippen used to keep his money. I hope I've thought of everything . . .'

He took her hands and kissed them, then held them to his face, unshaven and grimy after two days' nonstop travel: Venice to Turin, Turin to Geneva, Geneva to Paris. Stations that echoed in the dead of night and the sourness of railway coffee. The rhythm of steel wheels seemed ground into his bones. *Come home at once. Grippen has done something terrible.*

Lydia's telegram had lain on the front desk of the Palazzo Foscari Hotel for nearly twenty-four hours before he'd returned to Venice from Sarajevo. He'd passed the time between Venice and Paris planning how to bomb the Foreign Office and kill every living soul within it, for asking him to run that courier drop into Serbia. And then kill himself for agreeing to do it.

After he killed Grippen.

'You've acquitted yourself like a hero, best beloved.'

'I tried.' She abandoned the component atoms of the biscuit and began to align the silverware. 'Grippen's fledglings followed me one night. At least Simon guesses they were Grippen's. Two men and a woman. Simon says he doesn't think they'll harm me, that Grippen's hold on them is too strong.'

They had both seen Ysidro command his own fledgling to remain out of shelter in the first touch of the Arctic summer sun, until the new-made vampire flesh had ignited into unquenchable flame.

'I've said before,' Asher reflected grimly, 'that for people who stand in danger because they know too much about vampires, you and I know very little about vampires. Ysidro's probably right, but it's another reason I'd rather you stepped into the background. If Zahorec is strong enough to hide from Grippen, we don't know what else he's strong enough to do.'

Lydia was silent for a long time, making sure her fork was exactly perpendicular to the edge of the table, and that its central tines pointed precisely to the mathematical center of her coffee cup's diameter. 'Should I not have borne a child?' she asked at length. 'Knowing about them what I knew—'

'Never think it.' He grasped her hands again, as if to force her to meet his eyes. 'We will not transform ourselves into the dead for fear of them. Nor for hatred of them. You've seen where that leads.'

She looked aside. The electric light of the platform lamps outlined her features against the twilight that now filled the cavernous spaces around them. 'It's one thing to say that of ourselves. We can choose. Miranda . . .'

'No child can choose.' He rose from his chair and came around to her, drew her against him, delicate in his arms as a bundle of twigs. He remembered the Boer children in the concentration camps during the African wars, shock-haired, filthy skeletons with their bellies swollen from starvation: hostages to the demands of the diamond companies that called themselves by the name of Empire. Remembered, as he rode away from the camp into the warm African dusk, how the thin wailing of a baby had seemed to follow him for hours across the veldt. Their fathers in the commandos had not ceased fighting the invaders.

But he could not speak.

*You could hunt us down eventually*, Ysidro had said to him once, *were you willing to give your soul to it . . . to become obsessed, as all vampire hunters must become obsessed with their prey . . . Are you willing to give it years?*

He had not been.

*And this*, he reflected, *is what came of that . . .*

He became aware of a man standing at the far corner of the café kiosk, a slender gentleman in evening dress, spidery pale hair trailing down his shoulders. For a moment Asher's eyes met his, pale as yellow champagne, across his wife's red head.

When he blinked, Ysidro was gone. Nor was Asher, who had been on trains continuously for nearly forty-eight hours and was half blind with exhaustion, entirely certain that he'd seen him at all. In either case he knew that even if he sprang to his feet and darted to the place he'd find nothing.

'Come.' He stood. 'Let's get something real to eat – Vidal's is just over on Broad Street and they make the best onion soup you're likely to find in London – and then go back to this Temperance Hotel of yours and get some sleep. In the morning I'll get myself up as a loafer and go down to Stepney and have a look at Henry Scrooby's pub. If Grippen trusts him enough to put property in his wife's name he may trust him enough to put him in charge of guarding a couple of captives. What's that?'

As he picked up the packet of McClennan's latest information a small envelope slipped from between the pages, addressed to Mrs Marie Curie care of the Ladies' Christian Hotel in a hand unlike any that he'd seen on any of the reports. Good-quality notepaper, he observed automatically as she tore the envelope open: linen rag, tuppence a sheet, *finest for all polite correspondence . . .*

Behind her thick spectacles he saw Lydia's eyes widen. Silently, she handed him the sheet.

> *Mrs Curie:*
>
> *Please forgive my intrusion, but it has come to my attention that you are urgently seeking information about a man who came to this country at the end of January, with outsize luggage.*

*It happens that I am myself seeking such a man. Could you grant me the favour of a meeting, tomorrow afternoon, the fourteenth of May, at the café at Claridge's Hotel, at two? Please feel free to bring trusted friends with you. Would it be too great an imposition, to suggest that you wear a white hat, so that there will be no mistake in identity? I will likewise wear a white hat, and will bring proofs of my identity and bona fides.*

   *Thank you, more than I can say,*
   *Mr Edward Seabury*

James went in first, attired in proper morning dress of gray and black (*and Heaven only knows*, reflected Lydia distractedly, *how he happened to have THAT in that little satchel of his!*) and festooned in one of his collection of fake beards (*I KNEW he was doing a job for the Foreign Office in Italy!*) to make sure Dr Millward wasn't lurking behind a potted palm in Claridge's lobby. He also carried a stick, purchased that morning at Selfridge's where they'd acquired a white hat for Lydia, since as a redhead she never wore such things. If it was necessary for Lydia – waiting outside the great hotel's bronze doors – to simply walk away without entering, James would emerge from his reconnaissance stick-less, and they would rendez-vous back at the Temperance Hotel via separate cabs.

As a schoolgirl, Lydia had quizzed James (only she'd called him Mr Asher then) about being a spy. It hadn't taken her very long to figure out that her Uncle Ambrose's friend was leading some kind of a double life, probably because between her clandestine scientific studies and her hated lessons in deportment, dance and piano, she was leading one, too. She'd found the intricate play of logic, obser-vation, and secrecy fascinating and exciting, certainly an improve-ment over deportment, dance, piano lessons and dress fittings.

Now she felt only fear.

*Seabury CAN'T have told Millward . . .*

She felt sick at even the possibility.

*He knows the man. He isn't stupid. He has to know that if he breathes a word about Cece Armistead being seduced by a vampire, Millward will go straight to Noel . . . Noel who was flirting besot-tedly with Cece on Saturday night and yesterday morning . . .*

*Noel blurts all to Cece. Cece goes to Zahorec.*

*Zahorec goes deeper underground – after guessing about me.*

*If Zahorec kills me, Grippen will have no reason to keep Miranda alive.*

*Or Nan.*

Lydia closed her eyes. *Ned Seabury CAN'T be that mesmerized by Millward . . . Can he? He HAS to understand the stakes . . .*

She whispered a prayer to a God she didn't precisely believe in: *Don't let them come to harm.*

She had dreamed about Zahorec again last night. Dreamed of him by candlelight, charming and smiling, drinking wine among his friends and laughing, until across the room he'd seen a woman. Tall and queenly, full breasts braced tight by the flat front of a boned bodice, cold aquiline face framed by a collar of wired gauze. Her dark eyes had met Zahorec's smiling blue ones. Her face, stern when she had entered, had softened under his lilting glance.

Lured by his warmth, or pretending to be. Predator masquerading as prey.

He had left his friends, reached out to her. He might even have been deceived by the softness of her fingers answering his grip.

'Lydia, darling!'

Lydia opened her eyes with a snap in time to see Lady Gillingham toddling toward her in a golden-beige hobble-dress so narrow as to barely permit ascent of the hotel steps. 'Darling, it's been simply *ages* . . . Is it true Isobel's having Emily's court dress made by Worth? I think the man's overrated, myself – you should see the *shocking* frock he turned out for Loïe Varvel! It cost a hundred and fifty guineas and makes her look positively *pudgy*, darling – not that she'd be anything to brag about under any circumstances. Not everyone has your lovely figure.'

She slid an arm around Lydia's waist. 'And who was that *outré* creature I saw you with yesterday at the Metropole? What on *earth* did you say to him, for him to actually kneel and kiss your hand? My dear, don't *tell* me you're going to give that husband of yours something to worry about at last?'

Lydia had the presence of mind to roll her eyes. 'He's a student of Professor Asher's,' she explained in her kindliest voice. 'And yes, he does do things like that . . . But his uncle is a specialist in migraines, and I needed to ask him a few questions on the subject . . .'

'Oh, you poor *darling*! And here I thought you just cooked one up the other night to escape from that *frightful* affair at Wycliffe House!'

'I'm afraid not,' replied Lydia. 'My doctor recommended regular rest in the afternoons, so as soon as I've met with Ned Seabury – who I understand knows a specialist in Brighton – I'm hoping to get back to Oxford . . . Oh!' she added, as the Claridge's doors opened. Among all the black-and-gray-clothed gentlemen of the world – even in fake spectacles and a fake beard and walking with the slouch that took three inches off his height – she knew Jamie by the way he moved. He was still carrying the cane he'd bought. 'I think I see Mr Seabury now . . . Please excuse me.'

She hurried up the steps, not exchanging so much as a glance with her husband as they passed one another.

In a murmur no louder than the rustle of leaves he murmured, 'He's alone.'

'Mrs Asher!' Ned Seabury sprang to his feet, and even without her eyeglasses Lydia could see he was taken aback. Apparently it had never occurred to him that his fellow vampire seeker might be someone he already knew.

He snatched off his bleached straw boater, but her own white straw hat seemed to leave him in no doubt that she was, in fact, the 'Mrs Curie' whom someone – *it HAS to be one of Teazle's operatives* – had told him was seeking the same traveler that he himself sought. Belatedly he bowed over her hand.

'Before we speak,' said Lydia firmly, 'have you told Millward anything? Anything of your suspicions, of this meeting, or anything you guess or know or think you know?'

'Nothing.' Seabury held her chair for her, then sat with his athlete's grace.

Lydia closed her eyes again. *Thank you . . .*

'Please don't misunderstand him,' begged the young man. 'No man walks this earth stronger or more steadfast in his opposition to the nameless and ancient evils that hunt the night. But he sees the duty that a man owes to the whole of humankind, and pursues it as he sees it—'

'Without thinking who might be hurt.'

'That's not . . .' He paused and shook his head in vigorous denial.

'It is just that he thinks of the many before the few. As I should.' Shame momentarily shadowed his face. 'Were I stronger . . .'

'Then I need to ask you –' Lydia cut off his self-recriminations – 'on your honor as a gentleman, I need to beg you – to swear to me by all that you hold sacred, that today's meeting is to go no farther. Not to Dr Millward, not to Lord Colwich, not to Jamie – Professor Asher,' she corrected herself self-consciously, 'when he returns . . . to no one.' She was fairly certain that Jamie was, in fact, sitting quietly within earshot of the entire conversation, having returned to the café in his usual unobtrusive fashion.

But everything – her own survival, Miranda's, Jamie's as well – depended on remaining, in Damien Zahorec's eyes, simply a friend of Cece's, and not the wife of a folklorist familiar with vampire lore.

And there was no guessing, in the small circle of London society, who would talk to whom.

'Of course.'

A waiter brought tea, biscuits, and cucumber sandwiches.

'I gather . . .' Seabury hesitated, as if unsure how to broach the topic of the Undead. 'I gather your reason for seeking the man calling himself Ludovicus Bertolo is similar to my own?'

'And I gather *you* encountered one of the detectives I hired in the course of your own researches?'

Again he looked discomfited. 'Please don't complain of the man. I used every subterfuge to get the information out of him. I had to learn whatever there is to know of this . . . this creature. This *thing* masquerading as a man. It was clear to me that you – that *someone* – was able to pay for information that I'm forced to gather laboriously by myself, and time may be of the essence. Bertolo must be stopped.'

Lydia nodded slowly. 'I've tried to think of a way to separate Miss Armistead from him without rousing his suspicions,' she said. 'But she's . . . she's *entranced*. It's enough to make one believe in magic spells. I don't think she'd listen to reason – God knows what he's told her about himself! And . . .' She hesitated, raised worried eyes to the young man's face. 'And I'm afraid Lord Colwich is . . . is either entranced with Miss Armistead, or with her father's money. At least he gives the appearance of being so. And if we spoke to him . . .'

'It wouldn't do any good.' Anguish twisted his brow. 'Bertolo – Bessenyei, he called himself in Italy – won't give her up. He can't! Not as long as he thinks he can lay hands on it.'

'Lay hands on what?' Lydia regarded him in some surprise.

'On the book.' And when she continued to look blankly at him, he lowered his voice almost to a whisper, as if he feared that at two-thirty in the afternoon vampires would be lurking behind the palm trees in the café of Claridge's Hotel. 'Have you ever heard –' he leaned across the table, his face deadly earnest – 'of *The Book of the Kindred of Darkness*?'

# TWELVE

'**O**h.' Lydia blinked. 'Oh, that. It's a hoax, isn't it?'

It was Seabury's turn to look blank. Then he snapped, 'It's nothing of the kind! *The Liber Gente Tenebrarum*—'

'—was published someplace – Geneva? – sometime in the seventeenth century, Jamie said, to take advantage of this big craze they had then for witchcraft and the occult, as a sort of reaction against the growth of science. We talked about it one night, Jamie and I and his teacher from Prague, Professor Karlebach, on our way to Peking last year.'

The dry breath of the Sinai wastelands came back to her at the mention of Karlebach's name; for a moment she saw again the triangular sails of the dhows on the canal behind the *Royal Charlotte*, the endless lines of camels and donkeys on the footpath.

*Miranda was with us, sleeping in the cabin . . .*

'Jamie read it when he studied with Karlebach back in the eighties. He said it was a sort of hodgepodge of vampire tales, with a lot of formulae and spells thrown in, that vampires supposedly used to let them walk around in daylight, or take on the shape of women's husbands in order to seduce them, that sort of thing.'

'The book is not *that sort of thing*,' Seabury retorted. 'It's no hoax. Vampires exist. They walk among us. Dr Millward has seen them, spoken to them—'

'Oh, so have I,' said Lydia. 'Professor Asher and I have fought them for six years now.'

Not the entire truth, perhaps, but it sounded better than *We're currently working for the Master of London*. She folded her hands and tried to look like someone who was on a first-name basis with Professor Van Helsing.

Seabury gasped. 'Why have you never told Dr Millward this? Professor Asher has never given the slightest sign . . .'

'Why haven't you told Dr Millward that Bertolo – his real name seems to be Damien Zahorec, by the way – is trying to entrap Miss Armistead?' Lydia tilted her head a little. 'You're afraid he'll do something silly that will get Noel killed.'

Seabury looked as if he were about to take exception to the word *silly*, but in the end only closed his mouth, and sighed. In time he said, very quietly, 'I can't risk it. But I see no reason why Professor Asher wouldn't be able to share his knowledge with Dr Millward. Even the awareness that he isn't fighting his battle alone would be, I think, of inestimable help. To know that someone else understands that these creatures exist, is aware of the danger . . . It is a lonely war that he fights, as you must know. His superhuman resolve has isolated him. Scorned and mocked for his beliefs . . .'

Lydia was of the opinion that Osric Millward was probably scorned and mocked for his company manners, and his habit of vilifying academic rivals in public print, as much as for his beliefs about the Undead.

'Professor Asher has a different approach to dealing with vampires,' she said tactfully.

'Has he killed many?' He sounded like a wistful boy speaking of a soldier uncle.

For a moment Lydia saw her husband in the lightless crypts of St Jude in Petersburg, injecting silver nitrate into the veins of those sleeping boys and girls, maiden vampires who had never tasted blood, never taken life. Saw their bodies burst into flame as he dragged them, one by one, up into the pale crystalline twilight of the summer dawn.

Saw him standing beside the bier where Don Simon Ysidro lay sleeping, a stake and a hammer in his hands.

She found she could say nothing.

'I'm sorry—'

She shook her head quickly. 'Tell me about the book,' she said. '*The Book of the Kindred of Darkness*. Why does Zahorec – Bertolo – want it, and what does it have to do with Miss Armistead? I presume her father has a copy.'

*He would.* It sounded like he'd bought every other example of early printed books in Europe.

Ned's brows knit. Other than lines of premature worry scratched deep into the outer corners of his eyes, he was remarkably like the boy of fourteen whom Lydia remembered, passing sandwiches at his parents' country-house party, back in the spring of 1899. That had probably been the last 'season' before his father's bankruptcy and suicide. Lord Colwich, she recalled – fourteen also and very conscious of his title – had always been at his elbow, producing with eager and laborious pride a full Latin quotation – they were studying Livy that term – to back up whatever scholarly tag Ned had tossed into the conversation.

The bigger boy had been a total nuisance, but Ned had displayed a kindness and patience rare in boys that age. Was that why the friendship had lasted, when all Ned's other contemporaries had 'lost touch' with him when he'd been obliged to leave Eton? Why Noel had used his own social eligibility to force ajar the door of the world Ned had lost?

She saw them again, in the bow window of Lady Brightwell's, heads together as if nothing and no one else were there . . .

Yet only days later Noel had passed him unseeing, to flirt with a rich man's daughter.

So what was the truth? In the young man's silence, she read the doubts that he wouldn't frame even to himself.

'Bertolo – Zahorec – wants power,' said Ned slowly. 'That's what the book contains. The secrets that give one vampire power over the others.'

*I want a list of every bolt hole he's got*, Grippen had said to her. *Every lair, every cupboard . . . every cellar . . . and that's all I want of you. You're not to put foot in any of 'em, nor tell man nor woman, livin' nor Undead, where they lie . . .*

'Have you read it?'

He shook his head. 'Not the real one. There's a late forgery of it, published in French, in Paris, in 1824, that's supposedly a trans-lation. I suspect the 1637 Geneva text that it sounds like Professor Karlebach has is inaccurate as well. But the great French occultist, the Comte de Saint-Hilaire, had the 1680 Antwerp printing in his collection, and it was that collection – Saint-Hilaire died last spring – that came on to the market in the summer, when Titus Armistead was in Europe.'

'He spoke of that the other night,' Lydia recalled. 'At tedious length . . .'

Seabury's lips tightened. 'He prides himself on the things he buys,' he agreed grimly. 'They all do – American millionaires, I mean. They ship paintings home by the boatload to prove to the newspapers they're not swine. Rockefeller got such a terrible reputation, between buying Congressmen and hiring thugs to quell the unions, that he's hired an advertising man to polish his "image" with the press. Given the number of strikers Armistead has had his own "detectives" beat up or shoot, he could do with a little of that himself. In any case,' he sighed, 'Armistead was in Paris when the collection came on to the market, and he asked Noel to go with him to take a look at it.'

'He knew Noel, then?

'He was recommended as a man who knew about paintings,' replied Seabury in a flattened voice. 'And Noel is a Viscount. For all that stony grimness Armistead is a fearful tuft-hunter, and he's pleased as punch to see his daughter marry into the nobility. And Noel is very knowledgeable about incunabula. Saint-Hilaire's collection included some very fine fourteenth-century manuscripts, and about a hundred early printed books. Armistead purchased the entire thing.'

'And this was how Noel and Miss Armistead got to know one another?'

Again that constricted silence, and the unspoken memory of Colwich and Cece, gorgeous in gold braid and powdered wigs, flirting outrageously in the electric glare of the Wycliffe House ballroom.

Before Cece slipped away to meet her vampire lover and let him into her father's library . . .

'Sweetheart!'

Lydia turned her head with a start, to see her friend Josetta Beyerly threading her way toward her among the tea tables. An ivory-fair brunette whose figure would have been called voluptuous by anyone with the temerity to treat her as an object of beauty instead of intellect, Josetta had spent a good portion of her thirty-five years teaching French and English to the daughters of wealthy provincials, until a small legacy had permitted her to return to London. At the moment she looked ruffled and rather pink, her straw hat askew and smudges on her sleeves and gloves: the purple-green-and-white ribbon around her shoulder amply attested that she and her fellow suffragists had been demonstrating at Parliament again. But her voice – and her face, when she came near – held only concern.

'Is everything all right?' She caught Lydia's hands, then glanced past her with a warm smile, 'Hullo, Ned! I won't keep my girl but a moment . . .' She lowered her voice, looked down into Lydia's eyes. 'I haven't heard from you, which isn't like you—'

'I'm well.' *My daughter has been kidnapped by vampires and Jamie and I might get ourselves killed trying to find her . . .*

*Smile.*

Josetta's brows tugged together, as if she read the lie. 'There are times,' she said at length, 'that I want to slap your aunts. Jenny Boyer tells me you've been blackmailed into putting that poor little niece of yours through her paces this Season . . .'

'It's not so bad – except for Isobel expecting me to foot the bill for things like new gloves and ballet tickets.'

The older woman stood for another moment, studying her face. Remembering, maybe, everything Lydia had told her over the years about the workings of her family, since the nights they'd huddled together in the dark of that frightful dormitory at Madame Chappedelaine's . . .

'Don't listen to a word they say to you, honey.' Josetta put a gloved hand to Lydia's cheek. 'Whatever you do, you're not going to ruin Emily's life . . . or theirs. We'll be over at the corner table,' she added more briskly, nodding toward the blobs and blots of purple-green-and-white, like bedded-out flowers in the sunlight by the long windows. 'Plotting – we will ask a question in Parliament and we'll *make* them answer . . . And you . . .' She turned to Seabury, and whipped a leaflet from the satchel at her side. 'You come to our demonstration this evening! Steps of Whitehall, seven o'clock, and tell that horrid old professor of yours if he'd ever actually talk *to* a woman instead of just *about* them, maybe he'd learn a few things.'

Seabury grinned, and took the leaflet. 'That horse has been standing in front of that fountain for years, not drinking,' he said.

'Him and every other man in his profession.' Josetta patted him on the shoulder, and strode away in the direction of her friends.

For a moment the young man sat, folding the leaflet, first in one direction, then in another. Lydia was silent, watching his face.

'The odd thing is,' he said, after a little time, 'Noel hadn't a good word to say of either Miss Armistead or her father, when he went with them to view Saint-Hilaire's collection. He found Armistead *père* vulgar and Miss Armistead's romanticism tedious – for all his quest for independence – and those frightful waistcoats he wears – Noel can be a terrible snob.' A smile, reminiscent and forgiving, brushed Seabury's Cupid lips. 'He was simply murderous on the subject of Armistead's pretentions to gentility, and about how Miss Armistead would go on and *on* regarding spectral lights and ghosts and old tales of teleportation and travel through time in a trance state . . . We'd walk down the Boul' Mich and he'd do imitations of them . . .'

'You were in Paris, then?'

'I'd gone to see Noel. I was worried about him – about what friends had written to me. It's true he went through a *phase*, as I think they call it these days, of living on absinthe and opium before he left England . . . trying to live the artist's life. You must – or at least I think you must – know what it's like to be the only child, to be expected to do and be something that you can't possibly do or be without surrendering your soul and your sanity.'

His dark glance questioned, and Lydia looked aside from it, sick with the recollection of her Nanna's discovery of Lydia's old copy of *Anatomie Generale* that she'd hidden under her mattress, with its colored plates and precise descriptions of things eleven-year-old girls weren't supposed to know about or think about or *want* to know or think about.

Her father had been away and Valentina had had her locked in one of the attics for twenty-four hours without food, drink, lights, or a chamber pot, to teach her refinement of thought. For years after that Lydia had dreamed about being the only person in the world who had fingers, and trying to hide them because the people in her dreams kept wanting to cut them off.

It had never occurred to her that boys went through that, too.

That the heir of an earl who wanted to do something besides be an earl would have to fight, as she had fought.

And worse, she supposed, because she at least was intelligent. She knew Noel wasn't, particularly – or even that good a painter.

And after she was thirteen, she had known that Jamie, at least (or Mr Asher, as she'd called him then) would understand.

She said, 'I do know.'

Another small sigh escaped him. 'I suppose I should be glad. Before he became enamored of Miss Armistead, as he is now, he was going the pace fearfully hard. Now he seems . . . more content. And of course though they'd never say so, his parents are sobbing with joy that he's marrying the Silver Eagle Mining Corporation.' He looked down into his untouched and now tepid tea. 'But he isn't the man I knew.'

In the pause that followed, the voices of the women at the next table drifted to Lydia's ears: '. . . climbed on top of the *wardrobe* to get away from him on their wedding-night!'

She hoped James was paying attention to that conversation as well as to her own.

'And where does Bertolo – or Zahorec – come into it?'

'That's just it,' said Seabury. 'When I reached Paris in November, Noel introduced me to him as a new friend: scholar, artist, connoisseur, bon vivant. He'd just arrived in Paris the previous week, had met Noel at the Cabaret du Néant and they'd taken one another to their mutual bosoms as kindred souls. Noel does that.' For a moment the smile returned to tug at the corner of his lips. 'Develops enthusiasms about people. I thought nothing of it. And he is fascinating – Bertolo, or Zahorec, or, as it turned out, Bessenyei . . . Count Bessenyei, he called himself in Florence. I quite liked him . . . until I accidentally learned that he'd been one of Miss Armistead's suitors in Florence. Cece's father had purchased a partial copy of the *Liber Gente* there also, the English John Aubrey translation that is supposed to be based on the lost Paris text of 1510. I gather her father had "Count" Bessenyei's finances investigated by his tame detectives and it was found he was only recently arrived in Italy from the Balkans, and both his bank account and his bona fides were fairly sketchy. Miss Armistead conspired to keep her father ignorant of "the Count's" presence in Paris. I suspect it was he who told Miss Armistead to recommend Noel to her father.'

'That it was he who brought them together, you mean.'

'I don't know!' He raked his fingers angrily through his hair. 'Sometimes it seems to me . . .' He shook his head despairingly.

Lydia was silent.

'I say, *of course* all the landlords in Ireland don't live there,' proclaimed Lady Savenake at the next table, loudly enough to be heard all over the café. 'Who would want to live surrounded by a lot of bog-trotting potato-eaters who sleep with their pigs?'

'Noel changed.' Seabury's voice was suddenly small. 'About a week after they were introduced. He started dreaming about her – reading books about the destinies of kindred souls, and writing to Dr Millward about reincarnation. He asked me, did I think one's . . .' His eyes shifted and he groped for a moment to phrase a thought that dared not speak its name, at least not in the presence of a lady. 'Did I think one's deepest habits and inclinations were only something one had learned in this lifetime, and that they might simply be a sort of garment one was given, like the color of one's eyes? He started smoking opium again, heavily, and drinking absinthe with Miss Armistead in places like the Café l'Enfer and L'Heure Verte. I had already extended my leave twice, but in the end I had to return to London or lose my position.'

His forehead creased with distress, at the thought that he had abandoned his friend for so mundane a cause.

'But it was nothing I could put my finger on. Sometimes he seemed as troubled by these dreams of her as . . . Well, as I admit I was.' He picked up his cup again, set it down. 'Then shortly before I was to leave, it began to seem to me that Miss Armistead was . . . was *wasting*. I know it sounds melodramatic and for a week I tried to tell myself that it was only jealousy: an overheated imagination. For all I've studied with Dr Millward – for all he's revealed to me about the Undead – it wasn't anything I actually expected to *see*. But I realized that Miss Armistead always *did* wear scarves, or collars that covered up her throat. And when I thought about it, I never saw Bertolo during the daytime. He made a great fuss about the bourgeois being slaves to the clock and how the mere thought of rising before five in the evening gave him migraines, but those last few days I was in Paris, I studied him closely. That's more difficult than you might think,' he added ruefully, 'in some ill-lit bistro when everyone has had a few drinks . . .'

'And when you can't be quite certain,' finished Lydia, 'that you're seeing what *is*, or what you only wish were true: that someone you dislike is a demon rather than simply another man.'

Ysidro standing on the prosaic pavement of Queen Street, arms folded, head down. Whispering of sleep to a houseful of people . . .

'Did you come to any conclusions?'

He shook his head. 'The day before I left, I bribed her maid. Hellice, her name is, Hellice Spills.'

Lydia recalled the dusky satin of the girl's thighs against the pinks and golds of Cece Armistead's coverlet, and the general ridiculousness of a young man wearing Lord Mulcaster's green velvet livery coat, a powdered wig, and no trousers.

'She confirmed that Miss Armistead had known Bertolo – Bessenyei – in Florence. That Miss Armistead was still meeting him secretly. She demanded every penny I had above my bare passage money; I had to hide in the baggage compartment on the train up to London. She also said that her mistress has had "spells" of weakness and pallor, ever since they were in Florence. "It's like the witches are riding her," she said. And she confirmed that she'd seen wounds in Miss Armistead's throat.'

'Did you speak of it to Noel?'

'I sent him a note that evening, saying I had to see him. Later he told me he'd gone with the Armisteads to St Cloud. I had to leave – I didn't even have money for a room for the night by that time – and when he returned to England the first thing I heard was that he was engaged to Miss Armistead, and was moving into Dallaby House. While I was crossing the Channel I'd recalled Noel telling me about Armistead buying a partial copy of the *Liber Gente Tenebrarum* in Florence. Until then, it didn't make any sense: why a vampire would choose a victim who's being watched over by a doting father and five or six gun-toting detectives, rather than some poor flower girl whom no one will miss. When I got back to England I got a catalog of Saint-Hilaire's collection from Dr Millward. And there it was: another copy of the book. It's what he's trying to find. What he's trying to get his hands on.'

'More than that,' said Lydia quietly. 'He's trying to separate Cece from her father, and keep her in England. Vampires have an incredible power over the minds of the living. They can influence them, convince them to go against their own best interests—'

'Dr Millward has told me that, yes.'

'The old ones – the strong ones – can manipulate peoples' dreams. Use them to make you think you've fallen in love, or that events – someone you meet, something you see – have some kind of mystic significance. It's how they hunt.'

*As Simon does?*

*DOES Simon do that?*

*And if he's doing it to ME, how would I tell?*

'You know this?' Anguish burned in Seabury's eyes.

'I know it.' She steadied her voice with an effort. 'Heaven only knows what kinds of visions he's sending Noel about Cece, or what Cece dreams about Noel at night. But you can see why speaking to either of them would be perilous.'

'I realized that when I saw them come down the gangplank of the *Imperatrice* together. Bertolo came over only a few days after they did, with a "valet", a Frenchman named Fournier. Fournier died very soon after that, committed suicide, the police say . . .'

Lydia shivered again.

'Bertolo only had one trunk with him,' Seabury went on. 'I'm guessing he has to have shipped several ahead of him, of his native earth, to lie in . . .'

'Oh, they don't do that. That's just an old wives' tale.'

The young occultist again looked shocked and a little miffed.

'I would guess he's purchased others since he's been here. The problem is finding a safe place to put them, a place that's absolutely secure, where there is no chance of daylight reaching him, or of anyone finding the trunk, opening it untimely.'

'But how do we find such a place?' he cried in despair. 'What can we do?'

'Well,' said Lydia, 'I'm working on that. Until such time . . . Oh, *bother!*' The slim, tall figures making their way towards the table could be no one but Aunts Lavinnia and Harriet: Lavinnia's favorite dragonfly-brown silk was unmistakable. 'I will *not* be quizzed about why I obliged Lavinnia to chaperone Emily to Lady Stafford's reception last night . . .'

She got to her feet, caught up her reticule. 'Can you arrange for me to meet Miss Spills?' she asked quickly. 'Tell her I'll make it worth her while.' She slipped a half-sovereign from her bag, laid it on the table. 'And if you value your life – if you value Noel's life, or mine, or my husband's – don't tell Dr Millward *anything*: not of this meeting, not of anything we've said, nothing. Get yourself three silver chains.' She pushed up her lace cuff, to show him the thick links where they crossed the veins of her wrist.

'So long as the vampires of London thought Millward didn't

know what he was talking about, you were safe. That might not be the case any more. So mind your back, when the sun goes down.'

# THIRTEEN

'**A**re you sure that this *Book of the Kindred of Darkness* is a hoax?' inquired Lydia, when James fell into step beside her as she turned the corner into Moulton Lane. 'Ned Seabury seems to be taking it very seriously.'

'Ned Seabury takes Osric Millward very seriously,' Jamie pointed out. He frowned, long, curling eyebrows incongruous behind the horn-rimmed spectacles. 'Karlebach always spoke of it as a hoax . . . and just because Grippen is himself a vampire, doesn't mean that he isn't being hoaxed as well.'

'It certainly sounds like he's seeking something in Zahorec's lairs. Something he doesn't want me – or his own fledglings – to find.'

Beside them, traffic streamed west toward Holborn and the City: blue, green, yellow buses of different lines, hackney cabs darting and clattering between luggage vans, motor cars, costers' carts. Along the side of the street an Italian with a monkey cranked 'Un di, felice, eterea' out of a barrel organ.

London at three in the afternoon.

'As I remember,' said Jamie thoughtfully, 'the book contained most of the old folk myths about vampires that one finds all over Central Europe: the holes in their coffins, that eating soil from their graves will banish them, that wolfsbane or garlic or Christmas rose will keep them at bay.'

'The wolfsbane and garlic part is true.'

'Yes, but much of it simply isn't. As far as I know they do cast reflections in mirrors, and they can't turn themselves into bats or wolves or mist. They seem to vanish only because they trick your mind into not seeing them leave. It's been years since I read it, but even at the time that I did, some of the formulae it contained – how some vampires will walk in daylight after coating themselves with

a mixture of honey and gold dust, or how they'll drink pearls pulver-
ized in the blood of a priest to render themselves immune to the
effects of silver – sounded ridiculous, or at least impossible to test
without putting the vampire into mortal danger.'

'Wouldn't that be exactly what someone would want to lure
vampires into believing?'

'You mean that it's a hoax on vampires?' He paused on the
sidewalk in front of a stationery shop. 'Surely they'd know it.'

'I suppose.' Lydia sighed. 'Did Dr Karlebach correspond at all
with Millward on the subject, do you know? He never mentioned
him while we were traveling together.'

'That's probably because in his most recent article, Millward
referred to Karlebach as "a racial degenerate".'

'Oh!'

'On the other hand,' Jamie went on, as they approached the
jostle and clamor of Oxford Street, 'people are still paying fortunes
for relics of the Lost Ten Tribes of Israel that were dug up in
Michigan. And now that I think back on it, the author – who is
given as Iohanot Vallisoletum – described fairly accurately the
structure of vampire nests. He spoke of them existing in cities –
Paris, London, Bruges, Toledo – which I found interesting because
the Greek and Balkan tales of vampires all take place in villages
or the countryside. And as I recall, John of Valladolid – whoever
he was – attests that the vampire state is spread by *corruption of
the blood*, not merely the fact of being bitten by a vampire. So it
does sound as if he had some experience with vampires.'

A little diffidently, Lydia asked, 'Might Don Simon know about
it, do you think?'

'I would lay money that he does. He's often said he's made a
study of the vampire state; he can't not have heard of it. But whether
he'll tell you the truth about it is another matter.'

He spoke matter-of-factly, but Lydia could feel in his careful
glance his awareness that – much as she loved him – she loved Don
Simon as well. She'd told Jamie about the Tiffany mermaid and
understood that while the trinket in itself was nothing – Don Simon
was an extremely wealthy man – a pale shadow fell between them
at the mention of the vampire's name.

And she knew quite well that despite the fact that were it not for
Don Simon, neither she nor Jamie nor Miranda would be alive, the

Spanish vampire's word could not be trusted. Not on all matters. Almost certainly not on matters concerning himself or other vampires.

'It does seem,' she went on after a moment, 'that Zahorec might be on the trail of the book. If he's has been living like Count Dracula in some crumbling castle in the mountains killing peasants, he probably doesn't have a stockbroker and couldn't come up with the cash to simply buy the thing when Saint-Hilaire's collection went on sale. He seems to have latched on to Cece in Florence, which is where Mr Armistead bought another copy of it, as well as a First Folio of Shakespeare . . . of which he already had three, from what he told me Saturday night. Surely one would do.'

'Not if you're an American millionaire,' returned Jamie, amused. 'For one thing, most extant copies of the First Folio are incomplete, so if you want to know everything that's in it, you need to see more than one. At ten or twelve thousand pounds apiece that can get to be an expensive hobby.'

'Ow!'

'Even if one paid a tithe of that for a good copy of the *Liber Gente* . . .'

'One can still see why Zahorec would go after Cece.' They stepped around a pair of men washing the windows of Allenby's Fine Soaps. 'Though most of the older vampires seem to be phenomenally wealthy, he doesn't seem to be. If he fled from the fighting, he may have had to leave most of his assets behind. I wonder if he told that poor "valet" he hired who and what he was?'

'He'd have needed some kind of contact with the daylight world when first he left the Balkans,' said Jamie. 'I wonder where he did come from. Useless to try to find out now, with Bulgarian troops all over the mountains . . .'

They emerged on to the crowd and hustle of Oxford Street, and he raised his stick to signal a cab.

'I'm going to send you to Regent Street,' he went on, 'to purchase a new hat in the arcade. When you've done that, can you convince the shopkeeper to let you leave her premises by the back door? Take another cab back to your hotel. We're being followed and I want to see which one of us he goes after when we split up.'

Lydia said, 'Bother,' and didn't look around. Completely aside from the fact that she didn't have her spectacles on, she was fairly

sure she wouldn't be able to glimpse a reasonably competent professional even if she could see. 'Why would anyone be following you?
You've only just got back to England.'

'I'm wondering that myself. Too much to hope he hasn't got a
good look at you . . .'

A cab detached itself from the rank across from the Post Office,
its driver seemingly oblivious to the safety of pedestrians and the
ire of motor cars alike.

'Will you be meeting Ysidro this evening?' His voice was
suddenly neutral again. 'Or this tame clerk of his from Barclays?
Then I'd feel a great deal safer if from the hotel you'd go straight
back up to Oxford for the night.'

'What are you going to do?' She caught his hand as he helped
her into the unsteady vehicle, resentfully aware that for Jamie's
follower to remain unsuspecting, she couldn't argue or linger . . .
and that Jamie knew this.

'Exactly what Grippen expects me to do. Act like an outraged
husband. We're certainly never going to be able to convince him
I'm not in town.' He pressed his lips to her hand, and turned to
give the driver the address. 'Our friend seems to be about medium
height, dark hair, heavy build, brown tweed jacket, three-and-ninepenny bowler hat – a description which fits about a quarter of the
population of London. He may in fact be working for Grippen. I'll
come up to you in the morning if it's safe. Watch out for
yourself.'

He stepped back. Lydia was aware they were being observed,
aware that she should simply sit back in the cab and let it bear her
away . . .

But she was aware also that if Jamie was going to look for
Grippen, there was at least a chance that he wouldn't come back.
She leaned out – causing the driver to jerk his horse to a stop again
with an oath – and caught her husband's hand. 'Jamie—'

He turned back, that careful calmness already in his face and
demeanor: armor that had protected him long before he'd put it to
use as a spy. *No wonder he and Simon get on so well . . .*

For a moment they regarded one another in silence, as if that
pale shadow were not in both of their minds.

'Jamie, don't let's let this – the vampires, and dreams, and mistrust
– come between us. Don't let it pull us apart.'

Even sheathed in a very proper gray kid glove his hand had a warm strength to it, firm and adept.

'Don Simon . . .'

He cupped her cheek with his other hand. 'My only fear is that you'll be hurt, best beloved,' he said, and a ghost of a smile touched his eyes. 'I know you're not going to run off with him.'

Her single quick laugh came out like a sob, at the thought . . . Absurd? Tragic?

Nothing so simple as that.

He'd been a man grown when first she'd met him, a college lecturer and – she had rapidly come to suspect – a spy on Her Majesty's service, and she herself a schoolgirl, living her own double life like a spy in enemy country. It was he who had shown her the path that led to her dream of education and training in a field of knowledge which had fascinated her for as long as she could remember. She recalled how scandalized she'd been with herself, when first she'd thought of him as *Jamie* instead of as *Professor Asher*. When first she'd wondered what his lips would taste like on her own.

Trust and love had come first, a woman's passion only later, with womanhood. With Simon it was different.

She whispered, 'I'm glad you understand. Because I don't.'

He leaned across the wheel and kissed her, his lips and mustache tasting of spirit gum and Claridge's Hotel coffee. 'The only thing that will pull us apart is death,' he said.

As the cab darted away into the maelstrom of Trafalgar Square she leaned out to look back, but Jamie had disappeared already in the crowd.

He was good at that.

It took Asher only moments to ascertain that Bowler Hat was in fact following himself rather than Lydia. The man pursued him when he took a cab to Porton's Hotel in Bayswater, where he registered under his old work name of John Grant. There was a tea shop across the street: just as well to know where to find his pursuer, instead of wondering. He was in morning costume, correct for tea at Claridge's but less so for slipping out the back way and walking over to Prince's Square to take a cab again (one couldn't very well ride a bus in a top-hat and swallowtail coat) back to the Temperance

Hotel. He changed cabs twice without seeing any sign of pursuit, and in the last one removed the spectacles and false beard. Lydia had introduced him last night to the desk clerk as her husband and it wouldn't do to arouse the man's suspicions by a discrepancy of appearance.

Owing to these precautions, by the time he reached the place she had already been and gone. She had left for him the list of properties that Lionel Grippen had owned six years previously, when first their paths had crossed, which he'd studied that morning while Lydia dressed – at her usual fascinating length – to go to Claridge's. These lay mostly in the oldest portions of London, the City or the East End: *We feed on the poor.*

There was a note from her also: *Returning meet Rolleston 1. Tea at the Metropole 3?*

He wired her confirmation at the Oxford house, then resumed his false whiskers and a different pair of spectacles, changed into the rough tweeds and soft cap of a working man, and took the Metropolitan Line to Stepney. The Scythe, on Oak Street, was easy enough to find. It was the largest pub in the district, and at this hour of the afternoon jostled with sailors, soldiers, and stevedores in a musty fug of low voices and cigar smoke. He retired with an Indian pale ale to a corner of the tap room and spent about an hour, speaking to no one but taking note of the faces as they came and went.

It was the time when the neighborhood regulars would begin coming in, to get pails or bottles of ale for dinner or to have a pint before going to whatever grimy rooms were occupied by their families. Asher sat close enough to the bar to hear one of the men greet the woman behind it as Miss Violet, and ask after her ball-and-chain: Miss Violet laughed and retorted, 'Lord, I feel like as if I'd rented 'im out . . . and for a good price, too!'

When Henry Scrooby, Proprietor (as it said in chipped gilt letters on the front door's glass) arrived the resemblance was visible between himself and Miss Violet: crisp brown curls, sharp brown eyes, trim small stature though it was the brother that was the slighter of build. He was handsomer as well; Miss Violet had a nose and chin that could have been copied from the sculpted bust of one of the homelier Roman emperors. Asher moved deeper into the shadows, and took note of the fact that four men came in to give the publican money – with the matter-of-fact air of men repaying a loan – and two appeared to be borrowing it.

A man at the center of the neighborhood economy, then, like many pub-keepers. *Like the centurion in the Bible, he saith unto one Go, and he goeth; unto another Come, and he cometh . . .* Asher had seen the man's counterpart in shabby working-class neighborhoods from Peking to Lisbon. At least he didn't glimpse Mr Three-and-Ninepenny Bowler among the customers.

With the sun still well in the sky he departed, choosing a moment when Scrooby's back was turned. Pub-keepers on the whole were observant men and he wished to run no risk of being recognized at some inconvenient time. He took the roundabout route going back to Blomfield Street, on the District Line to the Embankment and then changed trains twice more, and walked the final quarter-mile, to make sure he didn't have company. At the hotel he changed clothes again – a corduroy jacket as rough as the one he'd just put off, trousers just as pilled and seedy, and boots as shabby – removed the beard and spectacles, and with darkness settling over London, set forth for the East End.

It was time to talk to Grippen.

In addition to his new raiment, he wound extra chains of silver around his throat and wrists, and wrapped three or four more around his left hand, so that a slap from it would burn a vampire's face like a blow from a blazing torch. Up his right coat sleeve he slipped a foot of iron rod with a knob at one end and a ring at the other, in case he met someone a little more mortal.

Grippen, he guessed, would be expecting a furious husband to storm to Lydia's defense. But what the Master of London's new set of fledglings would do if they guessed his involvement with those who understood vampires was another matter. As was what they thought they could get away with when his back was turned.

So he made his way to the ancient riverside parishes, to Priest Alley and Belly Court, to Fox and Goose Yard and Love Lane. What had been an old inn not far from the Tower, undestroyed by the Fire and built on foundations more ancient still, crammed these days with well over a hundred Romanian Jews . . . *Does he still collect the rent from this place, though he sleeps here no more?* In the narrow yard the women were still at work pasting together paper boxes for a penny the dozen by the light of burning grease as the men came home from searching for jobs in the sweatshops.

Were Francis Houghton and Nicholas Barger – both of Rood Lane – fledglings he'd made since the murder of half the nest in 1907? Or were they simply Lionel Grippen under another name?

He moved eastward, past the Tower, to brick mazes and old warehouses, cheap boarding houses packed with sailors, immigrants, whores. In a nameless court he passed what looked like a tumbledown church, transformed into a boarding house for Lascar sailors, chewing betel and watching the white man with speculative eyes. The philologist in him picked out accents and voices: the slithery glottal stops of Bow Bells Cockney and the dropped 'r's and broad 'a's of Bromley and Deptford . . . *What's a Yorkshireman doing selling oysters hereabouts?*

Grippen would be watching for him.

Asher hoped he was right in his guess that the Master vampire would rather use than kill him. That he wouldn't shatter Lydia's usefulness by murdering her husband in the middle of the mission he'd commanded her to fulfill.

*IS he searching for the Liber Gente Tenebrarum?*

*Is it, therefore, genuine?*

A girl of fourteen, cocky in a new pink hat ablaze with silk roses, slipped her hand into his. 'All at a loose end, guv? I can tell you a story that'll 'ave you weepin' wi' joy for a shillin'.'

'Just spent me last on a woman that 'ad me weepin' wi' sorrow at the sad tale she told.' He very quickly withdrew his hand from the moist little grip: though he had nothing in any pocket that could be easily accessed, he'd learned a long time ago that one thing you didn't want to do in these streets was let either of your hands be trapped.

Her pert smile disappeared and she used a word sailors would have hesitated to pronounce, and disappeared like flotsam into the crowd around a pub door. Asher walked on.

Fog had risen, stinking of the river. Down lightless turnings he glimpsed the flaring illumination of the docks, where colliers, barges, merchantmen were unloading. The Fleet River flowed somewhere hereabouts, deep beneath the ground in its channel of brick. One could still get to Roman catacombs through the old sewer channels that had once served St George's Wapping.

Were they keeping Miranda in such a place?

Terror of such a thing ground through him, distracting his thought. *I will kill them . . .*

Present and clear as if she were cradled in his arms he felt the extraordinary silkiness of her baby hair – orange-red as poppies – against his lips, smelled the sweetness of her skin, when he'd kissed her before leaving for Venice. He'd loved Lydia almost from the moment he met her, his deep affection for the child merging into love as he'd seen her grow from girl to womanhood, but the love he bore his daughter had been instant and total, a sort of soul-deep daffiness that defied description or challenge.

He could not put her image from his mind. Sleeping . . . gravely searching his study for her alphabet-blocks . . . snatching at milkweed pods with tiny hands in the garden . . .

*If I don't get her back . . . if I can't get her back . . .*

Years of work for the Department had taught him precisely how many things could go wrong with the most foolproof of arrangements. . . .

At the last minute he realized he was surrounded – *Jesus, I didn't even hear them!* – as shadows materialized from between the buildings of the narrow court into which he'd somehow wandered in his abstraction, as hands grabbed him from both sides by the arms. He tried to wrench free but was slammed like a rag-doll into the brick of the wall behind him, and in the near-pitch darkness, discerned the shape of a man who stepped in front of him, and the steely glitter of a drawn knife.

'Help me . . .'

Damien Zahorec's voice, barely more than a whisper among the murmur of the leaves around her.

'Lydia, help me . . .'

Yew leaves. Lydia identified them, with the clarity of eyesight that she invariably enjoyed in dreams.

The garden maze at Wycliffe House. High over her head, she could see the ragged line of the bushes against a sky black and clear and bannered with stars, a sky such as she had never seen in London in her life. No glare of street-lights reflected on river fog and smoke. It was like the sky at sea, jeweled infinity down to the horizon.

'I need you . . .' There was desperate weariness in his voice, the weariness of the prisoner she'd seen in his cell.

She followed the maze's turnings, the way she remembered from childhood. *He'll be in the belvedere at the center.* Smelled recent rain on the leaves, and from the damp gravel underfoot. In the weeds of the lawn at the maze's center her stiff satin skirts whispered on curled brown leaves. Damien Zahorec rose from the broken plinth of the miniature temple, and the linen of his shirt hung open to show his jailer's bite-marks on his throat. Infinite loneliness seemed to surround him and yet in a small corner at the bottom of her heart, Lydia was aware that this was artificial, like the radiant blondness of her stepmother's hair.

A very good job . . . but a job, nonetheless.

'Why did you run from me?'

'You sounded like you had other fish to fry.' She threw a wistful note into her voice. 'This is a dream, isn't it?'

His face gentle and a little sad, he held out his hand to her. She put hers behind her back, remained where she stood.

'Don't be like the others,' he pleaded. 'They look at me and see one who is beyond salvation, beyond hope. Or they want to use me. To use these gifts that I have, these abilities that I swear every waking moment that I will not use . . .' He spread his hands, begging.

'I don't understand.'

There was a thing that vampires did. Lydia had experienced it before: a crushing sleepiness, a period of blank unawareness that wasn't exactly sleep, as if the mind uncoupled itself from her awareness . . .

And then she was in the circle of pillars, and in his arms. His grip was gentle, careful, yet crushingly strong, his lips on hers soft and cool as rose petals. (*How does he keep his fangs out of the way during a kiss? Or do I just not notice?*) Her whole body responded, with a cresting frantic awareness of the shape and strength of his back under her hands, a thousand times more powerful than the passion she felt in Jamie's arms. She let him tilt her head back, kiss her throat and her breast. The nip of his teeth was feather-light on the skin, not drawing blood – a testing, to see how she'd take it.

Her desperate body ached for more. (*He's influencing glandular reactions on the nerves in some fashion . . .*) His body pressed hers against the wall. (*What wall? We're in a circle of pillars . . .*) His breath hot against her neck. (*Vampires don't breathe . . .*) His hands doing things to her, calling responses from her that she'd never dreamed possible. She was aware of her heart racing. (*A hundred and twelve beats per minute*? She wondered if she had a watch in this dream to time it.) Her knees trembling and growing weak. (*At a hundred and twelve beats per minute that's no surprise . . .*) Aware of the tangy salt smell of his flesh, and the scent of the pines beyond the window. (*Window?*)

She opened her eyes and saw they were in his prison cell.

'She's coming,' he whispered. 'She'll take me, change me. Force me under the shadow of damnation . . . Make me her slave. Lydia, I'm begging you. Help me.'

Though she knew transition to the vampire state to be voluntary – although the alternative was death – she gasped, as she was fairly certain Cecelia Armistead had gasped before her, 'What can I do?'

With a convulsive sob he thrust her from him, and she saw that they were definitely in his cell. He pushed her behind him, away from the door as it opened, and the dark woman stood framed there, the dark woman who'd smiled to him when as a living man she'd encountered him at that candlelit gathering. She saw Lydia (*how much of this is a dream?*) and her face twisted. 'Who is this?' She reached toward Lydia with a hand tipped by long vampire claws, and Damien caught her wrists.

'She is no one . . .'

She flung him aside with the terrible strength of the vampire, and as Lydia backed away (*oh, God, what if this isn't a dream?*) Damien sprang up, seized the woman's arms. 'Ippolyta, don't . . .'

The woman Ippolyta turned upon him, seized his arm with a grip that drove her nails into his flesh. She dragged him to her by the hair at the back of his head and thrust him to his knees, kneeling over him while she released her grip for the second it took to rip his throat with her claws.

His eyes met Lydia's in that last mortal second and he gasped, 'Run!' and Lydia fell back another step as the vampire woman fastened her lips on the spouting wound. Her black hair fell from its twisted braids, half covering his face; the black silk of her garments billowed around them like a cloud, the jewels in it flashing like half-concealed lightning. Lydia saw his hand grip the woman's arm, frantically trying to thrust her away, then clinging as if he felt himself swing suspended over the blackness of a deeper abyss.

'Lydia, run . . . and wait for me. I will come . . .'

She woke trembling, her whole body reverberant with the memory of his lips, his hands, his strength . . . his blood black-red in moonlight . . .

*What a farrago of nonsense!*

The dry pungency of garlic filled the darkness. Beyond the windows of her bedroom she heard the dim chiming of the Great Tom bell in Christ Church College's gatehouse. Heard birds begin to sing.

*If he thought I'd fall for that I think I've just been insulted.*

But the taste of his lips lingered in her memory as the first stains of day infused the sky.


# FOURTEEN


'You Asher?'

The hands that crushed the silver links under his shirt-cuffs into his flesh were warm. The bodies pressed against his on both sides stank of the living, not the dead. Someone dug at his throat with fingers like tanned leather and pulled his collar away, grabbed the handful of silver chains.

'Looks like,' grunted a voice accompanied by a wash of beer and dental caries.

Other hands tore open his cuffs, stripped the silver from his wrists and his left hand.

'Oi'll take them,' said the man in front of him, a deadly quiet voice with a south Irish *dh* to his speech. 'Grippen said he'd be wantin' 'em.' He held out his hand and Asher heard the protective metal jingle as it went into the man's palm and pocket. 'And that one you kept out, Jem,' added the Irishman, and the man holding Asher's arm cursed unimaginatively and handed it over.

'It's real silver.'

'And Grippen's real easy to fool, ain't he, then?'

The would-be thief didn't even attempt a rebuttal.

'Let's be havin' no monkey tricks then, Professor.' The Irishman yanked Asher's neckerchief free of his collar, used it to bind his eyes.

'I wouldn't dream of it.'

In the clammy darkness somewhere nearby, he smelled the whiff of blood.

The stink of sewage and coal smoke and the river; the occasional brush of wet bricks against his shoulder or sleeve. Voices yammering. A woman screamed *Spendthrift!* and *Godless drunkard!* in Romanian and a man yelled that he owed nothing to a shrewish whore. Neighbors shouted at them both to shut up. Someone played a barrel organ, a shrill rickety approximation of '*Il balen del suo sorriso . . .*'

Ships hooted on the river, not more than a few streets away. *The old inn near the Tower . . .*

Steps underfoot, deeply worn in the centers, slick with moisture and stinking of vomit and piss. A door creaked and he smelled the musty reek of filthy bedding on top of the other myriad stinks of poverty, overcrowding, degradation. An uneven floor beneath the crunchy sponginess of soiled straw.

The men holding his arms fell silent and Asher smelled blood again, a moment before Grippen's claws scratched his face in pulling the blindfold down.

'Leave him go.' The Master of London's voice was cold slag. 'And get out.'

The feeble gleam of a dark lantern showed Asher brick support piers crumbling to nothing, and between them what might have been two dozen makeshift bunks in a space barely larger than his parlor in Oxford.

The bunks were empty. From the darkness that clotted the farther end of the room a draft breathed the scent of deeper underground, mud and wet rock.

'The Russkys want back in,' said one of the men behind him. ''Fraid we'll steal their blankets – faugh! Ol' 'Atter at the two-to-one wouldn't touch 'em wi' a bargepole—'

'Tell 'em, the man that comes in now, wears his blanket for a shroud ere morning.' Grippen put a hand on Asher's shoulder, hooked dark claws against the skin of his neck. The men murmured and retreated. The screaming argument outside grew louder for a few seconds as the door was opened, and the cold fog flowed down the stair.

Then stillness.

'You've a rare craving to get your veins opened, Professor.'

'I've a rare craving for a word with you.'

The broad nostrils flared. 'And cocky with it.'

'I want you to leave my wife alone,' said Asher. 'And return our daughter. I'll do whatever it is you ask me to do – find this Zahorec and kill him –'

*If it's the book he's seeking, let him think we misunderstand.*

'– and give you a list of where he's been hiding, but give her back to us. You've no need to hold her prisoner, for me to do as you ask.'

'Huh.' The noise was a grunt rather than any attempt at a laugh. 'The minute you have her you'll discover on a sudden that what I ask is what you can't do on any consideration, and I haven't time to prove to you otherwise. You'll get the brat back when I've what I want. She's well.'

'Prove it.'

'And you prove to me I'll live forever and go to Heaven when I die.'

'I think we can both see how promises about *that* worked to make you a good and holy man in life.'

The vampire growled within his throat. Massive in the grubby frock coat of forty years ago, his gaudy vest of Chinese silk stained and spotted with old blood, Grippen reminded Asher of the lions that roved the veldt in his African days: eyes intelligent but without the slightest resemblance to humanity. Still as shadow.

'Fear for our child has stolen Mrs Asher's sleep,' Asher went on. 'You know – none better – that in such a state one makes mistakes.'

At the word *mistakes* Grippen moved his head a little. Mistakes – inattention through weariness or distraction – were the vampire's power, what he lived by, hunted by. He knew indeed how deadly they were.

'You say our child is well. But what about the nursery maid you took to look after her? She's young, and frightened – and probably not frightened enough. She may try to escape, and run afoul of those who have them in keeping. What if your fledglings start one of their damned games with her, what if they lie to you, tell you she escaped or tried to escape . . . What do they do with her, with my daughter, when they go hunting?'

He watched Grippen as he spoke, and though the Master Vampire had some of Don Simon Ysidro's quality of stillness, yet he saw him relax, just slightly, when Asher spoke of the fledglings.

*Lydia was right. She's being watched over by the living.*
*He has that much sense.*

'You leave that to me.'

'I can't.'

'You'll have to.' Fangs glinted with the lift of his lip.

'Will you do this, then?' said Asher, when the silence had gone on long enough for the Master of London to turn over all possibilities in his mind. 'Have the nursery maid write me a note. Tell her that if what she says in it is the truth, she's to mention Lydia's favorite book in it. If she's being forced to lie, she's to mention my favorite book.'

'And the chit'll know these?'

*If she's not so exhausted that she can't think straight . . .*

'She will.'

The vampire growled again. 'There's a reason I want your woman doing the job for me, Professor, and not yourself. You say you fear this girl of yours will try to escape, or try to get the child out of there, through not being afraid enough. *Not afraid enough* is what I see in your eyes. Fathers get stupid, when it comes to their girls. They do stupid things. A mother I can trust, to do as I bid her without thinkin' she knows better than me what I want.'

'I won't have her in this,' repeated Asher stubbornly. 'I can deal with your fledglings. She can't.'

'*I'll* deal with my get.'

'You haven't seen her,' said Asher. 'She can't continue.'

Grippen stood silent, big head a little to one side, barely more than a monster shadow in the dimness. As if he sensed the lie. 'Then I'll say to you as I said to her. You find me this Zahorec's lairs. You don't speak of 'em, not to the livin', not to the dead. When you find a lair, you don't put a foot across its threshold—'

'Why not?'

'You'd learn soon enow why, an' you put foot in one, or e'en left the scent of your breath where Zahorec could smell it. He butchers and doesn't care where he leaves the remains or who knows it. Two he killed last night, at the head of All Hallows Pier, and a woman and her two brats in a house on Priest Alley t'night before. The constables are runnin' about squeakin' with their aprons over their faces and the quicker you find me where he lairs up the better for us all it'll be.'

'Why not get Millward, then?' demanded Asher. 'You could do it without his knowing who he's working for.'

'Millward?' The vampire snarled. 'I'll not have that quim-faced jolterhead poking about below the city, nor his pasty little punks. They've learned enough as it is, about old crypts and old drains and old tunnels that the Underground dug and walled up and forgot. Nay, you do as you're told and not a dram's weight more. And if you play me false in this, Professor—'

'No,' said Asher quietly. 'It's you who's played me false, Grippen. You said to me once that a man whose own ox has not been gored doesn't make a persistent hunter. And you were right in that, to my everlasting shame. In six years I've known you and your kind walked London's streets – fed on London's poor and London's innocent – and multiplied yourself like rats breeding in the darkness. And I kept my silence and held my hand, because of Lydia, and later because of my child. I would not risk their lives – I would not risk my happiness – to go to war with the Undead. Take them from me and I guarantee you I will cause as much damage to you as I can before you kill me . . . and after you kill me, Zahorec will still wait for you in the dark.'

Grippen struck at him. It was like dodging the strike of a cat but Asher at least saw it coming, turned his body and stepped clear of the clawed, heavy hand as it flashed by his face.

The vampire's eyes blazed – clearly he had not expected to be dodged – and the next instant – but there was no 'instant', only the crushing black weight of darkness that closed on Asher's mind like a fist – Grippen struck in earnest. Impossibly, Asher found himself waking – only he could not imagine how he could have slept – as Grippen forced him to his knees, crushed and twisted his right arm in a brutal grasp as he tore the sleeves of jacket and shirt to the elbow. Asher tried to slither free as the vampire's claws ripped the flesh of his arm. He gouged at the dark eyes with his free hand only to have that wrist caught, too, and effortlessly wrenched around behind his back with pain that held him immobile as the vampire drank.

Asher woke up again on the floor, not certain how long he'd been out.

Grippen laughed and wiped blood from his mouth. 'Don't take on, man, I've done you no hurt. You'll not even turn into one of us foul abominations, or whatever the story is. There's more in that than just the blood. Get up.'

The floor swooped and spun. Asher fought to breathe, fumbled at the remains of his neckerchief with shaking hands, to staunch the blood that still ran from the torn vein in his wrist.

Grippen yelled, 'Mulligan!' and the door creaked in the darkness behind Asher.

'Yeah, Dr G?'

'Get Greene to take our friend here home. See he gets there safe, mind. Where be you sleeping, Professor?'

He suspected he wouldn't make it as far as the Tower without being assaulted by other denizens of the neighborhood. In any case he could change hotels when the sun was up. 'Porton's. Moscow Road.' He jerked the knot of his makeshift bandage tight with his teeth. 'Bayswater.'

Someone yelled, 'Tommy!' into the fog-muffled darkness of the court.

Head swimming, Asher nodded towards the men, asked softly, 'Do they know who you are?'

'Would they care?' Grippen chuckled. 'All they know is I'm the man what buys up their debts and gets the Jews off their backs. Or a few on 'em, I'm the man gets 'em what they need, every now and again. The art of holding a slave is seeing which men go about with chains on 'em already, Professor. I just pick up the trailin' end.'

*And then I'll be free?* Ysidro's tame bank clerk had whispered to Lydia, with tears in his eyes. *And then I'll be free?*

Mulligan and another of the men took him under the arms and led him to the door. Asher recognized the place from earlier in the night. The square spire and pepperpot towers of St George in the East were just visible above the sagging roof lines. Ragged laundry draped the old inn's galleries, and behind the few windows that hadn't been bricked up to avoid the window tax of a century ago, only the dimmest of grimy yellow light bleared. Children played in the gutters, though it was past midnight. The couple who'd been screaming at one another were still doing so.

From the slippery stair of what looked to be the ruin of an old chapel, Asher glanced back over his shoulder down into the crypt. Grippen was gone, but it seemed to him that his eyes still gleamed in the shadow.

As they shoved him into the evil-smelling cab that waited at the end of Sun Alley for him, the Irishman said, 'You're lucky, mate.'

Asher just had time, by the sickly glimmer of the cab's lamps, to observe the cab's number, before Mulligan yelled Asher's destination to the driver – Greene, Asher remembered his name was – and the vehicle lurched into motion.

A four-wheeler, with the front wheels slightly narrower than the rear.

Not that it mattered any longer.

He closed his eyes.

As interviews went, it hadn't been as bad as he'd feared it might. He pulled his torn sleeve over his bandaged arm, shivered in the night's clammy chill. He'd learned some useful things.

Most importantly, he'd drawn the master vampire's attention from Lydia to himself. With luck, that was a situation which would last long enough for her to track down where Miranda really was.

# FIFTEEN

Even without spectacles, Lydia gasped '*Jamie!*' when he came near her table at the Metropole's café the following afternoon.

'I'm all right.' This was a complete lie and he knew it as he took the chair beside her. Despite thirteen hours of sleep and several pints of cider and broth, even the walk from the cab into the hotel had exhausted him.

She scrambled for the silver case in her reticule, unheard-of behavior in so public and fashionable a venue. Behind the thick rounds of glass her eyes widened in shock as she realized what must have happened to him, and she turned as pale as he had been when he'd looked at himself in the mirror that morning to shave.

'I'm all right,' he repeated, and put his hand over hers. 'Grippen has a ring of human helpers in the East End, led – I think – by the publican Henry Scrooby, and by an Irishman named Mulligan. They're the ones guarding Miranda. I doubt his fledglings even know where. Grippen himself has a lair off Sun Alley in the City, about a quarter mile south-west of St George's. I think Miranda and Nan were taken away in the cab of a man named Greene – number 1349 – not that it matters now . . .'

When she still did not reply, only gazed at him with tears filling her eyes, he added gently, 'This is war. I took a wound. I've come closer to being killed for information less valuable, and for the sake of people whose heads I would trade on silver platters – I'd even buy the platters – for a single doll to give Miranda.'

'Of course.' She wiped her eyes, then glanced guiltily around them, pulled off her eyeglasses, and concealed them again in her handbag, a vanity that Asher found both endearing and exasperating.

'Next time this happens I'll wear a little rouge.'

Her smile flickered into being, ducked out of sight. 'Oh, don't! Nothing looks worse than rouge when one is pale: like paint on a barn! And besides, you'd probably run slap into Uncle Ambrose and your reputation would never recover. I met Mr Rolleston this afternoon.' From her handbag she pulled a slim packet of papers. 'Damien Zahorec opened an account at Barclays in Sofia on the eighteenth of October of last year—'

'The day after Bulgaria, Serbia, and Greece declared war on the Turks.'

'Well, he seems to have been on the run, or else this woman Ippolyta has control of his money. Not only had there been no previous contact with the bank, but his initial deposit was in gold and silver, worth about a hundred and thirty-five pounds. He went on almost immediately to Venice, where he withdrew seven hundred lira. A few days later he deposited five hundred and fifty lira, and three hundred French francs. He withdrew another hundred and fifty lira when he arrived in Florence on the twenty-eighth of October, and deposited six hundred lira there on the second of November, and thirty-one pounds on the tenth.'

'Sounds like he's robbing his victims.' Asher poured coffee for himself in the cup the waiter brought, and noted how heavy the pot seemed. 'Either that or gambling. I wonder what the local masters had to say about that.'

'It would be easy for him to hunt tourists. Trains run from Venice to places like Verona and Padua all the time.' Anger touched her cheekbones with red, for the families whose Uncle Clarence or Tante Eugènie never came back from abroad. 'The odd thing is, I stopped at the University Club on the way here and checked the old newspapers at the library. The cities of Tuscany and the Veneto are smaller than London, but I didn't find anywhere accounts of extensive killings or disappearances at the time that Zahorec was there. My Italian isn't very good, but I do know words like *assassinio* and *saugue.*'

'Full marks for you, Dr Asher.' He kissed her hand. 'I wonder what changed?' He took the papers, studied the cramped, minuscule handwriting.

'I wondered that, too. The Armisteads reached Florence on the twentieth of October, and went on to Paris on November fifteenth. Zahorec followed them almost immediately. He'd met Cece in Florence and been warned off by Mr Armistead. In Paris he wasted no time becoming bosom friends with Lord Colwich, whom he then introduced to Cece. Then on December the thirtieth –' Lydia turned over the page she was reading – 'seven hundred and fifty pounds was paid into Zahorec's account by Lord Colwich—'

Asher's eyebrows shot up.

'—which Zahorec immediately laid out to purchase a property called Thamesmire, three miles downriver from Woolwich.'

'On the railway line,' Asher remarked into the ensuing silence. 'Half an hour from Waterloo station. And well outside of what might be considered Grippen's hunting ground.'

The light strains of the café's pianist floated over the well-bred chatter of the patrons: 'Eine Kleine Nachtmusik.' Asher reflected for a moment upon some of the murkier honey-traps he had witnessed in his service to Department and Queen. Such affairs were always safer if one had both sides of a couple ensnared.

Lydia shuffled the papers. 'There's reference here to repairs Zahorec has ordered on a house which he evidently owns in Keppel Street, though there's no mention of him buying it. There seems to be another in Marlborough Road, which can't be more than a hundred feet away. Colwich put fifty pounds into Zahorec's bank account just before he left for England in January – Zahorec had only a hundred and thirty in it at the time – and since then money has been paid, in the amount of fifty pounds a week – either directly from Colwich's account or in almost-identical amounts in cash – into Zahorec's account.'

Asher said, 'Hmmn.'

'I'm meeting with Hellice Spills – Cece's maid, you know – in

a tea shop in Finsbury Circus at five.' Lydia took a sip of her tea.
'I'm quite prepared to blackmail her, but it really doesn't sound like
it will be necessary. I'm only sorry Don Simon and I didn't look
more thoroughly through the house while we were there Monday
night. We might have found the accountant doing something
disgraceful as well.'

She fell silent, turning Rolleston's close-scribbled page of notes
over in her fingers with the same abstraction with which she arranged
and rearranged silverware. Then she sighed, and produced a folded
note from her handbag. Asher recognized Don Simon Ysidro's spiky
sixteenth-century hand. 'This was waiting for me at the hotel this
morning.'

> *Mistress, I beg forgiveness. I continue to seek one at the Bank*
> *of England willing to serve, yet stone hath not yet yielded to*
> *water. Ever your servant, Ysidro.*

'I hope whoever he finds for me there isn't going to be like Mr
Rolleston,' she went on in constrained voice. 'Though I suppose
any bank clerk willing to violate professional confidentiality to a
total stranger on the strength of something he saw in a dream isn't
likely to be completely sane. This morning, when Mr Rolleston
handed me these notes, he poured out his heart for half an hour
about how I mustn't be afraid of him despite the things he's done.'

Another long silence, her attention seemingly absorbed in turning
her cup in its saucer. Afternoon sunlight lengthened across the gold-
rimmed café china, and at the next table a woman said, 'To be
honest, I didn't know who he was. At Jenny's house-parties, how
*would* you know . . .?'

'Is this the sort of thing you did when you were spying?' Lydia
asked at last. 'Put together lists of people you could use . . . people
who may not have had any idea of who you really were or what
you really wanted?'

'This is precisely what we did.' He laid his hands over hers, met
her eyes, as if steadying her across slippery ground. In her face he
saw the revulsion that he himself had felt, at the deceits which
comprised professional spying. *Seeing which men go about with
chains on 'em already,* Grippen had said. *I just pick up the trailin' end.*
*Ambush a man in an alley? Righty-o, guv!*

*Haul an unconscious girl and a baby away from a house in the middle of the night? Sure thing!*

*Meet a lady in a green dress an' tell her about some stranger's finances? Not my funeral.*

For a moment Asher remembered the velvety green of the African veldt, and the people who'd trusted him, back during the war: people who'd assumed he was a German professor of linguistics, in Africa to study the kaffir dialects. People who'd shared their fears about their husbands and brothers, riding with the commandos . . . to a man who'd promptly reported to Lord Kitchener the location of those husbands and brothers. And who had then exclaimed and sympathized and comforted those farm women, when they'd wept for men killed or men transported away to hard labor in Ceylon . . .

*All in a day's work, mate.*

'You can't always choose your weapons in a war,' he said quietly. 'Particularly not in a war that's fought in darkness and silence. Most of the time you have to pick people who won't ask questions, people who don't look farther than what they get out of it – whether what they get is money or protection or vengeance or the pride they feel in doing "what's right", God help us. I did get Grippen to say he'd provide proof that Miranda and Nan are well. I don't doubt they are, but I want to see how long it takes for the proof to arrive. In the meantime, I . . .'

'Don't.' Lydia laid her fingers to his lips. 'I dreamed about him – about Zahorec – last night again. It was frightful tosh,' she added quickly. 'But it's probably better that you tell me as little about your movements as you can.'

Exhausted as Asher was, he took a cab from the Metropole to Keppel Street, to have a look at the addresses Lydia had given him. The house Damien Zahorec owned there – however acquired – was, like most in the neighborhood, tall, brick, and fairly new by London standards, though like everything else in the city it was dark already with soot. An alleyway from Leader Street brought him around to the rear of the row, and showed him that as he had suspected, that house and the one in Marlborough Road backed on to a common yard, barely larger than the kitchen of his house in Oxford but shielded from view by a tall fence and a ramshackle shed.

Fence and shed – to judge by the cleanliness of the wood – had been erected since January.

And as far as he could judge, both houses lay near the course of the river Westbourne, whose bricked-in channel flowed deep beneath Dallaby House as well.

By this time he was dizzy, but knew that he had to finish his investigation in the same period of daylight. If Zahorec heard his footsteps outside one dwelling, he might just recognize them the following day outside another, and wonder if someone were showing interest in both.

The sensible thing to do would be to go immediately out to Woolwich and have a look at the house called Thamesmire, then return to the hotel and sleep.

Instead he hailed a cab. The instruction 'Dean Street' got him a disgusted look at the quarter-mile fare and a *sotto voce* stream of Cockney imprecations as the driver climbed back on to his high seat. The neighborhood of the Inns of Court was primarily given over to solicitors' offices, but among those Georgian facades was one that bore the signboard: *Artemus Sophister, Books*. A small rack of battered volumes – Russian editions of Tacitus from the previous century with missing pages, von Junzt's *Unaussprechlichen Kulten*, and the autobiography of Aaron Burr – just outside the door seemed to offer proof of this assertion to doubters. Within, the shop was a maze of stacked boxes, piles of volumes, and bookshelves standing in front of other bookshelves with barely space for the proprietor to slither between.

Artemus Sophister himself hadn't changed much since Asher had gone to his lectures at Oxford, tiny and grubby with his unkempt hair trailing down his back and his pale blue eyes blinking from behind massive spectacles, smoking what was probably his fortieth cigarette of the day – every book Asher had ever purchased from him had reeked of tobacco – while he perused a crumbling volume in Arabic. He looked up when Asher entered and his eyes widened with pleasure. 'Asher! Good to see you, man . . . It's been, oh, what, five years?'

'All of that.' Asher clasped the nicotine-stained claws.

'Still at your travels? Heard you'd gone to St Petersburg . . . Find anything interesting?'

Sophister meant, *any interesting books*, so Asher didn't trouble

him with either the beauties of the city or the horrifying inefficien-
cies of the Secret Police, to say nothing of the St Petersburg nest
of vampires. 'I had barely time to look around me.'

'A waste,' sighed the bookseller. 'A sheer waste. A true scholar
never ceases the quest for knowledge. *Sed nil dulcius est, bene quam
munia tenere, edita dictrina sapientum templa serena . . .* When I
went to Paris last summer, I dare say another man might have frit-
tered away his time at such places as the Opera and that other place
– what's it called? – the place with all the paintings. And that time-
waster would have missed – completely missed! – come here and
have a look at what I found there . . .'

He caught Asher's sleeve, hustled him to one of the boxes
beside his overflowing desk, where books resided in an explosion
of straw. *If he drops his cigarette*, Asher reflected, *the whole place
will go up . . .*

'The *Encyclopedia Donkaniara*! All volumes of it . . . And the
1674 Geneva printing of the *Pantofla Decretorum*! Only missing
two signatures . . . Now here – here . . . wait a moment . . . No,
over here . . . Isn't it beautiful?' He hefted the crumbling brown
volume in his hand. '*Bishops' Antidotes for Aphrodisiacs*! Just *sitting*
in a barrow on the Right Bank! *Tempus edax rerum . . .*'

'Tell me,' said Asher, 'about the *Book of the Kindred of Darkness.*'

Behind the spectacles the pale eyes widened. 'Why do you ask?'

'Has someone else asked you for one recently?'

The bookseller emitted a thin giggle, like the call of some
unknown bird. 'You might say so. You don't think this shop is
always this frightful, do you?' He gestured around him.

Asher bit back a self-evident *Yes* (the place didn't look a bit
different than it had five years previously, and was in fact tidier
than Sophister's rooms had been when he'd been a Lecturer at
King's College) and asked instead, 'What happened?'

'It was that American.' He poked at Asher with a twig of a finger.
'No one can tell me differently.'

'Armistead?'

'You know about him, then?'

'I know he bought a copy of the book in Paris. In fact he bought
Saint-Hilaire's whole library—'

'Trash.' The bookseller waved dismissively. 'The most shocking
rubbish. *Tenet insanabile multos scribendi cacoethes et aegro in*

*corde senescit.* Anybody could sell the man anything – I did myself, a frightful mash-up of old signatures stitched together with a forged preface that was supposedly Temesvar's *On the Use of Mirrors in the Game of Chess* . . . I'd be surprised if his copy of *Kindred* was genuine.'

'Did Armistead buy one from you?'

'Armistead attempted to *steal* one from me,' retorted Sophister bitterly. 'The man's a complete thug. *Ingenuas didicisse fideliter artes emollit mores . . .*'

'I should think he's wealthy enough to buy whatever book he wants.'

'It's what *he* thinks also.' With the stump of one cigarette still dangling out of his thin gray moustaches – Sophister's unkempt Prince Albert only increased his resemblance to a senescent goat – the bookseller pulled a tobacco pouch and papers from his shirt pocket, and began to roll another. 'I'd had an order for the book from another client back in November, a Romanian nobleman living in Florence. But the fellow put about a guinea down on it and then never kept up the payments. It's the seventeenth-century Prague printing – the genuine one, not the 1835 forgery, missing the title page and the last signature. I have the forgery also: the so-called introduction by Nostradamus is written in completely modern French, and they didn't get the binding right. *Dixeris egrege notum si callida verbum reddiderit iunctura novum* . . . Where was I?'

'Armistead.'

'Ah, yes. I told Armistead I was honor-bound to inform Count Bessenyei that I had another purchaser for the book – for which I was asking a hundred and seventy-five pounds – and spang, on the money, two nights later the shop was broken into and ransacked.' He caught Asher's arm, led him to the back premises, where a number of very old volumes lay open upon a table and where the glass panes of the lockable bookshelves that ringed the walls had all been broken. 'With special attention paid, you will observe, to the incunabula. They passed up the Arentino, so obviously they were in quest of something specific—'

Asher noticed that his old friend hadn't yet got around to sweeping up the broken glass.

'And you think Armistead was behind it? Did he get the book?'

'Heavens, no! The really valuable stuff I keep elsewhere at night.' The older man puffed on his new cigarette to kindle it at the end of the old. 'But it was obviously a ploy to push me into selling immediately. He offered me three hundred guineas.' Sophister made a long arm for a faded volume at the far end of the table. 'Armistead had already paid some frightful sum in Rome for the Aubrey translation – six hundred and fifty guineas, I think it was, and half the signatures missing.'

He opened the stained calf binding. The title page was indeed missing, but inside the front cover someone had written in faded ink:

*Liber Gente Tenebrarum.*
*Johanot Vallisoletos.*
*Prague – 1687*

'Not bad for something that was supposed to be a hoax to begin with.'

Asher carefully turned a page, studied the graceful 'lettre de somme' type and the corrupt, idiosyncratic Latin. *Know you then that the things called vampire were known and abominated among the Romans, and dwelled in the cities of their empire, even unto Narbo in Gaul, and Lutetia, though farther north they did not go . . .*

'Who was John of Valladolid?'

The bookseller shrugged. 'Supposedly a student in Prague in the latter part of the fourteenth century, who made a bargain with the vampires in that city . . . You're familiar with the conceit of the book? That the Undead live in rookeries, rather like penguins, under the command of a sort of Chief Vampire? Rather ingenious . . . Yes, well, John of Valladolid was a Spanish student who claimed to have been a servant of the Chief Vampire – someone has to deal with the tradesmen during the daylight hours, I should imagine. You're the folklorist, Asher. You'd know better than I.'

'The edition I read – the Geneva text of 1637 – contained nothing about the author. My old teacher Karlebach in Prague had it, as well as the nineteenth-century forgery. They were substantially different—'

'Oh, heavens, yes! The book is notorious. Nearly every edition differs wildly from every other, and some vampire expert or other – was it old Millward over in Bayswater? Frightful bore on the subject . . . *Difficilis, querulus, laudator temporis acti se puero . . .*

Stingy, too. Anyway, he told me that most of the so-called "formulae" in it go clean against every vampire legend in folklore.'

'The ones in the Geneva text certainly do,' Asher agreed thoughtfully. 'And the Latin was seventeenth century, nothing like what they used in the Middle Ages. It screamed *fraud*. I'd heard there was an older text—'

'Several!'

'—but I'd never seen it.'

He turned another page and blinked, almost shocked. Had this paragraph been in either of Karlebach's books?

*The Master of London is Rhys, that was minstrel to the Dukes of Burgundy before the Plague that devastated the whole of the world. He was made vampire by the lady Chretienne de la Tour Mirabeau, who also came out of the Realm of Burgundy in the reign of Edward Longshanks, the first of her kind to dwell in London . . .*

He couldn't recall.

He scanned the corrupt Latin, thickly mingled with sixteenth-century vernacular Czech.

*The hold of the Master Vampire over those whom he has begotten is absolute, and cannot be comprehended by those who have not had experience of its strength. For to such of the living as will drink of a vampire's blood, when they die, the Master Vampire will take their souls into his mouth, and there hold them until his victim dies. With death the body changes into the flesh of a vampire, and into this new-changed flesh the Master will breathe the soul again. Yet a part of his victim's soul he keeps . . .*

The formula for breaking the hold of the Master upon the fledgling, Asher noted, didn't look like what he remembered from the Geneva text . . . and in any case he doubted whether that concoction of herbs and mercury would do anything but make whoever took it thoroughly sick. And as for the instructions for making a tincture of silver, yew leaves, and the urine of a black dog, which would permit a vampire to step out into sunlight unharmed . . .

'From what I recall of the prologue to the 1702 Antwerp text,' Sophister went on after a time, 'Johanot – or John – of Valladolid returned to Spain from Prague around the year 1370, and became a canon of the cathedral in his home city. He perished of the plague before his thirtieth year. But the text of the prologue is very corrupt.' He shook his head disapprovingly, 'And in a Latin completely different from the main text – absolutely peppered with nominative absolutes. The earliest edition – the one printed in Burgos in 1490 – describes him as an Arab, and the Spanish printing done in Toledo four years later has nothing to say about him at all. So you pays your money, as they say at the fairgrounds, and you takes your choice.'

'And have you heard further –' Asher gently turned more pages – 'from this Count Bessenyei in Florence?'

'Nary a word, but it's early days yet. *Fugaces labuntur anni . . .* I only sent the letter off last week. Mind you, I've dunned the man twice for payments . . .'

*As Death's shadow changes all things, so the vampire is no longer man or woman. Blood he seeks, and without the kill he loses that facility which he has, to cast a glamour on human sight and human dreams. Yet even when he has fasted only a short while, still he hungers for the kill with the lust of starvation. No other thing is to him so important as this: not the love of family nor honor, neither learning nor art. Having given up his soul for the promise of more life, he finds that without the soul, all that remains is appetite. All which colored life takes on the single hue of blood.*

Asher thought, *Ysidro told me this, and it was new to me. I would know it, if I had read this passage before.*

*Whoever wrote this has spoken with vampires.*

'And what is your connection –' Sophister drew a long breath of nicotine – 'with Titus Armistead?'

'What makes you think I have one?'

The bookseller nodded toward the front of the shop, where a man was just turning from the window. 'Because the fellow who's been hanging about the street since you walked in was with him when he and Colwich came last week to buy the book.'

# SIXTEEN

In Lydia's experience, maids – her own, her family's, and those of her friends – could mostly be bribed.

Since the time that Valentina Maninghurst had married Lydia's father, Lydia had heard her exclaim repeatedly on how loyal her maid, Cubitt, was. 'She's like one of those Biblical servants, faithful unto death . . .' and, 'There's nothing Cubitt wouldn't do for me . . .' Despite the fact that Cubitt was accepting a regular stipend from Aunt Lavinnia, to keep Lavinnia informed about Valentina's behavior, finances, lovers and movements, this was a view of personal maids widely held among Lydia's acquaintances.

Aunt Louise, before she'd moved to Paris, had paid the servants of a number of her social rivals (and of her own sisters and sister-in-law) a few shillings a month, just to keep them on her side. (*Heaven only knows what she's doing along those lines in Paris society!*) Valentina had one of Aunt Harriet's housemaids in her pay, only Lydia was aware that Aunt Lavinnia had 'turned' the woman – in Jamie's expression – with a small rise in salary, and so could feed Valentina misinformation as necessary.

Across the table from Lydia, Hellice Spills gave her a dazzling smile as she slipped the two guineas Lydia had handed her into her bag. 'Don't you worry, ma'am, I know exactly where Clagg keeps the account books and I'll have what you need to know 'bout those houses his Lordship's bought by the end of the week.' Evidently Ysidro had been correct – Hellice Spills either did not recall meeting Lydia in the upstairs hall of Wycliffe House on Monday night at all, or didn't recognize her. Or, just possibly, didn't care. She clearly no more needed to know the reason for the request than Messrs Teazle and McClennan did, and there wasn't the least necessity of mentioning Lord Mulcaster's footman.

*And why not?* Lydia reflected. She knew for a fact that the faithful-unto-death Cubitt was paid, per year, about half what Valentina spent on a pair of shoes. Why shouldn't she steal a feather here and there to render her own nest fluffy and warm against cold nights to come?

'Is this something the servants all know about?' she asked, in the voice of one fascinated by the facts of below-stairs life. 'About Lord Colwich buying property for – well – his *friend*.'

'Lordy, ma'am, servants know everything.' The girl looked wise, and took a sip of the coffee Lydia had bought her – surprisingly good, despite the unprepossessing air of Lady Sydenham's Parlour on Finsbury Circus. 'Back when we went down to South America with Mr Armistead to see his wife's family, I remember thinking everything would be different in a different country. But it's pretty much the same. If somebody finds something out, it's all over the Room before dark.'

'Even if it's about someone else's family?'

'*Especially* if it's about the family Miss Cece's going to marry into. I hear tell from Mr Gervase – that's Lord Colwich's man – that His Lordship the Earl was fit to be tied when he heard about his son buying these places for gentlemen he'd met in Europe. He never bought more than a cigarette case for his other boyfriend, Mr Gervase says – even if it was solid gold. A house, that's different. You want to know what he paid for all these places?'

'If you would, yes, please.' With the air of doing so almost accidentally, Lydia slipped a gold half-crown from her handbag and laid it on the table.

The girl picked it up unselfconsciously, and Lydia guessed that this was the sort of information that a matchmaking parent could easily use to break up an engagement so as to hitch her own candidate to one or the other party.

'Why would he do such a thing?' she wondered aloud. 'It seems an extraordinary thing to do, particularly as I know the Crossfords aren't wealthy.'

'Well, ma'am,' observed the girl, with a nod of her head – carefully coiffed, Lydia was fascinated to note, in a manner she had never seen before, her nappy red-brown hair straightened (*chemically?*) and arranged in elaborate whorls flat to her shapely skull, shining with a glaze of some kind – 'that all depends on what you call "wealthy".' Despite far more vital matters demanding her attention, Lydia was dying to ask her about what she used. 'They look plenty rich to me. But pretty much anybody can take advantage of that man, ma'am, 'cause of the dope he smokes.'

'Does he, still?' Seeing him conducting Cece's friends through the paint-smelling salons of Dallaby House, she wouldn't have said so.

'You smell it on his clothes. Mr Gervase says he smokes it all the time these days, even when he gets up first thing in the mornin', but I think he says that, just to cover up that he don't keep his lordship's shirts as fresh as he might. My brother Jim back in Washington smokes it like that, startin' in the mornin'.'

'Every day?' Lydia recalled what Ned Seabury had said, how changeable his friend had become: *He isn't the man I knew . . .*

'Not every day, no. But more an' more often. He'll be bright and friendly up till maybe ten o'clock, and then he'll disappear, go back to that house Miss Cece's Daddy bought for 'em, where Mr Gervase tells me he's got a "meditation chamber" he's havin' the decorators fix up. I'm bettin' that's where he keeps his dope. Then I'm guessin' he'll sniff cocaine in the evenin's, to be bright and friendly again. You don't think Miss Cece knows?'

She cocked a rather protuberant brown eye at Lydia.

'And she's willing to marry him anyway?' Lydia tried to sound more shocked than she actually was.

'Course she is.' Hellice helped herself to the last biscuit on the plate. 'Miss Cece's been slippin' out to that garden maze to meet this *friend* of his Lordship. Her daddy wants her to marry his Lordship and be Countess of Crossford one day, so I'm thinkin' this way, she gets to be a widow 'fore she's thirty. A man livin' that way generally don't live long.'

'Damn it.' From the doorway of the bookshop's inner room, Asher could see through the front window of the shop. Though the small, leaded panes were old enough to warp the image he could tell by the color of the clothing, the height and stance of the burly little man who loitered inconspicuously on the other side of Dean Street, that this was the man who'd followed him from Claridge's Hotel the previous day.

It was well after five. Asher had hoped to delve into the bookseller's stock of newspapers – Sophister took, in addition to *The Times*, the *Standard*, and *Le Figaro*, assorted German and Italian weeklies and never threw out a thing – in the hopes of finding mention of killings in Paris last December, but it might take him time to shed his 'friend'. Sunset wouldn't be for another four hours, and then light would linger in the sky till almost ten.

There were vampires – Ysidro was one – who could remain conscious for short periods before and after the rising and setting of the sun, provided they were protected from its rays. If Zahorec slept in any of his London lairs, it behooved him to have a look at Thamesmire this afternoon.

'Damn it is right.' Sophister leaned a bony shoulder on the other jamb of the door. 'Armistead isn't a chap one wants to run afoul of. I understand from the newspapers that at least two men who've tried to unionize his mines met with convenient "accidents". You've done something to interest him.'

*Have I?* Asher wondered. *Or did he follow Lydia for some reason, to see who she met . . .?*

The thought made the hair stand up on his nape.

If Armistead had noticed Lydia, for whatever reason, it wouldn't take more than a chance remark about her for one of her aunts – or her egregious hag of a stepmother – to mention that their niece (or stepdaughter) had disgraced the family by marrying a folklorist. Of the Armistead girl he knew almost nothing beyond that she was sufficiently romantic and sufficiently gullible to fall into the emotional trap set for her by a vampire. But all it would need to arouse Zahorec's suspicions was the mention that Lydia, rather than being a naive acquaintance of no account, was married to someone who could be expected to know jolly damn well the signs of involvement with the Undead.

'Will you do me a favor? Three favors,' he amended, and Sophister grinned.

'I take it one of them's show you the back door out of here?'

'Got it in one.'

'Right this way. Would you like me to get a cab for you?' Behind the half-inch slabs of glass, the huge, pale-blue eyes narrowed for the first time. 'You're looking a bit seedy.'

'A touch of the Black Plague. I'll be fine.'

'Have it your way, old man. There's a cab stand in Red Lion Square, if you can make it that far. What else can I get you?' He opened a small door between the bookshelves, ushered the way into a kitchen unbelievably cluttered, soiled, jammed with old books and reeking of cat mess and tobacco fumes.

'I should like to come back tomorrow, if I may. I'd like to have a longer look at the *Liber Gente*.'

'Be my guest. You can have the upstairs, if you don't mind a little mess.'

Asher shuddered at the thought of any chamber the bookseller would describe as *messy*, but only said, 'Thank you. What time do you open?'

'Usually by ten, but come round the back any time.'

'Thank you,' he said again. And because he knew his man, he added, 'How many other copies of the *Liber Gente* do you know about? How many other printings? You say they're all different . . .'

'Well, there are similarities. I haven't made a study of the book or anything – that sort of thing really isn't in my line. Shall I make a list for you for tomorrow?'

'Would you do that?' Asher found himself leaning against the door jamb, as dizziness swept over him again. *Let's get this over with. You can rest in the train on the way to Woolwich.* Even the hundred feet or so to Red Lion Square seemed like miles.

In any case, it was not the state one wanted to be in when confronting a private detective in the employ of an American robber-baron.

Sophister walked him across the yard and handed him through a narrow passageway that debouched on to Eagle Street. From there it was a walk of moments to the mellow brown-brick respectability of Red Lion Square. Changing cabs twice and taking a short journey from Russell Square to Piccadilly Circus on the Underground to make sure he actually was unaccompanied caused him to miss the six-oh-five train to Woolwich. Thus, it was after eight before the cab he finally found at Arsenal station brought him to Thamesmire, an aptly named villa some five miles beyond the Arsenal, set in weedy grounds much overgrown with shrubs and trees. *And if I were Undead*, Asher reflected wearily – *which would certainly be an improvement on how I feel at the moment – this is exactly the sort of place I'd pick to hide in.* The property bordered the marshes, and the gate in the eight-foot brick wall which surrounded it was backed with sheet iron – newly installed, he guessed, climbing from the cab. He said, 'Wait here,' to the driver and began to work his way along the wall, which was in ill repair and would, he guessed, have a low or damaged place in it somewhere.

There were several. The worst damage was on the marsh side, where peach trees in the unkempt garden had run wild and were in the process of buckling the brickwork outward and caving sections of it from the wall's top. His breath laboring and swoony grayness lapping at the edges of his mind, Asher scrambled to the top of the wall, and down into the garden beyond. The house was a rambling pseudo-Gothic Victorian, with a free-standing chapel built to one side of it, though Asher guessed that this close to the marshes, it wouldn't have much in the way of an underground crypt. Every window was shuttered, but when he went close – walking carefully now, aware that he was already in the twilight zone where a vampire within the house might well be awake – and tilted one of the louvers, he saw that the windows had been bricked up inside.

Circling the house, he found the remains the bricklayers had left: clots of mortar near the kitchen door, boards smeared with its grayish residue, a huge area near the stables of broken bricks and scattered fragments and dust.

About a third of the house, it looked like, had been sealed. Something to tell Grippen, though Heaven knew how many other places Colwich had purchased for his 'friend'.

And though the last sunlight still gilded the house's absurd pinnacles and roof crests, shadow filled the garden, like the dark waters of a deadly pool. *It's time to get out of here NOW.*

He stood leaning against the newel post of the kitchen steps, trying to get his breath. *Damn Grippen . . .*

The peach tree and the broken spot in the wall seemed miles away. The cab around by the gate seemed unthinkably distant. *Get away from here. If he's here he'll be awake, waiting in the darkness of the house. Waiting until it's dark enough to emerge . . .*

*If I try to walk now I'll fall.*

For a long time he stood, gathering his strength and watching color fade from the sky.

He made it to the back of the garden. Saw the peach trees – there were four of them – beyond the snarl of overgrown rose bushes and waist-high weeds. With evening, mist was rising from the marshes, and the damp chilled him to the bone. *Another minute before I try the wall . . .*

A man stood beneath the peach tree as Asher emerged from the overgrown hedges, raised a pistol as Asher made a move to plunge back into cover. 'Don't try it.'

It was Mr Three-and-Ninepenny Bowler. His voice had the flat accent of the American West.

*Damn blast bugger . . .*

'Your cab's gone anyway,' Bowler Hat added. 'If we make a deal, I'll drive you back to town. If not . . .' He shrugged. 'My name's Wirt. You'll be John Grant, that's staying at Porton's Hotel? I want a word with you.'

# SEVENTEEN

'**N**ot here.' Asher lifted his hand in a gesture of peace, started toward the wall, and Wirt stepped in front of him again, pistol raised.

'I think here is fine.'

'Trust me,' said Asher. 'It's not. We need to get back to town—'

'Where you got friends? I don't think so. And I'm not a hundred per cent sure one of the other boys isn't on your trail as well. Five hundred dollars is a lot of dough.'

'Five hundred dollars for what?'

'For a vampire.' Wirt spoke as if the answer was written on a sandwich board across his chest and Asher had neglected to read it. 'That's your racket, ain't it?' He nodded in the direction of the house. 'They really real?'

'If we remain here,' replied Asher grimly, 'we run the risk of finding that out.' *I don't know what the hell you're talking about*, he was fairly certain, would only prolong a discussion that needed to be concluded – or moved to another venue – without delay.

'Good.' Wirt grinned, and shifted to block Asher as he took a step toward the wall again. 'He's the man I really want to talk to – or are there lady vampires as well?'

'There are. And I promise you, you don't.'

'Oh, I think he'll listen to what I've got to say.' Keeping his pistol trained on Asher, Wirt glanced around him at the darkening garden, as if expecting Count Dracula to emerge from the house at any moment in a silk-lined cloak. 'It's a straight business proposition, and if Mr Armistead's willing to pay five hundred dollars just for an introduction, you can bet the salary's gonna be worth it.'

'*Salary?*'

Asher knew he should be shocked, but he wasn't. What he chiefly felt – besides growing fear of what he was nearly certain whispered in the night around them – was disgust.

'Sure. Say, can they really turn into bats? Though how turning into a bat's going to help 'em deal with strikers in the mines is more than I can figure, unless Mr Armistead plans to use him as a spy. You know personally, I thought he'd read too many of those books he buys – you know he's got about four copies of that one about the ten gents?'

'The *Liber Gente Tenebrarum*?'

'That's the one,' said Wirt. 'But the old man didn't get that rich bein' crazy. He'll sit up all night in that strongroom of his, with this book in front of him and a pile of dictionaries on the desk, French and Latin and Spanish and what-all. Crazy. But he tells me – and I'm pretty sure he told a couple of the other boys – five hundred dollars if I can bring him a vampire to talk to. And if he's gonna feed him on those socialist bastards from the WFM, more power to him. I'm sick of dealin' with those whinin' rats.'

*WFM*, thought Asher. *Western Federation of Miners.*

*At least two men who've tried to unionize his mines have met with convenient 'accidents'*, Sophister had told him.

'Good,' he said. 'Fine. You go right up that driveway and knock on the front door—'

'Not so fast.' The detective stepped in front of him again, gun trained, and Asher could see he was both able and willing to use it. 'You're comin' with me. That pretty-boy kid of Millward's – he hire you to do his legwork? You and the red-haired dame? Old Millward showed me the door pretty fast, but I knew if I followed his boy he'd lead me someplace.'

'Where he'll lead you is an early grave. These are not people you want to meet.'

'Bub, anybody in Denver'll tell you that for five hundred dollars, Blackie Wirt'll kiss the Devil's ass. There's a lantern down by the foot of that tree.' He dug with one hand in his pocket and tossed Asher a box of matches. 'How about you light it up and the two of us walk up and knock on the front door together? Then if nobody's home, you can come along with me and talk to Mr Armistead yourself.'

Asher gauged the gathering dusk and wondered if he had the speed to make it to the wall. He had little concern that Titus Armistead would actually succeed in hiring a vampire to kill off strikers in his mines. Even Damien Zahorec, standing like a shadow within the man's very gates, wasn't about to declare himself, and having seen in Peking what could come of working alliances between the living and the Undead, Asher didn't blame him in the slightest.

But once he, James Asher, stood revealed as a vampire hunter – and as Lydia's husband – there was little chance that Lydia could get clear of the situation before Zahorec killed her.

The American flicked his pistol barrel toward Asher, nodded at the lantern. 'Light it. And don't think I wouldn't shoot you over it because there ain't a soul for a mile around and I'm betting nobody knows you're here. I took down the addresses of those places you went this afternoon so there's not a reason in the world you're worth keeping alive.'

*He's seen Lydia, too.* Asher knelt beside the lantern. *Whether he kills me or just leaves me lying with a hole in me for Zahorec to find, the next person he'll look for is Seabury's 'red-haired dame'. It won't be half a day before word that she's hunting him will get to Zahorec . . .*

With a sidelong slash of his foot he sent the lantern spinning away and dove for the nearest dark cloud of laurels. The pistol crashed, Asher stumbled, dizzy, scrambled to his feet again . . .

Behind him, Wirt yelled in shock and terror, and in the same instant icy and powerful hands closed around Asher's arms. Reflective eyes glimmered in the darkness and a cultured voice said, 'Well, well, well. What have we here?'

'You'll catch your death, sitting out here, ma'am.' Ellen handed Lydia the coat she'd asked for – a quilted silk cocoon-style with a collar of trailing monkey fur – and a heavy woolen shawl to wrap on over it, her square face lined with concern in the reflected glow of the kitchen windows.

'I'm all right.'

'No, you're not,' retorted the servant. 'You didn't have hardly a thing for tea and there's a fog coming up.' And, when Lydia neither replied, nor moved on the white-painted bench beneath the garden arbor, she added more gently, 'I know it's hard for you, ma'am, being in the house. It's hard for me, too. And for Cook and Mrs Brock and us all, walking past the door of the nursery a dozen times a day—'

'It's all right.' Lydia held up her hand to silence the reminder, but of course Ellen would never be silenced.

'But you worrying yourself into your sickbed isn't going to help anything. Mr James will take care of it. You know he will.'

*I know he will . . .*

*If he survives himself.*

The chalk-white pallor, the sunken look of his eyes, tore her like broken glass twisting in a cut. *This is war . . . I took a wound.*

*We parted at four-thirty. How long would it take him to see those places, and come here?*

For the past hour, sitting here in the garden, every passing footfall in Holywell Street had brought her heart up leaping.

Now dark had fallen, and it wasn't her husband for whom she waited.

'I'll be in in a little while.'

'You'll be in in fifteen minutes,' retorted Ellen darkly. 'Which is when your supper will be on the table. And if you're not I'll come out here and fetch you.'

She crunched back up the gravel path to the house. Lydia folded her hands in the extravagant fur of her sleeves, and closed her eyes. *Simon, please come. Please.*

The thought of going back into the house – of climbing the stairs, of passing the door of Miranda's darkened nursery – was more than she could stand. She felt that she would almost rather get blankets and sleep out here in the garden, and take her chances with bronchitis . . .

*She's with living guardians*, she tried to remind herself. *The publican from Stepney would surely have been in a position to find a woman to take care of Miranda . . .*

'Mistress?'

The voice spoke so softly she wasn't sure for a moment whether it was inside her mind alone, but when she put on her spectacles and turned her head, Don Simon Ysidro, arms folded, stood in the darkness of the arbor at her side.

She held out her hand to him and he took it, fingers strong and cold.

'Grippen wouldn't kill Jamie, would he? Even if he found him prowling around one of his lairs?'

'Having enlisted you to find Zahorec, he would be a great fool if he did.' The vampire seated himself beside her. 'Whatever else can be said of him, Lionel Grippen is no fool. Did he hurt him,' he went on, as if he read the events of last night in the emphasis she had put on the word *kill*, 'to "teach him a lesson"? A thing he is fond of doing, to the living whom he uses as his tools, though often they recall nothing of it later, save their fear.'

Lydia nodded, and poured out to him James' account of last night's encounter with Grippen. 'He wanted to divert Grippen's attention from me to himself, so that I can search for places where they may be keeping Miranda. Do you think Grippen even intends to return her safely?'

'At the moment I see no reason why he would not.' As always, Don Simon's voice was calm as a frozen lake. Lydia wondered if it had been so in life.

'And Nan?'

He was silent for a moment. Then he said, 'She is old enough to recognize her captors.'

Lydia shook her head mutely. The thought of another death on her conscience – as Margaret Potton's had been on it for four years now – was more than she could bear.

The calm yellow eyes returned her gaze, without attempting a reply. Then: 'I take it James has not yet returned?'

'He was going to look at three of Zahorec's lairs.' She handed him her notes of the addresses. 'That was this afternoon.'

'Then I see no reason for Lionel to harm him. This I take to be fruit of your encounters with Mr Rolleston? *Three* of them?'

'That we know of so far.' She wiped her eyes. 'Colwich bought them for him. I think Colwich has to be hiding him at Dallaby House. Cece told me there was an underground chapel there, that's supposed to be connected to an old priory . . .'

'St Mary Westbourne.' Ysidro glanced up. 'Grippen might well have a trouble to sense him there because of the underground river below it. As for Mistress Wellit . . .' A pin-scratch trace of disapproval touched the corner of his mouth. 'Will you go down to London again tomorrow, and wait, at six, in the café of the Metropole as before, wearing once more your green dress?'

'So you can induce some other frightful *creature* to do my bidding, under the impression that I'm Queen Mab in disguise?'

Something – distaste, disgust, wariness – moved behind the sulfur-yellow eyes. 'Has this Rolleston spoke amiss to you?'

'No,' said Lydia quickly. Though the vampire's voice changed not a whisper, what she glimpsed in his expression was truly frightening. 'No, he has never been anything but polite and respectful. But he . . . he's *loathsome*.'

Long hands folded, he seemed to be considering what he could say.

'I understand,' Lydia stammered, 'that he's probably the only one you could find at Barclays who . . . who could be got to do your bidding. I mean, if it's discovered he's handing out information about clients' banking activity . . . He's certainly not anyone I'd hire for *anything*. It's just that . . . He's admitted himself that he's done frightful things.'

'So he has.' Simon's glance met hers through long white lashes. 'But I promise you, Mistress, he shall not make a nuisance of himself. And when you have learned from him all that you will, he shall return to the place from whence he came, and trouble you no more.'

'Don't hurt him.'

In the vampire's silence she read what was in his mind.

'As you will, Mistress.' He kissed her hand.

When she went back into the house – considerably after the fifteen-minute grace period granted by Ellen, but she found the servants only just bringing supper into the dining room – she found also the college post, which Mick had brought over from James' study at New College. One missive caught her eye and she carried it at once to the lamps on the table: ordinary yellow foolscap, folded together rather than placed into an envelope, and sealed as before with red wax.

The jagged handwriting was the same, vertical sixteenth-century letters written with what looked like an ordinary fountain pen.

*Jms Cl Asher, New College, Oxford*

She cracked the seals, and a second, half-sheet of foolscap fell out, folded small.

*Thursday, May 15, 1913*
*Dear Mr Asher. I am well and so is Miss Miranda. We're taken care of, it's so quiet here, barring sometimes the train whistles, and fresh milk and fresh eggs for Miss Miranda, why a few nights ago I heard a nightjar. They even give me books to read, only this was a magazine, the Comprondooz of the Acadamy of Sciences with an article by Mrs Ashers favorite Mrs Curie, all about raydium and pishblen. Please don't worry. We are both well.*
*Nan.*

# EIGHTEEN

There were four of them. A man and a woman gripped Asher by the arms, and another man – tall, aristocratic, with smooth brown hair and an immaculate dark suit that screamed of Savile Row – constrained Wirt. The fourth, a kittenish girl who looked to be only in her late teens, was clothed in extremely expensive poor taste: gaudy, lacy, jet beads and sequins flashing on heavy green silk. She was laughing as she slowly untied Wirt's tie.

'Look, you don't understand,' the American said, almost stammering in his haste to get the words out. 'I'm on your side. I've got a deal for you, for all of you.'

'And we've got a deal for you,' purred the girl. She stood close to him, rubbed her hip across his groin. 'Don't we, Geoff?' She gazed up at the tall vampire beside her.

'I tell you, beautiful, I'm not the one you want. Titus Armistead – you heard of him? Richest millionaire in the States. He wants to meet you. Wants to work with you. You think this place is something?' Wirt nodded back toward the silent blackness of the house. 'This is nothing! Armistead'll give you whatever you want: silk-lined coffins, hydraulic self-sealed vaults . . . He's got judges, police chiefs, Congressmen on his payroll. You'll never have to worry about who you kill again!'

'Do we worry about who we kill, Geoff?' The girl slipped the tie from around Wirt's throat, draped it over her bare shoulder, and raised languid brown eyes to the tall vampire again.

'I cannot sleep within my coffin, sweet Penelope,' responded Geoff gravely, 'with the agony of my anxiety.'

Her fangs glinted as she smiled, and undid the buttons on Wirt's collar.

'I brought him!' Wirt jerked his head frantically toward Asher. 'I brought him for you . . .'

'Oooh, so kind of you.' She ran the tip of one claw along the pounding artery beneath the man's ear.

'You got it all wrong! You do a deal with me – you let me

introduce you to Armistead – and you're set for life! I mean – uh – you're set for eternity . . .'

'But we *are* set for eternity,' murmured Geoff, and ran his claws over Wirt's hair. 'Really, if we start killing everyone your imbecilic boss wants out of the way, how long will it be before someone figures it out? Before people start hunting us? How long will it be before one of your boss's own idiot helpers decides to use us against *him*?'

'We may be trying to get clear of ol' Grippen,' added the young man who held Asher's arm, in clipped Cockney, 'but God forbid we 'ave to move to America to do it.'

'Shut up, Jerry.' Geoff placed one hand on the side of Wirt's face, to turn his head. Penelope leaned close, baring her fangs as her lips touched the skin of the man's throat.

Asher saw Geoff's smile of gleeful anticipation.

Wirt twisted in the vampire's grip, jabbed an elbow into that expensive waistcoat, jerked himself free. Plunged away into the overgrown tangle of the garden.

Penelope, Geoff and Jerry exchanged huge grins of delight and darted after him, with the foxfire swiftness that, even without the sleepy inattention that the vampire can lay upon living minds, was nearly impossible to follow. Asher felt the pressure of sleepy darkness on his own thoughts and thrust it aside. The grip of the fourth fledgling, a sturdily built woman with a strong chin and a heavy, sensual mouth, tightened on his arms and he knew better than to try and break free. In the African war he'd encountered more than one lion and knew that flight only marked one as prey.

Standing behind him, she shifted her weight, and he guessed she was listening to Wirt's blundering footfalls among the jungle of laurel-thickets between Thamesmire House and the surrounding wall. It would be pitch dark in there. Even at this distance Asher could hear the sawing of Wirt's breath.

'*Are* you trying to get clear of Grippen?' he asked conversationally.

'They're idiots.' Her voice was a brisk alto, her accent Sussex overlain by a lifetime of French and German governesses. 'Without Lionel they won't last a year.'

'I don't imagine a fugitive Romanian is going to be of much use arranging local conditions, no.'

Her fingers tightened on his arms, bruising even through the sleeves of his jacket. Wirt would never, Asher knew, have been able to break free of Geoff's grip if he hadn't been released. By the sound of it the American was being driven, blundering through the dense leaves guided by touch and by whisper, crying out now and then as cold claws brushed him in the dark.

It wasn't often the Kindred of Darkness got a chance genuinely to play with their prey. They were making the most of this one.

'If you think he arranges them with us you don't know the man.' Resentment tinged her voice. 'We're only told, "Don't kill this man or that", "Don't kill at all five nights out of seven", "Don't kill this type of person or that" . . .'

'You think the Romanian wouldn't have that power over you?'

She laughed shortly. 'I'd like to see him try. You know a great deal about it.'

'Did you think Grippen doesn't?'

Her body shifted again, pressing against his back. He felt the cold of her forehead against his ear as she brought her lips close to his throat; felt her recoil in shock, at the silver he wore under his collar. She twisted his arm viciously.

Then, more carefully, she drew close again. 'You wouldn't happen to know the means by which Damien claims he can break Lionel's hold on us, now, would you?'

Asher said nothing. From the dark tangle of the overgrown garden he heard Wirt's voice sob, 'Don't! Oh, God, don't – please, stop it! Please! No . . .'

And a moment later, Penelope's sweet laugh.

*Don't think about it. You were probably going to have to kill him yourself.*

'Oh, God!'

*But not like that.*

He'd once spent seventy-two hours in a cell under the Okhrana headquarters in St Petersburg. During that time they'd brought in someone – to this day he had no idea who it had been, or why they'd needed the information they thought the man had. The torture had lasted most of a day.

'Or whether, when he's done it, he'll command us, as Lionel does?'

Screams ripped the darkness, agony, horror, frantic pleading lost in an animal shriek of pain.

Asher felt the woman behind him shiver. She could smell his blood, feel the warmth of it through his flesh and his clothing. Alone with her in the darkness – this woman who had the strength of a machine in her big white hands – he could tell she was listening to the sounds of the kill with the devouring instinct of a starved demon.

Would they never finish the poor bastard off?

Her voice was thick when she murmured, 'What is his secret?'

'What has he told you?'

'He says he's met the Devil.' One hand released his arm, slipped around his waist. 'And the Devil taught him tricks. He says he knows spells, can make elixirs. I think he's lying.' The cloudy sleepiness of her mind reached for his again, clumsy and heavy-handed, compared to the subtle inattention that Ysidro or Grippen could introduce, and easy to push aside. She thrust him back against what felt like the trunk of one of the peach trees in the blackness, stood in front of him, her face barely a blur. 'But I don't know what he's lying about. Do you?

'Answer me,' she added, when he kept his silence. 'Or I'll break your neck, and drink your blood and your soul as you die.'

'Is it worth it? I've seen what masters do to fledglings who displease them.'

She drew back a little. In the garden behind them, Wirt's voice had sunk to a steady thread of sound, a constant pleading 'Uhnn . . . uhnnn . . . uhnn . . .' broken now and then by a sob of agony.

'Are you one of Lionel's?'

'Would I have found this place if I wasn't?'

'I don't believe you. He trusts no one. Not us, not that publican in Stepney who gets his bully boys for him, not that Jew money-lender in Whitechapel he uses as a paymaster. No one.'

'He had no choice,' said Asher. 'I don't suppose you trust those others – your friend Geoff, and the little tart in the flashy dress . . .'

He heard her hiss in contempt. Then she turned, sharply, and in the dense blackness Asher thought he glimpsed movement. Nowhere near the broken whimpers of the dying victim. A trace of starlight showed him what he thought was the gleam of eyes.

The fledgling beside him whispered, '*Who is that?*'

There was fear in her voice.

Instants later the tall vampire Geoff appeared from another direction, Penelope and Jerry behind him. The latter two were giggling, like schoolgirls tipsy on champagne. Geoff wiped traces of blood from his lips, licked it from the tips of his nails. 'Have a nice chat with our friend, Mrs Raleigh?' His tone was that of a drunkard in mid-binge, with no intention of stopping until he's had enough. Asher's eyes had adjusted to the minimal ghost of starlight through the mists, and he could make out Geoff's long, pale face, the elongated white V of his shirt front, the ivory gleam of Penelope's shoulders.

*Wirt has to have come by motor car. It'll be by the gates.*

Mrs Raleigh turned to speak to Geoff, and Asher struck down at the hand still on his arm with his free wrist. Even through the cloth of his shirt he knew the silver would burn her – new-made vampire flesh was a hundred times more tender to the effect of the metal than Grippen's would be. She screamed, jerked her hand away, and he plunged into the darkness, knowing by instinct where the low place in the wall was, praying he'd get there before the others could surround him.

Like the lions on the veldt, once the chase started they wouldn't give it up. If they surrounded him – and vampires were faster even than the great African cats – they'd drive him, as they'd driven Wirt, prolonging his pain and terror for their amusement, relishing his knowledge that ultimately he wouldn't – and couldn't – escape. He blundered into the wall, barely glimpsed the lighter patch in the darkness that showed the low place. His breath labored in his lungs and his head swam. *At least outside the wall I'll keep my bearings . . .*

He dropped from the gap and nearly fell, blood-loss and exhaustion buckling his knees. A sort of dark confusion – he could put on it no more description than that – flailed at his mind, as if someone were trying to put a hand before his eyes, and he focused his concentration, as he sometimes could do when dealing with Ysidro. He ran with everything that was in him, stumbling on the muddy tussocks. Sometimes it seemed to him that he lost sight of the wall, and the bulk of the house – that he was lost in fog suddenly thicker than the mists of the night. That he *was* in Africa, fleeing lions, their musty animal pong in his nostrils. That he was dreaming.

He fought to keep his bearings, to remember the slope of the ground.

Claws touched his face, or he thought they did. Phantom lights flickered far to his left and it passed through his mind that a pub was there – safety was there – where he knew no building stood. In the darkness he heard Penelope laugh.

*Not far . . . Not far . . .*

A shadow on the wall, springing down. The flash of beaded sleeves, a pale face.

Ahead, the black bulk of a motor car, standing before the black bulk of the gates.

Someone was beside it, tall and slim and dark. Reflective eyes caught the starlight. Asher stumbled, turned, knowing he'd been headed off, seeking another direction to run. There was one more of them than he'd thought. Five, not four . . .

They were all around him, ghostly swirls of movement. Ferrety Jerry and Penelope like marsh fire incarnate to his left, Mrs Raleigh to his right and Geoff before him, a shadow-cloaked torero weaving back and forth, making feints to draw his attention. Asher backed a little, knowing the fifth vampire beside Wirt's motor car would take him from behind. There was nowhere to run.

They closed in.

A shadow for an instant – or longer, he wasn't certain – covered his eyes, and with a sense of sharp waking he found himself on his knees on the wet gravel. A voice like dark thunder cursed above him and the corner of a cloak brushed his face: 'Puking foot-lickers! The man's mine! Clot-heads! Rabbit-suckers! Leave him be! Hang the lot of you!'

Asher's eyes cleared and he saw Geoff sprawled twenty feet away. Before the tall vampire could regain his feet, Grippen – for it was Grippen standing over him – strode to his fledgling and kicked him with vicious strength that sent him another several yards.

Then with eye-blink speed the Master of London was on Penelope, wrenching her by the hair until she screamed, shaking her as a mastiff would a cat. 'Stinking drab, I'll teach you t'obey! Louse-ridden stale! Touch him, would you, filthy punk?' He flung her at Geoff. 'God's bowels! Clear off, the lot of you dirty paillards!'

Asher rolled over, aware that he breathed but with the sense that the air he gasped contained no oxygen. Grippen and his fledglings seemed far off in the dark mist, and he saw another shadow approaching him, barely visible as it coalesced from the night.

The pale whisper of a face . . . It may have been a hallucination.

It was gone in the next heartbeat, and Grippen dragged him to his feet, shoved him against the back of the motor car to prop him up. 'What cock-brained humor did you take in your skull, man, paddin' about in the dark like a moonling?'

'I came in daylight.' He nodded toward the house and the wall, though he was glad of the motor car to hold on to. 'The house is one of Zahorec's lairs. The man who kept me here past dusk is in the garden, dead.' His legs shook, and he wondered if he could convince Grippen to call him a cab.

*Probably not . . .*

'You been inside?' Grippen released his shoulder – he nearly fell – and looked back at the dark house with narrowed eyes.

'It was close to dark. I feared he'd be waking already, though if he was here,' he added, 'I think he'd have come out, when they started on that poor bastard Wirt.'

'Any of them go inside?'

'I didn't see. They surrounded us the instant it was dark, so they may have come from there for all I know.'

The vampire's fang gleamed as he raised his lip in a snarl. Then he nodded toward the black thickets. 'And what'd the American want, that he'd keep you talking till fall of night?'

'Much what you ask. Had I been inside, and what had I found there? I told him no, and nothing, and he wouldn't believe me. He had a pistol, much good it did him. He said he'd followed me from Millward's.'

'Did he, then?' The Master of London looked around him, at the dark road, the crumbling wall and rampant trees. 'Came from there, did they? Waitin' on him, ungrateful hedge-pigs.' He pushed Asher back against the car's bonnet again and turned toward the house, and in the darkness Asher felt more than heard something like the rustle of moth wings. The fledglings, watching from the mist.

Maybe something else as well.

Waiting for Grippen to turn his back.

To go to the house, to search it for something that he might not even know what it looked like, through who knew how many light-less, bricked-up rooms . . .

Somewhere he heard Mrs Raleigh make a throaty sigh, like a lioness purring.

Evidently Grippen heard it, too, for he whirled and bellowed, 'God rot the pack of you! Touch this man and I'll have your guts for garters!'

But he hesitated.

'He has at least two other houses in town,' said Asher, 'where he could keep – his *things* . . .'

Grippen regarded him, head tilted at the unspoken hint.

'Mrs Raleigh asked whether it was true, that Zahorec can free fledglings of their Master's hold. And asked me what I knew of it.'

'And what'd you tell her?'

'That I knew nothing. She said Zahorec claims that the Devil taught him how to free them.'

*So if you leave them alone here and they search the house, they won't know they're looking for a book . . .*

He willed Grippen to understand. Whether he succeeded – or whether the Master Vampire figured that out for himself – Asher didn't know. But Grippen snarled, 'That's cock.' He stepped back, raised his thick voice to a shout. 'There's no Devil and no saints either, and banker's brach and his sniveling suck-arse lordship Vauxhill and those other two, they're *mine*! My blood in their veins, their last breaths breathed into my mouth, their toad-spotted little souls here . . .' He shut his fist, as if upon those souls, like a handful of beans in his palm. 'A fledgling can no more not be his Master's than you cannot be your father's get. 'Tis what you are, flesh and blood and marrow! Get in.'

He pulled open the door of the motor car, shoved Asher inside. 'You look like skimmed whey. Where can I take you?'

'Moscow Road.'

'Of the four of them you'd think there'd be one with the brains to see you can't trust a lying Papist prating of the Devil and freedom, whatever freedom is that they talk of . . . Couldn't pick it out of a basket of apples!' He reached in through the door, set the throttle and advanced the spark. 'And no more loyalty than snipes in a bush—'

'Four?' Asher turned his head as Grippen, after jerking the crank, darted into the driver's seat with eerie speed to adjust the choke. 'There were five.'

'*Five?*' The vampire's mouth settled into a heavy line. 'You're sure?'

Asher wasn't. The shadow beside the motor car, the gleam of
eyes . . . The note of fear in Mrs Raleigh's voice: *Who is that?*

He was still trying to put together the memories when he woke,
as if from a trance, on a bench in London Bridge station, with a
train guard standing over him asking worriedly, 'You all right, sir?'

The clock between the platforms read nearly midnight. Asher felt
cold to his marrow and nearly sick with exhaustion . . . *Of course,*
he thought. *Even in a motor car, Grippen can't cross running water
of his own volition.*

*He probably took the train from here himself.*

As he boarded the Hampstead line to get across the river, Asher
caught a glimpse, far down the platform, of a tall cloaked shape in
the shadow near the stair, but it was gone when he blinked. He
watched for it when he stumbled off in Queen's Square, but saw it
no more.

# NINETEEN

*O*wing to the inability of the Undead to walk abroad in
daylight (save when they employ such elixirs as will permit
of it, at grave risk to themselves lest the effects wear off
*untimely), vampires employ the living to do their bidding. Some
they hire outright with divers bribes and rewards. Others, they lure
by appearing to them in dreams in the guise of those they honor
and love, or sometimes (heaping sin upon sin in the eyes of God)
in the shape of angels or saints, and command them to tasks, for
the sake of those for whom they care, or for the salvation of their
souls. Seldom do the Undead entrust the living with the knowledge
of who and what they truly are, lest their revulsion at working for
the dead, or their honor as men, or their care for their own souls,
at length overcome them and turn them against their evil masters;
and seldom do the dead employ a living servant for more than five
years, before killing him and all members of his family, to protect
their secret.*

Asher double-checked the patristic Latin against a lexicon
Sophister had lent him, and compared it with the similar – but much

shorter – passage in the Paris edition. That version – supposedly a retranslation of the lost 1510 text – he had almost concluded was a complete forgery, but his study of it through the morning had yielded a half-dozen passages that felt genuine, including the 'genealogy' of the London nest.

The Latin was fifteenth-century, very unlike that of the Geneva text.

He leaned the bridge of his nose on his knuckles, closed his eyes against the sunlight that filtered through the cat-clawed muslin curtains. *We're still alive.*

Upon his return to Porton's last night he'd left a telegram with the desk clerk telling Lydia where he was, and that he was well, a condition which still surprised him. He'd also informed the clerk that his wife would be arriving sometime the following morning, which hadn't prevented the man from giving him a glare of severe disapproval when, at ten-thirty, he'd shown Lydia into the room. *I've a lady here SAYS she's your wife, sir . . .*

For a time, Asher and Lydia had simply clung together in the armchair beside the room's little fireplace, like shipwrecked mariners who had somehow survived to drag themselves on to an island beach. *We're still alive.*

He'd read over Nan Wellit's note while Lydia unpacked a kettle, a tea caddy, a Spode teapot, two cups, two saucers, spoons, marmalade, sugar, and a packet of Mrs Grimes' batter-muffins (complete with a small pickle jar containing butter) from one of the two enormous carpet-bags she'd brought with her. (Light traveling, for Lydia. God knew what was in the other one.) He'd observed the smoothness of the young nursery maid's careful printing: block letters resting neatly on the lines, o's and a's shaped as they were in her infrequent notes to Lydia or Mrs Brock. *She's not in immediate terror or pain. She's had enough sleep.*

And she had her wits about her enough to put in markers: *fresh milk, birdsong, quiet, train.* Code-words: *We're in the country near a railway-line.*

One of his own agents in Berlin couldn't have done better.

'I'm meeting Cece's maid again at noon,' Lydia had informed him, as she'd handed him his tea. 'And Simon's B of E recruit this afternoon at six. So by tonight we should have a complete list of Zahorec's properties. Aunt Isobel is barely speaking to me for backing out of the theater this evening. Rumor has it that negotiations for Armistead's settlement on Cece have run aground and the whole match may be called off, and she's frantic to learn the details, and of course it wouldn't be proper for Emily to inquire. But I think we'd both do well to be out of London tonight. Shall I meet you at the train?'

Asher, who had waked a dozen times during what remained of the night thinking he heard Blackie Wirt screaming in the darkness, had nodded. Now in the stuffy, cat-smelling room above the bookshop, he wondered if Grippen had driven back to Thamesmire last night to dispose of Wirt's body.

*He'd have to. Nothing would bring the notice of the police more quickly than the discovery of a mutilated corpse in a suburban garden . . .*

And a tiny corner of his mind smiled at the thought of Lionel Grippen, born in the reign of Henry VIII, piloting a motor car through the streets of south London like a demon on hashish.

Even the prospect of bringing the police down on Damien Zahorec's lair wouldn't outweigh the risk of public notice. Of calling it to the attention of enough people to matter, that vampires existed or might exist. A fox cannot prevail against an infinite number of geese.

As Asher had suspected, Sophister's chamber contained copies of *Le Temps*, *Le Petit Journal* and *L'Intransigeant* dating back to the previous December (and probably to the Franco-Prussian War, for that matter). No mention of unusual murders in Paris had been made in any of these prior to Christmas. But after that holiday, all carried mention of disappearances in the poorer districts of St Antoine and the Left Bank, and of bodies found – mostly whores, factory workers, and late-walking students – in the Seine.

Zahorec reached Paris on December 16th. Nine days of staying quiet, feeding carefully, as he had in Italy.

*Whatever changed, it changed in Paris.*

Asher turned back to the yellowed volume, wondering if the answer lay there and if he'd recognize it if it did.

*It is the goal and the obsession of the vampire to conceal from the living what he is, and where he sleeps. For those who live longest have learned that no fortress exists, no army of retainers*

*can be formed, sufficiently strong to resist armed mobs in their
anger, once they understand the nature of their foe.*

That was in the Paris text but not in the Prague version. The supposedly medieval French used the modern word *armée* rather than the more ancient *pooir* . . . Did that make it a forgery? And if it was a forgery, did that make it untrue?

In the Prague version it said, *The strength of the vampire lies in the disbelief of the living, as much as in their strength and the glamour they cast.*

Asher turned the stiff pages, not daring to let himself think about his daughter, and where she might be. He recalled a colleague in Vienna who had urged him to kill a woman he knew in that city, because he had returned from a secret errand to find three telegrams from her under the door of his lodgings. He had not been supposed to be away at that time, and even if he came up with excuses why he hadn't answered, the seed of doubt had been sown.

'You can't even let 'em stand next to somebody who knew you in some other city, by some other name,' the colleague had said. 'Because somebody, sometime is going to say, *Oh, yeah, that feller . . . only his name wasn't Grant . . .*' And then they're going to ask themselves *why* your name was Grant in Geneva and Hoffner in Vienna, and whatever answer they come up with, it won't be good.'

The thought of Lydia, patiently watching Cece Armistead, waiting for the vampire's shadow to pass, turned him cold with dread.

Particularly if the mining baron were seeking a vampire for his own purposes. Even if Zahorec wouldn't involve himself in a partnership with a living man, Asher wouldn't have been willing to bet on the caution of the four fledglings who had cornered him last night.

Not to bet his life. Or Lydia's life, or Miranda's.

As Sophister had warned him, the room above the bookshop was frightful, stuffy and reeking of soured milk, unwashed clothing, stale cigarette smoke and cat. Old newspapers, books and fragments of books clogged every corner, heaped promiscuously with shirts, tea towels, bills, invoices, folders of unattached pages, and dirty plates. Through a half-open door a hallway could be glimpsed – choked both sides with collected sets of Dickens and bundles of detached signatures – and past that a bedroom similarly piled.

*The Undead flesh being impervious to the alterations of mortality, neither poisons nor medicaments can touch it, save only if they are mixed with a small quantity of silver dust.*

In the French text the explanation of silver's power over vampire flesh was totally different, derived from magnetism, salt, and the tides.

The Latin text went on immediately into a discussion of the relationship of the Undead *anima* with water – that whole signature was missing in the French text – though a little searching yielded a dozen pages of formulae by which vampires could dose themselves to do everything from walking about in the daylight to taking on the forms of living men and women. Many of these potions involved silver, garlic or aconite – wolfsbane – presumably in order to break the resistance of vampire flesh to change of any sort, but Asher wondered if these were the enterprising invention of a vampire-hunter seeking to get his prey to swallow a phial of silver nitrate.

Almost none of them existed in the French text. It, however, contained a warning that *divers elixirs*, taken to increase the vampire's mental powers, had the eventual effect of exhaustion, madness, or insane thirst for blood, followed immediately by a dozen anecdotes concerning live burial, and the mysterious disappearances of eleven Parisian children during the reign of Henri III. Annoyed, Asher turned the thick pages and scanned for the words *elissir, potio, pocion.*

*You'll see him sitting up all night in that strongroom of his*, Wirt had said, *with this book in front of him and a pile of dictionaries on the desk . . .*

*Looking for what?*

*A straight business proposition*, Wirt had said. *Mr Armistead's willing to pay five hundred dollars just for an introduction.*

*If he's going to feed him on socialist bastards from the WFM, more power to him . . .*

Asher sighed. He'd thought he'd uncovered the limits of danger, when he'd headed off attempts by the Austrian government – and the British – to employ vampires against their foes in what everyone knew was an oncoming war. Would the results be more, or less frightful, if private industrialists came to believe in them, and hired them as they hired men like Wirt and his cronies, to keep the unions in line?

> *The vampire exists as a state of appetite alone. They have the*
> *memories of the men they once were, but all trace of affection,*
> *of honor, of regard for other men or the law and custom of*
> *society, forsakes them and their sole concerns remain merely*
> *to kill and drink the blood of their victims, and to keep them-*
> *selves safe from detection by whatever means possible . . .*

Ysidro had said something of the kind to him once. Asher sought for the corresponding passage in the French text but found in its place a garbled passage concerning how Satan created quasi-souls and introduced them into the corpses of those whom the vampire killed, unless certain precautions were taken . . .

Yet the thought grew stronger in his mind, that whoever had written the original from which these two editions were taken – and neither bore more than a passing resemblance to the Geneva text he'd read all those years ago in Rebbe Karlebach's house – that man had genuinely known vampires.

*He probably DID work for them.* Like a Shabbas goy, as Karlebach had said: the gentile sometimes employed in the household of a wealthy Jew, to stoke up the fires and open and close windows on the Sabbath, lest any member of the household dishonor the day by doing work.

*If Lydia, or I, were to write what we knew of vampires – what we observed of them over six years of association with Don Simon Ysidro and the vampires of St Petersburg, London, Paris, Peking . . .*

Would it become the *Liber Gente Tenebrarum*?

*Seldom do the dead employ a living servant for more than five years, before killing him and all members of his family, to protect their secret.*

This passage was the same in both books. Asher recalled it also from Karlebach's Swiss edition as well.

He rested his hands on those stained pages, and his sheaf of notes concerning hiding-places, running water, lineages of vampire masters in the old cities of the Danube and the Rhine. In his mind he saw again Don Simon Ysidro seated in the study in Holywell Street, with Lydia unconscious on the sofa: *My name is Don Simon Xavier Christian Morado de la Cadeña-Ysidro, and I am what you call a vampire . . .*

Count Epaminondas Saint-Hilaire in Paris – said Sophister's

painfully neat block printing – had owned two copies of the *Liber Gente*, one the same 1637 Latin edition that lay before him on the bookseller's cigarette-burned desk, the other the first known printed edition, also in Latin, from Burgos in 1490. Four, Wirt had said, and one of them evidently in French: there had been a French edition printed in Paris in 1510, Sophister had written, of which nothing was known and no copies had ever surfaced. Both French forgeries were supposed to be taken from it, and John Aubrey had published an English translation of this text in London in 1680 – Balliol and Christ Church Colleges in Oxford, and Caius College in Cambridge, possessed copies. There was record of a Spanish edition of 1494 printed in Toledo, and two different Latin printings done in Geneva.

*This has to be what Grippen is seeking.*

The hold of a master-vampire over his fledglings – said the problematical French edition – could be broken by master and fledglings partaking of a Black Mass together, at which a black child without a single drop of Caucasian blood was sacrificed, or by dosing the master (*and how are you going to do that?*) with henbane, ox-gall, and powdered black pearls. The Prague edition gave three additional methods, all involving potions drunk by both master and fledglings in the dark of the moon on a bridge above running water (*presumably you have a living person get you on to the bridge . . . do you then kill him or her afterwards?*).

He wondered what the other versions said on this subject, and if in fact Damien Zahorec was going to have the temerity to suggest these rituals to Lord Vauxhill, and sharp-eyed Mrs Raleigh.

And, in their desperation to be free of Grippen, would they comply? (*Which still leaves the problem of how you're going to trick Grippen into drinking a cup of black dog's urine and garlic in the middle of Blackfriars Bridge . . .*)

*Is this what Zahorec is seeking, in the house of Titus Armistead?*

*If not these specific formulae, then one that WILL give him mastery over London?*

There was also, he noted, a method by which a vampire might – by use of a distillation of silver, graveyard earth, and the blood of a virgin boy – come to hold in his thrall vampires not his own fledglings.

The angle of window-light shifted. Pubs in Stepney would be opening, though it was too early for their owners to be working the taprooms themselves. Miss Violet would recognize him as someone who'd been in before and not a stranger – easy enough to get up a chat on the subject of other property owned by the publican, and whether members of his family had taken a vacation out of town on or about the eighth. *Amateurs always use their families.*

He rose from his desk, and made his way – nearly breaking his neck over the piled volumes of the *Patrologia Latina* – to the window. Dean Street was quiet. A cab rattled past, two lady shoppers strolled along the opposite pavement and paused to look into the windows of Clement Carghill, Fine Stationery.

Sunlight shone bright on sooty bricks, glinted on windows.

Yet the feeling that he was being watched hadn't left him: the sensation that had caused him to change cabs twice on his way here from Moscow Road and to leave his satchel at the toyshop on Regent Street where he'd bribed the counter-boy to let him change his jacket and hat and leave by the back door. Before parting from Lydia that morning, he'd arranged a fallback signal for the train station: *Red scarf, don't come near me, don't speak to me. Just get on the train.*

He hoped that precaution would suffice.

Lydia turned the page of the Café Metropole's menu with languid grace, not that she could read a word of its copperplate catalogue of poppy-seed cakes and *gateaux crèmes* at a distance of eighteen inches. On the far side of the little lake of white-draped tables, her stepmother, Valentina, sat likewise alone, likewise studiously absorbed in perusal of the possibilities for tea. Lydia might be blind as a mole, but she could identify her father's exquisite little widow anywhere, and had nearly shrunk under the table ten minutes ago when the older woman had entered the café.

Valentina had scrupulously taken a table as far from Lydia as she possibly could.

*Meeting a lover . . .*

She peeped up over the edge of the stiff white card: one glance at Valentina, one glance at the door. *Aunt Lavinnia will kill me if she learns I didn't put on my eyeglasses to see who joins her . . .*

A glance down at the packet of notepaper, folded small, which Hellice Spills had handed her over coffee at Lady Sydenham's Parlour Tea Shop and Sweets.

The list of properties whose purchase Noel Wredemere had arranged – and paid for – since the first of the year.

Her work for Lionel Grippen was done.

There were six of them, all in the Greater London area. Four in far-flung suburbs, though minutes by train and Underground from the crowded docks and slums. Had Colwich used his engagement to Titus Armistead's daughter as security for the purchases? The bridegroom would be in a sorry position, she reflected, if Armistead turned intransigent over the settlement and cancelled the marriage altogether. Cece – and Zahorec – would have to find a new means of getting her an independent establishment in London . . .

And they would almost certainly kill poor Noel.

She turned the list over in her gloved hands. The thought of Jamie going to have a look at these places – he would have to, to make sure there were no surprises in store anywhere – sickened her with dread.

*And then what?*

Lionel Grippen might possibly return Miranda to her unhurt – provided his human agents hadn't panicked. But the chances of his – or their – letting Nan Wellit go free were microscopic. And though everything in her wailed to simply hand the vampire the list of properties tonight (*Where? How? Even if I put an advertisement in* The Times *tonight it wouldn't come out until the morning*), she knew it would be a few days before Ysidro's promised clerk at the Bank of England came up with the locations of Grippen's holdings. Before she and Jamie had time to track down where Miranda actually was.

In those days anything could happen.

Tightly as she squeezed shut the door in her mind on the thought, a little whisper of it leaked through: *Get Miranda NOW, and hope they'll let Nan go as well* . . .

She knew they wouldn't.

*Will Ysidro help us stage a rescue?*

*Dare we even ask him?*

*One thing at a time.* She drew a deep breath, let it out.

Tomorrow night – provided Armistead didn't halt the marriage altogether – was dinner at Wycliffe House. Forty people, Aunt Isobel had said, and the Ballet Russe afterwards. Enough of a crowd to allow her to slip away for a more thorough search of the library for copies of the *Liber Gente Tenebrarum*. (*Drat it, that we didn't know to look for it the first time we were there!*) She was under orders from Isobel to seek out Lady May, who must (Isobel said) surely be so sick of the American and his daughter (and their detectives) by this time that she'd be delighted to tell all she knew about the settlement . . .

Movement on the edge of the café drew her attention. Though it grated on every sensibility she possessed, Lydia put on her spectacles. Across the café she'd already identified the unfashionable outline and colors of the man who stood on the shore of that lake of white tables: black and baggy and rather rusty-looking. Certainly not the garb of a gentleman coming to take a late and extremely expensive tea at the Metropole.

*Maybe I am supposed to be Queen Mab or the Spirit of the Woods and shouldn't be wearing spectacles . . .* but the last thing she wanted was to be surprised by another Timothy Rolleston.

The man who stood looking at her across the intervening tables was younger than Rolleston, and had the unhealthy thinness that Lydia had seen among the opium-smokers of the Limehouse. His ancient blue-and-white school tie was faded, his respectable, clerkish black jacket and trousers hung like a scarecrow's. Though he was clean-shaven and his hair was clean, he had the opium smoker's air of shabby self-neglect.

His sunken eyes, fixed on her, flared with shock: the red-haired lady in green, with the mermaid necklace gleaming against the white of her shirtwaist. With her spectacles on, she could see that shock change to horror, and despair.

*It's really real. The dream you had is really real. Whatever that creature, that being of shining shadow promised you in your dream, you're awake now and here she is, waiting for you exactly the way he said I'd be . . .*

*Asking you to violate everything you swore to your employers that you'd uphold.*

Her heart ached with pity for him . . .

. . . until he turned, with sharp decision, and strode toward the lobby doors.

Lydia sprang to her feet. In panic she wove her way between

the tables, cursing the dictates of good behavior (and the archi-
tecture of fashionable shoes) that made it impossible for her to
run – the lifelong training that forbade her to shout.

'Wait!' she called out, in that polite half-cry that comes from the
throat and not the chest. 'Please, wait!'

He was out the door twenty feet ahead of her.

By the time Lydia reached the sidewalk of Northumberland Street,
he was gone.

# TWENTY

**W**earing a red cravat, and reading an octavo edition of
Burton's *Kasidah*, Asher watched platform eleven
of Paddington Station until the eight-oh-five for Oxford
was safely on its way. He'd seen Lydia get on it, and watched the
other passengers for any hint of a familiar outline, any sense of
having seen a walk, a shape, a type of hat . . .

And saw nothing and no one that, in his spying days, would have
sent him fleeing for the nearest border without bothering to pack.

Lydia didn't give him a glance.

When the express arrived from Birmingham, and Asher went as
if to meet it, then left the station, returning only minutes before the
nine-fifty departed, with the last milky twilight barely lingering in
the sky. He waited until the train was actually in motion before
stepping on to it. No one followed.

The fact that he saw no one meant only that he'd seen no one.

The shadow he'd glimpsed beside Blackie Wirt's car – and as
he'd guessed, there was no mention in the newspapers of the
discovery of a body in Woolwich or vicinity, mutilated or otherwise
– lingered in his mind. The cloaked form in the Underground station.
The note of fear in Mrs Raleigh's voice: *Who is that?*

Not Zahorec, that was clear.

Would any of Armistead's other 'boys' have the wits to trace him
through Sophister?

The thought troubled him as the dark countryside streamed past
the window, alternating with the recollections of the smoky dimness

of The Scythe: sausages, beer, and enough neighborhood gossip to fill out a three-volume novel.

Asher watched the platform behind him when he stepped off the train at Oxford.

All the way along George Street he listened in the darkness.

A light burned behind the curtains of Lydia's room as he came down Holywell Street. He let himself in through the garden gate, heard her voice speaking softly beneath the arbor.

'Do you think you can get him to come tomorrow?' Behind her usual matter-of-factness he heard exhaustion and dread.

The glow of the breakfast-room window haloed them: Lydia on the garden bench, looking up into Ysidro's face, a shawl wrapped over the traveling dress she'd had on at Paddington. Ysidro standing, thin arms folded, gray clothing indistinguishable from shadow.

'What names do you seek, Mistress?'

She gave them: a catalog of how deeply she had penetrated the secrets of the vampire nest. The Spanish vampire had on several occasions risked incineration to help them, but Asher knew that his true loyalties were also wrapped in shadow. It was Ysidro – *with divers bribes . . . appearing in the guise of those they honor* – who had drawn himself and Lydia into being the heirs and successors of Johanot of Valladolid, servants of the Undead.

*And is all of this – or part of this – some chess game he's playing against Grippen?* Everything he knew about vampire nests whispered to him that there was at least that possibility.

'I feel such a wretch for not catching . . . Mr Ballard, did you say your clerk's name was?' said Lydia after a time. 'I did try.' It was a measure of her desperation – and her trust in the vampire – that she had her spectacles on. In the reflected lamplight she looked very like the gawky schoolgirl Asher had first met in the home of Ambrose Willoughby, the Dean of All Souls. 'I took a cab and drove round that whole area, from the Embankment up to Trafalgar Square. He fled the café as if he'd seen the Devil.'

'He may have believed he had.'

'Will you be able to bring him back?'

'Or can someone else be recruited?' Asher stepped from the darkness. Though he was fairly certain Ysidro had both heard and seen him coming, the joy on Lydia's face at the sight of him would have been enough to banish from anyone but a maniac any thought of jealousy . . . notwithstanding he was well aware that Lydia loved Ysidro.

The fact that he would rather that she didn't had more to do with his fear for her safety than conventional resentment of a wife's *ciscebeo*. As her arms closed hard around his ribcage, he asked across her shoulder, 'Am I being followed?'

The vampire's eyes for an instant lost their focus. 'I hear no one.' Then he held out his hand. 'I trust you are well?' The crystalline gaze lingered for a moment on Asher's face, as if he saw there everything that had passed since he'd come into the Palazzo Foscari to find Lydia's telegram. 'Madame informs me there seems to be more than one alien vampire in London – the second of whom has remained invisible even to Lionel's watchful eye.'

'I'm not even sure what I saw.' Asher glanced back toward the garden gate, and wondered if a vampire capable of hiding from Grippen's awareness would be any more apparent to Ysidro's. 'Has she informed you also that Titus Armistead is seeking to employ a vampire for purposes of smashing the miners' unions that inconvenience him? *Are* there vampires in the United States?'

'If there are, I have no desire to meet them. The thought of an American vampire's feeding-manners renders me queasy. Presumably he conceived his belief in our existence by reading the *Book of the Kindred of Darkness*?'

'You've heard of it?'

'Who among us has not?'

'Grippen's fledglings, to name four.'

Ysidro's long fingers moved, as if dismissing ungrateful hedge-pigs. ''Tis not a matter of which one speaks to fledglings.'

'Because it contains formulae that would break a master's hold on them?'

'James.' He tilted his head a little, like a mantis in the moonlight. 'Don't tell me you believe a word of that nonsense?'

'Damien Zahorec is acting as if he does. As is Grippen.'

'I never rated Lionel's intelligence above average. One doesn't speak of the book to fledglings because *they* would believe. Fledglings are so frightened at their own inexperience they'll believe anything. One doesn't wish to spend the next twelve decades trying to out-maneuver attempts to trick one into drinking rat-blood cocktails in the dark of the moon.'

'It would get tiresome.'

'Most of those mixtures contain silver or whitethorn, as you've probably observed. Not enough to kill a strong vampire, but some of those potions will drive him – or her – mad, and certainly weaken him. The book is a trap, James. Promulgated into the world – and spread down the centuries – as a means of killing vampires . . . or inducing them to kill each other or themselves.'

Asher grinned sidelong. 'It's deuced clever.'

Ysidro looked down his nose, like a fox not wishing to admit that foxes can be deceived, as well as surrounded, by geese.

'Zahorec seems to have swallowed it whole – though not enough to risk travel across open ocean for five days at the mercy of an American millionaire and his "boys". I wish I could reassure Grippen that sooner or later, his enemy is going to lay hands on the book and poison himself, but he seems to be taking great precautions to keep Lydia – and myself – from knowing what he's actually seeking in Zahorec's lairs.'

'Scant reassurance if Lionel's fledglings lay hands on it.' The twitch of Ysidro's aristocratic nostrils was a condensed firestorm of derision. 'Some of those recipes are genuine. The last thing he wants is to find himself another victim of Johanot of Valladolid's extremely clever little scheme.'

'I'm definitely starting to like Johanot. The problem is that like poison bait, the intended victim isn't the only one who's likely to die.' Asher laid his hand on Lydia's head as she seated herself again on the bench.

'I visited The Scythe this afternoon . . .'

'Not the first public house Grippen has used for his purposes,' remarked Ysidro. 'Though 'tis some sixty years since the last one. I hope you avoided the sausages.'

'They were . . . memorable.' Asher's quick grin faded. 'I had a long chat with Henry Scrooby's sister Violet, and sundry of their neighbors. Scrooby's wife, brother, and brother-in-law have all been away since the seventh of May. Everyone I spoke to attested to the terror and respect in which "Dr G" is held, but the general consensus is that neither Mick Scrooby nor Reggie Barns – the brother-in-law – can be relied on. Barns in particular is bad-tempered and impatient. Both are inclined to drink.'

Lydia's hand went swiftly to her lips, and when she folded it, almost at once, upon her knee, her face was nearly as white as the vampire's.

Ysidro only crossed his arms again, considering the words without expression. In life, Asher knew, the vampire had engaged in intelligence work himself, and would know what happened to hostages under the care of bad-tempered and impatient watchmen inclined to drink.

At length Ysidro looked down into Lydia's face. 'Tomorrow you will have the information you seek, Mistress.'

'Thank you.' She took his hand.

'When you learn that which you seek to know –' Ysidro's glance returned to Asher – 'speak to me, ere you make use of the information.'

Their eyes held for a long moment, and it seemed to Asher that behind the crying of the crickets in the summer darkness, he heard Millward's voice, and that of his own master Rebbe Karlebach – and indeed, Johanot of Valladolid: *They cannot be trusted. Their whole means of hunting and survival is deceit, and illusion, and the lies of the damned.*

'All right,' he said.

Ysidro walked them as far as the back door of the house, listening – Asher thought – to the darkness of the summer night. Only when Lydia had gone inside did Asher say, 'Thank you for looking after her. For all you have done.'

'Not at all.'

Their eyes met again. In his own, Asher suspected the vampire read his knowledge that if Miranda were killed, nothing between himself and Lydia would be the same again.

Into the velvet silence of the night the sound of the Great Tom bell spoke the hour. One o'clock, and the black sky over the old town's sleeping spires saturated with moonlight and stars. ''Twas my doing that Grippen came to know your names. And despite the neglect meted out to well over half the infants of this country,' Ysidro went on, 'who shiver under every bridge and railway embankment in London wholly unnoticed by most of its population, I understand your desperation at the thought of your daughter's peril. But lest you think me sentimental, I will admit that I understand also that should harm befall Miss Miranda, no power on earth will turn aside your vengeance upon every vampire of your acquaintance, myself included. And I understand also that you are a singularly difficult man to kill.'

'Thank you.'

'I would not wish to be obliged to make the attempt. Nor to have any of my . . . fellows –' he hesitated for a moment over the word – 'feel so moved, particularly since this pre-emptive defense would perforce involve you both.'

Asher said nothing. He had guessed this already.

'Tell me – if you know, and you may not . . . Did the tedious Dr Millward lose one whom he loved to the Undead?'

'I think he must have,' replied Asher in time. 'I hadn't thought of it before. I know his brother died young and unexpectedly in the early nineties – I was out of the country at the time. I know they were extraordinarily close. Even before that death he believed in the existence of the Undead, which I did not. So he always seemed a little crazy to me. By the time I returned to Oxford permanently his wife had left him, and he'd ceased to lecture. So far as I know he lives on what was settled on him in the marriage, and spends the whole of his time obsessively hunting down legends of vampires.'

'Indeed,' said Ysidro.

As usual, though they stood together beside the door, Asher did not see him depart.

Accompanied by Ellen and four portmanteaux of apparel appropriate for a morning at a garden show, tea with Aunt Isobel, a formal dinner, the Ballet Russe, and breakfast tomorrow morning – plus a spare green walking costume in case she had to meet a worshipper at the Metropole after all – and shoes – and hats – and rice powder, mascaro, rouge, rosewater and glycerin for her hands, Moondrops complexion *restoratif*, pomade, a copy of Haeckel's *Die Lebenswünder*, two issues of the *Journal Physiologique*, and seven pairs of earrings – Lydia took the nine-oh-five train to London the following morning, having missed the eight-twenty-seven. Resplendent in gray hair-dye, eyeglasses, a horrible combination of mustard-colored tweeds and a pair of enormous Dundreary whiskers, Jamie had ridden down to London earlier on his motorcycle to have another look at the *Book of the Kindred of Darkness*.

'Do you think Simon was lying?' she asked him, as he glued the

Dundrearies in place at the bedroom mirror. 'That the book really does contain the truth?'

'I think the book contains some truth,' Jamie had replied. He hadn't shaved that morning, and stubble – grayed also with flour – incompletely masked the slight red burns on his jaw and chin, where he'd glued his former disguise last night for his visit to The Scythe. 'He admitted as much. Be careful at Wycliffe House,' he added. 'Stay with the company, and declare yourself sick and get out of there as quickly as you can.'

'You don't really think Zahorec is really going to turn up at Cece's wedding supper?'

'I think if there's any danger Armistead is going to put a spoke in his wheel by calling off the marriage to Colwich, he may be unable to resist the temptation to find out what's going on.' He feathered streaks of flour into his own mustache thence to the fake foliage on his cheeks: Jamie sometimes joked with Lydia about the time she spent making herself presentable, but when he wore a disguise he was meticulous about putting it on, even if it was just to come and go from a bookshop unnoticed by a parcel of American thugs. 'He'd see to it that no one noticed him. He'll almost certainly put in an appearance at the ballet.'

'I don't think Mr Armistead is really going to call things off,' said Lydia after a moment. 'Not if he's hosting a dinner for forty people and taking twenty of us to first-tier boxes at the Ballet Russe. But he wants to tie all Cece's money up in a trust, and Lord Crossford got offended because he wants to touch Noel for the money to repair the roof on Crossford Hall. Aunt Lavinnia heard from her dresser that Mr Armistead and Lord Crossford had a frightful row, so in addition to seeing if I can get another look at the contents of the library, my assignment tonight is to find out about the settlement from Lady May.'

Asher shook his head. 'I think Zahorec doesn't know what he's getting into, tangling with those families. He'd probably be better off hiding in a country churchyard in the Midlands.' He selected from the corner a knobbed old shillelagh such as an elderly country-man might carry. 'Will you have time to meet me at the Bag o' Nails on Sloane Square at five? It's a perfectly respectable pub into which a lady may step without compromising her reputation.'

'Not if she has an aunt like Lavinnia, she can't.'

He kissed her, like being bussed by a holly bush. 'Fallback an hour later at the Temperance Hotel. I don't think even Aunt Lavinnia could object to that.'

'I think you're thinking of someone else's Aunt Lavinnia. Mine would and could and will.'

In truth, Lydia reflected some four hours later, as a blue-liveried footman helped her from the Halfdene family landaulet before the gates of the Chelsea Hospital grounds, it wasn't Aunt Lavinnia she dreaded meeting here at the International Horticultural Society's Flower Show so much as Josetta Beyerly. Other than their brief encounter at Claridge's on Wednesday, she had seen nothing of her friend, but whenever chance had taken her to the parks, she had seen the massed green-purple-and-white colors of the suffragists demonstrating before the palace or the Horse Guards, and the newspapers were full of accounts of disruptions of Parliament and social events alike.

'We will make them take notice of us!' Josetta had said to her, on more than one occasion. 'And we will make them admit to the nation – to all the nations of the world – what they are doing to women, what they would rather do to women before they'll give a woman the power to speak out.'

Lydia comforted herself with the reflection that at so early an hour as eleven, the full publicity value of a demonstration would be lost: why get yourself dragged away to prison if the newspapers weren't going to be there taking pictures? In any case instead of Josetta, she and Emily encountered the Earl and Countess of Crossford, and with them, Lord Colwich and Cece Armistead.

'It's outrageous!' Lady Crossford's nasal voice pierced the dimness of the orchid pavilion. 'Who does he think Noel is? An adventurer who's marrying you for your money?' Lydia spotted them easily in the sparse crowd: Lord Colwich had inherited both his height and his breadth of shoulder from his mother, and even to Lydia's myopic eye the grouping of her formidable shell-pink form, his 'artistic' green-and-yellow waistcoat, and the bird-of-paradise brightness of Cece's gold-and-tangerine frock were unmistakable.

'Lady Crossford, of course it isn't that—'

'It isn't as if we *needed* your father's money . . .'

In point of fact Lydia was well aware that they actually did. She crossed the pavilion to them, however, and, mindful of Hellice Spills' evaluation of Colwich, maneuvered herself close to Cece and her fiancé. Though it went severely against the grain with her, she nerved herself to put on her spectacles – purportedly to read some very small print on the show catalog – and looked up into the young viscount's face to ask, 'Why on earth would anyone deliberately breed a flower that smelled like that?'

And in spite of the diffuse light within the white cloth walls of the long tent, she saw that the Viscount's pupils were shrunk to pinpricks.

Lydia was so surprised she barely heard his response, which like most of Colwich's theories involved Hindu gods and aeons-deep recesses of pre-human time. She fell back from the main party, watched that tall, stout form as he moved among the tables of fragile Phalaenopsis and gaudy Cattleya.

*Cocaine on top of opium? At eleven in the morning?*

Nothing in his manner suggested opiates. He was talking fast and gesturing more wildly than Lydia had seen him do on other occasions, which did look like cocaine. Still wearing her spectacles, she saw Cece's worried expression as she glanced up at him.

*No wonder poor Ned Seabury says he's changed.* A change dependent on how much of what he'd taken on any given day . . .

*And what kind of dreams is he having, that make him grope for the opium-pipe first thing out of bed?*

Her own dreams last night had left her shaken: passionate kisses in Zahorec's arms, dizzying caresses that alternated with a curious succession of peril-and-rescue episodes involving the dark-haired woman whom he called Ippolyta. *She is holding me prisoner*, he had whispered, clutching her hands through the bars of his cell. *I've been here nearly a year. She'll drink of my blood, nearly unto death, then bring me back, slowly. She'll make me become what she is, a monster, damned . . .*

And Lydia had forced herself to remember, *This is a dream. A lure.*

*Did any of this really happen?*

*Does it matter whether it did or not?*

*She wants me*, he had told her at one point. *She says she loves me . . . Maybe she does. We were lovers; her love was passionate, insane.* He'd closed his eyes in the silvery moonlight – in that particular dream Lydia stood on a convenient snow-covered ledge beneath the window of his cell, clinging to the bars with a hundred feet of rock wall and another hundred feet of cliff-face below her, shivering in her jade-and-lavender silk. (*Why that dress? It's completely unsuited for climbing cliffs in.*)

*She said she loved me from the moment we met . . .*

Through the window Lydia had seen the bite marks on his throat, the blue of his eyes like aquamarine.

Had the woman Ippolyta – presumably, the Master of that particular area of Romania or Bulgaria or wherever it was all taking place – *really* lured him to her castle with threats to kill herself if he married the young lady to whom he'd been engaged? (*Where were the servants during all this?*) Or was that only something he'd told Cece?

Later, in another dream (he'd managed to get out of his cell somehow and meet her in the woods) he held her in his arms, gently bit her throat, tasted her blood, whispered to her, 'Don't be afraid. They lie, who say that we drink our victims dry. We need the blood, but only a taste, a sip. There are those who love the kill, those who revel in death . . . among us as among the living. Oh my beautiful one, I would never harm you . . .'

His hands – on her throat, on her face, on her breasts – were warm, his lips like honey and wine.

*Does he send me these dreams, and then turn his attention to Cece when I turn over or go on to dreaming about dress fittings?* She removed her spectacles and frowned across the pavilion at Cece, exclaiming over Julie Thwaite's new hat, secure in the knowledge that her own bridal ensemble was being made by Worth and boasted seven yards of point-lace train ('So vulgar!' Aunt Isobel had exclaimed over breakfast. 'Nobody wears trains any more!') and diamonds worth five thousand guineas . . . provided her father didn't cancel the whole affair.

*Or is it like a hectograph, and he's sending out identical dreams to the two of us at the same time, with just the names changed? DOES he use my name in the dreams?* She tried to recall. *What a gaffe, if in the midst of rescuing Cece from masked highwaymen in the moonlit snow he accidentally called her 'Lydia' . . .*

'And how is dearest Isobel?' The Countess of Crossford appeared at Lydia's side. 'Better, I trust?'

Lydia was frequently tempted, in her dealings with Lady Crossford, to answer such questions with *I'm sorry, Aunt Isobel was hacked to death by cannibals yesterday in the drawing room*, in the spirit of scientific inquiry. *Would Her Ladyship REALLY respond with, 'That's nice . . . Tell her I was asking after her'?*

But the Countess had already turned from her and leveled her *lorgnon* in her son's direction. 'Tell her I was asking after her . . . Poor lamb, you can see how he feels the insult!' Before a massed bank of Phalaenopsis Colwich turned suddenly upon Cece, snapped something at her with a gesture that threatened violence, then at once seized her hands when she drew back, stammering apologies: *I don't know what came over me . . .*

*Cocaine and opium before breakfast?*

*Passionate dreams that tell you you must do something you know you actually don't want to, like make love to a woman, or buy houses for someone you barely know, or divulge information about your customers' accounts?*

'And then will I be free?' the clerk Rolleston had whispered, desperately, despairingly.

*And then will I be free?*

'At least that *frightful* father of hers will be going back to the Wild West or wherever he's from once the wedding is over. But you know he's going to do everything he can to interfere with their lives! *All expenses over a hundred pounds must be submitted to the trustees* indeed! And as for buying them that miserable little house on Eaton Place, I'm sure Noel would be far happier living in Crossford House with his lordship and myself. He has *no* concept of how to hire servants or run a house, and . . .'

Lydia wondered if, after her meeting with Jamie, she dared make herself late getting back to Halfdene House in order to be at the Metropole again at six, in case the errant Mr Ballard had been lured, pressed, twisted into keeping his rendezvous with the Goddess in Green. *Isobel will murder me . . .*

*Good Heavens, in sixteen years I may need her goodwill when it's time for Miranda's come-out . . .*

Pain closed her throat like a crystal hand.

*Dear God. Dear God, let Miranda be in need of a come-out at seventeen . . .*

'Look!' Emily seized her elbow, pointing through the crowd in ecstasy. 'Oh, look, Lydia, there's the King!'

Jamie wasn't at the Sloane Square pub at five, with or without false whiskers. Nor had the clerk at the Temperance Hotel seen him, when she went there at half-past. She waited as long as she dared at the Metropole, stroking the jointed tail of her little bronze mermaid and wishing that, like Jamie, she could don false whiskers and ghastly mustard-colored tweeds and not have to worry about being descended upon by someone she knew.

'I have ordered the carriage for seven,' Aunt Isobel greeted her when at last she slipped into Halfdene House by a side-door and attempted to get up the stairs unobtrusively. 'Honestly, Lydia, considering the honor Lady May is doing Emily by asking her to be one of Cece's bridesmaids, I would have thought you would have made more of an effort—'

'Letter for you, ma'am.' Ross handed it to her as she started up the stairs.

The envelope was the stationery of the Bank of England. It had been posted at ten that morning.

It was addressed in a hand that was shaky and crooked as a drunkard's, or of a man laboring under illness or pain so great that he could barely form the letters.

But the letters were shaped in the fashion of the sixteenth century.

On Bank stationery within, those same staggering characters spelled out a list of names – Barger, Scrooby, Graves, Barrow – and of money transferred, properties bought, accounts under new names arranged.

With the same sense of sudden clarity she got when putting on her spectacles, Lydia suddenly understood.

Understood how Noel Wredemere had been induced to propose to Cece Armistead. Understood why Noel had turned from the friend he loved to a girl he scarcely knew with such blithe disregard. Understood why Damien Zahorec had no need of so wealthy a patron as Titus Armistead, and what he planned for Cece.

Understood everything.

And her heart turned to ice in her breast.

# TWENTY-ONE

*N*ests of the Undead haunted the unbroken forests of Germany and Gaul ere the coming of the Romans to the North. Among the Nervi and Atrebates they were worshipped as gods; among the Arverni and Ubii, special priests existed to protect against them, and in no case would travelers venture into the woods alone after dark. The first Master to dwell in Paris was Chramnesid, who preyed principally on travelers. He created Rigunth and Margareta to dwell with him in Paris and Godomar and Grimald who remained in the forests. Grimald later became a bandit-chief on the road between Paris and Bruges. Margareta became Master of Paris after Chramnesid's destruction and was in the days of the great siege of Paris by the Northmen succeeded by Egles . . .*

True or not true?

Asher turned the page.

Did it matter?

*The blood of cats, mixed with the distilled essence of the garlic root and the crushed fruits of the wood laurel will free the* ancelot (a late Latin word meaning 'little servant', presumably fledgling) *from his master's will. Yet to continue such potion over time brings madness.*

Why insert that caution, if the book – or even that particular formula – was a trap?

And how did it accord with the statement, elsewhere in the book, that the hold of the Master over the fledgling was absolute?

Or the accounts in both the Prague and the Paris printings, of fledglings who had indeed (in some fashion unspecified) defied their masters and set up rival nests?

*There weren't many cities of any size in Europe in 1360.* Asher scratched gingerly where the spirit-gum stung beneath his false whiskers. Paris might have held fifty thousand people, London perhaps half so many. Far easier for a predator – or a small circle of predators – to hide in, than in a countryside whose few inhabitants knew one another's faces from birth.

The cities mentioned in both texts were the cities that had existed in 1360. Nothing of towns like Amsterdam and St Petersburg, which had grown up since.

Voices in the shop below. A woman's soft alto, with the sing-song inflection of an Anglo-Indian, asked for John Ogilvy's 1656 translation of the *Iliad*: 'Pope's is all Pope, don't you know, not Homer in the least . . .'

He'd always had the impression that Artemus Sophister was a sort of hermit who spent most of his time brooding over his mountains of squalid arcana alone. Yet on and off, for most of the afternoon, he'd heard the distant tinkle of the shop bell, followed by requests for Munster's *Cosmographia*, or early editions of Donne.

The angle of the sunlight across the jumble of books, fragments of books, dirty plates and crumpled newspapers told him that it was approaching time to make his way to the Bag o' Nails, to meet Lydia for tea.

He glanced at his notes. Lydia would certainly pay a hundred and ninety pounds for the Prague printing, once Sophister had gone through the necessary legalities of returning the initial payment to Zahorec's last known address. *I'd better start tracking down the other known editions as well.*

*Who set this type? Who arranged these paragraphs?* His fingers traced the woodcuts of Paris, the purported portrait of Vladislas, Master of Prague in the days of Charles IV (though the style of the woodcuts wasn't that of the fourteenth century, but of the late seventeenth when the book was printed). *What text did they work from? Who did the translation?* The Czech-riddled Latin was nothing that a Spanish student would have written in 1370.

The Paris printing had a completely different explanation for the origins of the vampire, putting them first in *the haunted valleys of the Land of Egypt, whence these dark spirits spread, first with the exodus of the Hebrew in the days of the Pharaoh Rameses, later with the conquests of the land by the Assyrians, then the Greeks and Romans . . .*

A long passage detailed the foundations and anecdotes of the nest which had existed in Rome under the Caesars, in terms suspiciously reminiscent of *The Last Days of Pompeii*. And yet . . . Elsewhere in the Paris printing he found passages in what was definitely fifteenth-century Latin, listing the masters of Bruges and Venice:

*The master vampire most often chooses fledglings who have something he wants: property, or riches, or a skill which he seeks to use for his own protection or aggrandizement. Above all else he seeks those whose hearts are strong enough to hold to life through death, and whose wills can encompass the deaths of the innocent rather than surrender the shadow of life which is all that remains to them.*

This wasn't in the older book.

*It is the custom of many masters to keep these fledglings* (and here he used the much older Latin *pullae,* 'chicks') *ignorant of practices and abilities which grow in the Undead with time and with the consumption of human lives, lest their children grow strong and turn against them. Yet when the masters perish, through mischance or the outrage of men, then the fledglings are left without this knowledge, and so cannot pass it in turn to their own unholy get.*

*So comes it that I, Johanot of Valladolid, sinner and slave, come to write all that I have learned from the masters of the Undead, that this terrible knowledge, rather than that it be preserved only among these ancient minds without souls, shall come into the hands of the men who shall fight against them in the name of the Light which illumines the deeps of Time.*

Asher was still staring, startled, at this paragraph – the first and only reference he'd encountered to the author in either of the texts, let alone the testimony of the Spaniard himself – when he heard voices raised in the shop downstairs.

Shouting.

'I tell you there's no one here . . .'

*Damn it.*

Asher shoved both volumes into one of the half-dozen rucksacks that lay about in the mess, hooked the straps over his shoulder, grabbed his knobby old stick and made for the window. The stairway to the attic would carry the sound of his footsteps. A drainpipe ran a few feet to the left of the window – Asher never entered a building without checking all possible exits – and a swift scramble took him to the top. Keeping low, he went over the roofs, two houses north toward Eagle Street, his shoes slipping on wet moss and soot, then descended another drainpipe to a yard filled with the nameless clutter of a second-hand shop: broken boxes, rusted bicycles, a tangle of brass bedsteads and a wilderness of stray cats.

He climbed over the fence into the mews, cursing himself for having left his motorcycle at the Temperance Hotel. *I can get a cab in Red Lion Square . . .*

A man stepped around the corner, blocking his way. Asher turned in time to see a second man behind him, near the narrow gate that led back into Sophister's yard.

'Mr Armistead wants to see you.' The first man's flat accent reminded Asher sharply of the poor thug Wirt. Asher guessed he was armed, but not about to use a weapon in the middle of London.

'So your friend Wirt told me,' he returned, in the shrill and slightly querulous tones of a man twenty years his senior. He slumped unobtrusively, peering at the men sidelong through his phoney spectacles and leaning on his stick. 'I'd like to see him, too, but not with a lot of tame banditti standing around. Is he here?'

'He's in the car, yes.'

'Good,' said Asher. 'He can drive to Lincoln's Inn Fields and meet me by the north-east corner of the park. There are plenty of places there to sit.'

The man smiled a little. 'Anybody'd think you had something on your conscience, old timer.'

'I'm only worried about what might be on yours, young man. Or your employer's.' He turned, and with the slightly wobbly-legged gait of senescence, stumped off in the direction of the Inns of Court.

The shorter thug moved to stop him; the taller one waved him off. 'Go tell the boss that's where we're headed, Dougie. But honest,' he added, falling into step with Asher as he turned the corner into Eagle Street, 'all the boss wants is to talk to you.'

'Hmph. So your friend told me.' Asher dropped the stick, and under cover of retrieving it – the bigger thug simply stepped back from him, as if expecting a trick of some kind – pulled his gloves from his jacket pocket and put them on, fussily, as if particular about the dirt rather than hiding the fact that his hands were twenty years younger than his face or hair or voice.

'What happened to Wirt?'

'Since I object to being threatened, I eluded him in the dark. Last I saw him, he was standing out in the middle of the Erith marshes blaspheming his Creator's name and all his works.'

Evidently his reading of Wirt's character was close enough to the truth to convince his new companion: the man's expression changed from suspicion to disgust, and he shrugged. 'Bastard spent too much time chasin' Wobblies,' he grunted. 'Thinks the only way of dealin' with people is breaking heads. I told him a dozen times, that act won't play in England.' He nodded at Asher's rucksack. 'Them the books the boss has been after?'

'Not unless he's in quest of Donne's prose *Aeneid* and a French translation of Honorius of Autun's *Elucidarium.*'

A glib, detailed, and immediate answer, Asher had found, was often mistaken for truth. After dealing with the German Auswärtiges Amt and the Russian Third Section, lying to an American plug-ugly was like playing peek-a-boo with a baby. The man laughed. 'Crazy, if you ask me . . . But he's the boss.'

A big closed Daimler glided past them on their way along Red Lion Street. Only the shadow of a man was visible in its back seat. The vehicle waited for them in front of Lincoln's Inn, a tall man beside it, square, powerful, and ugly in a highly American suit. The man called Dougie stood beside him, with another of the same type, both smoking cheap cigars.

Asher regarded them without offering his hand to shake. 'Mr Armistead? Mr Wirt told me you wanted to talk to me.'

'You know what happened to him?'

'If there's any truth in the Bible, I assume God struck him dead with lightning, but that may be only wishful thinking on my part.'

Those cold brown eyes – small, and set too close together on either side of a nose that had been long ago broken – narrowed as they gauged him, but Blackie Wirt's fate obviously wasn't a point that made much difference to the American.

'Let's take a walk, Mr . . .'

'Wilson,' replied Asher. He turned and stumped away up the nearest path.

Traffic had thickened on Serle Street; with the ending of the day's session at the Inns of Court, robed barristers gestured as they strode the paths beneath the lengthening shadows of the trees. Armistead offered Asher a cigar – far better quality than those smoked by his henchmen – and when Asher refused, lit it up himself.

'Wirt tell you why I wanted to see you?'

'He seemed to think I'd be willing to help you find someone.'

'Are you?'

'No,' said Asher. 'I think you're a damned fool.'

'Because I believe these creatures exist? Or because I want to hire one?'

Asher stopped, faced him on the graveled path. 'Is that why you came to Europe? To find a vampire?'

'I didn't believe in them when I came over.' The mine owner blew a cloud of smoke. 'Thought they were a lot of hooey. Indians at the Peru mine talked some hogwash about 'em. My wife's grandma swore they'd lived in the mountains behind Lima back in Spanish days. But Indians think elves live in the forest and believe their lamas can talk to them. This's the twentieth century – well, it was still the nineteenth, then. But since I've been in Europe, I've read stuff that's changed my mind.'

Still those cold little brown eyes studied his face. Looking for something.

He didn't, Asher noted, ask him how he'd come by the knowledge that Armistead assumed he had.

'You ever heard of them in the United States?'

Armistead shook his head. 'I wasn't looking, then. But it's a big ocean. Even your fastest liner takes four days to cross it. That's a lot of running water. Running water *does* bug 'em, doesn't it? I'd hate to get back there and find they all live here.'

'And I should hate for you to get back there with your new employee and spread the curse of these things to two entire continents that have been free of them hitherto.'

'Oh, I wouldn't have any of that. No making more vampires. The man works for me, he'll do what I say.'

'Oh, will he?' retorted Asher. 'And what exactly will you say? *You kill whoever I tell you to and I'll hide you from the police?* Because if you don't think the police are going to take notice when the heads of every union that objects to fourteen-hour shifts and slave wages disappears, I suspect you're underestimating even their limited intelligence.'

'For one thing –' the American's grin was worse than his scowls – 'it ain't possible to underestimate the so-called intelligence of the American cop. And for another . . . even if they figured it out, you think they'd *care*? As long as they can't pin it on *me* – and I'm told these vampires can make sure it don't get pinned on *them* – I'm happy, the cops are happy, and I'll see to it the spooks are happy, too. Why not take orders from me? If you're gettin' your garters in a twist about this thing gettin' out of hand, I can promise you, buddy, it won't. Why should it? Anything they need, I'll give 'em and welcome.'

He took the cigar from his mouth, gestured with it. 'People who work for me don't lose by it, Mr Wilson. Ask anybody in the United States Senate.'

*Freedom*, Grippen had sneered. *They couldn't pick it out of a basket of apples . . .*

'We're not talking about a person.' Asher's voice lowered, as the shadows lengthened across the leafy walks and the angle of the sun shifted in the gothic windows of the Great Hall. 'We're talking about a blood-drinking corpse inhabited by the spirit of someone who thinks it's perfectly all right to kill the innocent in order to prolong his own life.'

'It ain't the innocent I'm asking him to kill. Just Wobblies and Communists who'd as soon chuck a bomb at you as look at you, the lazy sons-of-bitches. Now, do you know such a person, or don't you?'

'If I did –' Asher's gaze held Armistead's – 'is that really someone you want to know? Someone you want to bring in contact with your daughter?'

Sudden fury blazed in the cold eyes. 'He ain't gonna know I *have* a daughter.' For a moment Asher had the impression the American would strike him for speaking of Cece. 'She'll be staying here in England—'

'He'll know. They do.'

'And what do you know about it, old man?'

'I know them, Armistead. I've killed them, I've played cards with them, I've read their poetry and had them drink my blood. Don't let one of them into any aspect of your life or you will be the sorriest man on the face of this planet. And so will every member of your family.'

He turned away. Armistead caught his arm with a rage that was almost desperate. Asher had to remind himself that he was a gray-haired and slightly hobbling old man, and only turned back to glare at the American with an old man's futile anger.

'You let me be the judge of what's best for me and my family.

Just give me a name, and an address.' From his pocket with his free hand Armistead took a slim packet of banknotes, and slipped them into Asher's breast pocket. 'Where'd you meet them?' He'd collected himself again under a mask of calm, but Asher could hear the tension in that grating voice. 'They really what the book says?'

'More.' Asher wrenched his arm with deliberate lack of expertise out of the other man's grip. He took Armistead's hand in his and slapped the currency back into the gloved palm. 'Did you get to the part where it talks about how they'll offer you whatever you most desire, if *you* work for *them* and not the other way around? How they'll appear to you to be whatever you most trust? How they'll kill you – and your family – sooner than risk anyone guessing who and what they are?'

'I got that part from your pal Millward.' He held out the money to him again between two fingers of his hand. 'Who don't look to be doin' much better than you are for cash, pal. And you leave my family out of it. All I'm askin' for is a name, not a sermon. Believe me, I'll set it all up. If I can fix Standard Oil and the Chicago police force, I can fix a couple of spooks. I know what I'm doin'.'

'You haven't the faintest idea.' And turning, Asher strode off along Newman Row as the chapel clock sounded five.

Enough time, he thought, to meet Lydia at the fallback rendezvous in Finsbury Square. He was looking around for a cab when a four-wheeler drew up beside him. The door opened and Ned Seabury sprang out. 'Mr Barton, I've been—'

He stammered to a halt, stared at Asher disbelievingly. '*Professor Asher?*'

*DAMN it!*

Asher put on his most cantankerous expression and glared at him. 'Never heard of either of 'em, young man, but—'

Someone was behind him and he realized too late it was a trap. He started to turn when a hand grabbed him from behind and a rag was clapped over his nose and mouth, and he smelled chloroform as Seabury and another man (*it has to be Millward*) shoved him into the cab as his brain closed down into darkness.

# TWENTY-TWO

Dinner was one of those interminable affairs that began with two kinds of soup and proceeded to eleven courses thereafter. Lydia, the mere chaperone of one of Cece Armistead's twelve bridesmaids, was relegated to a seat two-thirds of the way down Wycliffe House's dining room, next to Terence Winterson, who could talk of little but what a smashing girl Emily was and how difficult it was to purchase decent haberdashery outside of London.

Around Winterson's shoulder, Lydia glimpsed Cece, ablaze in her diamond collar, seated blushingly across from the black-and-white block of Lord Colwich. He seemed as restless as he had that morning at the flower show, his gestures wide and slightly jerky . . . *More cocaine?*

Her glance went to the dove-colored midsummer twilight beyond the windows.

Colwich's voice drifted down to her, rather too loudly expanding upon the beauties of the family grouse moor at Kynnoch to Seaton Wycliffe – or at least Lydia assumed that was Lady May's cousin, since he was in about the right place for him, and was of about the correct shape and size. Without her spectacles, it was impossible to tell who was who up at that end of the table. In any case, Colwich didn't seem even to notice the absence of Ned Seabury.

The man who, of all others, he would have wished at his wedding.

Lydia wondered, if she should go up to him now and look into those blue eyes, what would she see?

But she didn't dare.

It was enough to know he was here, and would be going to the ballet afterwards with the family party.

She took a deep breath. Jamie, she reflected, would almost certainly take her to task about her plans for the rest of the evening . . . *But if Jamie wanted to order me to go back to the hotel once dinner is done, he could have taken more trouble to come to the rendezvous this afternoon.*

Across the table, the Honorable Reggie Wredemere elaborated

in excruciating detail how the settlement of Cece Armistead's three million dollars had been finally worked out between her father's lawyers and those of the Honorable Reggie's uncle the Earl. ('And a damned insult it was, too! If I were Noel I'd have torn the thing up and thrown it in his face!')

'Well, it's a bit late for him to back out now, isn't it?' crooned Valentina, aglitter with the diamonds that had belonged to Lydia's mother. 'Somebody's got to pay for the redecorations Noel's had done to that underground meditation chapel of his . . .'

*St Mary Westbourne is in the next street*, Lydia remembered, her heart beginning to pound. *And Dallaby House is only three streets from here. Once it gets fully dark . . .*

She set down her oyster-fork, her hands trembling too badly to wield the delicate little instrument. She wondered if Ysidro would be hunting tonight, and how she might reach him.

She closed her eyes briefly, and behind the lids seemed to see those crooked, staggering characters, spelling out all that she had asked to know about Lionel Grippen's lairs.

*Miranda . . .*

She had consulted Uncle Richard's *Ordnance Survey of Great Britain* at Halfdene House. Of Grippen's properties, only one – a farm called Tufton, a few miles beyond St Albans – lay close enough to a railway line that Nan Wellit would have heard the trains go by.

The footman replaced her oysters Florentine with *timbale du jambon farcie*; Terence Winterson asked her, What did Lady Halfdene think of his suit? He thought if he could not marry Emily he would very likely die.

Lydia poked once or twice at her timbale, and tried to formulate a reply. She'd wired the information about Tufton Farm to James at Oxford, not knowing where else to send it. The thought of what she proposed to do tonight terrified her (*but it's almost perfectly safe this early, with everyone at the ballet*), but her sense of urgency – of not knowing how much time she had left before something frightful happened to Miranda and Nan – pressed on her like a nightmare.

*Poor Noel.*

*And poor Ned.*

At eight-thirty, when the coaches came to the door to transport everyone to the ballet, Lydia found herself sharing – as she'd hoped – with Julia Thwaite, Terence Winterson, Lady Priscilla Sidford (sixteen, and in awe of Emily's Worth gown), Lady Priss's aunt Vorena, and Emily. The presence of Aunt Vorena relieved Lydia of any sense of guilt (*though Aunt Isobel will still kill me if I don't make it to the ballet by the end . . .*) when, halfway to Leicester Square, she exclaimed, 'Oh, curse! My bracelet – I left it in the downstairs washroom at Wycliffe! I know I did . . .'

Aunt Vorena's placid retort – 'Surely Lady May's footmen will put it aside' – was nearly drowned in the shrill cries of the three younger ladies of the party.

'I won't feel right if something should happen.' Lydia turned on her seat, and rapped at the window of the coach. 'Curtis, I'm *devastated*, but could you stop a moment and let me out? I must take a cab back to the house—'

'Mrs Asher!' cried Aunt Vorena. 'You'll never—'

'Now, it's perfectly respectable. Yes, Curtis, I mean it, please stop . . .'

'It's all right, Mrs Sidford,' soothed Winterson, 'I'll be happy to escort Mrs Asher . . .'

After ten minutes of argument, Lydia was on the pavement in her gold-and-turquoise silk, while young Mr Winterson hailed a jarvey from the press now jamming Piccadilly. 'I'm quite all right,' she assured him. 'Honestly—'

'It would be no trouble at all—'

'Emily would never forgive me if you missed the ballet.' Lydia gathered the silken billows of her coat and climbed into the cab. 'Go along now . . . I'll be at the theater in just twenty minutes . . .'

As soon as the Sidford carriage worked its way back into the flow of traffic, Lydia turned to slide open the driver's window behind her, and called out, 'Excuse me, sir . . . could you make that Walton Street instead?'

Pain woke Asher. Seeping cold, lantern glare, the reek of gin and sewage almost drowning the chloroform still clinging to his mustache.

But mostly pain.

He tried to roll over and gave it up instantly. His legs were trapped; it felt like his right ankle was broken, under the crushing weight of . . .

He blinked at it, barely visible in the clammy darkness. Stone blocks, with traces of ancient carving – Roman?

*What the . . .?*

He twisted a little where he lay on the broken tiles of an old floor, saw pillars holding up a roof that was lost in blackness overhead, and a portion of what had been a fresco, nearly obliterated with time and damp. A dark lantern burned six feet from where he lay.

The skin of his face stung, where someone had ripped away the concealing plumage of false whiskers. The fake eyeglasses were gone, too. His shirt collar was open, as were the cuffs of his sleeves. The silver chains had been taken.

'Millward!' he shouted. 'Millward, God damn you!'

'No, Professor Asher.' Osric Millward stepped through a low door in the wall to his right. 'God damn *you*.' He had a rifle in one hand, an American Winchester. His hawk-like face set like stone. Movement to his left caught Asher's eye. Seabury and another man – scarcely a boy, in a plum-colored Eton jacket, grim but visibly scared – stepped from the ruins of what had been another doorway.

*The boy must have been driving the cab.*

He knew exactly where he was. The Roman merchants' house that survived beneath the crypts of St Rood in the City.

'I've suspected for a long time that vampires use the living as their agents,' said Millward. 'I know they threaten, coax, bribe . . . They can command the mad, as they command wild beasts. They can bribe the venal, who don't know and don't want to know why their employers want what they want. They can seduce women –' he shrugged dismissively – 'and cow the weak, the degenerate, the superstitious: Lascars and Italians and Negroes. But for a true man, a white man in command of his faculties, to serve them, knowing what they are – faugh!'

Shame scorched Asher despite his fury.

'And for a long time I've known that this is the only way to catch them.' Millward's deep voice echoed among the broken columns, the wet darkness smelling of sewage and rats. 'Underground, where they hide – but among the streams and hidden rivers which will blunt their perceptions, limit their movements.' He slapped his rifle. 'I can hit a moving target by lantern-light at a distance of a hundred feet. So can Ned, and Roddy there. But from the first I knew we needed living bait. I think a man who'd take money to lead Armistead to vampires is an appropriate choice – and I can't say I was shocked to learn it was you.'

'It would have been appropriate,' said Asher slowly, 'had my dealings with the London nest been prompted by greed, or love of power, rather than duress.'

'What duress?' demanded Seabury shrilly. 'When Mrs Asher spoke of your "dealings" with the Undead, it sounded a great deal more like the understanding that comes from collaboration.'

'That's because you weren't paying attention. All that concerned you was to rescue your friend Noel from the clutches of Cece Armistead and her vampire lover – not to find out how deep Noel's involvement with that lover might be.'

'That's a—'

'If Mrs Asher wasn't frank with your assistant about the threat the Master of London is holding over our heads –' Asher turned back to Millward – 'it was because she suspected he'd do exactly what he did do: renege on his sworn word and tell you everything.'

'And why not?' retorted Millward haughtily. 'I know what the fresh bite on your arm means. Had your dealings with the Undead been those of an honest man, you would have taken me into partnership from the beginning. Instead you go straight to that poisonous American thug, Armistead, and give him what he seeks: a means to introduce the curse of these vile things to a new continent – two new continents! – which have never known the fear of the dark hours . . .'

'How do you know that?' Asher tried to shift his left leg beneath the stones, but the pain in his right stopped him, gasping, from even the attempt. 'How do you know there aren't vampires in every American city already, who don't need to go to work for Armistead any more than Cece's vampire lover does? I told Armistead to have nothing to do with the Undead; that his plan was a stupid one – something he didn't want to hear. I refrained from telling him that both his daughter and his prospective son-in-law were working for a vampire, possibly under duress, though it didn't sound like it to me any more than ours did to Seabury—'

Seabury reached him in three strides. 'You know nothing about it! Noel would never—'

'Check his bank account.'

The younger man lashed out with a vicious kick, which Asher dodged while he hooked Seabury's other leg from under him.

Seabury flipped backward and Asher caught his rifle as he fell, tried to twist to cover Millward and gasped in shock at the agony in his trapped leg. Young Roddy sprang forward, jerked the weapon from Asher's weakened grip and kicked him. Millward fired – Asher heard the shrill crack as the bullet ricocheted off the tile of the floor yards away – and Roddy scrambled back, tripping over Seabury. The two of them retreated in haste, leaving Asher half-unconscious on the broken floor.

He heard Millward say, 'It's eight o'clock.'

'If Noel gave money to the vampire it's because that bitch made him . . .'

'We'll talk about it later, Ned. The Fleet's just beyond that wall.'

Asher didn't bother opening his eyes. He knew where the ancient river ran in its bricked-in bed.

'So they'll be coming from the opposite way. Be ready for them.'

*And if you think a silver bullet is going to stop Lionel Grippen – or Damien Zahorec – you're in for a nasty surprise.* Asher debated about warning them but couldn't speak, almost nauseated from the pain in his leg and ribs and head.

*Lydia*, he thought. *Lydia's going to come in from her ballet outing with Armistead and the clerk will tell her I haven't been in. Sophister isn't on the 'phone . . . Will she go to the shop? Contact Ysidro? Not that anyone could find the vampire at will . . .*

Underground, Ysidro wouldn't be able to locate him.

The silence deepened, save for the hiss of the lamp fuel as it burned, and the occasional, far-off vibration of the Underground train.

*Damn all vampire hunters.*


# TWENTY-THREE

The lock on the side door of St Mary's Westbourne was so old – and so large – that Lydia almost felt she could have stuck her finger into it to move the levers, never mind the picklocks Jamie had taught her to use. She'd brought a candle and matches in her very small gold-beaded reticule, and the thread of light slipped eerily across the dark balusters of the altar rail, the chaste columns flanking the nave. Lydia found the door to the crypt easily, and descended, hand pressed to the glass-smooth stone of the central column.

As Ysidro had said, there was a second crypt beneath the first, accessed through a half-forgotten door behind the coal-hole: chillingly damp, circular and barely a dozen feet across. *We must be right on top of the old river . . .*

Even before she reached the bottom of the steps, she guessed it would contain a coffin.

And it did.

Her first thought was to wonder how the workmen had managed to get it down those stairs.

Her second, to wonder if it was empty.

It stood on a stone pedestal in the middle of the little room, lid off. (*If he's in it he'll have seen my lantern light and it's too late for me to run anyway . . . Oh, good. Empty.*)

*Surely if one is going to sleep in a coffin all day one would purchase a nice new one?*

A second glance showed her – nearly hidden in the gloom – a ruinous niche leading off the crypt, containing a second dismantled tomb. *Of course. He wants something that one would expect to find under an old church, in case someone came looking.*

*Turn around,* she thought. *Go back RIGHT NOW.*

But she remembered the crooked handwriting of the note she'd received. *Am I right?*

*Am I right about where he's been hiding? HOW he's been hiding?*

There was, as she'd guessed there would be, a second door to the sub-crypt, which led to a short flight of (newly mended) steps, and thence to what had to be the sub-cellar of Dallaby House. A workbench glinted with small jars, a wooden pharmacist's cabinet replete with tiny drawers. She unscrewed the cap of one big jar and made a face at the reek of ammonia. Others held only the faded pungency of crushed herbs. Another large jar was labeled silver chloride. Others were honey, gold dust, laudanum.

On a shelf above the workbench lay a yellowed, ragged bundle of pages, stripped of their cover and held together with ribbons like a Christmas present. Lydia held her candle close, but guessed what she'd see printed on the topmost soiled page, and she was right.

*Libro Tenebrarum Gente*

(Jamie had warned her about medieval Latin making free with word-order.)

*de Iohann de Vallisoletos*
*Antwerp 1680*

It looked thinner than Jamie's description and, recalling some of the treasures of her scholarly friend Anne Gresholm's library, Lydia lifted it gently and looked at the end. The stiff black-letter columns simply ran down to the bottom of the page.

The book was incomplete.

*He's trying to collate it. Like Jamie said about all those copies of Shakespeare's First Folio, to compare information in this copy with others, to find the truth.*

Gladder than ever that she'd taken the precaution of daubing herself with Jicky perfume in the cab, she opened a further door with infinite care. This one was new, and the stairway recently mended. The reek of opium reached her halfway up. *Meditation chapel indeed! How much is he smoking, for it to smell so strong this many hours after he's left?*

*Make this quick. If you stay in that room more than a few minutes you'll be drunk as a wheelbarrow just from breathing the air.*

The door at the top was elaborate, new masonry bright against the darkened stones of the old. The room beyond it had probably been a boot hole or a lamp room, now festooned with hangings of black and gold silk that must have cost Titus Armistead a pretty penny. A lamp wrought of a pierced ostrich egg sprinkled those glimmering tapestries with soft pink light. An ebony divan of fantastic shape, a carved ebony armoire, and a low ebony table crowded with empty absinthe bottles, laudanum bottles, open jars and boxes of gluey brown pastilles that smelled of opium and sugar. A pipe, an opium lamp, and an ivory dish of the brown opium pills lay among the mess.

And on the divan, snoring in a profound stupor, lay Noel Wredemere, Lord Colwich.

*But he's at the ballet . . .*

The stylish pumps he'd worn at the Flower Show that morning lay beside a chair. The dark mud that Lydia recalled from her own shoes still adhered to the soles. He was still in evening dress from dinner, and the clothes he'd worn that morning were draped over the chair: striped trousers, gray coat, that refulgent yellow-and-green vest. Lamplight caught something in the half-open door of the wardrobe. An identical vest, tailored for a slimmer man. On the wardrobe's floor, identical shoes, made for a narrower foot.

Lydia opened the door wider, held the candle high.

The wardrobe was full of sets of clothing, one half made for Noel Wredemere's chubby teddy-bear stature . . . and the other, not.

For a moment she was back at Ysidro's side in the upstairs hallway of Wycliffe House, facing Hellie Spills in the backstairs doorway . . .

'Get your hands up,' said Cece's voice behind her. 'Or I'll shoot.'

Lydia turned, and raised her hands.

Sure enough, Cece had a gun, a big American revolver. Lydia wondered if it was her father's, or if it belonged to one of his 'boys'.

Lydia straightened her spectacles. 'Do you honestly think you can get away with it?'

'There's nobody in the house—'

'I don't mean me; I mean Damien drugging himself awake and stepping in and controlling poor Noel like a hand-puppet during the daytimes.'

The girl looked down at her fiancé's snoring form with undisguised contempt. 'Are you kidding? It's exactly what Noel's always wanted out of life: someone to make all his decisions for him while he drowns his brain in a vat of dope. He's happier than he's ever been in his life.'

'You've only known him five months,' Lydia pointed out. 'But it's going to kill him . . .'

'He won't care.' She shrugged.

'And probably long before that happens, the elixir Damien is using to stay awake during the daytimes to control him will drive Damien mad.'

The girl's eyes flared with alarm, then quickly narrowed. 'No, it won't.'

'Did he tell you that?' Lydia went to sit on the edge of the divan, putting the snoring Noel in the line of Cece's fire. *What a horrible thing to do*, she thought – Cece looked so wrought up by her role as Tough Jane that she might shoot anyway – *but settlement or no settlement, with the wedding only a month away, she – and Damien – won't have any substitute plan for a dead suitor.* 'How many versions of the *Book of the Kindred* have you read? Most of them warn against that particular formula.'

James had actually only found one that did so, but Cece's eyes shifted as she struggled to hold her ground. 'How did you guess?' she countered at last, and Lydia raised her eyebrows and looked surprised.

'I didn't guess,' she lied blandly. 'Every printing of the book gives the technique by which a vampire can control the actions of a sleepwalker, though the stuff they have to drink to stay awake and do it is sometimes different.'

It was a safe assertion. At a guess this girl knew no more French than *the pen of the gardener's aunt* and no Latin at all. 'All of them say the sleepwalker has to be pretty much drugged senseless, though that 1637 Prague edition says that vampires can enter into the minds of the mad as well. I suppose drugged – or falling-down drunk – is easier to come by than schizophrenia.'

The haggard thinness of that pitiful Bank of England clerk returned to her, staring at her across the white-draped tables of the Café Metropole. The wandering, jagged letters on the Bank of England stationery. Opium had beyond a doubt opened that poor man's dreams to Don Simon's whispering, and when he'd fought against them – successfully – it had probably taken very little for Simon to get him to waken from his dreams towards morning and light up another pipe – or two, or three . . .

Enough to let Simon step into his mind, like a sober party-goer taking over the reins when the coachman proved too drunk to find his way home. And drive it all the way to the Bank of England. Even as, more and more frequently, Damien Zahorec had been tooling Noel around London like a rented gig.

When he wasn't convincing people, after the sun went down, that he simply *was* Noel . . .

'That's where all those legends come from,' she went on chattily, 'about this woman or that welcoming a vampire into her chamber under the impression that it's her husband. Or else it's just the vampire using that illusion that they do – that deception that keeps people from seeing their teeth and claws, or what their faces really look like . . . I don't suppose it was very difficult for Damien to get Noel to smoke himself silly in the hours before sunrise, then use drugs to keep himself awake into the daytime while he walked about in Noel's body, talked in Noel's voice. No wonder poor Ned thought Noel had changed.' She brushed gently at the dark lock of hair that fell over the young man's forehead. 'Poor Noel . . .'

*And that*, she thought, *is why Damien Zahorec chose him.* They were of a height, with the same coloring, almost the same build . . .

And of a social position that would make the substitution worthwhile.

Certainly it was by his build and outline and coloring that she'd identified him, at Wycliffe House and in company after dark when she hadn't been wearing her spectacles. She'd simply had the impression that this *was* Noel Wredemere, Viscount Colwich. People who had no experience with the illusory powers of a really skilful vampire wouldn't even be looking for the differences. They simply wouldn't notice that they weren't noticing what 'Colwich' looked like.

*Like me and Simon when we met Hellice Spills in the hallway. At night, Noel simply gets dispatched to his 'meditation chamber' and his pipe, and Damien plays games with illusion . . .*

'We're not going to hurt him,' Cece protested, her voice shrill. 'He's perfectly happy. And Damien's situation is desperate. He had to escape, had to get away . . .'

'From the war?'

The girl looked nonplussed. *Oh, come ON!* thought Lydia. *Even I know about the war in the Balkans!*

'No – I mean, yes . . . I mean, I suppose the war had something to do with it.' Cece stammered, like a schoolchild thrown off her stride in the midst of a recitation. Then her eyes flooded with tears, frantic that Lydia should understand. 'But it's worse than that! *She's* after him. The woman – the devil – who enslaved him, who forced him into being what he is! She held him prisoner, kept him in the dungeon of her castle for a year, trying to break his spirit . . . After she forced him to become a vampire, she made him bring her victims, made him hunt with her . . . Forced him into the state from which he now seeks redemption—'

'*Redemption?*' Lydia had been watching Cece's gun hand, gauging the distance between them, the size of the tiny room . . . and the time she had before Damien Zahorec himself appeared. *When I didn't turn up at the ballet he must have gone to see if I was investigating Wycliffe House, and sent her here . . .*

But at the word *redemption* she blinked, astonished at the degree of naivety. 'Is *that* what you think he wants your father's books for?'

The dim light flashed in Cece's diamonds as she drew herself up. 'It *is* what he seeks! It's in one of the books – he doesn't know which. How to return to being a living man. How to recover his soul. He has part of one book; he knows there are others. I'm the only one who can help him . . .'

'Which is why he started appearing to you in your dreams, back in Florence,' said Lydia gently. 'Because your father had the books. But what he wants isn't redemption. Just how to escape from Ippolyta, the master vampire who holds power over him. And how to obtain power of his own over the vampires of London.'

'You know about Ippolyta?' Her surprise would have been comical, if the entire situation weren't soaked in blood, and drugs, and madness, and death.

If Miranda's life – and Nan's, and Noel's, and Cece's, and Lydia's own – didn't hang in precarious balance.

*Here we go . . .*

In her kindest voice, Lydia asked, 'Did you think you were the only one he sent those dreams to?'

And in the split-second of disillusioned shock – of immobilized grief at the fissuring of everything she'd assumed was going on, and before outrage and denial and murderous reaction could set in – Lydia, who had hooked her foot around the pedestal of Noel's laden bedside table, shot it at her with all of her strength and at the same instant ducked sideways, in case Cece fired at her after all.

Cece didn't. The revolver flew from her hand as she sprawled backwards; Lydia had no idea where it landed, because she launched herself on the younger woman, grabbed her by the hair and one wrist, twisted her arm behind her back. Cece clawed viciously at her but fortunately was still wearing kid opera gloves. The American girl flailed, kicked, screamed curses, but terror gave Lydia focus and strength. She shoved the younger woman headlong into the wardrobe, slammed the door, and turned the key.

Noel hadn't stirred.

*I've got to do this* . . . Lydia straightened her spectacles, looked around for the revolver, which had skidded under the divan, caught it up, checked to make sure the opium lamp hadn't ignited anything . . .

*I'm forgetting something.*

She yanked open the door that led back into Damien's coffin chamber. His pitch-black, windowless crypt of a coffin-chamber . . .

*Candle* . . .

She re-lit it from the hanging lamp, hands trembling so badly she could barely keep it steady.

Inside the wardrobe, Cece was screaming, 'Damien! Damien!'

Lydia ducked through the door into the coffin chamber, gathered up her skirts, fled upwards through the crypts of the old church. *Jamie. He'll be back at the hotel by this time . . .*

She was in Brompton Road by the time she realized what she'd left behind in the hidden room beneath Dallaby House: her handbag.

She hadn't a farthing on her.

*Queen Street is only a few streets away . . . And the dead travel fast . . .*

Knees trembling so badly she felt she'd fall, Lydia walked up Brompton Road towards the park. *There'll be a cab stand near Tattersalls . . .*

What the cabbies thought of her – ashen-faced, shaking in her elaborate silken coat, with her long red hair hanging over her shoulders – she couldn't imagine, but she found one who, after considerable argument, agreed to take her to Finsbury Circus in trade for her earrings. (''Ey, Jack, you think them's really real?' 'Better get some-thin' better'n that for collateral, haw-haw.') The entire journey there, through the worst of the standstill evening traffic, Lydia expected any moment for Damien Zahorec to spring into the cab beside her, to catch her throat in those long, clawed hands . . .

*Jamie . . . Jamie, please be there . . .*

'Oh, hell, ma'am, I can't take your ear-bobs,' protested the driver, when he helped her to the pavement. 'You look like you had a bloody night of it as it is. You just send me the money when you can.'

He shoved a grubby fragment of a feed-bill into her hand, with an address in Brixton scribbled on it in pencil. Before Lydia could answer he led her firmly to the door of the Temperance Hotel and opened it, then returned to his cab and climbed, puffing (he must have weighed well over two hundred pounds), on to the box, and a moment later disappeared into traffic.

The room key was still behind the desk. 'Mr Berkhampstead's not been in,' said the clerk, and it took Lydia a moment to recall that Berkhampstead was the alias under which she'd rented the room. 'No, ma'am, no messages for you.'

Her hand was on the door handle of the room, her key in the lock, when she heard a noise inside. A clack – something falling over . . .

She felt like her very skin rose up all over her body.

*What do I do? Open it? Run screaming down to the lobby?*

She stood for five minutes, listening. (*If it's Zahorec, would I even hear anything?*)

Another clack. *It's the wardrobe door swinging.*

*But I closed the wardrobe.*

She fumbled in the pocket of her coat for Cece Armistead's revolver. *As if that's going to have the slightest effect on a vampire.* She turned the key, thrust the door open with her foot, gun held out before her . . .

Cold breeze from the window billowed her coat around her. Light from the street lamps below showed her the wardrobe open, every drawer of the little desk gaping, contents scattered. Papers like strewn leaves.

*Papers . . .*

*He knew where I was staying because he looked in my handbag. The dead travel fast . . .*

*Particularly when they don't have to argue with cab drivers or sit in traffic jams in Piccadilly Circus . . .*

She set the revolver on the corner of the table, lit the gas.

All the reports of Messrs Teazle and McClennan were flung everywhere. All her own notes, on them and from her interviews with Hellice Spills.

Simon's note on the Bank of England stationery was missing.

The one on whose margin she'd written: *Tufton Farm, St Albans.*

*He knows where Miranda is.*

*He's on his way there now.*

# TWENTY-FOUR

*imon left London in 1911. He didn't make new lairs.*

S    Lydia paid off the cab driver in Thames Street (with a mental note to send five pounds to the Good Samaritan of earlier in the evening), turned into the dark mazes of courts that had, in this neighborhood of the City, survived the 1666 fire.

Even after four years, she remembered the way.

A crumbling Gothic church at the end of a narrow yard. A winding alley, lightless in the river fog.

Her gold-and-turquoise shoes, never made for running and leaping and dodging vampires in, pinched her feet: blisters made and blisters torn. She knew she'd pay for this in the morning, but there hadn't been time to change.

*He knows where Miranda is. That's where he's going.*

The blackened half-timbered house was as she'd first seen it, in the dreary winter of 1909. *Simon, please be here . . .*

On the doorstep she called out, softly, 'Simon?'

It was black as a tomb. She tried the door, with its curiously new locks. Both were fastened. She stepped back, crossed the narrow lane – cobbles slick with the dung of horses and dogs – and looked up at the windows.

Behind the shutters, a thread of candle flame appeared.

'Simon . . .'

For several long minutes she shivered on the doorstep, waiting. Then, with a frightened glance up and down the dark street – though she was virtually certain that the last policeman to come by this way had probably been in Queen Victoria's reign, if not Queen Anne's – she lit her candle, knelt before the door, and started in on the lock with her picks. *I've picked this lock before . . .*

In any case, it was not the police that she feared.

The door-handle clicked. Lydia pulled out the picks, scrambled to her feet as it opened, nearly knocking over her candle.

'Simon!'

The scarred face framed by the long, colorless hair was more like a skull than a man's. 'Forgive me, Mistress.' His voice was barely audible, his touch like frozen bone.

'Simon, what happened?'

He drew her inside, stooped to gather up the candle. 'Did you get the list, Lady? 'Tis years since I tampered with elixirs to prolong wakefulness into the day—'

'He's found where Miranda is,' she interrupted. 'Zahorec. He's gone to get her.'

Stillness. The yellow eyes with their faint pleatings of gray regarded her over the candle flame. 'When?'

'Two hours ago. Jamie's . . . I don't know where he is; he was supposed to meet me this afternoon and didn't. We have to go; we have to go now . . .'

'Upstairs,' said the vampire. 'There's fire there. You're frozen.'

He wore, she saw for the first time, a quilted dressing gown of dark green velvet over a linen nightshirt, and had wrapped a Paisley shawl over that. She remembered him telling her once that when vampires grew old – or when they were hurt or starved, she had also learned – they suffered badly from cold. A little glow of firelight reflected from the upstairs chamber, a room almost completely walled in books. An armchair of much-worn purple velvet stood before that comforting blaze. She recalled it, from her first visit. Don Simon drew up another for her, and she saw him lean on its back as if his very bones hurt.

'Is that what it does to you?' she whispered. 'The elixir?'

''Tis passing off. I'm well.'

He didn't look well.

'Can I get you something . . .?' She stopped herself, blushing.

He cocked a very human eyebrow at her. 'Something to drink? 'Tis kind of you. I misdoubt we shall find a train so late, but you'll need to know for the morrow. There's a Bradshaw's Guide there.' He pointed a skinny forefinger toward the nearest shelf.

'But how . . .?'

She turned with the railway guide in hand, and though she'd been between Don Simon and the door, she now found herself alone.

A few years previously, Asher's old master in Prague, on learning that he was traveling with the Undead, had given him a bracelet with a set of sharp internal teeth, tightened by the turn of a screw.

The old man had warned him against 'that state you are in when you are not thinking of anything in particular. Perhaps you are a little sleepy . . . and off your guard. Pain will usually serve against the vampire . . .'

The best remedy against the vampire, the old man had gone on to say, was distance: the more of it, the better.

Pain served.

The night was interminable. Despite his recollection of Wirt's frightful death, the terror of waiting for Geoff Vauxhill and Penelope and Mrs Raleigh to appear from the darkness exhausted itself quickly. The throbbing pain remained. There was no way to lie, no way to turn himself, that wasn't excruciating. The weight of the stone blocks pinning his leg brought not only pain but the cold giddiness of shock that came and went. When Millward emerged from his place of concealment to refill the reservoir of the lantern – Asher guessed it must be nearly midnight by then – he asked him, 'Do you really think they're not going to know this is a trap?'

The vampire hunter looked so disconcerted that Asher realized, with a kind of weary exasperation, that the thought had never so much as crossed his mind. 'What do you mean?'

'Do you really think they'll see what looks like some drunken prowler down here – fifty feet below the surface of the ground – who got his foot pinned under a collapsing wall . . . What did you use to break the wall down, spanners? Levers? You're lucky the whole arch didn't come down on you. And you think a vampire is going to say, "What a lucky coincidence, just when I was feeling peckish"?'

'Men come down here. Seeking shelter, or ancient treasure . . .'

'Vampires hunt on the surface, you idiot,' said Asher. 'They can't hear through earth much better than we can, or project their thoughts through it. And the running water of the sewers, and the underground rivers, confuses them.'

'And you know that.' He said it as if it were a badge of contempt.

'Yes, I know that. And while I'm asking, just what,' he went on grimly, 'are your plans if one *doesn't* come along before daybreak? Are you going to kill me in cold blood?'

'You deserve it.'

'I deserved it long before I met my first vampire. Are you going to do it? Or get one of your disciples to? Tell him it's right because

I deserve it? Was this what they thought they were signing themselves up for? Not killing vampires, but killing a man in cold blood
because you, personally, on your own suspicions, have decided he
should die? Is that the kind of loyalty you ask of them?'

'Shut up.'

'Good answer,' Asher approved.

And, as the theologist stalked back to the round chamber that,
as Asher recalled, housed a well, Asher called after him, 'What time
is it?'

'Time enough,' retorted Millward. 'We have the night before us.'

Asher focused his attention on the dim blob of reflected lamplight
on the frescoed wall; on the distant rumble of the Underground; on
the pain. *Don't pass out . . .*

He knew how easy it would be.

And he knew, too, that though Geoff Vauxhill, the lovely Penelope,
and that ferret-faced vampire Jerry might not hunt underground,
Damien Zahorec would, for precisely that reason: because the others
wouldn't. Because beneath the earth, Grippen couldn't sense his
kills.

*The Undead cannot pass over running water*, Johanot of Valladolid
had written (or someone had written, purporting to be him).

*Even as the waters, which were the first created substances from
the hand of God, will reject the body of a witch when she is cast
into them, so will they reject the vampire, to the extent that he stands
helpless before a bridge, save at the moment of midnight, or at the
turning of the tide. Thus a man pursued by such a creature has but
to reach a river or a stream, or run into the fringe of the ocean, to
shake such pursuit . . .*

*Unless of course the vampire is in a carriage or a motor car,*
Asher reflected. *Driven by someone else.*

*Or has convinced some hapless mortal to load his coffin on to a
train or a trans-Atlantic steamer for him.*

He felt cold through to his marrow.

'Millward,' he called out after a time.

'Another word and I'll chloroform you again.'

'Vampires have a very good sense of smell. They hunt by making
you sleepy, or inattentive. They're beside you before you know it.'

No reply came from the darkness. *Wait until sunrise*, Asher told
himself, and prayed the man wasn't sufficiently obsessed – sufficiently

crazy – to kill him and then go after Lydia. He couldn't see Ned Seabury assenting, deeply as he revered his master. But until the night was past – until there was no chance of a vampire falling into the trap – he guessed he'd get no sense out of the man.

He rested his forehead on his crossed wrists, tried to will himself into the pain . . .

He was dimly aware he was dreaming. Dreaming of Thamesmire. Of fleeing through hazy darkness, of hearing Blackie Wirt screaming. Running, staggering, dizzy and terrified, praying he'd make it to Wirt's motor car beside the gates.

Seeing the slim dark form beside the vehicle.

Knowing he was trapped.

He saw her clearly now: a woman, tall and stately. Power came off her like smoke. Her black hair hung down her back past her hips, and her features, not beautiful, were strong and sensual and her dark eyes blazed with cold intelligence. Her hand moved, like silver in the darkness, and his pursuers dissolved into mist and moonlight. He knew she would kill him and yet a yearning for her swept over him, velvet and blackness. Not caring. Only wanting to touch her, to be near her . . .

*Lydia*, he thought. *Lydia dreamed about her, too.*

'Ippolyta,' he called out, and she turned her head, and he woke with the pain as if someone had chopped into his ankle with an ax.

She stood six feet from him, between him and the dark alcove where Ned Seabury and Roddy had taken their post of ambush. Roddy's arm, in its cheap plum-colored sleeve, stretched out of the shadow that hid the rest of his body, lying on the floor.

With a hunting cat's concentration she moved toward the tiny well room where Millward had taken his stand for ambush, and Asher knew to his bone-marrow that Millward was dozing. As Seabury and Roddy must have been dozing when she'd taken them, as sleep even now suffocated him, pressed his lungs breathless with a weight of dust, closed his mouth against a warning shout. Her dress was dark red, and by the lantern's dim glow her skin was flushed to human warmth with the blood of her kill. Blood stained her lips.

Asher drifted back to sleep.

Dreamed of Miranda. Miranda in the sunlight of a hillside yellow with autumn, crying – crying with exhaustion, with fear at being lost and alone. He could feel the heat of the place on his skin, smell the scrubby woodlands at the hill's foot, where a pale track of a dirt road ran. Spain, he thought, and wondered how she'd got there, and how he could possibly find her before it was too late.

*(Too late for what?)*

A young man was walking on that stony trail, and he stopped, turned aside to climb the hill toward her, he must have heard her crying. He wore a black robe and, Asher saw, chains of silver around his throat and wrists; there was gray in his hair, and a few streaks of it in the thin beard along his jaw. He knelt beside the child and gathered her into his arms. 'It's all right,' he said (only he said it in Spanish, and, Asher thought, late medieval Spanish at that). 'You are safe. It will be all right.'

Then he turned to Asher and said, in perfectly modern English, 'But you must wake up.'

Waking hit him like cold water and he shouted, 'Ippolyta!'

She swung around to face him, eyes inhuman as a hawk's. The next second – with the horrifying speed of the vampire – she was beside him, stooping over him, her hand in his hair dragging his head back—

*There's only one reason she'd come to England.*

In the High German of the Austrian Empire he said, 'I know where Damien is.'

Her countenance changed. Lost its murderous intensity and filled with a kind of brilliance, half rage and half triumph, even a kind of joy.

*Shoot her . . .*

'Where?'

*SHOOT HER, YOU NUMBSKULLS!*

'There's a house across the river from Thamesmire,' he said. 'Across from the place you searched the night before last.' *Damn it, Millward, are you bloody asleep?* 'He's been taking the train into London every night to kill, and—'

The crash of Millward's rifle in the confined space of the vault was like thunder. The bullet took her in the chest, close enough that Asher felt the sting of its passing on his cheekbone. She rocked back with the impact and a second shot roared, taking her from a different direction (*she must have missed killing Seabury, how'd that happen?*) and she was knocked sidelong, blood spraying Asher's face. The next instant they were running toward him, Millward from the well chamber and Ned Seabury from somewhere in the darkness toward the end of the vault, bending over him – 'Are you hurt, man?'

'Get her, you idiots!' yelled Asher, and they both turned. 'Finish her!'

Ippolyta's body was gone. Only pools of blood remained behind.

# TWENTY-FIVE

'Whose motor-car is this?' demanded Lydia, when Don Simon – now quite properly attired in his usual gray and a long black greatcoat that spread behind him like sinister wings – led her out the door of the house on Spaniard's Lane. The Sunbeam touring-car took up most of the narrow pavement, polished brass gleaming in the headlamps' reflection.

'That need not concern you.' He opened the door for her, offered her a gloved hand. 'Have you money to take the train back to Oxford? I fear we will need to abandon this vehicle at some point . . . Excellent.' He piloted carefully down the cobblestones. Lydia hoped the vampire was capable of causing the police not to notice a full-sized touring car in the same way that he could cause people not to notice himself . . . hoped also that sometime in the past six years he had actually learned to drive. 'How did Zahorec come to learn of your daughter's whereabouts?'

'He searched my room. He traced me to my hotel – I went into Dallaby House, found his lair . . . Simon, he's been . . . *possessing* Noel Wredemere during the daytimes, that's where he's been hiding. He's been taking drugs to stay awake, as you did with your Mr Ballard at the Bank of England, didn't you? Got him to smoke opium . . .'

'Had I the time to undertake a long campaign of dreams and clues and hints, believe me, Mistress, I would have pursued a less drastic course.' He turned up Thames Street, finagled through the traffic that even at this hour milled around the entrances of London Bridge. ''Tis not precisely "possession", thank God,' he added. 'Else

I would be confounded utterly, having not the smallest idea myself of how these transactions are recorded within the bank. And the effects of the elixir of wakefulness – a compound of silver chloride and cocaine – are devastating. Our friend must be strong indeed – desperate indeed – to pursue safe haven in such fashion.'

'He is desperate.' Lydia clung to the door as the Sunbeam skimmed between two lorry-loads of coal and dove into the vaulted blackness of the tunnel beneath Cannon Street station. 'His master vampire – I presume the Master of Romania or Montenegro or wherever he comes from originally – is in hot pursuit of him, a woman named Ippolyta . . . Or at least Ippolyta is what he calls her in . . . in the silly dreams he's been giving me.'

Even the knowledge that these exercises in romantic fol-de-rol had nothing to do with what she, Lydia Asher, actually wanted or needed or considered desirable, didn't serve to keep a blush from heating her face, and Simon, damn him, would sense it.

'In the night-times he just gets people to think he *is* Noel. That's why he chose him. Because they look enough alike, and he's of a respectable enough family for Cece to marry. But it's taking a toll on him,' she went on. 'He's erratic, the way he moves and speaks . . . He must be coming to pieces . . .'

'Hence his rate of kills,' surmised the vampire. 'The damage done him must be agonizing. Hence also his carelessness, and his need to acquire the services of a nest, to provide him with additional victims . . . Something the living would eventually question, no matter how much he was paying them. *Cagafuego*,' he added, in reference, Lydia presumed, to the coster who pushed his barrow out into New Bridge Street almost under the Sunbeam's wheels. 'And his need to acquire your services,' he added more quietly, 'at whatever cost. *Bueno*,' he added, as they swung on to Fleet Street. 'A decent street at last.'

He tromped the accelerator and the motor car sprang forward like a cheetah.

'Come on!' Millward snatched up the lantern. 'She's left a trail . . .'

Asher caught Seabury's arm as the young man turned to follow. 'Not going to stay here and shoot the next vampire that comes for me, Millward? That'll happen quicker than you'll find Miss Ippolyta.'

By the way Millward looked back at him, then at Seabury – by the sudden twist of expression on the faces of both the older man and the younger – Asher knew that in their eagerness to achieve their quarry both had totally forgotten his existence. Had certainly forgotten that he had, at the very least, an ankle so badly bruised and twisted that it would not bear weight.

Not to mention, he reflected bitterly as Seabury fetched a crowbar to lever the stone block from his leg, leaving poor Roddy's corpse where it lay for the rats to chew, until they had time to come back for it . . .

Using Seabury's arm, and the stones of the broken wall for support, he dragged himself to his feet. His left leg, which had also been pinned, was immediately flooded with pins and needles. The pain in his right, even from the smallest weight set on it, made him feel faint.

Millward cried in agony, 'You fool, she'll get away!'

'I'd come along to help,' Asher said through gritted teeth, 'except I appear to have carelessly cracked my ankle bone on somebody's gun-butt earlier in the evening. I presume that was to ensure I couldn't flee even if I worked myself loose? I think you owe me cab fare back to my hotel – and assistance in getting there, if you'd rather I didn't explain to the cabbie, and maybe to a policeman, how this happened.'

'We cannot let her escape! She's a murderess—'

'—a thousand times over, yes . . . Twenty thousand, actually, according to Lydia's calculations. I've let her take one try at me and I got her to stand still long enough for you to shoot her – and I even woke you up to do it. So unless you're willing to kill me in cold blood, as we discussed earlier in the evening, I suggest you see me home . . . Because I promise you, Millward, if you go after her alone you're going to be killed. Or do you still think I don't know what I'm talking about?'

It was the glance of anguish that Seabury cast – first in the direction of the shadows where Roddy's body lay, then at Millward – more than his own words, Asher guessed, that dragged Millward from his burning urgency to pursuit. *He'll leave a man to die* – which Asher guessed he would, crippled in the darkness underground – *rather than give up his hunt, but he won't risk losing his disciple's admiration.*

Rigid with fury, the vampire hunter slung his rifle, and put a

shoulder under Asher's arm. The Roman merchant's house lay near
Covent Garden, and was reached through crumbling brick drains and
an abandoned Underground station in Maiden Lane. Even with three
men to manhandle him along instead of two, it must have been a
nightmare when he'd been chloroformed and unconscious. *What a
tribute to Millward's determination to set a trap for a vampire.*

And to his disciples' devotion to his cause.

*Poor Roddy.*

He wondered how Millward was going to explain the death to
the young man's family – not to mention the police.

'If you're just going to leave your friend down there,' he remarked,
when they reached the Underground station and the hunters
concealed their rifles behind some boards, 'I'd suggest you go back
later tonight and remove all identifying objects from his pockets.
These things have a way of being discovered.'

Millward glared at him, speechless with rage, though whether at
Asher's sarcasm or his causing Millward to lose his quarry, Asher
was too weary to ask.

*And when I write my own version of the* Liber Gente Tenebrarum,
he thought, *I'll have to add the note that the Undead aren't the
only ones who bring about the deaths of their servants.*

Even at one in the morning, the streets around Covent Garden jostled
with farm carts, with herds of sheep and pigs and geese bound for
the shambles of Smithfield, with coster-barrows and market women,
beggars and thieves in quest of some out-of-hours refreshment.
Clammy mist haloed the gas lights and held in the smoke and stink
of the city. The only thing not present was a cab, and they had to
limp as far as the Strand, to find a dozing cabbie waiting for a few
dissipated revelers to leave the Savoy.

It was only as the man was pulling the rug from his scrawny
night horse that Millward finally spoke, jaw tight with fury. 'I acquit
you of deliberately engineering that she-devil's escape—'

'I can't tell you how honored I feel by your good opinion.'

The vampire-hunter's hand clenched. Asher had the impression
he was struggling not to strike him.

'I acquit you of engineering her escape,' Millward repeated. 'But
had you any manhood in you, you would have let us go on, to finish
what we began. I have no doubt she has got clean away by this

time, thanks to you. By way of atonement, you can tell us what you know of her hiding-places, and if she has others like yourself in London, who work for the Undead, to whom she might go—'

'I do not work for the Undead,' returned Asher quietly. 'Ippolyta – and I don't know her other names – is a newcomer to London and I'm guessing even the vampires of London wouldn't welcome her. What arrangements she's made here, I have no idea.'

'You know of Damien Zahorec.'

'Did Seabury tell you about him?'

'Of course.'

So much for one's word as a gentleman – something Asher had discovered, in his spying days, never extended very far. 'Everything?'

Millward frowned sharply. 'Of course. What was there to know? He was himself newly come to London, in search of the *Book of the Kindred of Darkness*. What more was there?'

'Nothing.' Asher threw a glance at Seabury – who looked aside – then climbed wearily into the cab.

'It'll be daylight soon.' Millward turned back to his disciple as if Asher had ceased to exist. 'She'll be helpless . . .'

'Don't count on that,' said Asher. 'The older they get, the longer after sunrise, and before sunset, they can remain awake.'

That got Millward's attention. 'It says nothing about that in the book.'

As the cab pulled away into the nearly empty Strand, Asher wondered whether the myriad lies in the myriad printings of the *Liber Gente Tenebrarum* had all been engineered by vampire hunters for the confusion of their prey, or whether some of them had been the other way around.

The driver helped Asher up the step of the Temperance Hotel; the desk clerk sprang to his feet: 'Mr Berkhampstead!'

And before he rushed around the counter to help him into a chair, he snatched the room key from the board behind him.

'Is Mrs Berkhampstead not in?' The exhaustion and cold that had swamped him in the cab vanished.

'No, sir. There's a doctor just over in New Broad Street . . .'

'Did she leave a message?'

The man paused on his way into the back room where the hotel's boy was doubtless sleeping: 'Why, yes, sir! It's right here . . .' He ducked through the door behind the counter. Had Asher been able to get to his feet and knock the man's head against the wall, he would have done so. As it was he could only sit in the worn green lobby chair until the clerk, and the young lad in his rumpled uniform, came back out. The boy darted away through the door, into the mists that had not yet begun to stain with the first daylight, and the clerk came around the counter again and handed Asher Lydia's note. 'She came in about ten, sir – looked to be bound for the theater – and went up to her room, then came right back down and went out.'

*Damn it*, thought Asher, his hands trembling. *Damn it.*

*Tufton Farm, Herts. 5 mi on Hatfield Road outside St Albans. Z learned of Miranda there, has gone to take her. I'm going to find Simon. Follow us.*

He crushed the paper.

*Damn it.*

# TWENTY-SIX

Don Simon switched off the headlamps beyond St Albans. Lydia reminded herself that the vampire could see perfectly well in the dark. Even with the moon waxing, the hedgerows rendered the road a perfect abyss, and when Simon halted the car she couldn't tell whether they were near a farmhouse or not. The whole night seemed thick with the smell of hay, without the more localized aromas of wood smoke or cows.

An owl cried, answered by the far-off barking of a dog.

'He can hear your footfalls if he is listening,' the vampire whispered. 'Yet I will not leave you here alone.'

Lydia wished she had the courage to say, 'Leave me here if it will make the difference.' But the words wouldn't come out. She clung instead to the cold fingers that wrapped hers, and tried to walk as silently as she could on ground that was invisible, uneven, and thick with last year's leaves.

Branches tangled in her hair in passing. Wispy moonlight showed the roughcast walls of a house: half-timbered gables, dormers like death-sealed eyes. Simon halted beside her, listening.

'None live in the house.'

He strode, soundless, across the graveled yard, Lydia stumbling at his heels.

*No . . .*

Two doors opened into the house from the stone porch. Lantern light beneath one of them seemed unbearably bright in the blackness. Simon pushed it open and a cat whipped past their feet, and away into the night.

The room beyond smelled of coffee, coals, bacon, tobacco, ashes. No blood.

'What make you of this, Mistress?'

The lantern on the table in the stone-floored kitchen showed a plate with part of a bacon sandwich on it, a dish of butter well-licked by the guilty puss. Coffee half-filled a pottery cup. Simon wrapped his hand briefly around it, went to look at the collapsed coals burning themselves out on the old-fashioned hearth.

'Two hours.'

A door beyond the stove opened into blackness. Lydia caught up the lantern, the light falling through to show her a stone stair going down. Iron bolts on the kitchen side of the cellar door . . . the familiar nursery smell of chamber pots and nappies penetrating even the earthen damp of the cellar.

*No . . .*

The room below was deserted. Tidy, whitewashed, almost bare, with a little heating stove in one corner (Lydia shut her eyes in a prayer of thanks) and a commode in another. A single cot was drawn up close to the heater. There were three blankets on it, one of which had been on Miranda's cot at home.

*No . . .*

She sank into one of the rickety chairs beside the little table. Cards scattered the tabletop – bezique, she noted automatically. Three hands. Three cups of tepid coffee. A fork lying by itself. A child's cup, a little saucer and bowl. A tin of biscuits and a stack of newspapers on a shelf, and a Bible: *Daphne Jean Robinson 1879* written on the flyleaf. *Nan must have asked for something to read.* That they'd obliged her filled Lydia with gratitude. *They hadn't been cruel.*

'None are here in the house.' Simon descended the stair – an extraordinarily long stair; the cellar was very deep. *No wonder*

*Simon couldn't hear them, sense them . . .* 'A motor car was kept in the shed, with cans of petrol and oil.'

'He took them.' Lydia turned the tiny spoon in her fingers. *Miranda touched this . . .*

She thought about laying her head on the table, weeping – like Niobe in the Greek myth – until she turned into stone and couldn't feel the loss any more.

'And their guardians – waking to find the cellar empty and their prisoners gone – fled, as anyone would who has seen Lionel in his anger. I smell no blood on the premises, and so take comfort in the fact that Zahorec at least did not murder your nursery maid. Yet having them prisoner, he will now use you – or try to use you . . .'

Lydia looked up at him sharply, in the lantern's dim glow. 'And Grippen will kill me,' she said softly, 'to keep that from happening, won't he?'

'He may try, yes.' He raised her to her feet. ''Twere best we were gone, Mistress. Unless his minions be complete fools they shall have sent word to him at once of what befell. Daylight draws nigh. I have a house near Hertford, where you can remain hid from Lionel, but word will have to be got to James, ere Lionel's men find him . . .'

He stopped, a few steps short of the door at the top of the cellar stair. '*Putada.*' He handed Lydia the lantern. 'He is here. Lionel. I can hold him I think until sunrise, but there is no lock on the inside of this door—'

'Come out, you mewling Papist,' growled the harsh bass from the kitchen. 'I should have thought I'd see you sooner or later. Bring the bitch with you. I need a word with her as well.'

The doctor – sun-burned and sallow from service in India – bound Asher's ankle and splinted it: the bone was cracked rather than broken, and shockingly bruised. 'What'd you do to it, man?' he asked. 'Looks like a carthorse trod on it.'

'Motor car.' Asher took another sip of the brandy the desk clerk had fetched for him. Veronal would have been far better, but was out of the question. 'The brake slipped off and my idiot nephew had left the thing in gear. Thing is, I must be in St Albans by eight—'

'It's not going to happen.'

'It must,' said Asher. '*I* must. If I don't . . .' He made himself look grave, noble, and not nearly as frantic as he felt. 'There's a woman's honor in it.' He laid a hand on the physician's shoulder: a simpler explanation than the truth and one that didn't involve a twenty-minute effort to convince people of the existence of the Undead, much less explain how he came to be working for them. 'I can't say more. I have a bike here; I can make the ride in good time if you'll strap me up.'

The doctor sniffed, and eyed Asher's loud tweeds – spattered with so much filth that Ippolyta's blood was lost in the general mess – and unshaven chin, but wrapped his ankle tightly, first in bandages and then in strips of sticking plaster. 'That's going to be the devil when you start your bike,' he warned, as Asher got to his feet – a fact of which Asher was already cringingly aware. 'The splint'll take part of the pressure, but if you make it as far as St Albans I'll be surprised.'

'Not as surprised as me.' Doctor and desk clerk followed him as he limped down the rear stairs to the narrow yard. The moon stood just above the rooftops. He wondered if Lydia had found Ysidro, and if he wasn't doing her some terrible disservice – or indeed, condemning her to death – by haring off at this moment.

How the hell had Zahorec discovered where Miranda was hidden?

*Damn Millward – and damn the lazy bastard who hasn't yet invented an electric starter for a motorcycle . . .*

The clerk strapped Asher's satchel on to the back of the bike, helped Asher to mount.

'Good luck to you,' said the doctor.

Asher pointed the front wheel at the gate, thrust the bike forward, pedaled three times – each stroke like a bayonet rammed up his heel – and the Indian's engine caught with a muffled roar. As he swept out into the dark of Finsbury Circus he wondered who he could ask about the patron saint of motorcycles, to whom he owed at least a sheep.

He swung around and headed up City Road for Islington and points north.

'So you've a house near Hertford, have you?' Grippen pulled a chair from the kitchen table, and pushed it roughly around for Lydia to sit in. 'I thought you said you were leaving this land.'

'And I thought you said you would leave Mrs Asher and her

husband in peace,' returned Simon. Lydia set the lamp on the corner of the table and surreptitiously slid her feet from the gold-spangled slippers. She'd nearly broken her ankle twice between the motor car and the farmhouse. If it came to a dash for her life, she refused to be like a heroine in a novel and trip on her own shoes.

''Tis no concern of yours, Spaniard.'

''Tis no concern of mine if your fledglings find themselves another master – deeply as 'twould grieve me to see you driven from London. I can recommend a number of minor cities in Italy whose masters might conceivably permit you coffin space.'

'I'd sooner lie in Hell than within smellin' distance of Rome – an' I'll drag that snivelin' Bohemian with me to the Devil's door sooner than stand by while he sets up for himself in my city! Yes, and them puking traitors—'

'Stop it!' cried Lydia. 'Both of you! Listen to me. Titus Armistead owns four copies of the *Book of the Kindred of Darkness*. Among the four of them, there's sure to be one formula that will break the hold of a master on his fledglings—'

'There's no such thing!' Grippen must have raised his hand to strike her, though Lydia didn't see it. Only that suddenly, Simon was standing next to her with his hand locked around the master vampire's upraised wrist.

Grippen yanked his arm clear. 'Nothing can break the hold of a master on his get. Not if the master's got any hair on his . . .' He glanced at Lydia, then at Simon, and finished: 'Chest.'

'And what will you do,' retorted Lydia, 'if one of those volumes also contains a recipe for the growing of that hair? For making himself stronger, if he isn't so already? He's been hiding from you all this time, Dr Grippen, by possessing the man who's going to marry Armistead's daughter. Controlling him when he's in an opium sleep. Taking his place outright when the sun goes down. Moving underground, only coming to the surface to kill. Through the girl, with Armistead's money, he's going to build a power-base in London. After the marriage I think he plans to step into Lord Colwich's identity completely, with the girl to cover for him.'

'Where's he gone, then?' growled Grippen. 'Him and this American slut? Looks to me like the answer to this puzzle is to kill her . . .'

He glanced at Lydia again, calculatingly, and then at Simon.

'And any other that'll give him aid. And you can't tell me, Spaniard, that this girl of yours won't betray you, if Zahorec but sends her a lock of her babe's red hair.' The dark eyes turned to Lydia. 'Would you, Missy?'

'I would,' replied Lydia steadily. *He'll know anything else is a lie, and so will Simon . . .*

'Any parent would,' she went on, looking up into his face. 'Surely you remember that at least, from your days as a living man. Had you not a daughter? Would you not have killed any man who harmed a hair of her head?'

The vampire looked aside. 'Greedy little bitch.'

There was pride, and deep affection in his voice.

'Which is why it would make more sense for you to help me catch him,' said Lydia. 'To help me get my daughter away from him would make more sense than it would for you to kill me. I mean, if you kill me, and kill Jamie, you might have to kill Simon also . . . at least I hope Simon would try to stop you from doing it . . .'

'I would.'

'You're a fool!'

'I'm not the one who made fledglings of a weaselly dandy and a scheming tradeswoman.'

'No, you're the one who—'

'*Stop it!*' Lydia said again. 'Don't pay any attention to him, Dr Grippen; he's just trying to annoy you. Listen. Before anything else Zahorec will try to get in touch with me, to secure my aid by threatening my daughter. Like the coward he is.' She spared a hard glare for the Master of London. 'But he doesn't know I've followed him here. He'll try to write to me, or contact me through some kind of middleman. While he's waiting for my reply he'll need to hide somewhere with Miranda. He knows I know where all his properties are, and he knows there's a good chance that I've told you. The one place he *doesn't* know I know about – because I didn't learn about it from banking records or bribing the servants, but just from knowing the family – is in Scotland.'

'Scotland!'

'And in Scotland,' Lydia continued, 'Miss Armistead can marry Lord Colwich immediately, without her father's consent. Right now he's trying to tie up her money so Lord Colwich can't touch it – probably somebody snitched to him about Colwich's use of opium. He may even suspect she has a lover. Zahorec has to be able to get at that money. If they present Armistead with a *fait accompli*, he'll capitulate. By what I've seen there's nothing he won't do for his daughter.'

'Armistead,' said Grippen. 'The cuffin that's got four copies of the book, so you say—'

'He does. He's looking for a vampire—'

'*Looking* for one?'

'To hire. To use as a paid bully-boy against the working men in his mines. Whether he'd do so if he knew his daughter was being courted by one I don't know. But the marriage will give Zahorec the upper hand. He'll use him – and he'll try to use me. And Stenmuir Castle – which belongs to Colwich's family – is close enough to Glasgow that within a few days Miranda could be taken anywhere, even out of the country . . .' She forced her voice steady, unnerved by the dark river of thought she could see racing behind those hard black eyes.

'We can't give him that few days. We have to follow him now, immediately, before he has time to get his plans ready.' She turned to Simon. 'Will you come with me?'

'Unto the ends of the earth, Lady.' He kissed her hand.

'God's blood!' Grippen stared at him, aghast with the dread that lived in every vampire's heart, dread of travel in daylight, boxed asleep in a coffin and knowing that the slightest accident would result in agonizing death. There was no animosity, no enmity, in his voice 'You're mad, Simon.'

Simon bowed. 'I need no heretic provincial to tell me so, Lionel. I assume – this house being a hiding place of yours – that you have a sub-cellar beneath the one in which Mistress Miranda has spent the past week, and a suitable trunk for travel?'

'I thought you'd a house in Hertford?'

'I cannot make arrangements for the journey – and for the disposal of Mr Grosvenor's motor car – and reach there by daybreak. Mistress . . .' He turned again to Lydia. 'Wilt you await me here?'

She glanced at Grippen.

'I should kill you now,' he growled. 'T'would be simpler.'

'No,' said Lydia calmly, and propped her spectacles more firmly on to the bridge of her nose. 'Actually, it wouldn't. We need help, Lionel. Zahorec is strong – I think only another vampire can match him. I certainly can't.'

She got to her feet, stood looking up at him as she had on the mist-drowned bridge over the Cherwell, not angry now, nor even conscious of much fear.

'The first trains to Scotland won't start running until nine. We can be there just after darkness falls. But we need your help.'

'Nay.' His pockmarked face hardened, and his glance shifted to Simon. 'You do as you like, man. But you'll not get me crated like salt beef hell-bound to the wilds of nowhere to meet that Bohemian blackguard. If you're off to St Albans to make arrangements for your journey I'll ride with you that far in that motor car, but I've an errand in London-town ere cock-light, and the night's waning fast. Lady . . .'

He took Lydia's hand, and kissed it with surprising grace. 'I was wrong snatching your brat, and I admit of it. I'll do what I can to amend it, but go to Scotland I will not, and travel with any living soul I will not, not to speak of lying anywhere near a scheming liar of a Spanish whoreson for so much as five minutes, let alone the whole of a day. Good fortune to you.'

It was always difficult to see vampires move. One moment, it seemed to Lydia that she was standing, barefoot on the cold stone floor, with the Master of London on one side of her and Don Simon on the other. Then she was alone in the lantern-lit kitchen, hearing from the darkness outside the whisper of voices:

'The least you can do is dispose of the motor car for me . . .'

'You stole it; *you* drown it.'

'Heretic . . .'

'Papist cur . . .'

And they were gone.

# TWENTY-SEVEN

In the dark frieze of houses, lights glimmered in kitchens, basements, areas: servants laying fires, making coffee, boiling water for shaving and baths. *Ysidro's agent at the Bank of England must have come through with the information.* Asher swerved past the glare of a trench where workers were laying electrical cable. *How did Zahorec get it from Lydia?*

The vampire had obviously learned that Lydia was working against him, if he'd gone to steal Miranda from Grippen . . . *How? From her dreams?*

He tried not to think about what he'd find at Tufton Farm. *Oh, that Dr G, he's a close one,* Violet Scrooby had said to him, over a companionable pint at The Scythe. *If you ask me he's up to some lay. Many's the night he's come in here, and chatted with Henry quiet-like. But I will say, what he pays Henry makes all the difference to Henry's girls, bein' sent to a proper school, and to Daphne's mum getting the care she needs, and her bedridden with palsy . . .*

His comfort at the barmaid's description of Daphne Scrooby (*Lord, quiet as a mouse and no bigger than a minute, but she'd rip the leg off the man who laid a hand on one of her girls, and beat him to death with the soggy end*) faded in the conviction that hers would be one of several bodies he would find in St Albans. Hers and Nan Wellit's.

*I will kill him,* thought Asher calmly. *Zahorec, Grippen . . . all their filthy get.*

Carts and vans filled with fruit and flowers from the countryside dotted Islington High Street, lanterns swaying as Asher flashed past them. The outbound road lay empty.

*Karlebach was right. Millward – ass that he is – is right.*

Blue dawn light showed him neat villas, standing apart each in its own garden. Then the long slope of Golders Hill, rolling green countryside and the smell of hay and livestock.

*Blood and darkness spread wherever they touch. Even the innocent – who don't even know what they are or that they exist – are pulled into that darkness and devoured.*

The church steeple of Barnet showed above the trees. Stone park gates to his right, guarding a glimpse of Restoration stonework, the blink of water reflecting brightening sky. Along the roadsides, between the fields, lines of stumps where the elm trees of his childhood had been cut down, sacrificed to the pressing economies of twentieth-century agriculture. *What does Ysidro think, of the England that is not the England he knew as a living man? What does Grippen think?*

*Or is that something that vanishes, when they pass into shadow?*

Did the original book, the book that had actually been written by that wandering scholar of Valladolid (*And what was a Spaniard doing studying in Prague anyway?*) speak of that? And his dream returned to him, of the wooded hillsides of Spain that was now yellowed scrub.

A square church tower and the ruins of a Roman wall, then a high street of sweet shops and greengrocers just stirring into life. The Hatfield Road, trees and hedgerows holding the damp chill of last night. A railway whistle sounded.

*If anything happens to Miranda, can we find our way back from that?*

Lydia after her second miscarriage, shattered and withdrawn . . .

Movement in the hedge. A flutter in the corner of his vision as he swept by, a figure with arms upraised. Even before he realized that the words she cried were, 'Professor Asher, sir!' his mind registered her dark skirt, white blouse, dark cape, and he skidded the motorbike to a halt – even taking his weight on his left foot, not his right: the jolt was agony.

'Professor Asher, sir! Oh, lord, is that you?'

She was running down the shadowed road to him as he turned the bike around, gunned back to her (*It can't be a vampire's illusion, it's broad daylight)*– and caught her as she flung herself into his arms.

'Professor Asher, sir! I did my best, sir, I did! I tried, sir, I tried . . .'

It was Nan Wellit.

He knew he should say, *It's all right, you're safe, I'm here*, for the girl was obviously terrified and exhausted, her hair tangled with leaves and her creased skirt a mess of stains and twigs from spending the night in the hedges. But the first thing he could say was, '*Where is she?*' and the words came out at a desperate almost-shout.

The young nursemaid burst into tears, and for an instant the world stood still between the future and death.

'I don't know, sir! I don't know! They took her—'

*Took her. She's alive.*

'Who took her, Nan?' Calm flooded him. *If they took her they mean to keep her, at least for the moment . . .* He stroked her tangled hair, as he had stroked Lydia's the first time he'd found that lovely and fragile schoolgirl weeping in the summer house at Willoughby Close, at the news that she was to be sent away from England. 'It's all right. We'll find her . . .'

'I don't know who it was, sir.' She straightened and stepped back from him, as if aware that one didn't clutch one's employer. From her sleeve she produced a handkerchief, to wipe her eyes. 'It was a lady and a gentleman. I heard him call her Para-something . . . Parady-vogel?'

'*Paradeisvogel*,' said Asher. 'It means "bird of paradise" in German.'

'*Mein Paradeisvogel*, he said. I was . . .' She wiped her eyes again, her hands shaking.

'Where was this? At the farm?'

'No, sir. That's just it. I'd run away, I'd got us out—'

'Is there anyone there now?' *Lydia*, he thought, *Lydia was ahead of me . . .*

'I don't know, sir. They fell asleep – Mrs Daphne, and Mick, and Reggie. All at once, they just put their heads down on the table . . . It was just the same as happened at your house, sir, the night we was took – taken,' she corrected herself. 'Mrs Brock just fell asleep sitting in front of the fire, and I got so sleepy myself, just like they say when you're little, that the Sandman comes and blows magic dust in your eyes . . . Poof! I was asleep. Was it sleeping gas, sir? It doesn't seem to have hurt Miranda afterwards . . .'

'Don't worry about it now,' said Asher. 'Tell me what happened.'

'Oh, yes, sir. We were playing cards at the table – they'd often come down to do so. Mrs Daphne was so fond of Miss Miranda, and told me all about her own daughters . . . So when I saw Mick, and Mrs Daphne, both fall asleep, just like that – and I felt myself so sleepy too – I thought, *This is the same as happened before.* So I got one of the forks out of the bureau and stabbed myself in the hand with it, to stay awake, and I got Miranda and went upstairs, and there was Reggie in the kitchen sound asleep too. And I felt queer, as if something terrible were about to happen, though that may just have been that I'd been down that cellar for so long. I . . . Oh!'

She turned sharply, and looking around, Asher saw Lydia emerge from a farm track a hundred feet further along the lane. Lydia in a dress of faded red-and-blue calico that was far too short for her, red hair bare and spectacles flashing in the dappled brightness.

She saw them, snatched up her skirts and ran toward them; shouted

'Jamie!' when she got near enough to be heard. And then, '*NAN!* Oh, God, Nan!'

Asher saw her slow, as she took in the fact that no child made up part of the little group in the lane. Her face convulsed with anxiety as she threw herself into his arms, then turned and caught Nan in an embrace of joy and relief. 'What happened? Did they let you go . . .?'

'No, ma'am. I was telling Professor Asher, they fell asleep, and I took Miss Miranda and got out of the house.' The nursery maid turned huge blue eyes back to Asher. 'It was dark, there wasn't a moon, but I swear I saw no one in the field. I looked, sir, I really did! Miranda was still asleep, and I felt so queer, like there was danger all around, that I didn't dare wake her lest she make a noise. I could barely to keep awake myself. All that time we were down that cellar, I'd creep up to the door and listen to their voices in the kitchen, and try to put together everything they said about what was around the house. I knew we had to be close to a railway line, because I could sometimes hear the trains when I did that. And they'd talk about there being woods nearby, and hedges and fields and a road into town, though it sounded like a fair distance to town itself because they'd take the motor car, every time.

'But I ran across the field making for the hedgerow, because I knew we could hide in the hedges, and follow them to the road. But it was like – it was like I'd tripped, only I don't remember tripping.' Her voice shook again and she blew her nose on her handkerchief once more. 'It's like I fell asleep on my feet. All of a sudden I was lying on the ground, and I looked up and saw this lady with Miranda in her arms—'

'Dark lady?' asked Asher.

'Yes, sir. Dressed fancy, in silk with beads all over it that shined in the starlight, and a big necklace of diamonds and pearls—'

'That's what Cece was wearing,' said Lydia.

'And there was a man with her, a tall man in evening dress. His hair was black, sir, and he was handsome, and young. I couldn't see his eyes in the dark, but I could feel he was looking down at me.'

'And because Cece was with him,' said Asher softly, 'he couldn't let her see him . . . harm . . . an innocent girl.'

'I stayed quiet, sir.' Nan's glance, terrified and miserable, went from Asher to Lydia, then back. 'I wanted to shout out, *Give her back to me*, but I knew they wouldn't, and there was two of them. And the gentleman, for all he was so handsome, he looked like a bad customer. He took Miranda from the lady – she was wrapped up in the quilt, and I don't think she waked, the whole time – and they went off across the field, to the gate that led to the lane. The minute they were out of sight I followed, but I heard a motor car start up, and drive away down the lane.

'I didn't know what else to do, sir. I thought Reggie and Mick would be out hunting for me, so I hid in the hedgerow until it got light. Then I started walking toward town, whatever town it is . . .'

Asher looked down at her, small and plump and seventeen years old, at her first job as nursery maid. She hadn't panicked, she hadn't put a foot wrong, she'd kept her head and would have made her escape – with her charge in her arms – had she not been hopelessly outmatched. He put his arm around her shoulders. 'You did splendidly, Nan. We know who took her.'

'It was Dr G that paid Mrs Daphne and Reggie and Mick, sir. I don't know who he is but I heard them speak of him. It sounded like they were afraid of him – and it sounded like they hadn't any idea why Miranda was to be kept. Mrs Daphne's husband's name is Henry, and he keeps a pub in London called The Scythe. But now she's been took – taken – by this other gentleman—'

'We know who he is, too,' said Asher quietly. 'And we have a list of places where they could be.' He turned to Lydia. 'He'll be getting in touch with you—'

'He knows all his properties are blown.' Lydia used the term they did in the Department. 'He found my list of his hideouts in my room, and my list of Grippen's. He must have guessed I was being forced to work for Grippen. Grippen was here, by the way. He has a crypt down under the old laundry, in what used to be a cistern, and lent Ysidro his coffin, though he refused to come with us—'

'Come with you?'

'I think I know where Zahorec has gone,' said Lydia. 'It's the only place they *could* go, the only property that wasn't on the list. They've gone to Stenmuir Castle, in Scotland.'

# TWENTY-EIGHT

When Asher returned from Watford later that morning in a carter's wagon – exhausted, half-nauseated from phenacetin that hadn't stopped his right ankle from feeling like it was being crushed between red-hot rollers – it was to find that Lydia had given Nan Wellit ten pounds and dispatched her in St Albans' only cab to the Bower Inn in Hatfield. ('It's quite the nicest in town . . .')

'She promised to stay till called for,' said Lydia, fetching tea from the great iron range in Tufton Farm's kitchen (she couldn't be trusted to make cocoa) while the carters bumped and manhandled the huge black metal trunk, quadruple locked, up from the old cistern deep beneath the laundry. 'And she promised not to get in touch with anyone at home, and to remain indoors. I let her think Miranda's kidnapping was for ransom, and that until you and I knew what the mysterious Dr G was up to, she wouldn't be quite safe and neither would anyone she spoke to.'

Asher caught her wrist, pressed her hand first to his unshaven cheek, then to his lips. 'To say that your value is above rubies, o Best Beloved,' he said, 'would still understate it. It is above light, above life, above breath. And far above phenacetin and tea,' he added, as he lifted the cup.

'There's probably some bread and butter around here,' she offered. 'It might settle your stomach.'

'What I need is something to settle my ankle.'

'I suppose phenacetin has the virtue of being a counterirritant.' Lydia began opening and shutting the doors beneath the counter and dish-cupboards on the far side of the big, stone-floored room. 'The idea is to make you so sick you forget about your ankle—'

'It's having a good try, but it hasn't worked yet.'

'I hope there'll be a pair of Daphne Scrooby's shoes somewhere hereabouts. Her dress fits me all right but I feel like a giraffe in it, and—'

Her sudden silence made Asher turn. She stood before an

opened broom cupboard, looking at what was on the single shelf inside.

Asher got to his feet, holding his balance on the back of the chair.

Lydia whispered, 'Oh—'

'It's all right.' He limped to her side.

There were two shotguns in the broom cupboard, several bricks on its floor, and, folded on the shelf, two sacks, one large and one small, some clothes rope, and a bottle of aconitine.

Poison.

Lydia said, in a perfectly matter-of-fact voice, 'They *were* planning to cut and run if anything went wrong.'

'Come sit down.'

She obeyed. Her face had turned chalky, as if her throat had been cut.

'Grippen would have killed them for it.' He didn't add, *I will, if he doesn't*, but when she looked up into his face he saw by her expression that she knew this.

After a long time she whispered, 'Will we always live like this?'

The carters emerged from the hall, carefully hauling the black trunk on dollies; maneuvered it out the door. Because it was Sunday there was no train connection in Watford. They'd have to catch the ten-thirteen to Inverness at Willesden Junction, with no more baggage than Asher's satchel – now bulging with Lydia's gold-and-turquoise evening gown – and Ysidro's borrowed trunk.

'Even if we get Miranda back, will we always have to spend our lives looking over our shoulders?'

'No.' His voice sounded flat to his own ears, like leather striking stone. He stood, put his hands on her shoulders, then framed her face in his palms, knowing there was no way he could promise. 'I promise you.'

*They must be destroyed.*

Long ago Ysidro had said to him that there could be no congress between the living and the dead. Now it seemed clear to him that they could not even exist side by side. Not so long as the dead preyed on the living, and the living – from the Titus Armisteads of the world on up to the Kaiser and the King and the men in Asher's own Department – sought to use the abilities of the dead against one another.

*They must be destroyed. All of them.*

Except, of course, he reflected bitterly, as Lydia helped him out to the wagon, that the only one among the Undead that he currently could destroy, here and now, he needed, if they were ever going to see their daughter safe.

He climbed into the back of the wagon, a sorry and shabby figure in his loud mustard-colored tweeds spattered with sewer-mud and vampire-blood, and propped his back against Ysidro's trunk. Lydia settled beside him in her too-short cotton-print dress, and set their satchel against the wheel of the tied-down motorcycle. His hand closed around hers, and as the cart lurched into motion he leaned back and shut his eyes.

There was a bookshop across the road from the train station at Willesden Junction, beside the garage where they left the Indian. Asher purchased another walking stick, and found Ordnance Survey maps of Argyllshire, twenty-five inches to the mile, with the intention of studying the territory that lay between Kynnoch Hall and Stenmuir Castle during the nine hours it would take them to reach Glasgow. Once on board the train, with his leg elevated on his upended satchel, Asher fell deeply and instantly asleep, to be awakened, somewhere between Birmingham and Manchester, by Ned Seabury saying: '. . . honestly, ma'am, we had very little choice. These things must be destroyed – and Professor Asher was in almost no danger.'

'If Professor Asher was in almost no danger,' retorted Lydia, 'why didn't you volunteer to be the bait yourself? Or is betraying one's honor as a gentleman venial compared with knowing more about the Undead than Dr Millward does? Which I gather was the justification your master used for nearly getting my husband killed.'

In a stifled voice, Seabury replied, 'He isn't my master.'

Asher opened his eyes. Lydia – still attired in Mrs Scrooby's red-and-blue calico – stood beside the half-open door of their compartment, while Seabury – who had clearly taken time to bathe, shave, and change into respectable tweeds while Asher had been haring down to St Albans with his ankle in sticking plaster – hovered in the corridor beyond. 'If he can command you to violate your sworn word,' said Asher wearily, 'and put the life of an innocent man in jeopardy, solely on his own judgment and command, yes, he is your master, as surely as any vampire rules his fledglings. Did you find the woman Ippolyta?'

'No.' Seabury drew a shaky breath, brushed aside the dark curl that hung over his forehead. 'You were . . . quite right. She eluded us in the sewers.'

*No wonder you needed to change clothes.*

'How she could have done so, with two silver bullets in her . . .?'

'You're lucky she didn't kill you both. Vampires kill more, to strengthen themselves if they need to heal. It's why Zahorec started killing in Paris, after he began taking drugs to control Colwich. And when you went back to the vault, was your friend Roddy's body gone?'

The young man started. 'Did you know it would be? You could have warned us—'

'Would it have kept Millward from hunting for Madame Ippolyta for what remained of the night? He'd put me out as bait for her on the strength of my having *talked* to a man who was trying to hire a vampire. If I'd told him that I was pretty certain the London vampires would dispose of a suspicious corpse, he'd probably have shot me. What takes you to Scotland?'

'Noel.'

A stout man in tweeds almost as garish as Asher's passed along the corridor and Seabury stepped into the compartment, as if taking Asher's reasonable tone for welcome. In the better light his face was haggard, his dark brows standing out sharply against a pallor of weariness.

'Noel came to my rooms this morning, on his way to catch the early train. He said Cece had gone up to Kynnoch last night – the Earl of Crossford's shooting place, you know . . .' He hesitated, then laughed shortly. 'You must know, of course. I assume that's where you're going . . .'

'Are they staying at Kynnoch Hall?'

'Well, he said Stenmuir, but it can't be that. He was . . . He seemed exhausted, and confused . . .'

'Did he tell you he and Cece were going to be married in Scotland?' Lydia put in.

Seabury turned shocked eyes on her – shocked but aware. 'I didn't . . .' he stammered. 'I couldn't . . . Noel was confused, as I said. He'd been taking opium, laudanum, who knows what. He shook so badly he could barely sit still. Yet there was something about him . . .'

Sudden tears flooded his eyes.

'This is going to sound completely mad but it's true . . . I thought that he seemed himself again. And I don't mean that "himself" is necessarily a . . . a soused, unshaven opium-eater. But it's as if . . . as if Noel were really Noel, and not . . . not whoever it's been, it's sometimes seemed to me . . . As if I were really talking to the person I've known all these years . . .'

'I understand,' said Lydia softly. 'You were.'

'What?' His gaze searched her face, and for a moment he seemed to struggle, wanting to ask but not wanting to know. Then, 'He said he wanted to see me before he left. To warn me against Zahorec – though Noel has no idea that I know Zahorec is a vampire . . .'

He passed his hand across his face. 'Yes, he said they were getting married, in the Registrar's office in Glasgow. He said, *Don't let yourself be drawn into our set, Teddy. Even if I invite you, don't come.* I said, *Can't you cut the connection?* And he shook his head. *It's too late for that. It's too late for me. I'm in too deep. But you get out.* He seemed to think . . .'

The young man broke off again, looked away. Lydia's glance crossed Asher's: *When Zahorec got on the train for Scotland, it was too far to control him, wasn't it?*

Either that, reflected Asher, or whatever Zahorec was taking to remain awake into the daytime was finally taking its toll.

But entangled in family demands, in promises he only partially remembered making, in dreams and the recollection of dreams, Noel Wredemere obviously considered himself bound to go through with Cece Armistead's plans.

'He took the early train up,' Ned continued after a time. 'But the more I thought about it – and about what you'd said, Mrs Asher, of how vampires can manipulate the dreams of the living – the more I thought, *I have to get him away from her.* From them. From Zahorec. God knows what he's going to tell his parents . . . But I have to take him back to Paris. Take him to Spain, or Italy, or China if I have to.' He shook his head, like a man trying to waken from deadening sleep. 'Does it sound as mad to you as it does to me? I feel as if I'm fighting for Noel's life – and for his soul.'

They reached Glasgow at ten. The sun had gone down, but light still filled the sky. 'Simon said he'd follow us,' murmured Lydia, as Ned Seabury took the instructions she'd given him and left the station to find one of the several companies in the city that rented motor cars. 'He wired ahead, to make arrangements for the motor car. Also to rent a house, where we're to store his trunk. Drat these shoes!' She stumbled – for the tenth time in the course of the day – in the delicate gold-and-turquoise slippers she'd worn to the dinner at Wycliffe House. Though Daphne Scrooby's red-and-blue dress fit her – albeit with serious deficiencies in sleeves and hem – and Lydia had even found a corduroy jacket on the premises, Miranda's jailer, 'no bigger than a minute,' had feet to match her stature.

Asher looked at the black trunk, loaded on to the porter's barrow, ready to be delivered to a rented house on the old High Street. *Every kill he makes from this day forth*, his old master Karlebach had told him, *will be on your head* . . .

Was the fact that he needed the vampire's help – that he dared not kill him – made more, or less, maddening by the knowledge that in his way, he liked Ysidro? That they understood one another, as he had seldom found anyone – other than Lydia – to understand his thoughts? Sick and exhausted from the effects of the elixir he'd taken (*The same stuff Zahorec has been taking all these weeks?*) Ysidro would doubtless hunt in Glasgow's teeming docklands before following Asher and Lydia down the road to the western land of lochs once known as Lorn. Only blood and death could heal him.

But looking worriedly for that terrible knowledge in Lydia's eyes, Asher saw only the coolness that masked her anxiety. Nothing existed for her now, he realized, but the chill single-mindedness of a hunter, who must achieve her prey or die.

Glasgow was a seaport, one of the biggest in the world. Flushed out of London, Zahorec would be seeking another refuge – and seeking a place to conceal Miranda, where neither Lydia, nor any vampire whose help she might be able to enlist, could find her.

What Zahorec needed now was human allies whose obedience he could trust: without prevarication, without lies, without the slightest fear that they would dare betray him. *A mother I can trust*, Grippen had said, *to do as I bid her* . . .

By tomorrow – Tuesday at the latest – he would have found someplace, put some scheme in train. Cece's three million dollars would be secured to Colwich, whom Zahorec could manipulate – or, in the hours of darkness, simply replace.

*We have to take him tonight. We have to find her tonight.*

*Or,* his heart told him, *we will never find her. And we will be his slaves.*

When he and Lydia came out of the old house on to the cobbled High Street, and locked the door behind them, they found Ned Seabury waiting for them in a rented Ford, its headlamps glowing yellow in the last blue of summer dusk.

Leaning heavily on Lydia's shoulder, Asher climbed into the front seat. They set out into the twilight, and the road to the hills of Lorn.

# TWENTY-NINE

Just beyond Dumbarton, with the moon not yet risen above the peaks of the Arrochars and slate-black rain clouds sweeping in from the sea, Asher caught the gray glimmer of a shadow beside the road. He signed Seabury to slow as the headlamps revealed Ysidro's thin form.

'I am a friend of Noel's from Paris.' The vampire avoided the reflected light as he offered Seabury his gloved hand to shake, and climbed at once into the rear seat beside Lydia. 'Do you travel to Stenmuir?'

Looking back at him, Asher could see the scars on his face, the glint of fangs as he spoke, and as Seabury put the Ford into gear he saw, too, the young man's shaken expression.

'There's no road to Stenmuir,' said Lydia, since Seabury appeared unable to reply. 'The summer I came here for the shooting – not that I ever actually shot anything, but anything was better than staying back at the Hall with my stepmother and Lady Crossford – it drove the servants mad because one couldn't get the wagon with the lunch supplies anywhere near the Castle. They'd have to make three trips in the dog cart and then lug everything up the Castle hill by hand. But the view from the top of the tower was breathtaking.'

Her spectacles flashed, like twin moons in the dark. 'You'd probably better drive to Kynnoch, Ned, and see if we can get horses.'

She turned to Ysidro, shivering slightly in his black greatcoat at her side.

'There should be no problem achieving horses, Mistress.'

Seabury shot another glance at his uncanny passenger, then returned his attention to the road. 'I know them at the stables.' He wet his lips. 'Antrim – the head groom – is a little fond of the bottle, and if this is one of his nights there's a good chance I can take four out unnoticed.'

'I suspect,' purred the vampire, 'the man will be deep asleep.'

Asher hoped Ysidro was right. He looked exhausted and ill. Still, Zahorec had been using such an elixir from December to May, and had been able to put down everyone at Tufton Farm.

'Make that two horses,' Asher said. 'Ned, I'll want you to go up to the house and speak to Noel. Don't let Cece know, if she's there. Don't let anyone know. Wake him up if you have to, lie to him if you have to, but get him away from Kynnoch. Take him back to Glasgow tonight – back to London, if you can. He'll probably be doped, but he'll also probably be himself.'

Ned nodded jerkily. In his eyes was what they both knew Dr Millward would do: stop the car, get out, and say, *You cannot take the help of the enemy without turning toward the shadow yourself.*

*Not even to save your friend?*

*Not even to save your daughter?*

*And your wife*, Asher reflected. *And yourself . . .*

Seabury's gaze went back to the road. He drove on in silence.

*Was that why Johanot of Valladolid went back to Spain?*

*And did his flight do him any good?*

Fleeting moonlight revealed the eerie landscape of rock summits and bare boulders, blinked on the waters of Loch Lomond. *You take the high road, and I'll take the low road*, the old song said: the low road being, Asher knew, the paths that the Dead walked. *And I'll be in Scotland before ye . . .*

*Because the Dead do indeed travel fast.*

Far off in the darkness, rising wind bore the howling of dogs.

'That will be the pack at Kynnoch Hall,' Lydia whispered.

Asher felt as if the skin crept on his body.

'What is it?' whispered Seabury. 'What's happening?'

'Some chance noise, mayhap.' Ysidro, who had sunk into

meditation, raised his head a little. 'Or perchance they sense that ill things walk the moor tonight.'

'What weapons have you?' Asher had seen the long gun-case Seabury had loaded into the back of the Ford.

'Shotgun and pistol.' Loaded with silver, Asher guessed. They were what he'd carried to hunt vampires in the sewers below London last night. 'And Roddy's rifle.'

'Let us take them. We'll need them more than you.'

Clouds gathered, broke; swept the motor car with a spattering of rain as it turned on to the track toward Kynnoch Hall. The howling of the pack grew louder, dying when some kennel man, perhaps, came out and whipped them silent, only to break out again. Ysidro, arms folded, listened without a sound.

They surmounted a hill crest. Moonlight showed them a huddle of roofs, touched with a few lights low against the earth, where servants washed up after late tea. A single lantern gleamed where the stables must be. Seabury began a careful descent over tarmac buckled and rock strewn from winter downpours. A glance at his watch showed Asher that it was just after one.

'Two horses?' whispered Seabury. 'Not three?'

'Saddle no beast for me.' Ysidro's soft voice came from out of the darkness. 'I shall follow afoot.'

'All right.' Seabury asked no reason. No horse would bear the Undead and few mounts would even endure a vampire's touch. The clamor of the pack continued unabated, but no man's shadow now crossed the lantern light beside the stable door.

In the rear seat of the Ford, Ysidro was motionless as pale stone.

Only after Seabury had braked the car, sheathed his dark lantern, and picked his way afoot toward the stables, did the vampire lift his head. 'No child dreams in the Hall,' he said. 'There are some, sleeping here and there in the night – villagers, at a distance, I think. Without knowing the child I cannot tell one from another.'

'Thank you.' Lydia touched his arm.

''Tis naught. Think what fools we should have looked, mounting assault upon an empty castle while our quarry was left behind us here.' He turned his gaze out into the darkness, where tor and heath and Munro blended with piled cloud in a wall of black. 'I shall play the scout, I think, before you and behind. The dogs do not lie. Undead walk the moor tonight.'

'Zahorec?'

There was something bird-like about the movement of the vampire's head – *Listening? Scenting?* Something un-human.

'More than one.' A broken fragment of moonlight showed pale brows pinch over the aquiline nose.

'Could Grippen have followed us after all?' Lydia's voice sank to a whisper, as if she feared the Master of London might hear them. *No unreasonable concern . . .*

'He has living men aplenty at call,' agreed Ysidro softly, 'who would take five pounds, or ten, to travel to Scotland with a trunk and ask no questions what it might contain. The world e'en abounds with those who would do so for nothing.'

'Is that how you got from Italy to London in two days?'

'The dead travel fast, Mistress. And the living sometimes stand in desperate need of whatever the dead can pay them.' Rising, the vampire leaped lightly over the side of the open car to the stony drive. 'Whether 'tis Lionel out there, or whether this Zahorec has made a fledgling, either of the American girl or of someone else, I cannot tell. Perchance it may be one of the old vampires, the spirits that haunted the moors and caves time out of mind here and preyed upon the villages. 'Twere best I keep behind you, and best we all pray – to whoever we think might listen – that through weariness I am mistaken in my perception, and that we shall meet only one foe tonight.'

Then he was gone.


'They're sleeping like the dead in the stables.' Seabury, when he came up the path leading two of the Earl of Crossford's hacks, was waxen with strain. 'Not only in the stables, everywhere! Every hound in the kennels is giving tongue and nothing! Not a kennel boy, not a groom, not a servant from the house . . .'

He looked around him, the white of his eyes showing all round the dark pupils in the dim glow of the dark lantern. Flakes of silver rimmed the streaming clouds overhead; the baying of the hunting pack drifted on the night like the smoke of spreading fire.

'The noise will wake the house again soon,' said Asher. 'Get Noel out of there. If Miranda isn't in the house I'm guessing that Cece isn't, either. Tell anyone who tries to stop you that Armistead's threatening to disinherit his daughter completely unless Noel wires him tonight. We'll leave the motor here for you; you'll probably need to refill the petrol. Once you're away from the house tell him about Zahorec: that he's a vampire; that he's been controlling Noel; that he's planning to kill Noel and take his place. That's if you need to. He may be too dopey to care.'

The young man's lips tightened, but he didn't disagree.

Asher gathered the reins in his left hand. Seabury caught him around the waist, took his weight while he balanced on the running board as a mounting block, got his left foot in the stirrup. Then while Asher recovered his breath he handed him up one of the rifles, the dark-lantern, and the walking stick he'd bought at Willesden. The rainy wind was rising, driving the clouds before it toward the moon.

'Good luck.'

'And you,' said Asher quietly. 'Even if we manage to kill Zahorec, you know, it won't be the end of Noel's griefs. He'll still be the man you tried to save in Paris, with that man's family and flaws.'

'I know that.' Seabury smiled crookedly. 'And I suppose . . .' He paused, as if looking at his friendship – his love – for that tall, clumsy nobleman who only wanted to paint and read and be left alone. 'Do vampires have this sort of problem? Loving, and trying to help people who don't want to be helped, and getting their affairs into a mess? Do you know?'

Asher said, 'They don't. Their existence is very simple: protecting themselves at all costs, the hunt, and the kill. That's why people become vampires.' He reined away, toward the barely seen Corbett of rock that Lydia had pointed out to him as marking the way to Stenmuir. Night lay on the moors like the foreshadow of death, as if all the world had been tipped over into an eternity that moved with invisible peril.

It was only hours until first light.

He smelled wood smoke before he saw Stenmuir Castle itself: not a castle, as Lydia had said, but a square gray manor house grafted on to the original tower of what was in those parts called a fortalice, a small fortress built to defend against border reivers. With the disappearance of the moon again Lydia had dismounted, leading both horses by a slit of lantern light. Tiny as a lone fragment of glitter adrift in the ocean of the night, a window glowed against the cloud wrack.

Roof line and tower took shape against the ragged sky. A suggestion of broken timbers, the black spoor of some old fire. Beside the ruin of a pair of crumbling gateposts something white moved in the gloom, and he heard a horse whinny in fear, and the *tink* of harness-brasses. A chaise stood near the gate, empty. Its lights had been doused but their metal was hot to the touch. Asher whispered, 'Ysidro,' but the vampire failed to materialize.

Scouting at a distance?

Lying with a broken back after an encounter with one of those vampires he'd sensed? Unable to move and waiting for first light to ignite his flesh?

No way to tell.

Asher's own mount jittered against the lead rein. The wind? Or something else? Five miles away across mire and stone, the dogs could still be heard baying at Kynnoch Hall.

He slid from the saddle, handed Lydia the rifle. 'Follow me.'

'Don't be silly!'

'You can move quicker.' He took a step, almost fell, stood for a moment clinging to his stick and wondering if Millward's idiotic scheme of last night was going to end in the entire Asher family and their Undead godfather getting killed.

*I can do this . . .*

He took a deep breath, shifted his hold on the cane and the shotgun, and limped agonizingly up the crag on which the little Castle was built. Steps had been cut where the path was steepest, but he was sweating by the time he reached the door.

It was unlocked. A candle burned beyond a door to his right, and the suggestion of voices, of footfalls, murmured overhead. Feeling as if he had been rationed only a certain number of paces for the night, Asher dragged himself through the great entry hall to the half-opened door of what had probably been a dining room. An enormous table was all that remained of its furnishings, and on it lay a woman's crimson leather handbag, a candlestick with candle burning, a Thermos, a picnic basket, and four books.

Worn leather covers glinted with faded gilt. They'd been wrapped in a silk shawl and he hadn't the slightest doubt what they were.

*Cece must have found where her father hid them, and stole them when she fled.*

The thought was only a passing one. The important fact was that there was no one in the room.

*Wait for them here?* The picnic basket and Thermos promised a return. Getting up the stairs – and then coming back down them – were going to be exercises in agony that he might well not be capable of making without a fall. The banister was long gone; the drop from the gallery above would be wicked.

But the utter stillness of the night raised the hair on his nape, and morning's nearness after the short summer night was a goad even sharper than the pain in his ankle. *She's meeting Zahorec here with the books. They're upstairs now . . .*

He dragged himself up the first two steps, strained his ears to listen. A woman said something, indistinct through the intervening stone and wood. Another voice, also a woman's, replied.

Then like the stab of a silver knife into his flesh a child's voice: 'Go home . . .'

'Hush,' snapped an alto voice, with the slight inflection of speech that Asher recognized as characteristic of American southern blacks. 'We gonna take you home soon, honey.'

The sound of his daughter's voice heated every atom of his flesh, as if he'd drunk brandy. Wild and murderous rage . . .

*They're waiting for him. He must have gone to kill. With dawn this close, he'll be here very, VERY soon . . .*

By putting his shoulder to the paneling on the stair, and keeping his weight on the risers, he was able to climb, more or less steadily, and without a sound.

'. . . all depends on what your daddy's gonna say about that little girl,' continued the black girl – Hellice, Lydia had said her name was. 'You say she's this Charlene Savenake's baby given over into your care – though I never heard Lady Savenake had no other daughter but Sylvie—'

'Whose daughter she is, is none of your business, Hellie,' said a lighter voice – like a soubrette who'd had elocution lessons. 'She's in my care—'

'Then why keep her secret from your daddy? Why send me out here with her all today? I'm not sayin' you're wrong, Miss Cece. I'm just sayin', your daddy could fire me without a character, and then where'd I be?'

The upper floor of Stenmuir was far more ruinous than the lower.

Much of the roof was gone, and the walls of several of the rooms. When the clouds shifted Asher saw the tower rising above them, little more than a hollowed shell, floors broken away and inner doors opening into nothing. None of the banister that once had circled the gallery above the hall survived. The hall below was a pit of night.

Keeping to the wall where the stronger flooring would take his weight without creaking, Asher angled his head to look through the door of one of the few intact chambers that opened from the gallery. By the light of a single lantern, Cecelia Armistead had to be the dark-haired young lady in a flame-red walking costume more stylish than practical. Hellie – what Americans would call an octoroon – stood beside a camp chair in a corner where a couple of carriage rugs had been thrown.

Miranda sat curled into the corner on the carriage rugs. Her red hair was tangled and uncombed, her dress dirty, but she watched the two women without fear, as if she were just calculating her moment to run. Asher could almost hear her thinking, *I'm only a baby, how far can I get and is it worth getting slapped if I get caught?* Her face was bruised: someone had slapped her recently and hard.

Smoothly, Hellie continued, 'I just want a guarantee, Miss Cece—'

Through the door, Miranda's eyes met her father's, widened in shocked joy—

And she didn't make a sound.

A stride took Cece to her servant and she caught Hellie's arm. 'Don't you try to blackmail me, you black bitch—'

Miranda bolted for the door as Asher stepped around the doorpost, leveled the shotgun on both women as they turned. 'Stand right where you are.'

Both Cece and Hellie expressed their feelings in a way that Lydia's Aunt Lavinnia would have deemed only to be expected of Americans. Miranda grabbed his leg and pressed her face to it. 'Papa'. He could feel her shaking.

'Your mama's downstairs,' he said quietly. 'Go quickly – stay by the wall . . .'

*We're going to get out of this after all . . .*

Behind him in the dark Lydia screamed, 'Jamie, look out!'

# THIRTY

A sher turned his head and Hellie grabbed her mistress and shoved her at him, the American girl's weight catching him on his right side and collapsing his weakened leg like the blow of a hammer. He tried to roll clear, but Cece wrenched the shotgun from his hands and reared herself back, fired it at him as he threw Miranda out of the way – to his life's end he was never sure how he managed it in the confusion. Ricocheting pellets tore his arm and scalp; he heard both Miranda and Cece scream. As he tried to get to his feet someone flung herself past him, almost tripping over him in a rush of skirts.

The next instant a numbing kick to the ribs sent him almost over the edge of the gallery. He grabbed the broken stub of a baluster, dragged his legs back from over the black drop, and saw, by the flaring glow of the lantern, Damien Zahorec at the top of the stair, holding Lydia by the waist and one arm.

Cece, on her knees and clutching a bleeding arm (*the ricochet must have caught her, too, and serve her right*), sobbed, 'Kill her!' A revolver lay near her on the floor (*Lydia must have had it in her hand*) and Cece grabbed for it. In the same instant Miranda wailed, 'Mama!' and ran toward Lydia with arms outstretched.

Lydia twisted in Zahorec's grip and smote him across the eyes with the silver chains wrapped around her left wrist, lunged for her daughter when the vampire dropped her with a shrieked curse. She might have reached her, had not Cece fired at her – missing her by yards, but Lydia dodged aside, and the next instant, with the near-invisible swiftness of the Undead, Zahorec had overtaken her, knocked her spinning with a sidelong slap, and scooped up Miranda in his arms.

The child screamed, bit, thrashed like a demon, but the cold clawed hand wrapped around her throat and Zahorec shouted, 'Stay back!'

Lydia, halfway to her feet with a look in her eyes that Asher had never seen in his usually matter-of-fact young wife, froze, crouching. Cece swung the pistol toward her and Zahorec shouted again. 'Drop it!'

Such was his power over the American girl that she too stood still, though she didn't let go of the weapon, or lower its aim.

'Cecelia,' said the vampire softly. '*Caro*. I have told you I have need of this woman – stay where you are, Lydia, *meine Liebling* . . . This is your so-brave husband?' The blue eyes flickered down to Asher, who had got his elbows under him and was struggling to breathe. In the soft old *hochdeutsch* of the Empire he continued, 'Don't be foolish, *mein Held*. I want your beautiful one alive and willing, and if you make me kill you then I shall be obliged to kill her also, and your lovely child. Surely you have seen how it is, and what it is that I need.'

'And what,' panted Asher, 'do you need?' He could probably, he calculated, reach the vampire if he lunged for him, but if he did so he knew Miranda would die. Lydia, too, the moment Zahorec took his attention from the hysterical girl with the pistol.

*Watch for it*, he thought. *You'll only have a split-second . . .*

'I need what all men need,' replied Damien gravely, 'living or dead. I need my freedom.' In the lamplight he looked far worse than Ysidro had, skeletal and alien, with his dark hair falling over his eyes and his powerful form bony and shrunken. The silver chain on Lydia's wrist had left a suppurating welt across his forehead, as if he'd been struck with a red-hot rod. He did, in fact, bear a superficial resemblance to Noel Wredemere. Asher wondered for how much longer he would have been able to muster the strength to maintain the illusion. How much longer he'd have been able to make love to Cece Armistead in her dreams.

'For three hundred years I have been a slave – three hundred years! Suitable penance, my old confessor would say, for one who used to boast that I could enslave any woman whose eyes met mine . . .'

His glance returned to the dark-haired girl in crimson, her revolver still trained on Lydia, but her eyes on Zahorec's face: suspicion, incomprehension, jealousy, adoration.

'A jest worthy of the Devil himself. They said Ippolyta Vranica, sorceress and heretic and ruler in her own right of the mountains beyond Zara, had a heart of obsidian, impervious to the smiles of a man. Of course I had to have her. Never did it cross my mind to wonder at it, that I never saw her save after the sun was down . . . too late I found the reason. Queen of the vampires of the Dinarics, she would not let me go. What would you have done, Englishman?

With the life bleeding from me, drop by slow drop, she dangled me over the abyss of death and offered me the choice: to be her creature, her servant, her lover for eternity. What would you have done?'

Asher dragged himself carefully to a sitting position. 'I've met the lady,' he said. 'But if it's freedom that you seek, what need have you of Lydia's services, or mine? What need of the London nest, or the *Book of the Kindred of Darkness*? Where did you get it, by the way?'

'In my days of daylight and breath,' replied the vampire, 'I was a scholar of sorts. I read it as I read *Pantagreul* and *Utopia* and the dialogs of Plato, and thought of it no more than of those other fairy tales. It was in my house in Venice. I recalled it with bitter longing, all those years of enslavement in the mountains. When the soldiers came and Ippolyta fled, it was the first place I made for. Like everything else it had been sold . . .'

'What are you talking about?' Cece moved closer to him, the revolver still aimed at Lydia's heart. 'I brought you the books, all of them. And I got Noel here. He's back at the Hall, he'll marry me tomorrow . . . Why isn't it "possible" to get rid of her now?'

'Beautiful one,' said Zahorec gently, 'I have need of her—'

'Why? What can she give you that I can't?'

'*Ein Gehirn*,' muttered Zahorec, *sotto voce*, but replied coaxingly, 'She is a scholar, beautiful savior. She has skills that I need.'

'I can learn them.' The American girl's eyes were wide with the burning focus Asher had seen in soldiers going into the veldt. 'Is it true what she told me? That you've gone to her as you came to me? That you kissed her as you kissed me . . . Made love to her as you made love to me . . .?'

'Honestly,' protested Lydia, 'I hardly asked him to—'

'You shut up!' Eyes blazing, the American girl swung to face her demon lover. 'Did you promise her what you promised me? That she'd be yours forever? Did you tell her you love her, as you told—'

Asher heard nothing, but Zahorec's head turned with a snap. Following his glance, Asher saw the maid Hellie, still standing a few yards away, even as her knees buckled, and a ribbon of blood uncurled down her shoulder and breast. Without an instant's hesitation Asher flung himself at Zahorec's legs, knocking him over, rolling. He heard Miranda scream and Cece's revolver fire and felt rather than saw Lydia lunge, too.

Her feet hammered the wooden floor, fleeing from the gallery through one of the black doors. Claws sank into the back of his neck and a knee ground his spine, but after that first split-second of pinning him, Zahorec didn't move.

Asher smelled blood, a lot of it.

He knew what had happened as he looked into the blackest corner of the gallery, and saw the maid Hellie slither, dead, to her knees and then to the floor.

The woman who straightened up behind her faced Zahorec across the body, proud pale aquiline face calm as marble and streaked with blood. The dark dress she'd worn in the Roman ruin last night glistened with it; besides the gunshot wounds in neck and breast, her flesh was crossed with the slash-marks of claws.

*She must have met Ysidro . . .*

Ippolyta kicked Hellie's body casually over the edge of the gallery. Asher heard the meaty smack as it hit the stone floor below. A glance – with Zahorec kneeling beside him, crushing him to the floor, he couldn't see much more – showed him no sign of Lydia or their child.

'Damien.'

Zahorec loosed his grip, and stood. 'My lady . . .'

In the old high German of the Empire, she said, 'Thought you to leave me?'

Cece fired, emptying the rest of the revolver – Asher didn't think the bullets even hit their target. Ippolyta turned towards her with eyes like the sun in eclipse. 'Little whore. Kill her, Damien. I want to see you do it.'

She still spoke in *hochdeutsch*, but when Damien turned toward Cece the girl saw in his face what he meant to do. She screamed, 'Damien, no! I love you!'

He stopped, features convulsed with pain. 'Don't you understand,' he whispered, 'that the love of the Undead is not like the love of the living?'

*A statement not entirely accurate*, reflected Asher. *They look identical so far.*

Damien sprang toward the girl, but either because he was unwilling despite the force of his master vampire's command, or because the elixirs he'd been taking had eroded his speed and skill, Cece saw him coming. She fired the empty pistol at him, then flung the weapon in his face, doubled from his grab and darted into the blackness of another of those blank-eyed gallery doors. Asher heard her footfalls clatter on the ancient floors, searching a way downstairs.

'Fetch her.' Ippolyta's guttural voice was cold.

Damien averted his face as if from a physical grasp, and as if physically dragged looked back to meet the black glow of her eyes.

'Bring her back here. I'll fetch the other bitch. I want to see you kill them both.'

Damien moaned, 'No . . .'

'Do it.' She walked toward him, stopped beside Asher and looked down into his face, then smiled. 'And we'll kill the little girl, too.' And she kicked him over the edge of the gallery.

He was half-ready for this, and if she'd been a living woman he'd have grabbed her ankles or her skirt, to drag her over after him. As it was he grabbed for the stumps of the burned and shattered balusters; he heard Damien's footfalls, bodiless as the scratching of a wind-blown tree, as the vampire darted away to catch Cece, but only felt Ippolyta's going.

*Lydia.*

*Miranda.*

*It's fifteen feet to the floor. If I let go I won't land well; I'll never get up the stairs again . . .*

Shadow moved on the stairway. Then a hand cold and bony and strong as the Grim Reaper's locked around his wrist and dragged him up; another caught him by the back of the jacket.

'Which way?' It was Ysidro.

'That door—' There was blood on Ysidro's hands and clothing: it had indeed been he whom Ippolyta had fought. He looked as if he'd got the worst of it, but at least he'd slowed her down. 'She's gone for Lydia and Miranda—'

Then he was lying alone on the edge of the gallery, Ysidro not even a wisp of smoke vanishing through the door he'd shown. Shaking, Asher crawled to where the shotgun lay, fumbled several silver-nosed bullets from his pockets before finding a shotgun shell, shoved it in the breech. Ysidro looked badly wounded, Ippolyta also . . .

*She'll summon Damien.*

He dragged himself to the wall, used it to get to his feet. How much additional silver it would take to incapacitate the vampire queen he didn't know, but he guessed Ysidro would need every shred of advantage, and the clouds were clearing enough to give him a reasonable chance to aim. Through the black doorway where Lydia had fled with their child he could see moonlight now, and his fear was replaced by certainty. That way led to the stair that wound up the old fortalice tower. Railless stone, spiraling up floor above broken floor.

He leaned his shoulder to the wall, forced himself up a step, then two. Dizziness swamped him and he sank to his knees so as not to fall. A shadow bent over him, massive and smelling of blood – A hand like cold, clawed iron dragged him to his feet. *Damien. He must have killed Cece, to heal himself from the silver-burn* . . .

A flake of moonlight showed him the face of Titus Armistead.

And he saw that Titus Armistead had become vampire.

The American's eyes caught the thin light like a cat's. The grizzled hair had almost completely returned to the dark of his prime, and his skin had the white-silk smoothness of vampire flesh. Fangs gleamed wetly as he asked, 'Where's my daughter?'

He answered the father, not the vampire.

'Zahorec's hunting her. He'll bring her to Ippolyta alive.'

'Ippolyta?'

'His queen. The one who made him vampire.'

'Where's she?'

'Ahead . . .'

'You're Wilson.' The powerful arm circled his ribs, dragged him up the narrow steps. 'You don't look like him, except your eyes . . . Your flesh smells like his, your blood . . . And that's his clothes . . .'

'I'm Wilson.' The conversation in Lincoln's Inn felt like months ago. 'I see you found your vampire.'

'He found me.'

'I tried to warn you . . .'

The thin lip pulled back from the fangs again; Armistead smiled. 'Oh, no. I paid him to do me. That bastard'll bring Cece to this Ippolyta?'

Asher managed to nod. Badly as Zahorec needed a kill, he couldn't imagine him disobeying his Queen. Blackness fell away to his left beyond the brink of the narrow stair. To his right, wind keened through a window-slit where the lift of the land, scattered with glacial stones, lay formless in a darkness thinning to ash.

'Good. It takes a devil to fight a devil, Mr Wilson – if that's really your name. The book taught me that if nothing else. There was nothing else I could see to do, to save her.'

Stone rattled down from above, clattering off the broken rafters that were all that remained of the tower's floors. Miranda screamed, 'Mama!' Armistead dragged Asher up out of shadow and on to the parapet at the tower's top, where Ysidro and the Lady Ippolyta struggled on the last yard or so of stairway against the first stains of gray in the sky. She was a queenly woman, and of a height with the Spaniard, powerful with a vampire's power. Lydia lay on the parapet just beyond them, where she had crawled in a last effort to get away from the Master of the Dinarics, Miranda clasped tight in her arms. Her dress was torn, where Ippolyta had snatched at her. Blood streaked the rips, and her face, and her tangled unbound hair.

Armistead let go of Asher's arm, and with the eerie weightless power of the vampires sprang across the gulf of the empty tower that separated them, twelve feet from the stairway to the parapet, his gray Inverness cloak billowing behind him like wings.

'Give her to me.'

Lydia's spectacles flashed in the sinking moonlight as she looked up at him, her arms tightening around her child. Feet away, Ippolyta drove Ysidro to his knees on the parapet's edge, claws buried in the back of his neck – she'd strike Lydia next and strike with the speed of a bullet.

'Give her—!' The fledgling vampire – the mine-owner who'd lived a lifetime by hard-headed greed – stretched down his hands, clawed and hairy and strong . . .

And he too, Asher knew, needed a kill. Needed two kills, if he was going to take on Ippolyta and Zahorec both, if he was going to save his own child.

Lydia shrank against the stone, clinging tight, threw one fast glance at Asher—

*Dear God, I can't make this decision—*

He saw his dream again, Johanot of Valladolid reaching down to gather Miranda into his arms.

He nodded, and would have turned his face away so as not to see, but he couldn't. Miranda clinging to his neck, Armistead launched himself back across the void to the stairway, landed a few steps below Asher and set the child down.

'Take her down,' said Armistead. 'I'll—'

Lydia screamed, 'Simon!' and Asher looked up, to see Ysidro writhe from his opponent's grasp. But Ippolyta was swifter than a snake, striking at him before he could catch his balance. His foot slid on the stonework, slippery with both of their blood, and he fell, down into the empty hollow of the tower. Before he was even out of sight she was across the space that separated her from the narrow ledge where Lydia crouched, caught her by the hair and bent over her.

Armistead tore the shotgun from Asher's hand, brought it up even as Ysidro, catching some broken rafter below, swung himself back up to the parapet. Ippolyta screamed, jerked her hand back from the silver on Lydia's throat, face inhuman with rage. Armistead fired, and Ysidro jerked back out of the way of the silver deer-shot that ripped through the flesh of the vampire queen's face and breast. The force knocked her out and back off the wall, and as she went over she caught Ysidro by the arms, whether to save herself or only with the intent of dragging her enemy to his doom Asher could not tell.

Lydia cried, 'Simon!' again and grabbed for them as they tottered on the edge, but she was too late.

As they plunged down off the parapet, Damien Zahorec shrieked, 'Ippolyta!' as if his soul were being ripped from his flesh.

He stood below them on the stair, Cece pressed against his body, one arm around her waist and his other hand closed on her throat. She was sobbing with terror, her red gown torn half off her shoulders and her creamy skin marked by claw-rips and scratches. She raised her dark eyes and wailed, 'Daddy! Oh, Daddy—'

'Let her go,' said Asher quietly. 'Your lady is dead.'

Zahorec's voice cracked in wild laughter. 'Is that all you know about us, *mein Held*? You think a fall like that will kill Ippolyta Vranica? Break her back, yes. Break her legs, yes, and all the bones of her body, so that she lies in agony looking up at the sky as it grows light . . . yes. But kill her? Never!'

His blue eyes pressed shut, and again his face spasmed. 'She will have her vengeance,' he whispered. 'I feel her in my mind, in my bones . . . In agony, but strong unto the end. She holds me here. Even now as the sun rises, she won't let me flee. She won't let me leave this place until I do as she commands. She will feel me drink this girl's life, ere the flame burst out on her flesh . . .'

From his pocket Asher took one of the silver-tipped rifle bullets, flung it full-force at the vampire's face. The silver itself would have stung him, not even penetrating the flesh, but Zahorec, exhausted already, reacted without knowing what had been thrown. Turned his head, his attention, his focus, and in that split-second Armistead struck.

Cece screamed, pulled herself free as Zahorec grappled with the American. Fell to her knees and scrambled to put her back to the stone of the wall, away from the sixty-foot drop below the stair. The two vampires grappled on the narrow steps. Had Armistead tried to wound or kill or even hurl Zahorec down as Ippolyta had been hurled, he probably could not have done so, even weakened as the older vampire was. But he only held on to his opponent, by the wrists, by the arms, by the throat, heedless of the other vampire's claws and teeth. He shouted, 'Cece, run!' but she didn't move, only stared up at them as they writhed against the paling sky. Trapped at the top of the tower, Asher backed against the parapet, put a hand over Miranda's eyes, knowing what was going to happen.

Far below him he heard a bestial scream, and the roar of fire at the foot of the tower.

Armistead was burning, too, the oily heat of the flames beating on Asher's face. Screaming – but hanging on.

Asher didn't know whether it was the flames that sheathed Armistead that ignited Zahorec's flesh, or the still-distant sun's light suffusing the sky. Whether the older vampire would have been able to make it to shelter, had not the cleansing fire spread from the flesh of his opponent into his own. Cece screamed, 'Daddy!' as both vampires fell to their knees, a doubled spout of flame, then tipped sideways off the stair. Plunged into the central gulf within the tower like Lucifer plunging into darkness.

Asher kept tight hold of Miranda, but Lydia crawled from the parapet where she had lain, went to the edge of the broken floor and looked down through the tangle of shattered joists at the blaze below.

It was Asher who said, 'We'd better go.' He would have carried Miranda if he could, but it was all he could do to keep himself on his feet. The sturdy toddler held his hand, stepped carefully down each step of the long stone curve unassisted. Though it was Asher who was lamed and bleeding, it was Cece, doubled over in sobbing hysterics, whom Lydia had to assist down the steps, through the ruined upper floor of the house, down the stairs into the house's hall and – at long last – to the bench outside.

Limping far behind them, Asher paused in the hall. Through a doorway he could see into the bottom of the tower, where the two locked forms had subsided into a sullen mound of charred bone still flickering with blue flame. He doubted there would even be enough left of Titus Armistead's clothing and effects for anyone to identify. He kept his hand on his daughter's head, kept her face turned away. Then, still holding to the wall, he dragged himself around to the dining room, where the candle was guttering out on the table and the blue twilight of morning trickled through the shuttered windows, gleamed gently on the gilt trim of four old books.

Asher supported himself on the table's edge as he emptied the picnic basket Cece Armistead had left there: sandwiches, apples, a pocket flask. He opened the books one by one, briefly, and put three of them into the basket.

The fourth he concealed under his jacket.

The sandwiches in his pockets – Miranda carrying the Thermos – he made his agonized way to the door. On the bench beside it Cece wailed like a beaten child. Asher watched her impassively, feeling very detached from himself – like a very old spider, he reflected, that has been stepped on many times.

Lydia fell to her knees, crushed Miranda against her chest, shaking with shock and cold and reaction. Asher sank down on to the end of the bench, put his arms around both of them.

*We're all alive*, he thought, and it was the only thought that would go through his mind. *We're all alive . . .*

Public-school chivalry and common decency told him he should comfort Cece but all he wanted to do – for the rest of his life, if possible – was hold his wife and his daughter against him, feel the softness of their hair against his lips.

At length Lydia asked, 'What's in the Thermos?'

'Probably coffee.' Smoke filled the air, and the smell of charred flesh.

Lydia unscrewed the cap, gave Cece a drink, and took one herself before returning the flask to Asher. 'I'll be back.' She clung for a moment more to Miranda, then kissed Asher, stood up, and walked away around the corner of the house.

He rested his head against the stone of the wall behind them. Miranda, with the simple healing miracle of childhood, had fallen asleep in his lap; Asher wished he had the option of doing the same.

Instead, a little awkwardly, he put his arm around Cece Armistead's heaving shoulders, patted her gently, but could find no words of comfort, no words at all. She kept sobbing, 'Oh, my God – oh, Daddy – oh, Damien,' and turned her face to weep into Asher's chest. It had not been her fault, he understood, that Damien Zahorec had made her his target, and she would have had to be an extraordinary woman to resist his seduction. Still, he felt infinitely distant from her and from all the sweet stillness that surrounded them. Mostly all he could think of was that there was still the hill to get down, to the chaise and the horses at the bottom.

Lydia came back around the corner of the house, a long stick still in her hand. The end was charred, as if she'd used it to probe through an ash-heap.

'There's only one skeleton there at the foot of the wall,' she said. 'It's still burning, but the pelvis is definitely a woman's. I think the bones should be consumed,' she added, 'by the time anyone gets here.'

# THIRTY-ONE

I t took three weeks for the cracked bone in Asher's ankle to heal. He spent the time quietly in his study in Holywell Street, preparing his notes for the start of Trinity term, studying fourteenth-century Spanish verb tenses, and playing finger-puppets with Miranda. He limped up the stairs to her nursery three and four times a night, but Nan Wellit – with whom, for the first week, the tiny girl insisted on sharing a bed 'like we did downstairs' – reported neither nightmares nor disturbed sleep.

Evidently Miranda had inherited Lydia's phlegmatic temperament. Asher's own sleep was not so restful.

Lydia sent word to her Aunt Isobel that Miranda had been taken ill and that she was no longer at liberty to chaperone Emily to regattas, ballets, and the races, thus missing the spectacle of one of Josetta Beyerly's suffragist compatriots who threw herself – fatally – beneath the hooves of the King's horse just before the home stretch at Ascot. She did go up to London to attend Emily's engagement party to Terence Winterson, and heard her aunt exclaim from her bath-chair throne, 'I do not grudge one moment of the labor and trouble I went to this Season, to bring this about . . .'

For the first week of term Asher used a cane, and told sympathetic students he'd stepped off a curb in Padua.

Just before midsummer a back-page advertisement in the *Telegraph* mentioned that The Scythe pub in Stepney was up for sale, its owners – Mr and Mrs Henry Scrooby, and both of Mr Scrooby's brothers – having disappeared. A day or two later a small paragraph remarked on the suicide of bank clerk Timothy Rolleston, in whose rooms the hair ribbons of at least twelve little girls were found, tidily pasted into a scrapbook.

Shortly after that, when the days were longest and everyone who was anyone was flocking to Henley on the Thames, Asher quietly set about gathering syringes and ampoules of silver nitrate, stakes of hawthorn-wood, and a surgical saw. Since 1907, when first he had become acquainted with the reality of the kindred of darkness, he had been aware also that to become a vampire hunter – to follow in the literary footsteps of Abraham Van Helsing or the actual ones of Osric Millward – was to become obsessed. To enter into the world of the Undead himself, pursuing their shadows to the exclusion of the world of the light.

If the vampires, in their quest for eternal life, ended by shrinking that eternity to nothing but the search for prey and the efforts to control all things around them in order to remain safe, so, he had observed, did the vampire hunters of his acquaintance also live for nothing but the hunt.

Still, on the third of July, starting when first daylight flushed the sky at five and moving where he could through sewers, Underground tunnels, and London's submerged network of rivers and ancient crypts, he visited every one of Lionel Grippen's lairs. Asher had killed vampires before. Mostly it was a matter of dragging their decapitated bodies to where light would fall, if a shutter or a door or a manhole-cover were opened, and then opening it. Only a few seconds of direct sunlight would suffice to ignite the Undead flesh. Heads severed to separate the central nervous system, hearts staked and veins injected with silver nitrate, they would then go on burning in the darkness as he walked away.

He found in Grippen's lairs the lovely Penelope, the foxlike Jerry, and Sir Geoffrey Vauxhill.

In none of them did he find either Mrs Raleigh or Lionel Grippen.

In the house to which Lydia gave him directions in Spaniard's Lane, he found no trace of Don Simon Ysidro, nor even of the sub-cellar and crypt which she described. He wasn't entirely certain he had the right house.

He rode his motorcycle back over the hills to Oxford. And dreamed that night of Africa.

There was a camp he'd make on the veldt, on the land of a Boer farmer named Van Der Platz. The only son of the household, sixteen-year-old Jan, would ride out in the evenings, to talk with the man whom he knew as Professor Leyden of Heidelberg, about what life would be like beyond the confines of chores and church, about places where black men weren't assumed to be cattle and women weren't treated like brood-mares, about books to read that weren't the Bible. Then Jan would ride home, and Asher would sit sometimes for hours outside his tent, listening to the far-off lunatic yikking of hyenas, gazing at the gold African moon.

He often dreamed of the place, as he did tonight: the glow of his lantern catching in the long grass, the humming of insects in the twilight. On the camp table before the tent lay the *Book of the Kindred of Darkness*, and across the table from him, on the other camp chair where young Jan had sat (Asher knew) earlier in the evening, perched Don Simon Ysidro, elegant as always in Savile Row gray.

'Do you think it an accident,' the vampire asked, 'that Lionel's disloyal fledglings all happened to be sleeping in Lionel's lairs today?'

Disgust swept Asher, and anger that even his vengeance had been used for the Master of London's convenience. He pushed aside the scribbled notes of old Spanish morphology that littered the table, flung his pencil at Ysidro, who didn't even bother to dodge. 'Is he watching me?'

'I don't think so.' The vampire shrugged. 'Are *you* watching *us*? Once *la niña* was safe I suggested to Lionel that you'd do something of this nature, as soon as you were on your feet again. He's been rearranging his holdings all month. It vexes him, but I pointed out to him that 'twas no more than what he had asked for, and all for the best. Even the dead must move with the times.'

'Does he think he'll escape the reckoning for what he's done? That any of you will?'

'Yes, in fact, we do. You sound like your friend Dr Millward –
who has, by the way, disowned that poor *bonachón* Seabury when
Seabury and his friend left together for the South of France. Do
you really want to turn into him? To hunt us is to hunt smoke,
James, as I have said to you before. Prior to the death of his young
brother in 1882 Millward did quite good work in the translation of
proto-Jewish inscriptions. Once he became a vampire hunter, he
became as you see him. A fanatic, and a bore, incapable of having
a relationship that does not turn upon the Undead in some fashion.
Not a happy man and not a particularly effective vampire hunter
either.'

'That's no reason to let you go on killing.'

The Spaniard raised colorless brows. 'You do not "let" us, James.
We do as we must. We do as we do. 'Twas Lionel who returned to
London that night and made Armistead vampire, you know. Guessed
– or recalled under the goad of Mistress Asher's words – the man's
true purpose in seeking for a vampire. It takes a devil to deal with
a devil, Armistead said, and we all of us underestimated him. From
reading the books he understood what was happening to his daughter,
weeks before. It was, as he said, the only thing that he could think
to do, to save her. Would you do as much, to save Miss Miranda?'

Asher recalled the man's screams, and how even as his flesh was
consumed he had not released his grip on his daughter's predator.

'Yes. Yes, I would. And to save the children of other men, from
Grippen . . . and from you.'

'*All whom war, dearth, age, agues, tyrannies / Despair, law, chance
hath slain,*' quoted Ysidro. 'Can you save them? *Earth's face is but
thy table, there are set/ Plants, cattle, men, dishes for Death to eat.*
If saving the world from death were truly your heart's calling, James,
you would have remained in the Department. The Kaiser will kill
more than ever we did – he, and your Prime Minister, and Messires
Poincaré and Clemenceau in France and all the rest of them.'

'That's the answer of a thief who wants to go on helping himself
to other men's goods.'

''Tis the only answer I have. Will you publish this?' The long
nails brushed the brittle brown paper of the book between them.

Asher shook his head. 'I know as well as you do that to prove
to the authorities that vampires exist would only set them hunting
them to hire them, like Armistead told his men he was doing. Do

you think these Americans – these Vanderbilts, these Rockefellers, these Fords – wouldn't try it, if they knew?'

For a time there was only the hiss of the lantern's hot metal, and the sough of wind through the veldt. Then he asked, 'That one is the original, isn't it?'

'How did you guess?'

'Because the language is right. The date of publication is 1494 – one of the oldest editions, though the earlier Latin one is substantially different. But that's fourteenth-century Spanish: when Johanot of Valladolid supposedly lived. It has to be a direct copy of what he wrote.'

Ysidro smiled. With lantern light giving color to the pallor of his flesh, he looked, Asher guessed, as he had in life: a young Spanish gentleman who traveled to London for a little diplomatic spying, and who never found his way home again.

Asher thought, *He has a copy, too. Somewhere in that dusty library that Lydia described . . .*

'What will you do with it, then?'

'I'll keep it,' said Asher. 'In a silver reliquary, like Armistead did. Possibly the same one he had. I'm told Cece is selling up his collection before going back to the States. And I'll study it. And use its knowledge, to destroy whichever of your kind crosses my path. Including yourself.'

'James . . .' The vampire held out his hand to him. 'I have known this of you for many years now . . . and I will endeavor, as I have for many years now, not to cross your path. Might I bid Mistress Lydia, and *la niña*, farewell ere I go?'

Asher recalled Ysidro's thin form locked in the grip of lady Ippolyta, as he'd pulled the other vampire away from Lydia on the parapet against the growing light of dawn. Knew in his heart that it was only luck that the Spaniard had been able to either catch some window-ledge or projection of the tower, or that he had not broken his neck or his legs in the fall and had been able to crawl to safety before the sky grew bright.

Had he been, he reflected, a true vampire-hunter, a true champion of what was right instead of a man used to compromising with shadows in order to win achievable goals, he would have said, *I'll kill you before I'll let you touch my daughter. Get you back into darkness where you belong.*

And he knew Ysidro would have gone.

'Of course.'

Ysidro turned toward the tent and lifted the mosquito-bar, and sure enough, as Asher had guessed would be the case, Lydia lay asleep on his cot, dressed in one of her lace tea-gowns, her spectacles laid down on a copy of Weismann's *Germ-Theory of Heredity*, Miranda curled up asleep in her arms.

The vampire knelt beside them, gently kissed Lydia on the brow, and laid his clawed hand on Miranda's cheek.

'Don't abandon your treasures, James, to chase shadows you never will catch,' he said quietly. 'I did so once, and have for three hundred and fifty-eight years regretted it. They need you, as your heart needs them in order to go on beating.'

Bending, he kissed Miranda's cheek, eyes shut, like a man breathing the scent of a rose.

Then he straightened, and stepped out into the darkness, holding the mosquito-netting aside for Asher to follow.

'Light and warmth are very brief, James. Darkness is long.'

And he melted away into the warm African night.

Asher stood for a time, looking out over the veldt; the place, perhaps of all places on earth, that he had loved the most. It was a part of his heart and his bones that he could never share with Lydia, for he had known it before they were wed: the smell of the grasslands, the dry softness of the nights. Across the sandy wash, in its stand of willows, he could see the Van Der Platz farm, and knew that behind the barn among the trees Jan's body lay in a pool of blood, killed not by a vampire, but by Asher himself, in the name of King and Country.

He went to the table, where the *Book of the Kindred of Darkness* lay, and remembered what Sophister had told him about Johanot of Valladolid: that he'd died caring for others in a season of plague. He had been a servant of vampires. Had this been his penance, to record all that he knew of their secrets, for whoever needed in future to chase shadows?

He closed the book, carried it back into the tent, laid it beside the cot. Then he stretched out at Lydia's side – in waking life of course the cot would never have accommodated two, but in his dream it did so easily. His wife and daughter wrapped in his arms, he lay long, listening to the darkness, and waiting for sleep, and daylight.